You

You

A Novel

Joanna Briscoe

BLOOMSBURY
NEW YORK · BERLIN · LONDON · SYDNEY

Published by Bloomsbury USA, New York

All papers used by Bloomsbury USA are natural, recyclable products made from wood
grown in well-managed forests. The manufacturing processes conform to the
environmental regulations of the country of origin.

Every reasonable effort has been made to contact copyright holders
of material reproduced in this book, but if any have been inadvertently
overlooked the publishers would be glad to hear from them.

LIBRARY OF CONGRESS CATALOGING-IN-PUBLICATION DATA

Briscoe, Joanna.
You : a novel / Joanna Briscoe.—1st U.S. ed.
p. cm.
ISBN-13: 978-1-60819-483-4 (pbk.)
ISBN-10: 1-60819-483-3 (pbk.)
1. Women music teachers—Fiction. 2. Mothers and daughters—Fiction.
3. Self-realization in women—Fiction. I. Title.
PR6052.R4457Y68 2011
823'.914—dc22
2010046928

First U.S. edition 2011

1 3 5 7 9 10 8 6 4 2

Typeset by Hewer Text UK Ltd, Edinburgh
Printed in the United States of America by Quad/Graphics, Fairfield, Pennsylvania

For Clemmie
with love always

One
February

Iᴛ's ʜᴀᴜɴᴛᴇᴅ, she thought.

They emerged from the lanes on to the upper reaches of the moor, and Cecilia understood that the baby girl was still there: there in the sodden cloud shadows, there in the bracken.

Once she had thought that her baby lived in her own mind only, projected on to passing buggies and strangers, the back of a dress glimpsed and lost. Yet the child had stayed here all along, here where the wind blew and the ponies' manes made limp flags. She had never gone away.

They drove across several miles of countryside – mother, father, three daughters – to a hamlet in a river valley near the centre of the moor. The children pushed out of the car to approach their new home on foot, the older girls languidly disgruntled as they lifted their mobiles skyward in search of reception, the youngest impatient in her desire to capture a Dartmoor pony. A noise more raw and round than anything they'd heard in London filled their ears, roadside streams racing, lone birds fat and savage with sound.

Cecilia followed them towards the house of her childhood, now her own new home. It was the same, joltingly the same as it had always been, changed only by distortions of memory that receded as the stone reality confronted her, but she walked up the path through the garden as hesitantly as an intruder.

'Is it strange to be back?' her middle daughter asked, the river torrent behind them loud in the air.

'No,' said Cecilia untruthfully, stroking her daughter's hair, and she had an instinct to run back down the path.

They reached the porch and she pushed open the door, the knocker slamming against it with disquieting familiarity. She felt seventeen again in a moment: slender and omnipotent and powerless. The old log smoke against granite, a scent forgotten even during two decades of rumination, shot back into her bloodstream as she stepped inside, and she knew with all certainty that if she had returned to her old house in order to lay a ghost, it would turn and find her first. The hall seemed stained with it, with what she had done.

Two

The House

H ER CHILDHOOD was supposed to be about innocence. When Cecilia Bannan was a girl, she considered herself happy. It was only later that she wondered whether her upbringing with its extreme isolation, its perceptions almost entirely informed by books, had left her dangerously naïve. In that place and time, anything could happen. The great liberal experiment of the Sixties and Seventies, so well meant, had its consequences. Children were layered into old cars like animals, allowed to roam the moors, raised on spring water and brown rice in the company of goats and peripatetic idealists, and sporadically killed by bogs or farm machinery. In that unkempt Eden in which romantic impulses could bloom, Cecilia didn't guess the intensity of her own desires.

It was the beginning of the 1970s when her parents, Patrick and Dora Bannan, bought their dilapidated Dartmoor longhouse with its spread of barns and outhouses at the end of a steep-banked lane. The low-slung building with its thatch and glow of stone, its wind-beaten curves and rounded porch, seemed to idle and doze, as though still settling into 800-year-old foundations. Patrick, the second-youngest son of a prosperous Dublin textiles family, and Dora, née Dorothy, a Kentish deputy headmaster's daughter, had decided to move their growing family to the middle of Devon where artistic communities flourished and children could exist unfettered by convention.

Dora, unpacking, her hand-turned bowls already retrieved from crates to hold grapes; paintbrushes and recorders instantly as accessible as toothbrushes; the tabby with its buttered paws obediently resident on a rocking chair, sighed at dust and planted kisses as she discussed her children's countryside future with them. 'This means, you see my darlings, that you can swim every single day; in winter if you choose. You can paint on the old walls, ride ponies . . .'

She wore a thick cord button-through skirt, her hair lying in a pale plait down the back of her Guernsey, and cooked while transporting a baby. Candlelight amplified mug shadows through that flagged cavern of a kitchen, gradually warming as the Aga belched its first ashes of the season, meat hooks curving from the ceiling and the dresser looming like an oak beneath which the children scribbled with felt tips at the corner of a table so large it had been constructed there at the beginning of the century and couldn't be moved. Cecilia, aged three, plump in a brushed-cotton dress and stout boots, barely dared to walk beyond the kitchen into the darkness of rooms where she could be lost and soaked by the ghosts that surely crowded the shadows.

She and her elder brother opened the window in the early hours of the morning to the rush of the water, distant owls, bats, moths: a kind of three-dimensional darkness of living things and papery collisions. She felt that she could run for ever across screaming floorboards, mud, grass, slate, into wardrobes, along passages, and it would never end, she would never find every cranny, every secret of that place.

Later she looked back and wondered: where were they at that time, the people she would love and long for in her life? One a man who was twenty-two to her three. The other not yet born.

Within days of moving in, Dora and Patrick realised that the simple upkeep of the house, precariously mortgaged and acquired as precipitously as they had found each other, would drain their resources. And so in those first weeks, they hastily filled spare rooms and outbuildings with the strangers who bobbed around the moor in search of cheap accommodation and surfaced at a rumour of a barn or studio, a little employment, a beautiful view.

'Who are all these people?' Cecilia asked.

'Neighbours,' said her mother tentatively.

'Why do they live in our house?'

'Only a couple of them do.'

'But why? Do they live with us?'

'I suppose they do. Just for a little while.'

But the men with foxy beards and fluty women in dresses resembling aprons, the hippies and mud-caked artisans who fetched up at Wind Tor House stayed on, their tobacco, gouache and miso thickening the air, their irregular rent paid in inexpert dry-stone walling or an afternoon's digging or a casserole dish of mulled wine at one of the many parties that spontaneously occurred. To the Bannan children, they and the farmers' families scattered over the hills were civilisation.

Cecilia, the second child, was a red-haired stubby girl with a rosebud mouth, an indistinct nose and a sweetness of nature that endeared her to her parents and their friends. At four, she was sent on a bus along three miles of lane to the local primary school, where her older brother Benedict was already happily failing to learn to read among illiterate ten year olds. Bored by tales of Pat the dog, Cecilia wrote orphan stories while her contemporaries doodled in a babble of neglect and left early for harvest. At home in the afternoons, Benedict, Cecilia and Tom the toddler fought, drew, piped, quilted, wove and fashioned wooden objects, smilingly encouraged by Dora, who offered them no choice but to converge in artistic endeavour. At that time – before the great mistake – Cecilia adored her mother and father equally.

'You are my little peg creature,' her father Patrick told Cecilia.

'What do you mean?'

'You're a peg doll. Look at your big eyes, your round little head.'

He called her Arrietty and Darrell Rivers after the books she read. He cherished her for her affectionate ways and misguided fantasies:

skewed ideas of the world that made him laugh, but which caused mild concern in Dora. He kept an old-fashioned pinball machine requiring thumping and rocking in one of the bedrooms, an unreliable jukebox in the hall, a 1930s racing car decaying in a barn. He made his pottery, sold to friends and visitors, and patched up the lodgers' accommodation; he turned conversation into lyric, entrancing and infuriating Dora, who was just beginning to fend off the knowledge that this almost excessively captivating member of a successful Irish dynasty was in fact a drifter. In a flurry of activity, she had the largest barn converted into an artists' retreat on borrowed labour and charged London-based writers and sculptors higher rent, employing girls from the village to change the dark-brown bed linen. Patrick made speculative plans for a summer pottery school.

Aged eight, Cecilia sat in her monkish room over the front garden of Wind Tor House awash with hay fever as she immersed herself in the Borrowers and the Bastables and Miss Minchin. She still had the freckles-and-milk faintly sinusy look of a redhead. She was ferociously determined to excel: to discover treasure; to become a species of child genius; to find her own Heathcliff upon the brooding moors.

'I must find work,' she said to herself, filled with anxiety over family fortunes. She made a pledge out of the window and watched it land at the top of Corndon Tor. She wondered whether she could earn a decent wage during the summer pantomime season like Posy, Petrova and Pauline, the Fossil girls; but a professional engagement would require an education at an academy or seminary of some sort, preferably run by a Russian, and she didn't know how to find one. Were there ballet classes in Widecombe? She would have to apply post-haste to the Wells.

Ballet practice – 1 hour night. 3 hours Sat and Sun, she wrote on the timetable above her bed.

Her father did not seem to have a regular job, like other people's fathers.

Be good, she wrote in secret mouse writing on a corner of her timetable, because if Beth March could be so good, so very, very good, she could attempt to rein in her flawed nature. *'Do better and be better'* – Emily Brontë, she wrote on the other corner.

Help mother, she added. Sara Crewe had slaved among coal scuttles for Miss Minchin and held her head like a princess all the while, so she herself could help sweep the Aga ashes for her poor overworked mother and devote an hour a day after her homework and ballet to scrubbing, brother care and log carrying.

Circus studies, she wrote tentatively, for perhaps she could make a bob or two as a circus girl. She had no idea where one learnt the skills or found a circus with which to run away, but the majority of the lodgers could teach her juggling and she would practise her somersaults.

Ice skating, she wrote. A white-muffed girl from *Bunty*, her elongated sketch of a leg raised in star-spangled air, sailed past her. If she studied hard and showed aptitude, like Harriet of *White Boots*, she should be able to take her inter-silver before the year was out. 'No carpet knight,' she murmured, but what was a carpet knight?

Piano practice – 1hour; 4 hours weekends, she wrote, and this she could do, for an old woman thumped out scales in Widecombe church hall for those who cared to learn, and care to learn Cecilia did. Her own mother supplemented her lessons, and had begun to teach her the cello.

Her father seemed to knead and fire in his pottery barn, but where did he sell the pots?

Wares, she wrote, uncertain of how to express her commercial imperative. She could produce her own bowls, make taffy, tap maple syrup or sell lemonade from her window to passing cyclists.

Wolves howled outside, savage and yellow-eyed on the wolds. Water poured off the fields, bubbled beneath the lane and rushed along the gully in front of the garden. The fogs rolling down from the moors could smother lambs and young children. Spirits and demons followed the Dart and smugglers signalled from among the gorse at night. It would be best if she could unearth some ingots. How else would they fend off penury? What if they had to make shoe polish with soot and dresses from curtains? She shivered in delighted martyrdom. She saw herself standing stiff in the classroom, unable to sit in her cone of brocade as children laughed, poked and pulled her hair, while shortly thereafter the headmistress summoned her to her study to inform her that her parents were dead.

At Wind Tor House, chaos reigned: spare rooms, utility rooms, potting sheds, cottage and barns were filled to capacity with tenants renting, scrounging, bartering. Nine neighbouring children would appear for tea, parents uncertain of their whereabouts; in the summer, caravans sloped in the mud, packed with students seeking work in the artists' barn, trailing patchouli and damp clothes. Patrick's stereo system thumped across the valley with no one to complain, cottages dozing by the river; birds crying; the Beatles booming. There were parties: a Christmas celebration, guests arriving on horses, skidding in old Land Rovers; a summer gathering that spilled to the river, adults naked in the water, draped over fields; Patrick picking up his guitar, drunk children catching the ponies at night. It was, Cecilia feared sometimes, too rich, too wild, too free.

'I've got news,' said Dora one summer evening, brightness disguising weariness.

'Oh yes?' said Patrick, looking up, his mouth twitching in apprehension, then straightening with tangible effort.

'I've got a job. Music teacher. Haye House.'

'A regular income,' said Dora when he failed to respond.

He was silent. He exhaled. 'That's great,' he said.

Patrick, now in his mid-thirties and already emanating strands of disappointment, was almost openly reduced. The confidence that was rooted in his birth family's prosperity and his own charm butted daily against reality, resurrected only at night with music, with company, or among the children who were his loyal companions. In an attempt to escape the industry that supported three generations of his family, he had incongruously trained as an accountant in Dublin, but had never practised. Unlike his taller red-headed brothers with their unquestioning participation in the family business, he, the physically slighter but mentally faster rebel, was now beginning to flounder, a sense of embarrassment as perceptible as nervous sweat beneath his old boyishness, his essential philanthropy. His brown hair was patched with grey. He knew that he lacked purpose and that he should have persisted with his earlier career, but it felt too late already. His wife was by this stage infinitely more practical.

'Subsidised fees for teaching staff's children,' said Dora in a controlled manner, glancing at the three alert faces at the table. 'Considerably subsidised.'

'Haye House?' said Cecilia suspiciously.

'Haye House,' said Dora, unable to contain her satisfaction.

Haye House, the progressive school some eleven miles to the south, where the Dart spread and gave rise to water meadow and sheltered garden, was the institution almost uniformly aspired to by the Bannans and their more bohemian acquaintances scattered across the moor. Haye House was the social and scholastic ideal. Patrick's parents, embracing an expedient solution to a private education, had already offered to pay the reduced fees.

The school was famous, or infamous: fading rock stars' love-children mingled happily with their extravagantly monikered legitimate half-siblings; scions of attenuated European dynasties and colonial offspring mixed and mated with the children of more local wealthy families of an artistic or educationally opinionated bent, or with those simply imbued with the latitudinarian values of the time. Cash-strapped hippies with the right connections and subtly defined credentials – a tone of voice, a way with a plectrum, an invisible but dogged instinct for nepotism – managed to secure themselves healthy subsidies for their dirty-haired broods, to the puzzled irritation of their more industrious contemporaries. Over the years, accidents, precocious record deals, drug addictions and frequent recourse to child psychologists had further ruffled the turbulence of academic life.

Cecilia caught sight of the circles under her mother's eyes as she talked to her family. 'You're tired,' she said, and Dora slumped a little before she gathered herself and kissed the head of the daughter who had always assumed responsibility for fragile family harmony as though she were the oldest child while the real firstborn happily shirked it.

'You're a lovely girl,' said Dora quickly. 'What do you think? I think you'll love it.'

Cecilia dropped her gaze. She spent her evenings plotting to apply for a scholarship to a school such as Malory Towers: a school with a uniform, prefects, medals and flying colours. She hadn't so far dared to tell her parents of her wishes.

'Do I have to go to Haye House?' she asked so quietly that no one heard.

'I – I –' said Cecilia on their first journey to Haye House, still wishing to explain that she treasured other, more navy-blue desires. But she could barely form the words. It would be akin to expressing a preference for Sunday School over Drama Saturday or Battenberg cake instead of flapjack. Because Haye House was what she wanted, of course. It was what all children wanted: smoke and jam smears, kayaks and wall hangings. Down they plunged, gripping each other in the car, along high-hedged lanes frequently blocked by snow and wild pony-jams, through tunnels of green that led to the Dart. Cecilia looked out of the window, a red-haired, clear-skinned person pressing her face to a rush of leaves with all the opportunities in the world awaiting her.

'Hey you guys, walk around, soak in the place, take your time, hang out,' a teacher called Idris, originally named Ian, said to the new pupils on arrival. 'Make merry,' he added.

James Dahl was not yet teaching at the school by then, but Cecilia wondered later whether she might, by some tiny chance, have glimpsed him that day, visiting his wife's friends in the Art Department. She often dredged her memory, searching for a flicker of him between the trees and stripey jumpers, as though running and running after a disappearing figure in a dream.

Three
February

ON THE evening of her return to Wind Tor House, Cecilia held Ari, the father of her children, for a long time. She was darker now, her redhead's complexion with its ability to freckle given to shadows, the skin settled more tightly on her bones, so that the structure of her face only faintly resembled that of childhood. She rested her head on Ari's shoulder, unable to express to him or to anyone else the claustrophobic, somehow *shaming* aspect of stepping backwards and coming home. There was an indefinable sense of failure. She instinctively wanted to avoid her contemporaries who lived locally, as though she still had something to prove.

She had chosen to do this, she reminded herself. Circumstances had conspired, but she had made the choice to come back here. Yet the country seemed alien, making her newly afraid of its remoteness, its overwhelming silence, and the proximity of her mother, who lived in a cottage on a bank beyond the back vegetable garden. Now that she was here, she was hit by a jittery dread of what she would ask Dora, and when. It had been easy to devise her approach in London, but even a glimpse of Dora in the garden made her stiffen with guilt and antipathy.

Cecilia led Ari through the dully lit passages, nudging open doors, teasing him as he ducked and tripped on uneven slopes and steps while the girls thundered about downstairs.

'This was my parents' room; this was my room ... this was the baby's,' she said, stepping into a small bedroom at the end of the house.

'What?' said Ari brusquely, turning to her in the gloom.

Cecilia looked at him in momentary confusion.

'Please don't start,' he said. His expression tightened.

She hesitated. 'Ari ...' she said. 'I meant my youngest *brother's* room. When he was a baby.'

Ari paused. 'OK, OK,' he said, putting his palms up in front of him. 'Big apologies. Come on.'

'God, Ari,' said Cecilia.

'Sorry.'

They walked in tense silence.

'This is *weird*, hick girl,' said Ari more lightly, bowing his head beneath a lintel on a landing where pine smoke suffused the air and small panes chattered with wind. 'Where are the sirens? Hoodies? Where's the Thursday recycling van? The deafening chucking of glass and cursing?'

Cecilia was silent.

'Well?'

'I don't know if I can do this,' she said in a rush, stopping and taking his arm and stroking it, pulling at the hairs distractedly. 'It's very, very strange. Have we made a mad mistake?' She caught sight of Dora's cottage hunched behind a hedge beyond the back garden, and swallowed. 'Am I in fact a lunatic to have come here? Have I dragged us all?'

'Too late, too late ... It's fine,' said Ari, and pressed the back of her neck.

'I need to look after her,' she said, glancing at the cottage again. 'I really don't know if she's going to be OK, whatever she says ...'

'She will be.'

'You don't know that.'

'Be brave.'

'I am,' she said heatedly.

'Yes,' he said. 'If anything – you're that. Brave. Stroppy.'

'I'm not.' She rested her head hard against him. Her hair fell over her cheekbone, its waves still gathering at her shoulder in a shadowed reddish brown. She wore dark pink and much black, and in this place of leaking barns and damp plaster, she looked decidedly urban; more defined and drawn than the bright blurry child she had been.

'I have to go,' said Ari reluctantly as the light fell.

'I know,' said Cecilia.

She felt an instinct to tug him back, or simply to ask him to stay, but he had to return to London during the week for work until June, and then he would take up the post he had long contemplated at the University of Exeter. She would stay with the girls and write her latest children's novel at home. She waited by a sitting-room window and watched his headlights disappear, standing there after the beam had been swallowed by trees until all she could see was lichen-draped branches knitting darkness. The radiators clanked and remained tepid, and furniture shrank in corners, newly insubstantial in such large rooms.

'Come back,' she murmured.

She went to bed long after her daughters, creeping and shivering and feeling for light switches, and pictured Ari in the car on the motorway. It was shockingly cold.

A creak seemed to echo her words near the end of the room. She felt, already, as though she was shoring back animals and ghosts.

She had forgotten that country darkness was absolute. The house was animate with settling plaster and contracting beams, dense with condensation and stone. As a child here, she had kept her head under the blankets in terror, the place too alive with shadows and the accumulated drifts of human history to contain nothing but air.

The river's flow was audible; the buckled thatches of cottages dripped in the tuck of the valley; Wind Tor House was hemmed by streams, pouring off the fields, bubbling under the lane. With the exception of her mother and one old couple by the bridge, the neighbours in this remote hamlet were now unknown to her.

She lay down and tried to sleep. It was after midnight. She thought about the big mortise keys for the house and the country habit of leaving doors unlocked. Time glowed on her clock, fifty minutes passing in shaking jolts. Fragments of her childhood came to her in distorted images, and it felt once more like a form of madness to be here again, whatever Ari's job and her mother's state of health, and, underlying it all, her own compelling need to lay ghosts. Her mind, she had sometimes thought over the years, would never rest until she returned. Despite motherhood and adult experience, she realised that she was, in some small but tenacious way, arrested in that time, her emotions still caught in her late teens, the values and sources of excitement of that period affecting her to this day.

She stared upwards to find the ceiling through the shifting darkness. A layer of grey began to settle on her consciousness. Then she heard footsteps outside on the lane that was barely more than a loosely surfaced track running between the front garden and river field, and she wrapped the sound into her half-sleep, too warm to move.

She heard the steps again. She sat up, remaining motionless, and waited. Minutes passed.

Rising, shivering, she made herself creep blindly towards the window where she pulled back the sheets that she and Ari had hitched over curtain poles and sat on the sill, pressing her eyes to the glass, detecting shreds of blowing cloud among the blue-blackness. She caught the noise again. Was it a dog? A wild pony? Feet were lightly dislodging small stones on the lane as they moved. She widened her eyes against the night until they hurt. Could she be seen herself, the whiteness of her nightclothes a dull glow behind the glass? The thought made her shiver. She was able, perhaps, to detect the palest glimmer among the spaces between the fence railings on the river field. There was silence outside, her own blood pulsing in her ears.

She made herself return to bed, the irregular beat of her heart hurting her. The house settled and scratched; there were mice and pigeons in the loft, she remembered, and she longed for the warmth and the comfort of Ari in bed with her. This place was too big, the children too far away, the river rushing audibly.

And one question kept running through her mind, however hard she tried to banish it as she edged towards sleep.

One thought: will she come back to find me?

Four

The School

A T HAYE HOUSE, Cecilia's brothers flourished on a regime of nicotine and collage-making while she rebelled by attempting to work. She was a freak, she thought increasingly as time went on. She didn't want to smoke or mix vodka-based drinks with Valium. She couldn't talk to people in the required casual manner in which understatement was threaded with mockery. She couldn't even pretend to relax in a school where class attendance was voluntary and children swarmed naked across the lawns. She couldn't pluck at a guitar; wear scarves on her wrist; launch herself, black-coated, on a rope into a pit in the woods; don a bowler hat or a dress made of lavatory paper, or doodle Jimi Hendrix lyrics on her margins. She couldn't not care.

She begged to leave. She would settle for the indifferent girls' grammar near Plymouth with its pudding-faced daughters of local industry clad in ink-uniforms; she would board in another county; she would attend her best friend Diana's entirely delightful-sounding Catholic school just north of the moor where girls attended daily mass and studied Greek. At Haye House, she truly suffered. She was a monstrous misfit in a place where she tried so hard to absorb the dominant culture and was simply unable to do so. As soon ask the lame to walk.

'Of course you'll be staying, darling,' Dora said, for there was in her mind simply no alternative to that lush and scruffy sanctuary where pupils were addressed as 'kids' and 'people' and teachers were called Karim and Dobbo, Blimmy and Jocasta. In Dora's world, in which, ideally, Cecilia would wear her embroidered jacket to join other children for door-to-door wassailing on ponies and spend evenings of improvisation in Haye House's theatre, dissent was simply an affectation.

After a time, Cecilia realised that Dora, who had been given as rigidly and conventionally English an upbringing as it was possible to experience in post-war times, and whose method of rebellion was to merge Sixties progressive thinking with a sensibility attuned to the Arts and Crafts movement, held theories on education, aesthetics and childrearing that were as coaxingly draconian as they were apparently liberal. But Dora was so kind, so busy, so patently exhausted, that Cecilia barely dared to bother her. And so she endured her enforced and expensive schooling. She pretended that she was Sara Crewe or Tom Brown or a pupil at Lowood while her contemporaries jammed, played bongos, called themselves Communists, hugged or ignored in greeting, and girls in tight waistcoats wore so much black eyeliner that Cecilia caught merely an appraising glint as she passed, her back stiff with self-consciousness.

Dora Bannan taught music O level, cello and piano at Haye House, fetched little Tom from the junior school, returned to collect Cecilia and Benedict, then drove them home and wrestled with the gritty fumes of the Aga to cook supper. Patrick would meanwhile have fixed a dripping tap, dug the foundations of a drainage system at the suggestion of a lodger, planned to repair the thatch himself, and possibly fired his kiln. Pots and decorative beasts stacked up on the windowsill of his barn were admired by the rare passers-by who wandered down that lane, a sole sale often involving a long chat over a coffee and flapjack with a tour of the grounds thrown in.

His passions, thought Dora, looking at herself in the mirror one day – her light-brown hair still long; her mouth full; some sex and spirit still to be detected, she thought cautiously, beneath the tarnish – were his guitar and his children and the life that they had created: the existence that had adhered itself to them and their house over the years: children's plays performed with a weekend's notice, requiring the night-sewing of velvet capes and owls' ears; her own Saturday-morning music groups that sprang up, unpaid for, involving virtually unknown children with pageboy haircuts ferried to the house; charades on smoky evenings scattered with slumbering toddlers and teenagers and loud hilarity that kept out the battering winds, the bogs, the cows shifting in the lane while the Aga hissed with potatoes and Patrick sang tunes learned in youth and, as the evening wore on, Irish rebel songs. It was what she had wanted so fervently upon meeting Patrick's large family; it was the opposite of her own buttoned-in Kentish childhood and she was still, she told herself, learning to accommodate the chaos, to live with the exhaustion.

The tabby was joined by two strays, horses chomping in the fields, the children petitioning for a dog.

'Who's paying?' said Dora to Patrick, uncharacteristically.

Dora had once been entranced by him. She had gone to Dublin in nervous youth – her first trip abroad after music college; her escape from small-town life and parents who still called her Dorothy – to take up a job she had seen advertised in *The Times* for an assistant in the Bannan family's outlet shop. There, selling rugs and tweeds in a lavender-scented converted cottage, she, like many an enthusiastic young summer worker before her, had been enveloped by Bannan hospitality as she was chatted to in passing, fed soda bread and carrageen, included as a matter of course in their evenings of unbridled entertainment in the family house outside Dublin. She never wanted to leave. She watched August passing with anxiety; she let her plaited hair loose for the first time and caught that summer's sun. She longed to belong to that family, that spiralling Catholic dynasty with its offshoots and in-laws, its much-mentioned touch of Huguenot ancestry, its traditions and largesse.

Patrick Joseph, PJ, one of eight, played guitar and banjo, could improvise any song request, segued from classic Spanish melodies to tunes from the Burren, and was cheerfully determined to forge his own path. Dora – thin, a little colourless, musical, repressed but hopeful of change – had suspected within days of arrival in Ireland that she would fall for one of those sons, and found the second-youngest hypnotic, experiencing love as certain and destined the moment it occurred. Patrick's modest height was offset by his strength. He was sinuous, fast-moving, showing amusement and displeasure with equal rapidity; he was eternally busy, could shoulder a vat of dye or carve her a ring out of the ancient Bannan ash as easily as he could hum complex harmonies to background music while collating figures. Dora's own parents were suitably ruffled by this alliance with an Irish Catholic, however moneyed, and Dora enjoyed her first act of rebellion more than she had predicted.

It took over a decade of marriage for her to understand a simple fact: it was a family she had fallen in love with: a well-meaning but domineering and ever-expanding clan that now annoyed her as much as it, or the idea of it, had once enraptured her. She had begun to realise that the family slipped injections of cash to Patrick in addition to the school fees, recognising another truth she had ignored: that PJ Bannan, loving father adored by children and cleaved to by friends, born on a pad of wealth, was unlikely ever to be financially independent.

She tried to calculate when she had begun to tolerate him.

When winter drew in with its fogs that killed hikers while ponies drowned in the mires and children lost fingers in farm machinery, all three Bannan children maintained more forcefully that the ancient warren of a house was haunted, even the older and more rational Benedict avoiding the boiler room in darkness and the section of the upper floor that led along a passage to the loft of a barn. For Cecilia, there were places where she held her breath as she ran through shadows. There were pools of darkness and fitful spirits to appease.

Cecilia – surrounded by the slow-moving hippies whose ruminations she soon scorned; by Haye House pupils who inhabited a different planet, and by village children who ran in packs and knew how to turn sheep from their backs – had few companions other than her old confidante Diana, the daughter of Dora's childhood friend Beatrice.

'Diana is my best friend in the entire world,' Cecilia said in solemn tones when Dora hesitantly touched upon her isolation. 'We are blood sisters. We're like Jane Eyre and Helen Burns,' she said grandly. 'There is no one else on this moor, after all. Nothing but *absolute heathenism*.'

'Why heathenism?'

'Emily Brontë. *Wuthering Heights*,' she said.

'Oh,' said Dora.

'You see,' said Cecilia.

She wished so fervently to be good, to look after unwanted children; she read orphan books, mused upon water babies, ragamuffins, upon foundlings and motherless mites. She begged her mother to adopt an African baby and Dora considered the practicalities.

Home was her escape from school, her haven of crouching ceilings, old floorboards and fireplaces as big as rooms, of settles and ledges and window seats where she could tuck herself with her legs wrapped in curtain and read and read like the girl Jane Eyre.

'What are you reading, Celie?' her father enquired, and she told him. He, like Dora, always shortened her name, despite Cecilia's protests that this made her sound like a seal.

'What are you writing?' he asked, and she hesitated.

'A children's book,' she replied.

'Ah great. For your brothers?' he asked.

'. . . Maybe,' said Cecilia, royalties swimming in front of her mind; thoughts of glory, revenge, money for roofs and heating and clothes; money to send Dora, bountifully, on a holiday.

She was now writing for an hour and a half each evening about Gabrielle Blanche Chevalier de la Dupont, the French orphan educated in Paris who was fluent in English and brilliant at ballet, resident with her guardian in a house of polished antiques and mysteries: a girl whose piled-up hair snaked to below her knees when unravelled, and whose excessively thin body and dark-blue gaze alerted concerned neighbours to her dreaming nature. She hoped fervently to sell the novel to Penguin, London.

'I need – I need – to leave Haye House,' said Cecilia, falteringly, to Dora that night, and Dora smiled.

'How would you travel elsewhere?' she asked gently.

Cecilia was silent. 'I don't know,' she said, guilt tangling with helplessness, and she leaned her head against the shutters, inhaling the pine and praying for continuance, pressing her forehead harder, sending thoughts and tightly muttered pleas for family safety vibrating through the wood and the glass and into the constellations beyond. She stroked her future babies, somewhere up there in the dark infinite sky.

She first saw James Dahl one afternoon break when she was standing outside the art department reading, her features still unfocused with a transient plumpness, her mind constricted with her own inadequacies. He was walking through the granular gloom of the drive, dark with pines, that wound its way to the school.

'Who's that?' whispered Nicola, a studious outcast who had attached herself to Cecilia in hope of discovering a kindred spirit.

'I don't know,' said Cecilia. 'A teacher from a different school?'

'Perhaps he's a father.'

He was tall and thin, though his shoulders were broadly angular. He seemed quite emphatically to have emerged from another era, his style inconsistent with his actual age. His hair, a dark blond grading to something more colourless, looked clean in this place of unwashed tangles and fell forward on his forehead in the manner of public school boys who don't know what to do with their appearance once mothers and matrons have ceased their ministrations, just as his clothes bore the faltering formality of a once privileged boyhood. His eyelashes were conspicuously, thickly dark, contrasting with his essentially fair colouring, and added to the impression of alertness or sensitivity. His nose seemed to Cecilia to be like a statue's: large and almost perfectly straight, his mouth precisely formed. His trousers, held up with the kind of belt that Cecilia imagined in amusement his father would have worn fighting in India, fell in almost concave creases against his stomach, and his jacket pocket was lined with pens. She saw that his forearm was slimly dense with muscle.

He seemed so incongruous in this haven of drumming and kite-making that it didn't occur to her that he could be considering a job there. His wife, as she found out later, was an old friend of the head of art. As Cecilia watched James Dahl making his way towards a side entrance, head slightly bowed as though apologetic for his height, she detected a trace of melancholy or simple seriousness in him that she found interesting.

I saw him when I was a child, she always thought. I glimpsed him when I was a girl. She liked the fact. She liked the fact that it disturbed her.

Five
February

DORA WOKE at dawn the morning after Cecilia moved back to her childhood home. As she gazed at the little section of Wind Tor House visible from her bedroom window, tired and weakened by a lumpectomy, a sense of trepidation was followed by a surge of joy. Her barely known grandchildren had arrived. Those beautiful girls.

Cecilia woke soon after and understood in that bleached dance of light and silence where she was. Despite her apprehension, she felt a rise of happiness: almost bliss, white-clean and shivering, at the thought that she was here, that she had dared to change her existence so utterly that she was on the moor with her three daughters in the place that had weighted her dreams.

She turned her face towards the mattress into darkness.

The baby would be in her twenties now. Twenty-three.

She looked through the window at the field sloping to the river, the late winter sky like chilled sea, and eight-year-old Ruth, her youngest daughter, stormed across the floorboards, her eyes lowered, and threw her arms hard round Cecilia's waist.

'I got lost in the corridors,' said Ruth in a series of blowing breaths as Cecilia stroked her and kissed her hair. She pulled her to her and aimed for a cheek still faintly protruding with young childhood with its miraculous skin scent. Ruth succumbed, then wriggled away. She was plump, and shy, and would look no one in the eye.

'You have to remember which way to turn at the top of the stairs. What's the matter?' Cecilia said, holding Ruth's head to see her face.

'It's haunted.'

'What? What is?'

'Here. *Here*,' mumbled Ruth, rubbing her face into Cecilia's arm.

'Oh you mad girl, lovely girl, it's not.'

'I heard noises.'

'Where?'

'Everywhere.'

'The whole house creaks, you know. There are streams gurgling away, floorboards settling. That's all. You don't really know the country. That's the thing; that's all.' She wrapped her further into her arms.

'No. But – it was later,' said Ruth, drawing in her breath. 'Outside as well,' she said.

'Really?' said Cecilia.

'Yes.'

'A pony,' said Cecilia. She paused. 'Wild ponies come down the lane.'

'It was someone walking,' said Ruth, and began to sob.

'I love you,' said Cecilia, hugging her. 'I'm going to drive you all over the moor later and show you round. We'll have a big trip! A sightseeing tour. And a big fat cream tea.'

Ruth blushed and scampered, heavy-footed, ahead.

Cecilia passed a window seat set in a curve of the staircase where she had so often sat to think about James Dahl, and was reminded of him. For years in London, he had been a rare and unwanted memory. Where was he? she wondered. Haye House had bowed under its own troubled excesses at some point in the early Nineties, admissions falling as progressive ideals all but expired, and a more traditional school had taken over the building. He was most likely, she knew, to have returned to the house he had always considered home in his beloved Dorset, but she sometimes wondered, with fleeting unease, whether he could still live and work in Devon. It was possible. She had made herself contemplate the idea before moving.

She walked downstairs into the main sitting room, beamed and sloping, so low and unevenly plastered with its exposed granite walls and cavernous fireplaces, it seemed to have been caved out of the earth.

There they were, the three girls, like a noisy spell, alighting on window seats and crates: their heads a cluster of different colours: red, dark and pale. Cecilia went and hugged them all in turn as she always did, physical with them as she continued to be even though they were older and intermittently resisted her. She clung to that image, that storybook trio of girls. She attempted to fix the picture into her head – a portrait, reaching to the edges of the frame – but however hard she tried, an airy space, a shadowy outline that needed to be filled, slid and hovered just behind.

Six

The English Room

CECILIA WAS almost fifteen when she saw him for the second time. There he was, talking to a woman in the sunken garden, the tall grave-faced man she had once seen as she stood with Nicola while he walked up the drive. She recognised him immediately, though he was a little different from the figure in her memory who had lightly mutated into a 1940s illustration, a wounded silent soldier from a children's novel. In reality, he was more contemporary, a normal man, yet starkly dissonant in this context.

He and the woman walked across Cantaur's Fields to Neill House, and the news rapidly spread that new teachers had arrived. Cecilia could barely believe it to be true.

'Who's that teacher?' she asked that evening. 'I mean, he's new.'

'Who?'

'He's very tall and thin.'

'You must mean James Dahl,' said Dora.

'Who is he?' said Cecilia.

'He's an English teacher.'

'Oh . . .' said Cecilia.

'He's been brought in to control the badly behaved masses,' said Dora cheerfully, with a glance at Benedict.

'He can piss off then,' said Benedict.

'Oh, he's really quite an interesting chap,' said Dora. 'A bit serious. His wife's come too; she's something of an artist.'

'I don't want to be "controlled",' snarled Benedict.

I do, thought Cecilia, wishing for homework timetables, lists, prize-giving days, a punishment book. She pictured a volume of rules in glowing leather on a lectern in the main hall. She imagined the serious James Dahl, tall and erudite, teaching her.

'Are there other well-known ghosts, or – metaphorical hauntings . . . in literature?' Cecilia asked Mr Dahl, her new English teacher, as the class discussed Banquo.

'*Woo hoo*,' called out a boy with a peroxide fringe.

'Well,' said Mr Dahl, addressing his desk and twisting his head a little away from the row of faces in front of him. His dark lashes seemed to form a protective veil as he looked down. 'It depends on what one construes as a "ghost". You could do no better than to start with *Wuthering Heights*.'

'Seen the film. Crap,' commented another boy. Cecilia winced. James Dahl ignored him. He spoke, instead, of Henry James and Wilkie Collins, of W.W. Jacobs, Edgar Allan Poe, Robert Louis Stevenson, Shakespeare and Washington Irving, compressing his words into a series of near-stutters followed by short runs of impassioned fluency as he ruminated upon the subject, seemingly forgetting who had asked him the question.

A former English master at a boys' public school in Dorset, James Dahl had been brought in as head of the English department to introduce some discipline and to improve the school's lacklustre results in a subject in which the governors felt it should perform, though its risible science grades were a source of indifference. The former head of English had died, inspiring a predictable flurry of rumours about drug addiction, overdoses and suicide. James Dahl, his style so opposed to the Haye House ethos, was persuaded by a promotion with a considerably raised salary, an ambivalent desire for the first real professional challenge of his life, and the offer of a position for his wife.

His arrival was treated with disbelief, followed by protest and mirth.

'Jim!' they called out in class, encountering a quashing lack of response. 'Jimbo. Jimmy-Boy!'

English classes, conducted until that point in Haye House's usual lounging and matey teaching style and dedicated to creating experimental narratives in a variety of media, were now formal sessions, and pupils were indignant that the new geezer should gag them with his offensively prehistoric methods. James Dahl taught as though he were instructing his own desk, holding an ongoing dialogue with its surface, eyes lowered and gestures occluded, his hair falling over his forehead, his manner hesitant and refined. Yet after the initial catcalls and outbursts of rebellion, comparative peace descended on his classes: an air of concentration and even of industry.

In an atmosphere of such tradition, Cecilia Bannan excelled. She was soothed to almost tearful relief that she had stumbled across a chance of a formal education. She revelled in his observations and comparisons; in the historical contexts he encompassed; in his clearly instinctive understanding of rhythm and scansion; she stored the Latin phrases he occasionally used, scribbling them on a corner and looking them up later. She had already taught herself some Latin; she had learnt the Greek alphabet to exercise her mind. She wondered whether she was a genius. Or hosting a brain tumour.

The Dahls' two sons were boarding at school in Wiltshire. Elisabeth Dahl, a trained art teacher who had spent the majority of the previous decade raising her sons, had accompanied her husband to Haye House to fill a position as a housemistress for Neill House, the scuffed and echoing red-painted series of bedrooms, common room and kitchen facing the lower stretch of Dart that meandered past the end of the grounds. She also taught a limited number of sculpture and graphics classes in Haye House's art department, and a small spare studio was at her disposal. She had studied sculpture at Chelsea School of Art, later specialised in typography, and still produced large canvases incorporating hand-painted lettering. Elisabeth, like James, was an anomaly at Haye House; one who, with her understated elegance and almost chilly expectation of good behaviour, could only instil a modicum of restraint in an institution that occasionally threatened to implode.

'And what does your husband do?' Elisabeth Dahl, an angular eyebrow raised, asked Dora one day in the staffroom: an underheated section of the school into which pupils were apparently free to wander at will. She wore a dark grey suit and a thick silver bracelet. Dora gazed at her clothes. Elisabeth habitually twisted the classical lines she adhered to, mixing tweeds or precisely cut trousers with bright stones, or large opals, or a weapon of a brooch.

'He – he trained as an accountant,' said Dora, giving herself time to think. 'He ... makes pots. Quite amateur stuff,' she said hastily, reddening at her own treachery. 'In comparison with ...' she said, nodding at Elisabeth. 'And we have – we let out lots of the barns around the house and so on to people. Artisans. The unwashed.'

Elisabeth laughed. She gave Dora a look of open curiosity. Dora went to the staff lavatories, where she pressed her hand to her forehead in shame, self-censure tangling with fury at Patrick, who had recently developed a scheme to make paper from bulrushes and was paying hippies to help him wade into the mud to harvest the plants before hammering and dampening them into dung-hued pulp. He appeared to work ever longer hours while bringing in diminishing profits.

Every weekday morning, Dora navigated the sunken, scrambling lanes that led from the moor to Haye House, the only classical music teacher in a school that employed the part-time services of four guitar instructors, two saxophonists and one tabla tutor who could double up as a modern-dance coach. Dora collected neighbours' children on the way, piling them on to laps, stuffing them beside her cello into the luggage space of the ancient estate car whose heater was broken and windscreen wipers limped. This and a mildewed VW camper van were kept at Wind Tor, tax and insurance unpaid. The moment an engine was heard coughing into life in the silent valley, a beard or muddy hem would appear in hope from behind the foliage.

As the term went on, Dora became increasingly anxious to leave promptly for Haye House.

Almost ideologically lenient over the years, she started to insist that her children gather on the front path by eight twenty. This changed to eight fifteen. Cecilia stood there trying to neaten Tom's hair and shivering: Cecilia her transformed daughter, an alarming child-woman who would surely attract boys with this sudden blooming. Benedict was now tall and scabrous, still radiating the gruff self-consciousness of late adolescence.

'Chill out, Mum,' he said.

'Has the snow plough been?' Dora asked, looking anxiously up the lane as the moorland snow swept in.

'We can't tell yet,' said Cecilia, idly sucking pieces of Tom's hair.

'Has anyone *heard* it?' said Dora.

'Honest, Mum, you can't hear it from down here,' said Benedict. 'It's a big fucker but we're too far down the hill.'

Early on those winter mornings they piled into the car, children's breath an oat-scented fog, and Dora double-declutched on the snow-covered lane leading up from the valley, grinding up it in first gear, occasionally begging Benedict to sit on the bonnet to weigh down the front wheels; and in the yellow headlamp light and semi-darkness they moved in fits and starts through that ice-changed land towards tabla-playing with Jesse; towards nervous awareness in the corridors; towards *The Tempest*, *The Mill on the Floss* and *Selected Poems of Thomas Hardy*.

Lodgers, habitually carless in that wilderness where entitlement culture flourished, continued to loiter on school mornings prepared with gentle requests or more indignant assumptions.

'Any chance of a ride, Dors?'

'Any spare space going?'

'My cat really needs some help,' said an acupressure practitioner one morning, holding a yowling beast in her arms as she stood expectantly by the car door.

'*Hitch*,' replied Dora.

Once at school, she unpacked her instruments, and consulted her schedules. She rubbed cream on to hands that were eternally dry in winter, their soreness exacerbated by rosin, her cello strings pressing into cracked fingertips, and bit at her cold-dried lower lip. She had begun to keep watch, warily: on staffroom movements; on a section of the snow-fringed grounds that was visible from the woodwork room in passing; and on the cars lingering in exhaust billows on the drive.

She was more aware of her appearance than she had been for half a decade: the plait had gone, lopped inch by inch as she grew older, and her hair's pale brown ends sat more bluntly on her shoulders. Was she actually attractive? she wondered. Her pigmentation was purely English: light-sensitive, delicately freckle-scattered. Her skin was variable, its susceptibility to outside elements flaring and receding, its thin dryness either subdued with cream and scarves or revealed as a semi-transparent display of emotions and capillaries. She had never used cosmetics in her life. She applied a little plum-flavoured lip gloss filched furtively from Cecilia's room, noticing with the revelation of novelty how it caught light and suggested youth. Her bluey-green eyes seemed to echo that light, that cold light, suggesting cold depths, despite her outer warmth. She wore her long linen smocks, her corduroy skirts and old silk scarves in the bitterest weather as colleagues arrived in boots and mothy woollen layers or army clothes. If she was being noticed, then she felt compelled to dress well out of instinctive pride, even as she wished to repel the attention.

Teachers, rimy-eyed or yoga-composed, began drifting into the staffroom.

'You're looking peaky, darlin',' said Kasha, a jazz ballet teacher.

Cecilia, an oval of a face, long dark red hair, passed the staffroom door at that moment. Dora jumped.

'I'm *not*,' she said emphatically. 'I'm really not. Just tired.'

She went about her day, glimpsing her children at various points: Benedict, favouring eyeliner, who had increasingly retreated into the pulsing curtained world of his boarding friends' bedrooms, those expensive concrete cells in which pupils dozed and smoked during lesson time; Cecilia, who had begun, she thought, to come into her own as she collected her hard-won A-grades and fretted-over B-pluses, and her colouring settled into something richer and less reactive; and Tom, now in the senior school, who ran around happily in his felty jerseys, barely aware of the basics of the syllabus.

She moved from class to drama practice to staff lunch room to individual lessons, tense and strongly resistant and, despite herself, fascinated — fascinated in the midst of confused aversion — because she knew she was being admired.

'Your mum's looking sexy,' said Diana casually at the house one night.

'Oh, yuck! She is *not*,' said Cecilia. 'Please. Yuck.' She shook her head and the waves of her hair clustered with a shine beneath her shoulders. She stretched out her hand. Diana arched her back. They were sinuous with new vanity.

'She is. Look at her. I've never seen her wearing make-up like that.'

'No,' said Cecilia, a suspicion prodding at her before it faded. She pressed the sparking flipper on her father's pinball machine in passing as a guarantee of parental solidarity.

'Did you used to dread your parents splitting up?' she said, pausing and leaning on a windowsill.

'Yes,' said Diana. 'I thought it would be like ...'

'Like them dying,' said Cecilia. 'It almost felt it would be as terrible. Isn't that strange? I prayed ...'

'I did too, at mass.'

She had begun to pronounce it 'marse'. Cecilia shivered a little in disconcerted admiration. They had entered a new and thrilling snob phase.

'Parents can do so much ... and not know,' said Cecilia.

'When shall we have our own children?' asked Diana, leaning on the wide scooped sill and gazing at the tor in the distance. Shouts emerged from outside.

'When we're very famous,' said Cecilia, watching the sky. It was white and lined with recognition like a promise. 'When *hoi polloi* acknowledge our achievements; when we're in *Who's Who*. Then we can have some babies.'

'Yes,' said Diana, who was going to be an actress. 'We've got to have our careers.'

'Our brilliant careers.'

'Yes. I really won't be bothering with all that rep stuff. What's the point? You may as well just be famous immediately.'

'Exactly,' said Cecilia. 'What's the point of doing loads of *theatre in education*? *Mumming*. Oh yuck! All those embarrassing failures messing around in tights on barges to a scuzzy towpath audience. Just go to London and become famous.'

They giggled and muttered, spoke of peasants, of rabbles, of inbred commoners. They posed and gestured and laughed until Cecilia had to rest her hurting stomach against the windowsill, her mirth now perforated with guilt.

Diana fell silent. Cecilia gazed at her, at her dark hair flat like a painted doll's, her clear skin and newly larger mouth and nose seeming to Cecilia to belong to someone else, someone more womanly and cruder-featured.

'Supper,' called Dora.

'Busy,' shouted Tom from the garden.

The pond had iced over. Children had been skating on its surface, skidding as they anchored themselves to the rushes and hobbled out over frozen hoof furrows.

'If you don't come now, you'll have to do all the washing up,' called Dora newly impatiently, the end of her sentence tailing off with lack of conviction.

'Poor Dora,' said Cecilia. 'Utterly transparent.'

'I don't think she is, quite,' said Diana, pausing.

'What do you mean?' said Cecilia.

'I think she's kind of hiding something.'

'What? *What?*'

'I don't know . . .' said Diana.

'Well what?'

'She's different.'

'I know,' said Cecilia, barely opening her mouth.

'What is it . . .?'

'I don't know,' said Cecilia.

'I don't either.'

They were silent. A robin hopped on the gutter opposite.

'Who are you looking for?' Idris the woodwork teacher asked Dora just once as she walked along a corridor shouldering a music stand. She wore her best silk scarf and smock top, cuffs smeared with rosin.

'No one,' said Dora, instantly colouring. 'Have you seen how a few last leaves are clinging on? I loved the bird whistle Tom made in your class last term, by the way.'

'Cheers,' said Idris, and gave her a loud kiss on the cheek as he left for class.

'You're a graceful creature, our piano mistress,' said Elisabeth Dahl, coming up to her from behind. 'Prepossessing in ways you don't know.'

Dora jumped. She shook her head. She disappeared into a practice room.

She feared that her confusion was readable, she who had always easily slipped behind a cheery social persona. At hometime when there was much milling and chatting, when there were glimpses and blurred encounters, she felt the tendons in her neck stiffen with an embarrassed antipathy she attempted to suppress.

Dora couldn't tell anyone. It was imperative. Distraction had come upon her and yet she had barely noticed its arrival, its source was so outlandish. Elisabeth Dahl, that wife, mother, new housemistress at the school – above all, that *woman* – was nagging at her thoughts, staining them, unsettling her. That self-possessed creature appeared, quite inexplicably, to look down from her craggy heights and single Dora out, telling her things, announcing matter of factly in front of a group of colleagues that she was beautiful; that she was endearingly and preposterously naïve; that she held back the best of herself.

Dora was fiercely embarrassed. She walked round in a state of disbelief, certainties and then uncertainties assailing her. She returned to Elisabeth time and time again in her mind, questioning with a quiver of panic whether Patrick had noticed her air of inattention.

She would avoid Elisabeth at school, or simply not see her for some days, and then something of her equilibrium returned and she could only shudder at the memory. At other times, Elisabeth would walk briskly along a corridor and catch her eye and seem to appraise her, not glancing away, but gazing at her with a smile; with an edge, almost, of mockery, as though drinking her in. What an odd effect this person had on her, Dora thought. She, who had never desired women and never even considered the subject, sensed over time a discomfiting buzz of awareness in Elisabeth's presence that she had only ever experienced in youth with local boys; with Patrick; and briefly, potentially, with his brothers before she had settled upon the one she wanted and who emphatically wanted her. It reminded her of that old intensity of communication, that awareness of self in the glare of admiration, and she was captivated by the sensation. She almost wanted to *be* Elisabeth Dahl. And then Elisabeth would become less flattering for a period, seemingly less focused upon her, and Dora would thirst, ambivalently, for a renewal of her interest, and wonder what she had done wrong, increasingly certain that she had been discovered to be dull.

In more contemplative moments in the day, or in the heat of a chance meeting, she was, she thought, sporadically possessed, as though by an evil creature.

'What's wrong?' said Cecilia, the only time she directly asked her mother. She didn't know what she was asking.

'Nothing,' said Dora inevitably.

Cecilia shot her a glance. Dora coloured faintly. Cecilia turned away, embarrassed.

'What are you two talking about?' said Patrick, rising from his chair and stroking the cat.

Dora hesitated, then didn't answer.

She could barely look at Patrick. Almost single-handedly, she was required to maintain numerous offspring in what seemed like a series of catacombs sinking into the ground and sucking away her salary the moment it was paid. She could hardly find her children on its different levels with its little wells of steps, its twists and lofts. They were sometimes in the roof, like birds, as she called for them; at other times they were down among the cows, or sodden and shivering in the river. In that overstretched life in which every moment was absorbed by children or work, it was simple to avoid Patrick for several days at a time before tension arose between them, or she was driven by guilty self-awareness to focus her attention back on him.

The children were protective of their father without quite knowing why. Cecilia fetched him drinks and reacted to his jokes with fewer displays of eye-rolling cynicism, detecting something wounded about his narrow chest in his woolly jumper. Even as he teased and pottered, there was a flicker of watchfulness to him in this new less forgiving climate. He seemed deflated, less given to the bursts of enthusiasm that had stimulated his children.

Dora snapped at him. He walked out of the kitchen. Tom's mouth fell open. Cecilia winced. She ran to her teacher in her mind. She sat in her English class, the trees swaying outside the window, the cream paint collecting condensation, the harmonious well-bred tones of Mr Dahl guiding his pupils through a text, and all was right with the world.

After half-term, Dora returned to Haye House determined to excise her emotions. Her perspective had realigned itself during the week away with a juddering series of realisations as she had watched her family living their normal lives, her maternal focus altered in ways they could surely sense.

But once at Haye House – Idris kissing her twice on each cheek, the maths teacher known variously as Blimmy and Blim-Head sending a brownie he had baked spinning into the air for her to catch; once those parents, the rock dinosaurs and psychoanalysts and cabinet makers with their wives, mistresses and au pairs, had converged on the drive, dropped off children and departed; once inside the corridors with their nicotine scents and flimsy balsa installations

– she sought Elisabeth's gaze. The air was more rarefied than she had remembered.

That week, Cecilia looked out for Mr Dahl, as she always did now, but with more impatience. She needed a comment from him, a high grade for her *Tempest* essay, an encouraging nod or some other, non-specific form of salvation. He understood her. They never spoke outside classes, but with a certainty that was surely drenched in enchantment she knew that he recognised the way her mind worked.

For the first time, she noticed Mr Dahl's growing gaggle of admirers with a curiosity beyond her initial amusement. They fluttered unobtrusively around him: Nicola, Annalisa, and Zeno. They too were Haye House oddities. With the exception of herself and a pair of science geeks who tinkered sweatily in the lab and were ignored by teachers and pupils alike, these were the school's only studious pupils.

Nicola with her beatific expression and fringed frizz of cellist's hair, her clear skin sown with moles, already loved Mr Dahl: Cecilia could tell. Zeno, Zenobia, the disappointingly diffident daughter of a celebrity lawyer and his second wife, was more at home in James Dahl's classes than suffering the expressive anarchy favoured by his colleagues. The final member of that drear trio was Annalisa, a near-silent but marginally more attractive Swede given to flower-print dresses and hairbands who had begun to cling to Mr Dahl as her likely saviour in the pandemonium. Rigorously discouraging any form of personal friendship with his pupils, unlike a sizeable portion of the staff at the school, Mr Dahl was resistant to Annalisa's needs, and she followed him like an open-mouthed foal, silently crying out for pastoral care that he was unable and unwilling to offer her.

In the afternoon English class, rain falling softly among the pines on the drive, Cecilia's consciousness undulated to the rhythm of his voice as he read a speech of Trinculo's. She could float upon the air of concentration he demanded, an atmosphere that eventually tran-quillised the most sneering renegade.

He spoke to her through her alert daze.

'Cecilia,' he said. 'Perhaps you could explain Caliban's motives here.'

'Oh,' said Cecilia. And she blushed, and she explained.

'Cecilia,' he always called her. 'Cecilia.'

As no one else did, other than her father in his songs. He made her like her old-fashioned saint's name, her glassy Italianate name with its wings and flourishes. Celie she had always been to her family and therefore to most of Haye House. Now she was Cecilia, and elevated into blue cloudy saint's air where she could fly.

At home, she was infected with partial awareness that tension caught the air. Patrick was there at the table for supper, but he didn't reach for his guitar afterwards. Uncharacteristically, he washed up. Cecilia prayed for him. She read more, hiding within the crooks of her home.

At times the lodgers gazed at her, catching her outside the bathroom semi-dressed or wrapped in a towel, the sexual egalitarianism they professed quite abandoned as they appraised her with an open moist mouth behind a beard. A naked male hippie had on occasion left his bedroom open as she passed. She had to move swiftly around dark corridors and down steps, and she put a lock on her door.

She fought the iced air of the bathroom with kettles and the east side tank's entire supply of hot water, steam billowing into the stillness as she squeezed out the system's every drop of warmth. The moor blew out there, a scarred bowl to run over, a never-ending wildness. Was the howling the sound of gales, spirits, or the large cats rumoured to roam and hide in the gorse? Ice furred the frame of the window; the copper in the spring water that supplied the area stained enamel and fair hair blue-green, so she stretched out in the rare heat and imagined mermaids and swimming pools. She thought of Mr Dahl. She ate a small stack of penny sweets she had brought into the bathroom, and alternated *Anna Karenina* with *Fifth Formers of St Clare's*.

She saw in a passing moment what her childhood had been, perceived that it was about to end, and felt the weight of adulthood upon her. She seemed very old now. She picked up *The Mystery of the Spiteful Letters*, went on to *Middlemarch*, then settled back to think about Mr Dahl. Drips ran through the condensation inside the window that reminded her of his handwriting. Large-footed creaks started up in the passage and a lodger tried the door handle. She frowned in indignation and wondered what the indolent hippies would think when they heard that she'd become famous. She had almost finished writing a novel, and her body was elongating.

She arched her back, watching water run down her new astonishing curves. She could see a smudged impression of her features in a mirror: an oval-shaped face; her mouth now fuller; her precise eyebrows much darker than her hair; her hair and skin no longer discordant. With a surge of embarrassed excitement, she wondered whether she could one day turn beautiful, like Bathsheba, like Eustacia, like Anna Karenina, or the lovely Angela Favorleigh of St Clare's.

The next morning she looked out again for Mr Dahl, who was tall and considerate and affectingly sombre. *At first Tess seemed to regard Angel Clare as an intelligence rather than as a man*, she remembered. How could she have perceived him during his first weeks at the school only as a mind that guided her, an authority who wrote comments? When she saw him with his fringe falling over one eyebrow, the deprecatory posture of one accustomed to stooping beneath doorframes too low for him, her pulse changed its rhythm. It was the first sensation of anything approaching exhilaration she had ever experienced in that place.

She caught moley Nicola's eye. The possibility of future triumphs bubbling up into an irrepressible smile, she returned her gaze with a beam.

'I should like to go somewhere else with you,' said Elisabeth to Dora below in the staffroom, her words characteristically delivered as an announcement. 'Away from these stifling corridors. Are you free on Friday evening?'

'My husband. Patrick,' said Dora. 'I mean – I think he'll be at the pub. The children –'

'The pub,' said Elisabeth reflectively. Her lips slowly parted. She appeared to think about this, and was silent in a way that left Dora flustered.

'He has a group of friends – locals – there. Singing nights on Fridays.'

'Singing nights,' said Elisabeth again in an echo.

'Perhaps,' said Dora. 'Perhaps,' she said, floundering, 'you and – James – could come over for dinner?'

'Perhaps,' said Elisabeth lightly, and seemed to smile to herself.

There was, later, something of Elisabeth's smell – the spicy fig-like scent she wore, or a trace of the frosty rustle of her blouses against her skin – something known and familiar and subconsciously absorbed – that Dora detected on herself, because Elisabeth, always, stood close to those she was talking to; and it made Dora recoil with a spin of confusion in the kitchen. No *woman* had ever looked at her in this way, with that appraising eye contact, laced though it was with pride, with something held back. It filled her with exultation and repugnance in turn.

Yet for all Dora's aversion, she sometimes wanted to convey something else to Elisabeth. 'Don't see me only as a married woman,' she wanted to say. 'I am me. Perhaps I'm different things too.' But she could no more put the sentiment into words than crystallise it for herself.

'There is a woman,' she said tentatively to her friend Beatrice.

'Yes?' said Beatrice.

'She's at – the school. She works there. And she seems to look at me!' she said in a blurt, rising into hysteria.

'Look at you. Like a – ?'

'Yes,' said Dora.

'Oh, isn't that part and parcel of that school?' said Beatrice calmly. 'Anything goes. I don't really understand, but I'm sure it's connected to that liberal atmosphere.'

'Perhaps it is,' said Dora.

'Does she look at all manly?'

'Well she has short hair – properly short hair. Hard – how can I put this? Hard edges. But she is very feminine in a way. She's married to the head of English.'

'There have always been married homosexuals, I understand. But I don't know about women.'

'Nor do I,' said Dora, shaking her head, and she never referred to the subject again to Beatrice, her very closest friend in life, or to anyone else. Years later she thought that that was the principal legacy of her tightly sewn childhood: the ability to keep secrets; the necessity to conceal. Her parents had stitched that into her very fabric.

Patrick worked later each night in his pottery barn, and sometimes he failed to return to the house. Cecilia waited for him, listening from her room for the knocker's sequence of reverberations as the front door shut. She wondered how he could survive there in the winter storms that blew straight in from the higher reaches of the moor. The stream beside the barn frequently overflowed and flooded across the lane, gouging chunks of tarmac, carrying banks of pebble and mud. Fogs slid down and settled thickly in that river valley. She pictured him dying like an animal, just as her own hamster had expired of underfeeding and hypothermia, a fact that had tormented her for almost five years. Tears sprang to her eyes every time the merged hamster-father image rose to her mind. Patrick locked the barn door: he wouldn't allow his children to witness his occasional accommodation, but Cecilia balanced a stool on a hay bale outside the window and peered through the grime and twisted pottery animals, and what she saw broke her heart: a bed, neat, piled with duvets and blankets, cover after cover in a precarious puffed heap, an electric heater close to the mattress, a kettle and packet of biscuits. She thought then of his stories of all the times he had been picked up by the police when he had first come to England merely for being Irish; of all the times he had been assumed to be a labourer because of his accent alone. Anger merged with the sorrow.

Cecilia slotted against Mr Dahl's sketchily drawn figure in her mind. She brought him to her, a tall body, a broad chest, strong arms, sheltering her.

I will make myself perfect, she promised, tears streaking her cheeks until they itched. I will study under Mr Dahl and make myself a brilliant creature in his image, and very thin. I will become successful. I will buy my father a house by the time I reach the sixth form.

In the morning at Haye House, students were making loud music in the science corridor, sitting cross-legged on piles of bags. Amps vibrated on lockers. Nicola stood outside the top English room.

Cecilia stopped there. She had just been offered a choice between a canoe-making class, Brazilian dance and martial arts. She and Nicola glanced at each other.

'He's not well today,' said Nicola tentatively. 'Mr Dahl.'

'How do you know?'

'I heard Jocasta saying something that I *thought* meant he's got a cold.'

'Right,' said Cecilia, the prospect of missed lessons filling her with disproportionate distress.

'He's very clever, isn't he?' said Nicola in a tiny voice.

'Oh,' said Cecilia. 'Yes. I think so. Very.'

'I think he went to Oxford.'

Cecilia paused.

'What do you think of his wife?' she said, demonstrating her lack of concern by appearing to study the lockers.

Nicola screwed up her face. 'Horrible,' she said. 'Bossy. Stern.' She was silent. 'I don't think he likes her very much.'

Cecilia almost laughed. 'Poor him,' she said.

'Yes, poor him,' said Nicola fervently. 'He's so . . . He's such a good teacher, isn't he?'

'Yes,' said Cecilia, loitering. She caught Nicola's eye again and hesitated, Nicola blushed, and then they burst into simultaneous laughter. Cecilia couldn't stop. Tears began to run down her cheeks. Nicola laughed in quiet gulping gusts. Cecilia held on to the door, and every time she tried to stop, she could not catch her breath, her abdomen ached, and fresh laughter caught her. In a moment of silence, unable to breathe, she saw that Nicola's laughter also bled into tears.

'How long?' she said when she could finally speak, and then laughed again.

'Always,' said Nicola. 'Zeno too ...'

'From the beginning of term?'

Nicola nodded, her fringe obscuring her eyes as she looked at the floor. She shook her head. 'Since we saw him on the drive.'

'We were only children.'

'But look at him.'

James Dahl then arrived, nodding at the girls without looking at them, carrying his briefcase and beginning to hand out the class's Hardy essays before he sat.

I love you, I love you, I love you, Cecilia thought, jabbing the words into her margin. She glanced at the boys slouching on the desks opposite: pustular and intermittently purple: dismaying creatures she had never touched and barely talked to. She let herself catch a glimpse of the man at the end of the class with his authority and dark lashes and sense of faint, abstracted sadness. *James Dahl*, she wrote as a pledge.

Seven
February

S OMEONE WAS there on the lane beside Wind Tor House again that night. Cecilia stumbled to the window, almost asleep, and caught a movement as the trespasser hid among the tangle of teasels and long-dead grass at the top of the river field. She heard a rustle, and then there was silence.

She called Ari in London. 'I feel weedy for needing you,' she said, shivering steadily.

'Nonsense,' he said. 'Because I'm a *man*, you mean?'

'Yes,' she said. Her teeth chattered. 'Precisely. A bit pathetic.'

He laughed.

'One of those despicable creatures. Get over it. Have they gone?' he said.

'I think so,' said Cecilia, her small voice echoing in the large room, her nightdress ghostly around her in the darkness.

'Right. Call the police if they come back.'

'It's a sleepy little in-the-sticks station in Ashburton. They'll be in their beds.' Her breath rose as she stood there, her spine tight with the cold. 'They probably wouldn't even be able to find this lane. You try being on your own with three children all week,' she said heatedly. 'Sorry,' she said after a moment.

'It's only till June. Be patient. Call me and I'll speak to the police in Exeter,' he said.

'I don't like you being away. What if you *fall* for someone else?'

'Oh Cecilia. Don't be ridiculous. I won't. You know I won't.'
'You'd better fucking not.'

Dora couldn't sleep. Her breast was tender where her scar lay as she shifted in bed. Her cancer felt, at times, like the most terrifying intruder, so stealthy that an escapee from the prison would be a preferable visitor. She could hear someone walking by her cottage on the lane that led to the back route to Widecombe. A poacher, she conjectured, or one of the roaming dancers and travellers who lived for weeks or months at a time in a converted chapel at the end of the Widecombe lane.

She turned in her bed. Cecilia had come to cook for her that day, and she was still ruffled by the memory. She swallowed.

It had started: what she had known, and dreaded, and reassured herself wouldn't happen after years of barely talking. It was not articulated, but Dora knew. Cecilia was hungry, edging towards the subject of the past all over again. She was holding back, tending to a sick mother, being the dutiful daughter, but Dora sensed the banked-up emotion.

'I do wonder . . .' said Cecilia, looking out of the window at the bleached rise of moor below Corndon Tor.

'Wonder what?' said Dora before she had had time to think.

'How she is,' was all Cecilia said, and Dora was silent, and Cecilia was silent in response, and she cooked, and they talked of granddaughters and hospital visits and particular doctors and Dora's garden plans, but all the while Dora was reminded of the horrible complex mesh of emotions that time and resentment wove. She had been semi-estranged from Cecilia for so long, and she was reminded of why.

Now Dora felt her armpit and its small scar. Her physical strength was noticeably reduced since surgery, but she would not burden the hardworking Cecilia with household tasks more than she had to, so she had taken a village girl who was between jobs to drive her to radiotherapy and to help at home.

That day she waited, as she felt she had spent a lifetime waiting, for her beloved to show up.

★   ★   ★

Early in the morning, Cecilia searched the small lane that ran past the end of the house, largely used by farmers for access, or by villagers conversant with the narrow unnamed cut-throughs that led to the hamlets, although satnav was now directing drivers down there to much local consternation. She glanced at the lane's loose surface. She wondered what she was looking for. It seemed impossible when morning was pale blue on the fields that anyone could have been there during the night, but the memory made the skin on her arms tighten. She wanted to barricade her daughters inside to protect them.

She returned to the house, and there, before the light had soothed its wood and stone surfaces and revealed its grace, she sensed sadness in the whiny utility room, in the burpy pits of the boiler room with its sour plumbing and hiccuping. Even the white drift of light in her bedroom was fragrant with a passing flitter of new skin. She sat in the sitting room in the western end of the building and she put her head in her hands, crouching on a step before her family awoke, and cried for her baby.

Eight
The Pottery Barn

CECILIA AND Nicola arrived early for English and waited outside the room.

They paused before talking.

'Zeno says he was in his flat yesterday afternoon,' said Nicola. 'That's not on his Tuesday timetable.'

'Was he?' said Cecilia. 'I only just realised that if you stand on the Mound, you can see into the other side of his flat.'

'Oh yes,' said Nicola. 'His kitchen's on that side. And what I think is a spare room. I see his witchy wife in there sometimes.'

'Binoculars . . .'

'You can't do that! On the Mound?'

'We might be able to, hiding behind each other,' said the bolder Cecilia.

'I've seen Annalisa standing there once on tiptoe when she didn't think anyone could see her.'

'That pathetic bleating girl,' said Cecilia.

Nicola started to shake with laughter. 'Zeno spies on him playing tennis at weekends when he's here,' she whispered.

He appeared. Cecilia's heart thudded with such force as he rounded the corner that she felt momentarily faint.

Later, she hid in Haye House's wood, the Copse, where most acts of copulation and inhalation took place and where drug-fuelled classmates were given to swinging on a rope to hurl themselves suicidally into an old quarry thick with decaying beech husk. She crouched there reading a book and watched out for Mr Dahl's journey from Neill House across the stretch of grass above the river to the English department to teach the fourth form.

Instead, she saw the straight line of her mother's body against the green as Dora walked beside Elisabeth Dahl, her denim skirt protruding stiffly behind her, her necklace reflecting afternoon light. The two women were engrossed in conversation, both gazing ahead as they talked, paused and gestured. Dora wiped her hand across her face, and Elisabeth placed her palm on Dora's back, then dropped it. Dora moved away very slightly. Cecilia stiffened. They came closer towards the wood where she was hidden in tree shadow, Dora's face pale and frowning, her fingers twitching as she walked.

Cecilia, alert for ramifications involving Mr Dahl, absorbed the tone of Elisabeth's speech without hearing her words, and watched her decisive movements. There was an intensity to her interaction with her mother that was confusing. She wore a black skirt over black boots, a dark red scarf rising and subsiding behind her. Cecilia gazed in utter fascination. This was the body that had been held and, quite astonishingly, penetrated by James Dahl, the head enclosing a mind that contained every detail of him. Cecilia felt almost incapacitated with jealous curiosity.

'I saw you with Elisabeth Dahl,' said Cecilia that evening, a statement that had stalled in her mind before prodding at the atmosphere of the kitchen. The lights were low. The catflap banged.

Dora paused. Her skin pinkened. 'Right,' she said.

'I didn't know you – know you knew her so well.'

'I don't,' said Dora, turning round and facing Cecilia, her expression failing to relax. 'Not really.'

'You were walking across the lawn by the Copse. Talking,' said Cecilia. She focused on the flapjack crumbs on the table. She stood awkwardly by a chair, attempting to lean casually.

The redness rising through Dora's thin skin was visible even in the lamplight.

'So why were you talking to her?'

'I often talk to the teachers. Colleagues.'

'But you were talking – intensely.'

'Was I?' said Dora quietly. She drew in her breath. She turned around and began to put on the hand cream that she kept by the sink.

'It was about something!' said Cecilia, stabbing at the edge of the table.

'Well – We were discussing Gabriel Sardo staying sometimes at weekends. She's his tutor and will be his housemistress. He ... he doesn't want to board at weekends.'

'Right,' said Cecilia, pausing.

'They – Gabriel's parents are moving to Dublin.'

'You mean Speedy? Speedy Sardo?'

Gabriel Sardo, known as Speedy throughout Haye House, was a pupil in Cecilia's year. She had never spoken to him. He was smoulderingly modish: gangling and confidently taciturn. The idea of him at Wind Tor House was so unexpected that she could barely contemplate it.

'Why – why would she ask you?' said Cecilia, stumbling now. 'Why here, I mean? How?'

'Elisabeth is his tutor,' said Dora, speaking more calmly. 'I –' she said, glancing to one side, 'agreed, offered. Just weekends he can't get over to Dublin. Do you mind?'

Cecilia shook her head. 'I mean – I don't know,' she said. 'I don't know him.'

'Cool,' said Benedict, arriving in the kitchen and shrugging.

'Weedy Speedy,' called Tom.

'But I don't see why you would say yes to that,' said Cecilia.

'Why not?' said Dora.

'Why? Just because she *asks* you.'

Dora paused. Cecilia watched her swallow. 'It's only occasionally. Gabriel is a nice boy. We could do with the money, Celie.'

'I know,' said Cecilia, rifling through employment plans with shame.

'Don't worry about it, though.'

'You were talking to her for a long –' said Cecilia, tailing off in the face of Dora's expression. She glanced at the floor.

'I know that,' said Dora, and Cecilia glimpsed, as she so rarely did in her mother, a streak of determination, a chip of ice.

After supper, Dora stood by her bedroom window with hands still wetly sore from washing up, and found that she was shaking. She had been seen.

There was evidence there in the world. It wasn't just in her poor discomposed mind. They had been seen together and the sight of them had bemused their witness. Elisabeth had put her hand on her back out there in the dangerous air, and then they had agreed that they should attempt to minimise such contact and return to the care of their families. It was only when she was inside the school building again that Dora had stood in the staff lavatories and let hot tears emerge. Such intimacy wasn't sensible, and it wasn't moral, yet already Dora was hauled in by any hint of indifference or rejection or even lack of persuasion from Elisabeth.

Infatuation had developed in a series of swerves and horrified retreats, but on pausing to consider, Dora realised that she had been mentally seduced for some time, denying all evidence to herself. Elisabeth Dahl had shaken her. She was a force of nature who, for all her severe and sophisticated womanliness, possessed, thought Dora, the mind of a man. It confused her; it excited her. She dismissed it, denied it, pushed it away; and eventually it took root.

'Come with me to a concert,' Elisabeth had said only five weeks before, and Dora, steadily trembling and unable to eat all day, had left the children with Patrick for an early supper, then driven back the way she had come: down the river gorge, back past the school to Wedstone where Elliott Hall floated on embers of autumn light. She was thinner. She hadn't slept. She felt new speed to her blood. She had known as Elisabeth greeted her and they walked almost silently together through a series of doors to the concert barn, to the Rachmaninov followed by Lutoslawski, to the coughing, the bobbing heads and explosion of applause, to hot apple-juice scents, winding corridors, beamed medieval roofs; she had known that she was entering and accepting.

'So,' said Elisabeth after the concert, this creature who was so sure and so rarely expressed emotion. She was a shell of certainty: an elegant composition, shielded from mess or unwanted attachment by the fact of her tall husband.

She had guided Dora by the arm to a corridor that led backstage. There was no need to speak, though Dora feared that the speed of her heartbeat might prove fatal; and she had kissed her.

Dora could, even this evening, alone in her bedroom, be felled by recalled desire, images overlaying each other: mouths and hands, shocking little twists that made her weaken as sensations re-entered her body. The absolute self-disgust, the shock at what she had done in simply kissing a woman – and she would allow Elisabeth to do little more than kiss her – eventually followed the chilling of the fantasy, yet when she eased herself into her bed at night she wished with rigid hope that Patrick was snoring so she could hide under the blankets and think, embracing her allotted block of escapism. She shivered. Nothing like this had happened in her life. The sheer novelty of it shimmered through her guilt and shame.

Elisabeth's fig scent was detectable now in traces on an old paper hankie that Dora placed in a drawer. Her face was hot as she pressed her forehead to the window and she cried soundlessly, aware only of liquid spreading over her skin, its flow effortless. The hush and rattle of trees scored the river. An owl called. She was beginning to understand that she would never see Elisabeth as much as she longed to.

Having decided that perfection was attainable and that she would, through self-denial, aspire to it, Cecilia restricted her food consumption as best she could, aiming for a willowy slenderness that might attract the attention of Mr Dahl. She could never develop anorexia, she thought with a twinge of regret, because she found a state of even semi-starvation impossible, but she was encouraged when her periods became less regular.

Her childhood plans to become a prima ballerina assoluta had collapsed with a few frustrated pliés in a barn; she cantered across the moors on the ponies kept in the fields, but a precocious showjumping career had evaded her; even her novels, completed with love and great effort, had been rejected, and she had failed to provide for her family. She had not even been unwaveringly good like Thérèse of Lisieux. She sometimes thought she deserved to live as an orphan eremite in a cave in the Pyrenees, praying and self-mortifying. Now, she pledged, she would overcome her substandard early years. With her father to support, a married man to seduce, and an extraordinary career to wrest from the mud and youth that hindered her, only self-discipline and raw talent would carry her through.

Dora walked into the staffroom early the next day. She had been sick that morning; now she trembled with the empty-stomached after-effects. Jocasta, a history teacher, arrived in the staffroom balancing mugs of yogi tea whose smell currently made Dora want to gag. Elisabeth Dahl made Darjeeling instead and handed a cup to Dora, who was grateful. The headmaster, Peter Doran, arrived with a 1930s ukulele left to the school by a successful alumna. An old beatnik in crushed-velvet trousers, vaguely lecherous yet radiating a whiff of subdued misogyny, a glitter of homosexuality, he kept a series of largely blonde girlfriends in the headteacher's house on the grounds, obscuring their existence with a nod at decorum, and ran the school at a lordly distance while his deputy attempted to impose the establishment's comparatively few rules. Ignoring the timetable, Peter engaged Dora in an amateur musical conversation.

Cecilia made a timetable. She jogged in the mornings, or on the mornings she could force herself outside, almost retching with sleepy coldness as she rose and hobbled along the dawn-dark lanes. She ran up the steps built into the moss-covered wall that bordered the lane and led into a field high above, and there, ice sawing into her lungs, her cheeks fiery, she could see the valley, the blinking lights of others rising, catch a glimpse of Wind Tor and the moorland beyond, horses like rain in fields, thatches hunched, and here she held dialogues with James Dahl. Her hair blew behind her. She ran. Her heart thumped. She said fascinating things to him. He guided her. He was her mentor, her lover. She half twisted her ankle on frozen tussocks of horse dung; sheep clumped; cows lowed with terrible echoes and she was the only living human abroad: only she, she, a milkmaid in the fields, breathless and newly thin when she arrived back in the kitchen, where Dora sleepily stoked the Aga with Tom chatting beside her.

There was anticipation, because a miracle had entered her life. Her attachment to an admittedly unsuitable person anchored her. She went to school each day cushioned with hope, leaving behind disorder to enter a place of tampon sculptures and good-quality hash to collect symbols and evidence of glory.

'You are looking beautiful, darling,' said Dora one morning to Cecilia, unable to keep back the thought that came into her mind when she saw the blooming of her daughter, that period of transient splendour she had entered in which youth filled the outlines of womanhood.

Cecilia looked at the ground, her skin flooded. 'Thank you,' she said eventually. 'I'm not.'

'I think boys –' said Dora, pausing.

There was silence.

'*Boys what?*' snapped Cecilia to fill it, keeping her face downturned.

'Boys will want to go out with you.'

'They don't,' muttered Cecilia.

'I'm sure they *will.*'

Cecilia was silent.

'Don't you like anyone?' said Dora, aware that she was taking risks.

'No. I don't know. No,' said Cecilia, looking steadily to one side, frantically wishing to obscure her true attachment while unable to explain that boys showed no interest in her; that she couldn't speak to them; that they viewed her as a scholarly and undesirable yet somehow unattainable oddity who fell outside their mating and companionship radars. And that much as she longed for understanding, and though she was at heart scared of these guitar-strummers and moped-owners grown so tall and stalky, she also scorned them. There was no Heathcliff, no Darcy or Rochester among the student body of Haye House. Whereas *she*: she lived in a rosy suspended future shortly to storm into perfection. She felt herself step with fawn-like delicacy into the car. She sensed omen and dazzle all around her: in the glare of sky, the blur of leaves; in the twists of hair that fell back off her face, in her fall of eyelashes, the speed with which her hand could write and the blood rush through her body. James Dahl's eyes were almost perpetually on her through invisible psychic means. She conversed with him. She observed her own face in the car's side mirror, and rearranged her features and radiated her soul until she saw in that miniature reflection pure beauty. He saw it too.

When she descended from the car at the top of the drive, her certainty was tempered by the reality of the school.

Zeno was, as so often, waiting for her on the step.

'He *asked me how I was today*,' she said.

Cecilia and Nicola gasped.

'Zoom!' said Cecilia, taking Zeno's arm as they made their way to their little room, a former cleaning cupboard with a small window they had appropriated primarily for discussion of Mr Dahl. Here they perched on shelves to interpret the day's developments. Here they screamed and giggled, planned and theorised.

'Shhh,' said Nicola. 'He might hear on the way to the head's house. It's Tuesday morning.' They collided in a whispering heap. 'If one of us asks to go to the loo just before quarter past, we might see him. Pass a note. If not, we could look through the sixth-form loo windows at break.'

'*Some* of us have already seen him today,' said Zeno. 'He's wearing a greenish jacket, same tweedy stuff –'

'His hair's going to be cut soon. I bet you. I think the witch makes him,' said Nicola, raising her eyes.

'He looks like . . . someone from *A Room with a View*,' said Cecilia. 'He is quite old . . .'

'Ancient, yes. Thirty-five. But he looks like a poet! A young war poet!'

'He does not,' said Zeno hopefully.

'He's so *beautiful*,' said Nicola poignantly.

'I know ...' said Cecilia, pain lightly threading her excitement. 'What does he see in her?'

Zeno shook her head. 'She's a *hard cow*.'

'She's got streaks of *grey* hair,' said Cecilia, fingering a red wave of her own until it caught the light, and feeling that same indefinable essence of youth flex through her as she stretched. She yawned a little, intentionally, delicately.

'Do you think she knows? She's guessed?'

'She'd be *so* furious.'

Cecilia blushed in fear of exposure. James Dahl was painstakingly formal in the manner of the public school master he had been and would remain at heart. He limited his interaction with pupils to comments about prep or timetables; his wedding ring was prominent; at school events he sat beside his wife and exchanged solemn conversation with her, observed in a ferment of curiosity by his admirers.

Male voices could be heard overlaid by footsteps outside the cupboard. After a round of hushing, the girls silenced their spluttering and widened their eyes at one another. His voice alone, heard incidentally, was a gift that reverberated through a morning.

'What's today's fact?' Cecilia asked Zeno, more lightly. She coughed.

'Well, I've got something ...'

'*What?*' urged Cecilia.

'His younger son's called Hugh.'

'Hugh ...' said Nicola.

'*Really?* Are you sure?'

'Yes,' said Zeno, nodding. 'I heard Jocasta saying, "Elisabeth's son, Hugh".'

'Robin and Hugh,' mused Cecilia. 'Robin and Hugh Dahl ...'

The Dahl family. James, Elisabeth, Robin, Hugh. Had there been cousins, cats, grandparents, friends? A family history, thrillingly mundane? Cecilia longed to discover his birth date and his middle name, the initial letter of which was 'C'. She listed possibilities in a notebook containing observations, character studies, quotes both by and about James Dahl, and the scant biographical details attainable about a man who revealed so little. She could only glean information from her mother with the greatest of care, her friends plying her with questions impossible to ask but entertaining to discuss. The fact that this repository of knowledge was resident in her house was a source of painful pleasure, Dora's friendship with Elisabeth Dahl adding further frustration. How much did Dora talk to the man himself? What was the nature of their staffroom conversation, if it occurred at all? She seemed loath to mention him. When she did, Cecilia feared her own stiff expression was transparent.

Mr Dahl was a complex and large-scale project. The more information Cecilia could absorb about him, the more she would symbolically possess him. Her book contained floorplans of his flat in Neill House based on sightings from the Mound and covert explorations of the utility rooms and showers on the floor beneath, which were movingly scented with baking and other people's clean washing. In a moment of triumph, Zeno had ascertained his age through an overheard phone call at Neill House in which he had stated the year of his birth. But if no new facts were procurable, Cecilia and her cohorts burnished existing ones, their dialogue weighted with codenames and meaningful intonation. A glimpse of James Dahl was possibly more stimulating for the collectors' victory it represented than for the experience of the sighting itself, the hasty dissemination of news either by note or hint through the group – descriptions of setting, gestures and clothing repeated and repeated – suffusing the next few hours with satisfaction, or with a poignant feeling of loss because he was at large yet unavailable.

After discussing Mr Dahl all day, the girls rang each other in the evening to discuss Mr Dahl. Cecilia curled up in the cold on the prickly seagrass of her parents' room and watched her breath above her as if it made shapes of her words. Giggles ran down the stretched curls of the cord. She stifled laughter or exhilarating sessions of analysis as Dora called upstairs and her supper cooled in the kitchen.

At odd moments, Cecilia saw him and was stunned by the knowledge that beneath the commotion of her trio's worship, she loved him. She studied tennis reports and, because he played the game, effortlessly absorbed the sport's history. She read *Villette*; *The Professor*; *To Sir, With Love*. She tackled *Casino Royale* to immerse herself in the name 'James' and glanced at her younger brother's Roald Dahl novels for the electric tingle that swarmed along the letters of their shared surname when glimpsed sufficiently obliquely.

She saw him walking on occasion with his wife over Cantaur's Fields beside Neill House as she sat by the river, and she watched him bound in conversation, his gait subtly looser outside. Inexpertly, she imagined them having sexual intercourse. Elisabeth with her well-cut hair, her tailored shirts and skirts and strings of pearls, her authoritative manner that could subside into warmth, reduced Cecilia to a state of deference, yet in her near acceptance of her hopeless position she felt the stirring of determination. He, with his downcast gaze, hands deep in pockets revealing tennis-playing arms, his voice with its pleasing pitch, his diffident yet privileged manner; he was the finest thing she had ever encountered. She almost cried. She vowed. The others may be giggling schoolgirls, but she was a future wife. The world, which seemed charged with his name, swarmed with synchronicity that surely, yet barely believably, hinted at a future with him.

'I've got something to tell you,' said Dora at the end of the month. She was pale-faced as she entered Patrick's pottery barn. He was sitting on his stool embellishing a grotesque-featured creature with claws which seemed guaranteed never to sell. Why does he have to make them ugly? Dora thought absently.

'Yes,' said Patrick, looking up, then returning his gaze to his clay.

'It's cold in here,' said Dora, her voice weakening.

'It's OK.'

'Do you want –'

'What do you want to tell me?'

'I'm – I'm. I'm pregnant,' said Dora.

Patrick paused. His hands stiffened on the animal's torso. He began dousing it with water. He fetched more water and wrung out a cloth. Clay was smeared over the side of his chin, nestling among his hair.

'Whose?' he said, colouring.

'No. *No*. It's not like that. No. It's –' said Dora abruptly, blushing a fiery red. Tears came to her eyes.

Patrick turned his back to her.

'Yours. Ours,' said Dora. She felt her mouth tremble as she said the words. She feared she might cry. The glazing chemicals made her nose water. 'Really, Patrick, there is no – no –'

He waited. 'No –?'

'No other man.'

Patrick hesitated, his jaw working. His mouth was set and remained motionless. Then its rigidity crumbled and he smiled.

'There never has been –' she said, tailing off, the hypocrisy of her words boring into her. She blushed again.

'Ah, girl,' he said warmly, as he had said to her a long time ago, and she pictured him coming over to her and holding both her hands and then embracing her with a big kiss on the mouth.

He almost stood, then sat back down.

'Girl,' he said again, manifestly at a loss for anything further to say. He stood up, stumbling a little, and embraced her.

'Yes,' she said, and for a brief hot moment there in the cold in his arms she almost said, *I love you, come and save me*, but she couldn't because she had had what she had had.

'I'm, I'm,' he said, shaking his head, 'I'm delighted. It's crazy. What a thing. Are you sure, now?'

Dora nodded, not looking at him, and she thought about the hasty compromised coupling that had produced this state: the one time in months: a cunning trick played by fate and biology. It had been her resigned attempt to rescue a marriage. In truth, it had also been a competitive act, undertaken in both retaliation and perverse empathy because if Elisabeth was still unthinkably physically involved with her husband, then so would she be. She would do what she did.

Dora gazed at Patrick through the clear light that bore clay dust, and even though she could not anticipate anything more terrifying at this moment than having another child; even though she spent nights recalculating how many more lodgers she could accommodate if she put up partition walls in some barns and what their rent would come to, she gazed at his old shaving nicks, the clumps of clay stuck to his sleeves and fumbling skilled hands, heard his coughs and bodily rearrangements, saw decades of unbreakable patterns in a gesture, and knew that despite the reality of three children and the prospect of a fourth, she would never really love him again as she once had. His growing passivity made her want to howl in protest. She perceived him as forever the bawling penultimate child in a huge clan: forever a spoilt toddler born to a *droit de seigneur* charm, strutting through the semi-neglect endemic to large families. She would in effect have five children, she thought.

Patrick had never met Elisabeth, and Dora had carefully omitted to mention her name, assuring herself by rote on sleepless nights that a woman didn't count, that kissing a woman did not amount to infidelity. Caught unawares, however, she could be felled by guilt; it seemed the strictures of her girlhood remained. The terror of discovery was always present.

Dora and Patrick made uneasy peace. There was an expedient return to life as it had always been. Her period of resistance lay in the air, never acknowledged, but viewed as a beast of unknown hue that had done its savaging and could still leap. Dora feared that Patrick accepted it, whatever it was, with a sort of twitchy knowledge of his own shortcomings and she despised him for failing to fight. He could not win, she knew. But she had married her fortunes with his, and the trajectory of life in that house and the knowledge that she was pregnant propelled her.

A new cynicism hung about her. She compared her bewildering nascent relationship with her daughter's attachment. Cecilia's obvious crush on an unknown object amused her. She saw her daughter – over-responsive, attempting to study in the car in the morning with a book held above Tom's bed-knitted hair; tugging at her cuticles, and so carefully dressed in the limited number of outfits at her disposal – and thought that Cecilia's experience of love was similar to her own only at a simple level of infatuation, but she felt protective towards her.

Other teachers conversed with pupils about gigs and riffs, parties and motorbikes; about beautiful mathematical equations, grotty classrooms, drama spaces and jazz syncopations. James Dahl did not. Cecilia considered that she had held three proper conversations with Mr Dahl in her life. One was at the top of the school drive while waiting for her mother to collect her, when he had congratulated her on her O level results. She had noticed minute details of his face up close in the outside light: the fissures of adult discoloration on his white teeth as fine as lines drifting across a film; the variegated pigmentation of his eyes with their almost-black dots (she thought how remarkable his simple humanness, his rods and cones and lachrymal glands); the lines radiating from the corners of his eyes when he smiled.

The next was at a local fête downriver that she, Nicola and Zeno had attended purely because his presence was rumoured to be assured. She had borrowed Gabriel Sardo's telephoto lens for the occasion so that she and her friends could pose, pretending to photograph each other while focusing on a more casually attired James Dahl in the distant background.

She noticed a pair of long-haired pupils from the year below, instantly recognisable as the soulful variety of girl who would excel at English and who was similarly ruffled by his presence. One wore Laura Ashley while the other maintained the passive expression of a Victorian milkmaid, her lips parted, her hair draped becomingly over one cheek. Cecilia watched them in amusement and slight discomfiture. They loitered behind bushes; they shot each other glances; they kept within viewing distance of James Dahl. Competition sharpened her resolve.

'Cecilia,' he said later that afternoon when his path crossed hers, the light of sails carelessly playing on his face, his eyes a semi-transparent blue-grey behind the almost childishly dark lashes. 'How are you?'

'Fine thank you,' she said, blushing. His face was lightly tanned, turning his hair fairer. She saw golden stubble like sand on his jaw over his summer-coloured skin. She found him almost unsettlingly beautiful. He was discreet, she thought. In his reserve, he was statue-like; in the multi-coloured tones of his voice, he was human. The ear followed his voice.

'I was just musing upon various descriptions of events such as this in literature,' he said.

'Oh!' said Cecilia, her mind spinning into a search for references. '*Elizabeth and Leicester/Beating oars*,' was all she could think of to say in a mutter, swallowing his wife's name in embarrassment, but he didn't appear to hear.

'Think about it,' he said. 'I hope you enjoy yourselves,' he added as he walked on, and she glimpsed the hardness of his arm muscle pressing against his shirt as he turned towards Elisabeth who was accompanied, in a satisfying biographical touch, by a teenage boy likely to be the younger son.

Mr Dahl was not so old after all, Cecilia had thought for the first time. Thirty-six. It could have been twenty-six or forty-nine as far as she was concerned: a meaningless adult figure. Seeing him with his shirt ruffled by the water breeze, with no tie, his hair somehow informal in its sun-touched movement, he seemed not age itself, but simply a male figure imbued with hormones and body hair and effortless height. He laughed at something Elisabeth said and they looked together at a spot in the river.

In their third conversation, the one most treasured, most dreamed of in advance and then so lovingly recollected that the reality had almost disintegrated, he had stopped her one morning after class. 'Cecilia, could you stay for a moment?' he said matter of factly.

Her heart had hammered as she conjured all possible misdeeds on her part. Simultaneously, she wondered whether he was about to tell her that her literary talent now needed careful nurturing.

The dark trees swayed. A lark was out there, she fancied in her endless repetitions of the scene; an engine on the drive – whose? Two boys, Jason and Diego, were talking outside the door in their inauthentic London accents.

Mr Dahl wore his cream shirt, perhaps partly linen. He barely looked up at her.

'Cecilia,' he said calmly, gathering together the pens on his desk in a single sweep, then straightening his papers in one experienced movement, 'you wrote an admirable essay for me here, thank you. I think we should talk about university.'

'Oh!' said Cecilia. 'I . . . yes.'

'I would suggest you should be thinking about Oxbridge.'

Her pregnancy progressing to the point where she could no longer conceal it from her employers, Dora walked up the stairs towards the sheet-music cupboard. She kept to herself, frequenting the lesser-used corridors. As she approached the landing, she heard the voice of Elisabeth Dahl, so freshly lost to her even as she was still resisting her. She paused before she turned the staircase corner. Elisabeth stood beside the opened door of a stock cupboard, her leg and a section of fitted grey wool skirt visible to Dora. She was speaking to Cally Cooper, one of the science teachers, her voice rapid and lightly dismissive. Elisabeth's calf in its sheer grey stocking – and it would be stockings, Dora was sure – was almost as familiar to her as her face, and the shape filled her with pained desire. She leaned against the wall. It was almost unbearable.

'But,' said the science teacher, 'we haven't really discussed our last discussion . . .'

'I must love you and leave you,' said Elisabeth still rapidly but in a richer tone Dora recognised, a tone Elisabeth had used when she had murmured words that merged into kisses through her hair. Elisabeth's hand reached out towards the science teacher's as she turned away, the familiar nails glancing stubbier fingers.

Dora stood in the stairwell and had to catch her breath. She cursed the alien inside whose existence had confirmed for Elisabeth the unsuitability of their liaison, turning her cold in one moment, and then apologised to it, stroking her abdomen.

'I should have thought, then, that you have made your choice,' Elisabeth had said when Dora, floundering and stuttering, had broken the news of the pregnancy to her. 'You're a family woman to the end, my Dora.'

'It's not like that —' said Dora, but feebly, still ambivalent, aware of the rounded ache of the tears undoubtedly to come.

'The fact is there!' exclaimed Elisabeth richly. 'Let's not be naïve. And ... and, really, we can't continue to behave like schoolgirls sneaking into corners when we have families at home. Frankly, it's beneath my dignity.'

'Yes,' agreed Dora and yet already it was a sacrifice she would willingly have made: she would now have crawled into those hiding places, just to be kissed by this small assured woman.

She stared at the legs of Cally, who lingered as she closed the cupboard door.

The small room set aside for Oxbridge English was blue, curtained and abnormally unscuffed. There Cecilia began to study twice a week in the first term of the upper sixth. A teacher named Jane Greaves held the Tuesday lunchtime session, while James Dahl taught for ninety minutes every Thursday. In that room at the top of the school, Cecilia, Nicola and Annalisa studied alongside Lilith, the sneering and notably intelligent daughter of a retired actress and an accountant; and Nick, a German-speaking, oboe-playing self-appointed intellectual who resembled a middle-aged man in all but complexion. The teacher and five pupils sat around two desks pushed together while children shrieked operatically, rollerskated and sulked on floors below. The room, used for occasional staff or parents' meetings, was furnished with a small sofa and lamp, a framed Klimt in place of the usual batik hangings, and a ficus instead of the cheese and spider plants that swamped bedrooms and corridors beneath.

If she was happy in the A level English classroom with its trees floating to Mr Dahl's voice, now she was ecstatic. The experience was almost disturbingly joyful. During the period in which she, Nicola and Zeno had stalked, hidden, analysed, and collected sparse information, she had become accustomed to relying upon her imagination. Now she had been granted two double classes and one extra ninety-minute session a week with James Dahl himself. Amidst such excess, the desert that was the weekend came as something of a relief in the opportunity it afforded to digest and anticipate anew.

At home, Gabriel Sardo, that barely known boy from a frightening stratosphere, loped around the house and slept in the bottom bunk in Tom's room three weekends in four; Patrick no longer stayed the night in his pottery barn; Benedict had left school and appeared to be doing very little; Dora was exhausted; Cecilia walked the moors in order to talk to James Dahl in her mind, and otherwise she confined herself to her room.

By Monday mornings, she was dazed with reading, glutted with thoughts of Mr Dahl.

'Cecilia,' James Dahl often said. 'What do you think?'

And, sitting feet or even inches away from him, able to see the hairs on his knuckles, smell the cleanness of him, she spoke.

'Can you read for us?' he asked. 'Can you interpret that differently? See it, if you can, from a persecuted Puritan's point of view.'

The sun splashed from the metal of their ring binders and bleached sections of his skin, lay transparently on his fingernails or grew shadows from his pen. The leaves began to fall. Rain slanted outside the window that October; fogs drifted in from the moor and gathered in the gardens. Up in their afterthought of a room, sealed from the clamour of the school below, Cecilia often fantasised that term that if she blocked out Nick and the harsh stares of Lilith, she could be in an Edinburgh academy, a conservatoire, a Kensington seminary. It was as though she practised in a dusty studio in gelatine-coloured tights, her feet bleeding through her block shoes, her limbs fiery as she extended her tendons and pushed and pushed herself, her maestro Mr Dahl coming across her stretching herself to exhaustion in the half-light when others had retired.

Or she was a monk girl in a monastery by the sea studying all night until rose-fingered dawn touched her pallor. She was a hollow-eyed prodigy flirting with nervous exhaustion. She felt chosen; she felt fraudulent.

'Oxford and Cambridge set high academic standards,' said James Dahl. 'This can't be emphasised too much. Without wishing to put undue pressure on you all, you'll have to be extremely single-minded this term.'

His right forearm lay on the table, the hairs at his wrist visible. Cecilia glanced, as she sometimes did without meaning to, at the folds of material around where his penis must be, and blushed.

'Hardy's poetry incorporates some – some aspects of the late-nineteenth-century Gothic revival aesthetic, but in many ways it rejects it,' he said. His small class dutifully made notes.

'You don't need to write what I'm saying word for word,' he said. 'Just use it as a starting point for your own reflections on the work. Your examiners and interviewers will reward a combination of scholarship and original thought.'

'But sir,' said Annalisa in alarm, 'we do in class.'

'Do what?'

'Take down what you say.'

'That's fine at A level. This is a different standard.'

'Oh,' said Annalisa, her eyes and mouth matching circles.

By mid-October, her hand-wringing suffering magnified to unquenchable levels, Annalisa had dropped out of the Oxbridge class. In a wet outpouring of grief, she summoned her parents from Stockholm to the school for unnecessary discussions over the decision, while her love for Mr Dahl became ever more wiltingly forlorn. Eating-disordered and self-harming, drifting around the school in her flowery dresses and baggy Scandinavian tights, she began to talk about becoming a nurse or nursery teacher, voicelessly pleading with Mr Dahl to persuade her against such squandering of promise. He failed or refused to respond. Eventually she was sent to the expensive psychologist frequently employed by the school and assigned Dora Bannan as her pastoral tutor, a fact which inspired cruel mirth in

Nicola and Cecilia. Cecilia begged her mother to reveal details of their discussions, but Dora smilingly refused.

With Nick, Nicola, Lilith and Cecilia left labouring in the little room, lugging up books in their lunchtimes to avoid a library in which pupils smoked and caterwauled, the focus intensified. Cecilia felt purified. She was thin, fine, tuned to a pitch. Nothing else mattered but Oxbridge and James Dahl. The clouds scudded past the window, the room suspended high in the sky; the words were black and brilliant on the page, imprinting themselves on her mind with growing rapidity as her grasp of her subjects coalesced before unravelling again when a new layer of understanding deepened her vision. She read *The Hand of Ethelberta* in one night, skimmed *The Preface to the Lyrical Ballads* on the way to school, dipped into *Metamorphoses* and *The Golden Bough*, and took notes from a book of essays on Marvell in her first break.

One lunchtime in late October, Cecilia could read no more. She walked around the grounds, then left the school, as all seniors were entitled to do, and made her way to the nearby village with its local landmark, a medieval estate. Unaccompanied schoolchildren were banned from Elliott Hall and its spread of gardens, but Cecilia had been there on occasion with her mother and younger brother during lunchbreaks in earlier years. She mentioned Dora's name, and the woman at the entrance, all civility and patrician vowels, let her in.

The Garden! she thought, on glimpsing green through the weather-slubbed arches that led to the courtyard and slopes of lawn beyond. She began reciting Marvell's poem in her head and she was soothed. The tightness in her brain seemed to subside. *How vainly men themselves amaze / To win the palm, the oak, or bays*, she thought, walking along the courtyard path. Why did she strive so?

The winding lawns with their paths and topiaried borders sloped towards a herb garden, a sundial, a copse where bluebells grew in May. After the anarchy of Haye House, this place with its last herb scents, its birds and walls seemed to embody an ancient and more refined civilisation. She imagined James Dahl as he must have been in his college gardens in Oxford. A quadrangle. A slope to a punting river. A thin, fair young man playing tennis and loving unknown girls.

'Resting from uncessant labours?' said James Dahl, appearing on the path that led from the Japanese garden.

Cecilia gasped, tried to swallow the gasp, turning it into a small suppressed burp which even in that moment she knew she would spend years assessing for volume, persuading herself of its inaudibility and then waking to the hammering certainty that he had heard her.

'Uncessant labours?' she said dumbly.

He began to speak. '*Crowned —*'

'*Crowned from some single herb or tree,*' she said, quoting the same words a fragment of time after him and creating a jangling overlapping of speech.

She blushed.

'What do you like best in that poem?' he asked gently in an obvious attempt to save her from further embarrassment.

'I like — I like —' she said, coughing, 'the verse starting: *What wondrous life is this I lead!/Ripe apples drop about my head.*'

The sky seemed to rotate as a speeded-up film, clouds flying, birds large dark apparitions. His solemnity and height seemed enhanced in the white autumn light. The cedars of Lebanon rose in black behind him. She wished she had put on lip gloss and brushed her hair. Her coat was newly thin; she could feel air moving down her back, as though her clothes hung badly. She rubbed her tongue across her top teeth in case any remains of food lay there.

'*The luscious clusters of the vine/Upon my mouth do crush their wine,*' he recited. He swung the heel of his shoe against the path as he spoke. Stones scraped. All sound was amplified.

'*The nectarine and curious peach/Into my hands themselves do reach,*' said Cecilia, accelerating her speech into a gabble in case she had now overstretched the theme. 'I just came here for a bit of a break,' she added, to demonstrate that she understood that they had stopped quoting. She pushed her hair over to one shoulder.

'I'm resting – too,' he said.

'Oh! I'll leave you – let you –' she said, feeling blood pumping into her already flushed complexion.

He said nothing.

'*This delicious solitude*,' she blurted into the silence, following it with a small laugh, but he didn't take up the quote, and she jabbed at herself hotly in her mind for marring what had gone before.

'I wonder if Marvell had any inkling that his work would be known three hundred years later,' he said.

'Yes,' said Cecilia. 'Well,' she said after a pause. She pushed herself. 'He probably had intimations of immortality. But then so does every guitar-plucking fifth-former in Russell House.'

He smiled. They turned slowly. She walked beside him, uncertain of what else to do. She could see the tiny bobbles on the weave of his jacket. The movement of his arm in his sleeve as he walked beside her was visible, strangely intimate in its human normality. Her brain seemed to vibrate with the effort to find something to say. She heard her own breathing.

'So how are you finding the Oxbridge class?' he asked, turning away from her as he spoke with the curious tilting quarter-rotation of the head he employed when he asked a question or replied to an enquiry, as though avoiding unwanted focus. His lashes seemed to form an extra screen. 'Is it too hard?'

'No,' said Cecilia. 'Well,' she said. 'It is strenuous. Demanding. But that's the only way it can be. I suppose. It's such a short time. It's for such a short time, I mean.'

He paused. She occupied herself with staggered intakes of breath to divide his silence into smaller sections as a method for dealing with her embarrassment.

'I worry that pupils work very hard, but the truth is that they have to. There's so much competition –'

'And from far more academic schools,' said Cecilia passionately. 'From *proper* schools,' she said more fervently, not intending to show such emotion.

He glanced at her. 'Well, yes,' he said carefully. 'That's true. I believe that during most years Haye House has had no Oxbridge applications at all, or the odd pupil seeking tuition. It does need to be more specialist than that, I'm afraid.'

'Most people here want to take bongo classes or – or go to stained-glassmaking school!' said Cecilia. 'They want to travel round India or make experimental films.'

'Indeed,' he said.

'What an outrageous squandering of an education,' she exclaimed, kicking a pebble on the path.

His mouth moved slightly.

Cecilia blushed. 'I mean –'

'I fear it's not my place to comment,' he said.

'But *I* can,' she said in spirited tones. 'I find it inexplicable.'

He stopped. In the corner of her vision she caught his hair falling forward as he looked down. She couldn't see his expression. He rested his shoe on a plinth, and she noticed the crazing on its polished surface reflecting the light. 'Here's the *fountain's sliding foot*,' he said.

'*At some fruit-tree's mossy root*,' she said, and he laughed, and she thought how much she loved the rare sound of his laughter, and in its wake she felt a moment of intense happiness.

'You know those set texts by heart,' he said. 'You need something more – *muscular* now. Read *The Prince* by Machiavelli. Read as much of *Tristram Shandy* as you have time for.'

'I have,' said Cecilia with secret pride.

'Well that's good. Tackle a few of Donne's contemporaries? Lovelace and Rochester. They're not for everyone, but ... Also I'd recommend Milton's *Comus*. It's very beautiful. In fact, it has echoes of *The Garden: Bacchus that first from out the purple Grape / Crush't the sweet poyson of mis-used Wine* ...'

'... Gosh,' said Cecilia. She cringed at herself. 'It's beautiful.'

'It is, isn't it?'

They walked towards the outer courtyard, rooks calling as they passed through smoke drifting white in the white sky, and as she paced beside him focusing on the path, her speech became more relaxed, dialogue now eased by the rhythm of their footfall, just as conversation with friends took on a new fluency when oiled by night.

'What else do you read, Cecilia?'

'Oh,' she said, thinking, feeling the soaring of daring inside her. '*Cosmopolitan* and Enid Blyton.'

'Surely not!' he said.

'I do,' she said. 'Sometimes I can't read any more, except for that. My head is spinning. You should try some.'

'I believe Blyton's novels are said to contain compelling plots,' he said drily, and she exhaled through her nose in amusement.

'They're fantastic tales of thieves and smugglers, and deceitful schoolgirls, and dogs who can virtually talk and spiteful letters and things like that,' she said in a rush. 'They're almost gothic in their sensibility. I love them.'

'I see,' he said, pausing as though digesting the information. He glanced away again, lowering his head with the movement that made him appear to be excusing his height or his maleness, as though he were scrupulously aware of some traditional code of etiquette, and it occurred to her with surprise that he was shy. He seemed self-possessed; he appeared so experienced and quietly authoritative in class, his influence reining in some of the wilder excesses of the school, that the possibility of self-consciousness underlying his reserve had never occurred to her.

'And *Cosmopolitan* magazine?'

'*Cosmopolitan* is vaulting rubbish. I love it.'

'My my,' he said.

'Is lunch – What's the time?' she said, looking at her watch in her determination not to be a burden to him.

'I must be going,' he said.

'Yes,' she said, and she stood awkwardly, waiting for him to go, half-turning away to indicate her independence.

'Enjoy your reading,' he said, and he walked down the curved slope towards the hall. She stood on the higher section of garden and watched the back of his jacket, his old-fashioned gravy-coloured cords disappear through one of the arches, his hair a pale gleam. She leaned her head against a tree. She breathed deeply. She let five minutes pass, and then ran, sporadically leaping along high-hedged empty sections of the road, back to school.

Nine

February

AGITATED WITH nerves, Cecilia made herself visit Wind Tor Cottage to see Dora before she started her radiotherapy. Since Patrick's death, the cottage had been Dora's sunless retreat, the cello a dark gleam in a dusty corner, crockery gathering spiders on shelves, while Wind Tor House had been let out to lodgers, Dora wearily chasing late rent.

'Oh!' Dora said, looking up. She was stirring something in a pan.

'Nettles . . .' said Cecilia.

'Yes. I thought I'd try it again. Remember *Food for Free*?'

Cecilia screwed up her nose a little, then smiled.

'I thought you'd be working at this time, darling,' said Dora.

'I need to. But . . . I need, want to –'

Cecilia stopped.

There was something about Dora's mouth set thinly above a chin with a softening jaw. Something there. A glint of defiance, a coating of self-protection which momentarily halted her.

I came in to bring you this, she almost said, placing a mother-pleasing tin of Russian tea on the table, but she wouldn't let herself say it. There was a small silence. She felt, even in the depths of her pity, the old helplessness, the compromised fury rising up towards the person she had once loved more profoundly than anyone.

'You're looking a bit better,' said Cecilia, and she swallowed, and tried to disguise the swallow with a smile, and then she made herself stretch out and put her arms round Dora, hoping that Dora wouldn't feel that she was trembling. 'How are the scars?'

'Oh, still – still a little sore.'

'Are you taking all your painkillers?'

'Yes. I'm healing up nicely. Mr Kremer did such a fine job.'

'I'm so glad,' said Cecilia. 'I'll take you to your radiotherapy on Monday.'

'Oh no no! I've got this girl to do that. Katya. Thank you. She mows the lawn and shops too.'

'God! You didn't *need* to employ someone –' said Cecilia abruptly. 'Isn't that expensive?' She felt her skin flush.

'Oh no. I couldn't possibly –'

'I'll take you to the first session and then we'll discuss it. I wouldn't dream of letting someone else –' said Cecilia, shaking her head. 'How's the Tamoxifen?'

'Fine thank you. Just a very little bit of bleeding.'

'OK. Good.'

Dora glanced at her.

'You know,' Cecilia said, swallowing, 'one of – the reasons I came here. I wanted to look after you –'

'Thank you, darling. You know I'm more grateful for that than I can say.'

'I'm glad. And –'

'Ari's marvellous job!'

'Yes. Ari's marvellous job.'

Dora paused.

Cecilia breathed slowly to relax her throat in an attempt to normalise her voice.

'But I also –' she said eventually. 'I also came because I needed to come back; I . . . because I have to know what I can, whatever I can in my life about – about her.'

Dora paused again.

'You know that's not a good idea.'

'That's what you think. Yes, I know that,' said Cecilia, still gently. She struggled against tears.

Dora was silent.

'But – Please . . . Please.'

Dora shook her head. 'You know, you know that I think all this thinking and searching only brings heartbreak, Celie,' she said, and her voice faltered at the end of her sentence. 'I think that very strongly. You're given to it. It's all very old now . . . all this.'

'Please tell me what you remember,' said Cecilia. Patrick's grandfather clock ticked loudly in her ears.

'I've told you perhaps a hundred – more – times what I know, which is so very little, Cecilia,' said Dora, shaking her head, the tremor that so easily scratched her voice rising to the surface.

'What happened?' said Cecilia directly.

'I –' said Dora, and she took a step backwards. 'I can't remember everything.'

'You must be able to,' said Cecilia. She drove a fingernail into her own forearm.

'I can't remember,' said Dora. A skin of near-incomprehension formed like a cataract over her eyes.

'Please, Dora,' said Cecilia, holding her mother's shoulders, and her heart seemed to rise into her voice. 'You know I've spent a – lifetime suffering over this. I blame myself. But I have to . . . to ask you.'

Dora smiled blankly.

'I had my baby,' said Cecilia, ploughing on with audible desperation. 'You arranged the adoption. The *de facto* adoption. "Informal" doesn't even – even cover it. There are lots of bits of information missing, aren't there?'

Dora shook her head.

'I just want to know now who took her and what her chances of a happy life were.'

'You want to do investigation? More investigation work?' said Dora weakly, clearly struggling for words.

'Of course I do,' said Cecilia. 'Of course I have – always. It got – nowhere. But now I'm here, it seems more pressing, more – possible.' Tears sprang to her eyes. She blinked them away impatiently. 'I want to find her, to contact her. I want to love her, to say sorry to her.'

'No, no, no,' said Dora, shaking her head.

'I do,' said Cecilia.

'What would that do to your daughters?'

'I don't know . . . I don't know.'

'Exactly. It would be dreadful for them, Celie.'

'I don't think so –'

'I want to protect them,' said Dora.

'You hardly even *knew* them for years,' said Cecilia. She breathed deeply. She calmed her voice. 'Did you?'

'It wasn't my choice,' said Dora, hesitating. 'This isn't the way it's going to be, is it, Celie? That you've moved here and you're going to start raking all this up again?'

Cecilia paused minutely. 'Just tell me what she looked like.'

Dora moved through the cottage, stumbling determinedly towards a leaf fallen from a ficus. She clutched other leaves in her hand, tugged them from the stem, went to pour water, glanced out of the window.

Cecilia made herself look at Dora's back. A urine container sat on the window ledge, and Dora's hair was thinning. Cecilia moaned very faintly.

'You saw your baby,' said Dora eventually. She opened her mouth, then shut it.

'For a few minutes,' said Cecilia.

Dora said nothing.

Cecilia waited. Dora dropped her gaze.

'Please,' said Cecilia.

Dora hung her head. She stood still, then went and sat in the kitchen.

Cecilia gazed at Dora for a moment, pain softening her eyes, then turned, walked rapidly to the door and opened it, and Dora let her go in silence.

Cecilia ran to the house across the vegetable garden, hearing the phone ringing loudly through cold air, and when she spoke to Ari, she told him nothing of what had just passed, because she couldn't, though tears ran down her face. She was so distracted that he noticed and asked her what was wrong.

On the Friday of half-term, Cecilia drove her oldest daughter, the red-headed, focused Romy, to St Anne's girls' school, established almost a decade previously on the grounds of what had once been Haye House. While still in London, Romy had claimed that she would accompany her family to the bog-stinking sticks only if she could attend the expensive and academically selective St Anne's, and had secured herself a scholarship with daunting efficiency. Her parents had eventually capitulated, with some reluctance. The middle child, fifteen-year-old Izzie, scorned the very notion of St Anne's and chose the local comprehensive, while the youngest, Ruth, attended Widecombe Primary.

St Anne's rose before Cecilia like a polished, stagy version of Haye House, the buildings and grounds of the now defunct progressive school somehow rendered more aged and august with money. Large urns of flowers flanked the entrance, where once there had been purple-painted steps and twisty fibreglass sculptures. CCTV cameras glinted discreetly above the parapets. Cecilia felt diminished. She was, to her dismay, trembling as she drove into the car park, as though her mistakes glared, known to all; as though she had no power, even in adulthood, driving a car with her daughter.

'What's the *matter*?' said Romy, glancing at her.

Yet she was stronger now. She felt momentarily grateful for the authority age afforded and the knowledge it bestowed, however fallible. She caught sight of herself in the car mirror as she parked and saw in that concentrated slot of reflection how she had changed: her face more refined and her cheekbones more prominent as she had grown through her thirties and then into her early forties, her skin discomfitingly more tired, more shadowed round the eyes, her hair so much darker and browner, the scattering of freckles over her nose quite gone, and that wandering, receptive ability to blush and reflect every indignity thrown at her now mercifully almost controlled.

At seventeen, she thought, she had been notably naïve.

The path winding through a cluster of conifers – now taller and darker, as befitted the dark and crenellated nature of St Anne's – was where she had first noticed James Dahl. She had barely let herself think about him over the last years. And yet, she mused, perhaps, perhaps after all she was always thinking about him: always, some tiny strand of her mind flickering with a current that was him.

A deputy head in A-line taupe shook Romy's hand, introducing her to members of staff before classes began the following Monday, but Cecilia couldn't see the sombre formality as anything but a pantomime. The parquet so carefully restored was still covered in her mind with skidding durries and Tipp-Ex, the library they passed where uniformed girls would work with hair-twitching concentration was still the place where pampered children in orange cords smoked and launched themselves off bookshelves. Mr Dahl walked past in her mind, tall and serious, hazed with magic to his observers.

They were led outside.

'Oh look. How wonderful!' said Romy with newly patrician vowels, pointing at an art studio, and Cecilia, somewhat alarmed, could perceive her becoming already, in the space of less than an hour, a private school girl.

The immense geodesic dome that had once bubbled up like a fibreglass buttock in the middle of the grass had simply gone, the sweltering boom of its drama sessions atomised, leaving no traces at all on the lawn. The flagstones on which teenagers had sunned themselves quite legitimately by the pool instead of attending classes now bore railings and notices. Here Furry the school dog, edgy on his diet of tossed vegetarian sausages and magic mushrooms, had humped legs and suffered hairstyles. Now only a pigeon nodded and a recorded string concerto floated through a window. Few teachers were there among the administrative staff until lessons began on Monday, but the two or three who appeared summoned the memory of Elisabeth, Cecilia thought, catching a combination of well-cut wool and silk on a glimpse of back through a door that instantly made her recall the wife of Mr James Dahl.

Some of the staff, however, seemed young, young enough to be in their early twenties. Cecilia skimmed the hall as she did automatically when she was in a new environment, trying to find the one who slotted into the shadowy outlines of the child – now woman – she called Mara in her mind, following a spool of conjecture. Because, it seemed to her, the only route to sanity was to pursue those fantasies.

Her daughter could be anywhere, she knew. She could be anywhere. But she could be here, in the area where she had disappeared. She could have come back. She could have been here all the time. She was a trace of a person out there somewhere in the world just slipping her grasp. Cecilia was, forever, returning to Mara both in her mind and in notes she scrawled when she was in her study and meant to be working. It kept that imagined girl alive for her.

Cecilia saw her in cow-pitted meadows, in streets; she saw her hiding in bushes, or swimming in seas, or drowning while she, her mother, called out in despair; she saw her running away from her, turning to wave once more, disappearing across the fields, across the horizon, another horizon, and another, while she followed and followed.

She saw her in the pub. There was a barmaid in Widecombe who was, surely, around the age of twenty-three, who had a fresh-skinned eagerness and sensitivity, a sweet country look that Cecilia associated with a different strand of the girl Mara she so strongly imagined. There was a teacher at Ruth's school: a young teacher, just out of college, and Cecilia saw in her red hair remnants of the old colouring, and wondered whether her features bore something of her own. There was the girl who lodged near Widecombe and drove and cleaned for Dora who was about the same age, but whose looks were quite wrong.

I want you to know that I didn't give you away lightly, she wrote later in Mara's book: the book she kept for that first, unknown child, as she

did for her daughters Romy, Izzie and Ruth: books recording birthdays and events and observations. But while the others' albums were
filled with photographs and dated entries, the book for Mara was
almost entirely composed of speculation. *I want you to know that*, she
wrote, as she so often wrote to her, marking dates and mapping the
life she imagined for her, explaining the attempts she had made to
track her down, in uncontrolled fragments of writing that managed
to disturb her as she wrote them.

*You have grown up believing your mother abandoned you. That's what I
can't live with. I need you to know the mistake that this was. I want to look
after you. I write to you every birthday, but there's nowhere to send those
letters. I'm trying. I'm trying now. I will go on and on and on.*

*When you were born, you turned to me for milk. That's all I could give.
And I didn't even give you that. Milk.*

Ten

The Garden

W AS IT Barnaby who tipped her existence so far into chaos that she had done what she had done? Dora wondered later. Would Cecilia's baby have had a different future if it wasn't for Barnaby? Was life really so random? But an image of Elisabeth always entered the equation when she asked herself the question.

'I would now; I would, I dare,' Dora had wanted to say to Elisabeth, but it would have amounted to a begging, and she continued to ask herself whether, if Elisabeth attempted to seduce her fully, she would take fright. The idea of an illicit sexual liaison with another woman was so intriguing, she could barely stop herself from ruminating upon it, its repellent aspect enhancing the anticipation. But guilt and fear still dominated.

Patrick had recently taken to enquiring what she did during her lunch hours, and who her colleagues were, and who she had befriended, his questions apparently casually asked while betraying a tinge of aggression. Dora listed names, Elisabeth's always linked to her husband James's, and attempted to fashion anecdotes of them, as though life at Haye House were nothing but a soap opera with a cast of eccentrics whose chief narrative focus was Peter Doran the headmaster. She was, she thought, mid-story, no actress, and yet lies, once started, seemed to proliferate. Not lies, she hushed herself, hearing in her mind the voice of her mother. Omissions.

And still, Elisabeth occasionally turned to her with the full heat of her gaze, or touched her in passing, or said, quietly imperiously, 'Come here.' She stroked her even in public in the guise of relaxed bohemianism, and on rare occasions collided with her in a corridor and found a private place where they kissed, cool-mouthed and urgent.

What, thought Dora in the evenings, if Patrick were to discover? Discover the kisses, the fantasies that infected Dora's mind like a disease? What if he were to stumble, somehow, upon proof? Could he gain custody of their children? Of her unborn even? She stroked her stomach with a passing of nausea. He could never cope, but the clannish Bannans would close ranks, wielding wealth and family morals, the idea so terrifying to Dora that she pictured herself killing them one by one with a rifle in defence. She looked askance at Patrick and her mind hardened. She had never intended to be distracted. She had not meant to fall. She was, after all, a married woman and a mother. Patrick was either absent in his studio, or there, there, doggedly remaining in the kitchen as though placing himself as an obstacle to her private life. He was suspicious, watchful, and a streak of unpleasantness began to show as it never had before, making Dora even more careful. Or was she, she asked herself, simply deceitful?

As she made supper, she indulged the infatuation. Her mouth loose, her body heated and unstable, her vision glazed, she barely knew what she was doing as she boiled the pulses that had been soaking since the previous evening. She shivered with what felt like fever through coldness as she thumped out wholemeal pastry pizzas, sheer disbelief that her mind and body could, at least maddeningly intermittently, be desired by someone so sublime, making her mutter yelping clusters of words to herself and replay entire conversations in her head, prolonging the recollections with pauses for full gratification.

When her family began to come in, dropping jackets, chattering, complaining, trailing books and paper piles and rubbish, the fantasies peeled away one by one as every particle of her was demanded. But when she turned, turned towards a shelf to fetch a pan, they slotted back in front of her vision for stretched seconds.

Dora had barely known how to get through the later stages of her fourth pregnancy. In the car on the school run, she had breathlessly shunted the gear stick, her vision obstructed by steam and by the heads of shouting children, staring teenagers, a reading daughter, sheep clumped indignantly on the verges. She was irritated by the darkness of the tree-arched lanes alive with gnats. Newly sensitised, she could smell sour milk on the air. She noticed every chemical bin, every dead baby pigeon, every piece of corrugated iron pooled with puddles on the farm lane verges. She had cramp, and couldn't find a playing position for her cello. Yet in retrospect the pregnancy appeared as an interlude of free childcare compared with the chaos of the first eighteen months of her baby's life.

Barnaby had been born in a rush at home, the midwife still stuck on a lane between a French coach lost on the way to Widecombe and a farmer's van which had energetically reversed to avoid it, laming a pony. The National Parks sent a vet to the scene, exacerbating the traffic jam on the lane whose only landmark was a B&B sign above the hill descending to Ponsworthy. In the valley below, Barnaby emerged suddenly after eight hours of steady labour, assisted only by Patrick and a pair of brown-nailed lodgers, one of whom intoned about the home births she had attended while Dora wailed at the ceiling that she would never go through this again. The baby's head appeared.

'Come on, Dora, 'nother push for your midwife,' the lodger chanted. The grey streak in her hair flopped over her capillary-reddened cheeks.

'Fuck *off*,' hissed Dora.

'I've known plenty of women get uppity at this stage. Just relax. Lovely. Breathing ... In, out now, in –'

'Get her *out*,' bellowed Dora, wild-eyed, but moments later her son emerged in a slither and she was smiling, panting, her flesh fiery.

★   ★   ★

Dora began her maternity leave. She carried Barnaby at all times, feeding him assiduously, but he didn't gain weight as her others had done with their powdery thighs, their doughy bracelets of fat.

'He is harder,' she said with a smile after a day of fitful feeding. His demands, his sleeplessness, his mouth on her nipple, blocked out the now more remote Elisabeth for whole hours at a time: a gift that he brought with him.

'Each one is different, Mrs Bannan,' said the health visitor, a woman palpably past retirement age who organised the Widecombe WI children's Christmas parties at which Benedict and Cecilia had invariably succumbed to parent-shaming fits of giggling; and who negotiated the precipitous hills of the surrounding villages by bicycle, her face grimly set and her white uniform remaining spotless while her stockings were mud-splattered on arrival.

'He seems to feed all day, but he's not taking much,' said Dora, who had become yet thinner.

'He needs a bottle,' said the health visitor with a jaw movement that reminded Dora of her mother.

'Well . . .' said Dora.

She stoked the Aga with one hand, Barnaby hanging from her breast and grizzling while batting his head back and forth. She often sobbed. She cooked with him precariously tied to her chest since he cried if tilted towards an inanimate surface. She vacuumed with one hand, noticing the stealthy proliferation of animal and vegetable life that encroached: toadstools in the pantry twining from sooty sprays of mould at the base of the walls; birds and mice in the attic; cats slinking into the kitchen; foxes in the back garden.

'Elisabeth,' she murmured, almost hallucinating with tiredness.

When Barnaby was two and a half months old, the lodger who had helped with the birth drifted in through the open kitchen door, as lodgers tended to do, bearing a home-manufactured tincture of feverfew. Dora, her spine ringing, plumped Barnaby into her hands and stretched her arms.

'He's lovely, isn't he?' she said as she relaxed her shoulders.

'Here, here, baby boy,' the lodger crooned, cradling Barnaby in the crook of her arm. 'Whoopsy daisy, little star-gazer, there we are.' With a cloudy pipette, she eased a few drops of the tincture into his mouth.

'Oh I'm not sure about that,' said Dora hastily, snatching her baby back and dabbing at the liquid with a muslin.

'He'll be *great*,' said the lodger. 'You'll see. By tomorrow the small one'll have a great big lion-man's appetite, won't you, little boy?'

The baritone cough of a second lodger echoed outside among the foxgloves. A tall root vegetable gardener, a self-proclaimed Communist with a spray of red beard and laced boots, knocked on the open door.

'Chopped a few logs for you, Dora,' he said solemnly.

'Oh thank you. Thank you, Gid,' said Dora.

The man nodded. He stood there, saying nothing. 'Bea made this for you,' he said eventually, and handed Dora a knotty blanket, faintly oily to the touch, that smelled of sheep.

'Thank you,' said Dora again. 'I don't know what I'd do without you all.'

'Bea says poultices,' he said, nodding at the freshly grizzling Barnaby. 'For bringing down a fever.'

'Thank you,' said Dora again, and waited for him to leave.

Since Barnaby's birth, lodgers had arrived in the kitchen with gifts of astrological charts and offers of baby reiki; with papooses, dream-catchers and a hand-carved rocking crib that, too small for anything but a premature infant, was appropriated by one of the cats; and Dora had accepted such offerings, largely unused, with grace. Moll and her boyfriend Flite, who rented the cottage behind the back garden, volunteered for babysitting, the sole gift Dora really desired. Among Dora's older children, only Cecilia showed any interest in Barnaby, cradling him and kissing him repeatedly, but she was busy with her schoolwork and still the practical burden was barely alleviated.

That night, Barnaby kept the house awake with his projec-tile vomiting. He was put on formula milk the next day by the health visitor, an edict that elicited a stream of concerned visits from lodgers bearing herb-based solutions, goats' milk recommendations and cautionary anecdotes. When Dora went to bed while Barnaby lay in a new daze, she slept to escape her life, to escape Elisabeth.

In September, Dora Bannan returned to work. During the early months of her maternity leave she had indulged in hazy visions of school life: fractious Barnaby metamorphosed into a dungareed doll who was virtually transportable in her cello case, cooed-over by pupils and staff, and who would mutely play a xylophone in a corner while she taught her classes; but as an experienced mother she knew such musings to be rooted in self-delusion. Part-time work was impractical with older children to ferry home and a full salary to earn, and Haye House's liberal ethos and general turmoil simply did not accommodate the existence of babies.

Elisabeth Dahl and Dilys, a geography teacher, petitioned the governors for crèche provision on Dora's and future mothers' behalf, but met with blanket refusals on financial grounds.

'It's really, really scandalous,' said Idris, fingering his facial hair. 'If there's anything you need in the way of feeding or jiggling, piggy-backs and suchlike, just give us a nod.'

On what seemed the bleakest day of her life so far, Dora went from school to the neighbouring village of Wedstone to interview the childminder who lived in a bungalow surrounded by dying leylandia and plastic trikes. A mattress was propped against a wall, and the garden fence had been repaired with baler twine. Three small faces gazed through the window as she walked down the path and rang the doorbell to discuss hours, fees and nappy provision in a fug of cat.

'Sorry,' she muttered to Barnaby on the way out and rested her forehead against his cheek until he began to protest.

When she arrived back at school, she hid in a music room some distance from the staffroom and cried. To her considerable embarrassment, Elisabeth came through the door. Dora turned her face and busied herself restacking sheet music.

Elisabeth hesitated.

'How can I help?' she said.

'You can't,' said Dora in a muffled voice, still rifling through paper. 'Thank you.'

'I think it's very hard to leave one's child when one first returns to work,' said Elisabeth with the even pitch that had frequently silenced Dora's entreaties and could defeat the most aggressive dissenter.

'Yes,' said Dora with an unwanted sob, followed, to her mortification, by hiccups that wouldn't stop.

They both turned as another teacher entered the room. Dora moved away and tried to suppress the after-effects of her grief.

'Can't your – *husband* do some of the childcare?' said Elisabeth quietly.

'Oh,' said Dora, now attempting to smile through the tears that smeared her vision. 'I think and think about it, but frankly he'd be bloody useless. He'd – he'd play him songs all day on his blessed guitar, but there's a risk he'd lose him.'

'I see,' said Elisabeth, raising her finely arched eyebrows.

'The uselessness of men sometimes amazes me,' said Dora, looking up at Elisabeth wryly and feeling inept under her dark brown gaze.

'Yes.'

'Oh Elisabeth . . . Talk to me.'

'I am,' said Elisabeth, her face motionless. Then her mouth softened. 'No.'

'You chose this route,' said Elisabeth.

'I did not choose to become pregnant.'

Elisabeth merely raised one of the eyebrows. 'There is some choice,' she said eventually.

Dora shook her head.

'I miss you,' she said.

Elisabeth was silent.

'So –' said Dora then. 'Celie helps when she can. She dotes on him.'

'I hope so,' said Elisabeth. 'She's a very nice girl.'

'Thank you. She helps more when *Little Women* is on top of one of the book piles by her bed,' she said, hearing herself astonishingly and outrageously speaking to Elisabeth as though she were simply another colleague. Again, she wanted to protest, or to beg.

Elisabeth's mouth twitched. 'And the boys?'

'The boys ...' said Dora, and thought of Tom and the frequently absent Benedict, drumming, skateboarding, reading obscure comics and sitting around jabbing at sticks with carving tools or watching the small grainy telly upstairs in a miasma of farts.

'They come down to eat.'

You're beautiful, thought Dora.

'Boys eat,' said Elisabeth.

Dora looked at her watch and remembered Barnaby, who was currently in a studio with the jazz ballet teacher Kasha in a free period between classes. Since his birth, there had been dirty sinks, stacked-up washing, children's clothes requiring mending that were rotting against a pile of old horse tack in one of the utility rooms. Dora experienced a moment of vibrating panic that here was another mouth to feed, another body to save, another soul not to damage. God, she muttered in her head. Good God, please.

'Could your husband's family help with a nanny?'

'Really I don't think so. They help with the school fees. They have never offered more, though I sometimes think, privately, *help me*,' said Dora, shivering, knowing that by now the Bannans were aware of the futility of funding their son and were too astute to feed a bottomless pit. 'But –'

But she had learnt never to depend on a man, or on anyone else.

'Really,' said Dora, looking down at her feet, then glancing at the other teacher, 'for a while at least, I'll have to work and use a child-minder. She lives in an unpleasant house with expensive breeds of cat.'

'I do,' said Elisabeth Dahl slowly, 'I do wonder at people.'

You, Dora wanted to say, but could not say, you are the person who met my new son and said, 'They are dull at this stage, aren't they? Especially baby boys.' With no apologies, no congratulations, no gift for the baby, only perfume for me. Your nostrils faintly flared with distaste. You, a mother of sons. And you wonder at people.

★   ★   ★

As the term went on, Dora bit her nails and visited Barnaby at the childminder's each lunchtime. Instead of masticating wholemeal samosas alongside her colleagues as they discussed performance innovations or Peter Doran's sex life, Dora ate a cold slice of quiche alone on the lane on the way back, her hems dark with the hedgerows and her arms full of the shape of Barnaby.

Elisabeth was habitually evasive.

When the childminder was ill, Dora begged neighbours; she scrabbled for childcare, ringing home in her lunchbreak to make sure fragile logistics had somehow fallen into place; she occasionally considered asking Cecilia, whom she trusted more than Patrick as a babysitter, to stay at home for the day and look after the baby brother she adored, the teacher encouraging the pupil to play truant, but missed school days were viewed as catastrophic by her scholarly daughter and Dora could not bring herself to ask. Patrick became a better father the older his children grew, but the toddler stage simply failed to engage him.

One lunch hour when Barnaby had gone down for his nap early, Dora took a walk outside the village to Elliott Hall before returning to school. The progressive artistic nature of the place still pleased her at some profound level, the hall's barn theatre advertising *'Tis Pity She's a Whore* and a children's weaving lesson taking place in one of the medieval guesthouses across the courtyard. She thought, for a while, about Walter Gropius and his followers. She thought about all the locations to which the Bauhaus had moved, longing at some level to be in those places. She had discussed them with Elisabeth. She had been reading a biography of Bertrand and Dora Russell when she had discovered she was pregnant. There was a certain form of philosophical and artistic expression that had bloomed earlier in the century, and its ripples, she thought, could be found here. It was this, this far-reaching legacy that had brought her to this area and snared her, while the resident hippies' less cohesive babbling washed over her. It linked her to Elisabeth, who had such similar interests and aesthetics, while Patrick did not. She felt, now, as though her brain had died since her fourth pregnancy.

She crossed the courtyard and smiled at the heads bent over primitive looms. Smoke trailed across the walls from a bonfire behind the kitchen garden. A man, a timeless man in moleskins and wellington boots, prodded the fire and wheeled a barrow from a pile of branches.

Through the arch on the further side of the courtyard the gardens rolled in rich severity. Berries and evergreens splashed bare lawns. A duck passed in the sky. She followed it with her gaze and wondered whether Barnaby had yet woken. She stood against the arch as a girl ran down the hill and into the arms of her mother, who scooped her up and left. Two figures rounded the corner by the azalea path. Dora watched her own daughter and James Dahl walk slowly along, their bodies in profile as they followed the curve of the gravel. They were so delineated by the late autumn light that the air around the folds of his trousers was almost vibrant with clarity. Cecilia's hair was brighter, bolder in the muted glare. She wore no coat, Dora noticed, instinctively wanting to dress her. He was talking to her and she was listening. This, then, was who her daughter loved. It was suddenly ridiculously clear. Dora wanted to laugh and laugh; she felt unstoppable mirth, something close to hysteria: a surge of amusement that contained no trace of cruelty, and she leaned against the arch and tried to stop herself shaking. She found she had tears in her eyes.

She had pictured a rangy, pretty-featured upper sixth-former, a quartet of candidates springing to mind. She had briefly considered Daniel the school tennis coach, who attracted a small following. She frequently wondered about Cecilia's friendship with Gabriel Sardo. She would have assumed, if questioned, that Cecilia viewed her English teacher simply as the type of traditional pedagogue her funny old-fashioned mind seemed to crave.

'Stop it,' she snapped at her below her breath. 'Don't waste your love.'

Dora watched Cecilia's nervous lively gestures in the face of James Dahl's silences. He looked notably older than her unworldly country daughter with her almost dangerously desired vision of a future.

Dora gazed at this man who was loved by her love and loved by her daughter, and was unable, hard though she tried, to see what it was that they saw in him. How could they feel passion for him? He was too conservative, too tightly wrapped in a coating of privacy. His aspect was faintly colourless beyond the sooty contrast of his eyelashes, though he had, she supposed, a gentlemanly sort of male beauty. She preferred something more rough hewn, more expressive in a man.

They had stopped by a rose bush and Cecilia was talking, moving her head and arms rapidly, dropping her gaze to the ground, all movement accelerated. He was nodding patiently. He was a man in his thirties listening to the prattle of an intelligent schoolgirl, mildly enjoying it even and awarding her the respect her enthusiasm deserved. He was a married father perhaps two decades her senior.

'*Celie*,' Dora wanted to say, kindly and gently, 'come here right now.'

She thought of Elisabeth cradled in the arms of this man.

James and Cecilia began to walk again. She has left her coat behind on purpose, thought Dora, observing the waist of her daughter set off by a belt she had pulled in tightly, her legs still somehow childish in over-worn tights though they were meant to be womanly in the heels she wore. She pictured Cecilia that morning almost hopping between dry sections of path and lane, fastidiously pulling those heels away from the boot-wearing crowds in the car.

He leaned as though to hear her, his faded mac falling from straight shoulders. Dora watched her daughter: the formation of her head with its small chin and matching curve of a nose and those flying dark Bannan brows. Dora could hear nothing that they said. She watched a silent film: a man oblivious to the emotions of an infatuated girl.

An agnostic since her teens, she prayed for her children. She rued the wounds she had, inevitably, inflicted with her unknown obsession. She looked at her daughter and she felt love. *Adore someone who wants you*, she pleaded silently, kissing the spray of freckles remaining over her nose, reaching out in her mind to her and pulling her back to her by her hair, as though enacting some Greek myth.

* * *

Dora returned to Haye House and covered for a flute lesson, despite her frequent assertions to the school that she was not a wind instrument specialist. As she taught, she began to calculate whether she had enough rusks at home for Barnaby and decided she would have to use crusts. She glanced at her watch and wondered whether she could finish the third year's music class in time to pick him up before collecting the others.

She saw Cecilia walking alone by the drama department's geodesic dome, clearly caught in thought. Where was Nicola, her unfavoured best friend? Zeno Dannett, the other member of her old trio, was now viewed as mildly troublesome by the school. Instead of mooning around the grounds in silence, she had joined a gang that smoked by the river and energetically kissed and coupled on its banks. Staff found sections of foil down there, condoms and Rizlas. The nominal librarian, in reality a general studies teacher who occasionally discussed classification systems and spent school money on his favourite authors, laughingly enumerated the paperbacks returned with squares torn from their covers for use as cigarette filters.

Zeno had found passion beyond James Dahl. She had lost her virginity to a classmate with eczema who painted graffiti-influenced murals and expected sex most lunch hours. Her interest in her English teacher was now weighted with condescension: she discussed him from an amused distance, as though contemplating a film star slightly out of fashion. Annalisa the Swede wept and idolised with ever more ardour. Ignored by the boys in her year, Nicola remained virginal and devoted. Ignoring the boys in her year, Cecilia – who had only ever, with a sense of experimental duty, kissed two contemporaries, their adolescent slightness, their pimples and downy growth alienating her – felt her attachment grow even as she eschewed its more obvious manifestations. She was seventeen, and could no longer twitter and cluster like the girls in lower years who imagined themselves invisible as they trailed Mr Dahl.

By November, Cecilia had met James Dahl four times in Elliott Hall gardens. She walked there most blowing November lunchtimes on the chance of a sighting, assuring Nicola that she could study more easily in solitude and feigning oblivion to her hurt response. She glanced at Nicola as she spoke, considering her frowns and her moles, the anxious repositioning of wiry hair behind shoulders, the mind so often overlooked by others, and a shiver at the knowledge of what she could tell her ran through her. She felt the almost sickening power of it; the gathering of repeated temptation. But she couldn't tell her. It was far too dangerous. Diana was her only confidante, as she had been from early childhood. Fearing Nicola's presence and terrified of jeopardising in any way the pure thing, Cecilia had retreated into secrecy. She walked it off on the moors instead, bathed in it, wrote hidden page after page.

The third time she had seen James Dahl, there was bonfire smoke: a man throwing leaves, some children like fat-faced fairies pulling wool inside a building. She knew that she would remember all the details of these times.

'It's nice to talk to you,' he said at the end of their walk, and then left her to return to school.

Now she haunted the gardens. She sat huddled in her coat on benches writing notes; she crouched at the foot of the sundial reading with a tighted calf carelessly but elegantly displayed in case James Dahl should come past; she walked and read and drummed quotations into her head using spontaneously fashioned mnemonics, a whole system of visual and verbal links whose oddness would cause great humiliation if revealed. She was attuned to movement through the arches, any winter walker a smear of colour on the corner of her vision. She longed for him to arrive, just as, puzzlingly, she almost dreaded his entrance. He was, she thought, like her own self talking to her; but a better self.

That week, as she mounted the central flight of steps that rose beneath curves of bare branch, James Dahl entered the gardens with his wife.

Cecilia abruptly crouched down behind a cedar with her books, her heartbeat uneven and her breath visible in the air. All the resolve she had drummed into herself – be bold; be daring; push and push yourself – was punctured by this glimpse of reality. She repositioned herself, hiding among the branches that almost touched the ground and resting one knee on the earth so that she could be seen to be adjusting her shoe if found.

He seemed more human; he appeared more unguarded. His stride was faster. He mounted the large grass steps that formed a series of smooth ha-has beside his wife Elisabeth. They were arguing, Cecilia understood with a rush of invigoration that reminded her of being a child overhearing adults.

'No!' he said, more forcefully than he had ever spoken in the classroom. 'I don't think that's something we should necessarily even consider.'

'Don't try to influence me,' she said icily. 'I – I really don't think you have any right.'

Cecilia watched her intently through the branches. She frowned. Elisabeth's bewildering friendship with her mother seemed to have subsided some time before, but her own fascination with her love rival only increased as time went on.

'Christ!' he said.

Cecilia shivered, more alarmed by the idea of discovery by Elisabeth than by her husband. His hair caught a gleam of light through a gap in the old wall that wound around the stairs leading to a pergola, now disused. She studied him, spinning out the hot stretched seconds of observation available to her.

Elisabeth walked on ahead. She was frosty, dark-eyed, like a fierce but elegant animal, thought Cecilia. A mink. A slender wolf. Today she wore pressed wool trousers with a tight black coat, her hair smooth on the nape of her neck, its sections lying in layers, thick and motionless on her forehead.

'Darling,' said James.

Cecilia flinched.

'Yes,' said Elisabeth.

'I really don't wish to argue with you.'

'Nor do I wish you to,' she said as an uninflected statement that carried a dismissal of his words.

'I think we need to discuss this later,' he said, sounding weary.

'If you want to,' she said, hesitated minutely, and then walked off, fast and unerring, through the arch to the courtyard and out of the grounds.

Cecilia waited. She felt like a dirty, crouching child, measuring her breathing until James Dahl had finishing pacing down the steps and then walked up again. She heard him exhaling in the still air. Leaves crunched under his feet. Every sound and movement seemed private. A spider ran beside her. She stood, moved swiftly to a different section of the garden while his back was turned, and then walked along on the further side of the azalea path.

She heard him coming towards her.

'Cecilia,' he said when she rounded the corner.

She held a book in front of her as she walked. She made herself recite quotations under her breath, continuing, hot-skinned, after he had addressed her.

'What are you doing here?' he said.

'Oh,' she said, blushing more deeply. 'The same as usual,' she said, gathering her dignity. 'Working. I'm learning some quotes from Donne today.'

'So tell me your latest.'

'*These miracles wee did; but now alas, / All measure, and all language, I should passe, / Should I tell what a miracle shee was,*' she said instantly, blushing at the intensity of the emotion expressed.

'I fear you might have seen me with – with my wife,' he said, glancing at the ground. 'I'm sorry if you overheard our conversation.'

'Oh no!' said Cecilia. 'I mean, I didn't hear you.'

'I –'

'Not much,' she added, speaking across him. She drew herself up. 'Sorry. Sorry I – interrupted –'

'Well I'm sorry. It occurred to me you might be here. We silly ad – supposed adults – should conduct our disputes at home.'

'It doesn't matter,' she said in a small voice.

'No, we should.' He shook his head. 'I'm afraid that human nature is terribly flawed.'

'Oh –'

'But you don't have to know that quite yet.'

'Yours isn't,' she said spontaneously, then held her breath.

He smiled, his eyes catching the light. 'Yes it is.'

She looked down.

'Think of Milton: *Of man's first disobedience and the fruit . . .*'

'Think of Beth March,' she countered, instantly embarrassed at her childish reference.

'Alcott?'

'Yes.'

'Doesn't she die?'

'Yes –'

'The meek don't inherit the earth,' he said. 'I used to believe, hope – trust – that they might.'

'No,' said Cecilia, and an image of steely Elisabeth Dahl walking out of the gardens came to her. She stood taller and smiled directly, radiantly, at him. She was exhilarated by her own temporary boldness, so long planned, so long promised to herself at night.

He glanced at the ground. 'Perhaps I'm over-cynical,' he said. A smile creased his lips. His hair fell over his forehead. His features seemed more relaxed.

'No,' said Cecilia, euphoria running through her as she confirmed her pledge that she would possess him, nailing her vow to a certain crack in the bark of a tree she was passing as a symbol of her promise. 'The meek get nowhere. Nowhere at all.'

'No –'

'I have to go too,' she said, and slightly unsteadily, heady with resolve, she walked out of the gardens and left him standing there.

Eleven

February

URING HER first English lesson at St Anne's, the firs through the windows lightly misted with damp from the moors, the teacher, a tall, faded person with an old-fashioned accent, seemed to scrutinise Romy. He looked up at her with dark lashed blue-grey eyes. She caught his gaze; he looked away. His focus was generally fixed on the table or on some unspecified spot on the floor as he talked, his head bowed so that he had to glance up from beneath his eyelashes when he addressed an individual; he spoke in a low note, and guided his class with quiet certainty. Romy caught him appraising her again and she was disconcerted, instantly blushing, because he was ancient, and not overtly lecherous. Eventually she smiled awkwardly, and he rested his solemn gaze on her for one more moment, then looked away.

The rain now came in over Lundy and across the sea, over beaches and boats to swell the Torridge. It soaked the flatter lands to the north of the moor, then rose across Kitty Tor, clattering against the clapper bridges, pouring over clitter, driving the Dart with its weight. Rain filled Burrator Reservoir and sluiced the disused tin quarries near Huntingdon Warren, across Dockmell, Drywall and the Weir, making cows steam and thatches ache. It found the house and battered at the windows.

Ruth lay in bed and prayed for her parents to stay alive now they had come to this wild strange place. What if her mother's car tipped off a mountain and went flying and tumbling and tumbling into the river below? What if her father crashed into an Eddie Stobart on the motorway? She pressed her flesh as hard as she could bear and prayed. Her mother had kissed her so gently that night to put her to bed. She was her friend who always looked after her. She loved her mother's smell, the bits of brightness in her hair like red wood colour if she looked; she loved her cuddles, because all was safe as long as she was holding her as she said goodnight. She begged her for more, for more hugs, strokes, holds, couldn't bear to let her go, she was so soft and smelled of her, and then it was nine o'clock and she would say she must must must go downstairs, but she would beg, and always she'd stay a little longer, stroking her forehead, kissing her ear, chatting to her.

She had begun to walk out of school at lunchtime, because no one noticed, and the man was there, a big strange old man. He was in the fields and among the mossy trees around Widecombe, never on the Green. He offered her a chip, but she was too shy to take it.

Cecilia came downstairs before school. There they all were, her three girls, the flesh-and-blood girls: there was the tall and driven Romy with her back turned to her sisters and her mobile propped against a windowpane in hope, her hair flaring with threads of tiger and green in late February sun. There was Izzie the middle, adopted, child and the most troublesome, alert for stimulation. And there was Ruth, hoarding her Sylvanian Families and dirty dolls' bedding like a hamster.

Dora's hospital visit wasn't until the afternoon, and Cecilia had planned her timing. She would go there after dropping off Romy at school and ask her to the house for tea. After only intermittent contact over so many years, their relationship laden with seemingly irreparable wounds, this most fragile of subjects had to be treated with care and with love even, during a period of ill health with its possible ramifications. The cancer crouched over everything.

'What are you doing?' Ari would have snapped had he any inkling of her continued need to find reasons for the abandonment.

'Looking after my mother,' Cecilia said in her head, answering smoothly, the subject of that lost baby a tinderbox.

She could get very little past him. If he had been there in the week, he would, she knew, have sensed by now that Mara was haunting her more forcefully than she had ever imagined. That she saw her here in the fields, in the mud, in the river; that she addressed her in her head and in notes; that she chased her, chased her, chased her.

You're there where the gorse prickles your back, she thought, and she pressed her own nails into her flesh. *I think I see you, peeping over the riverbank. Try to find your first home. Come across the bracken. Try.*

Twelve

The River Island

JAMES DAHL entered Wind Tor House. He seemed to Cecilia to arrive in slow motion, splinters of him emerging spotlit through the door, then plunged into shadow by an intrusion of heads.

The autumn term had finished, Oxbridge entrance was over, and the Bannans were holding their annual Christmas party. Several neighbours and a group of Dora's colleagues arrived at the same time as Diana's family, the cold air in their wake making the fire flare and spit. James Dahl helped Elisabeth out of her coat, then took it back into the hall. The bodice of Elisabeth's dress revealed the faintest gradation of cleavage, and her habitual string of pearls had been replaced by a single large black pearl on a chain. She scanned the room openly in the fashion of a hawk surveying territory, then dropped her gaze and stood as though waiting to be brought a drink. Strained and wary, Dora obliged. She was aware of where Patrick stood as she greeted Elisabeth, glancing in his direction to ascertain whether he had noticed her. He would not dream that she could love a woman, she knew, but the image of the mighty Bannans returned to her and she glanced round for her children, only satisfied when she could see the faces of all but Barnaby, who was in bed.

Dora had been up late for several nights draping a ceiling-height tree felled by Patrick and Tom, clearing the fluff-sticky oil and spider remains from the wooden bowls piled on top of the dresser and filling them with grapes, cheese, roast chestnuts and chocolates already gigglingly filched by children. Lanterns lined the garden path.

Christmas lights tangled with holly on beams; candle and log flames left saturated shadows in corners. Haye House staff were uninhibited as they celebrated the end of term. Dora wove through them, cheery yet vigilant in her hostess duties. She caught sight of Elisabeth's cold fine profile now against a bookshelf.

Cecilia had instinctively failed to inform her two school friends of this year's larger version of her family's traditional Christmas party in case, by some gift of fortune that she didn't dare to expect, her mother might invite her old friend Elisabeth and her husband among her closer circle of colleagues. Here they were. The Dahls. Elisabeth and James.

Friends were pouring in, no longer knocking on the door, jostling, laughing and greeting as they dipped heads under lintels and clapped hands on backs, proffering drinks and dishes in a traditional collective effort, the Bannans' generosity so openly founded on financial uncertainty.

Cecilia sat beside Diana. She shook with a steady tremble as she and Diana tracked James Dahl's progress across the room. His presence was almost unbearable.

'Don't watch him so obviously,' Cecilia hissed, gripping Diana's arm.

Dora refreshed the mulled wine that simmered on the Aga with yet another cheap bottle bought at the Cash and Carry, moved into the sitting room and glanced at her daughter.

'Look at them,' she said to her friend Beatrice as she wiped glasses.

'I know,' said Beatrice.

'I don't know what one does with girls. At this stage.'

'Exactly.'

'How do you react to them? Are we supposed to rein them in? Look at Benedict. He's a boy still – an unwashed youth. He smells. I'm sorry. He's blundering, but she's aware. Do you think ...?'

'Virgins, the pair of them,' said Beatrice briskly.

'Yes,' said Dora, still watching Diana and Cecilia deep in conversation on a small settle at the other end of the room, absorbed in each other yet feverishly aware of their imagined audience, of the import of their gestures and muttered secrets.

'She's the one we always parade for the grandparents,' said Dora. 'The one least likely to upset them. The rest are such scruffs. I wonder quite what they'd think of her in that get-up?'

Beatrice laughed and Dora watched her seventeen-year-old daughter, her features almost transparent with youth, as though the new hormones in her blood were visible beneath her skin, its faint freckles like flecks of vanilla, her hair a contrasting dense red-brown. There was, thought Dora, something disturbingly young-animal-like, fawn-like, calf-like, about her, her arched mouth so full that it was held slightly open by the set of its own curves. In its translucency, Dora thought now, it was almost like glass.

Cecilia had, that afternoon, pinned and tightened a dark velvet dress bought in a second-hand clothes shop in Exeter. She wore lipstick, small diamond earrings and thin black tights. She had dressed in a careless good mood while engaged in a shouted conversation above the sound of the Doors with Gabriel Sardo, who was staying there for the beginning of the holidays. She had begun to understand which colours suited her, the clashes and opposites, the dusty pinks and moss greens that enhanced her, and so she displayed her colouring, no longer hiding it like a shameful rash.

'He's not talking to me,' muttered Cecilia to Diana in a voice of muted panic. 'It's already nearly nine thirty.'

The heat and volume were escalating; the floorboards jumped.

'He's your *teacher*. He's surrounded by work people. He's not just going to saunter up to you,' said Diana.

'I know,' said Cecilia. 'I know.' She glanced at her watch. 'Come with me. He's just not leaving that end of the room. Look how much he has to stoop below the beam. I'm going to make my way to the middle. Can I? Can I?'

'*Yes.*'

'Really? Can I?'

'*Yes.*'

Cecilia walked to the sofa, urgently speaking nonsense to Diana, her gestures lively and amused in an effort to seem engaged, to appear incidentally vibrant in snapshots caught by his eye.

'What?' said Diana.

'Nothing. Yes, well. It's a nice evening, isn't it? Fuck. Talk to me. I don't know. Come on. Look. Talk. Look at the fire. What shall I say?'

'I. Yes . . .'

'I'm –' she said, taking a big mouthful of mulled wine, then a smaller one, feeling warmth fanning through her blood. 'I'm going to go up to him.'

She approached the section of room in which James Dahl stood talking to a group of colleagues. He wore corduroy trousers, an open-necked shirt, a brown tweed jacket. His bleached-out 1940s appearance was exacerbated by the firelight, the flames rendering his hair and eyes a uniform pale sepia that painted out signs of maturity so that he looked disconcertingly youthful: he was a surreal celluloid apparition standing against familiar beams and books.

'Hello,' said Cecilia from too far a distance, and then coughed. She tried again, almost calling, finding she had little control over the volume of her voice. 'Hello.'

He turned around and glanced at her, looked away, finished a conversation, his manner considerate, old-worldly almost, then turned to her again.

'Cecilia,' he said, smiling and stepping towards her. 'Many congratulations on your offer,' he said warmly, and shook her hand. 'That is excellent news. Excellent. I was very pleased for you indeed when I heard.'

'Thank you,' said Cecilia, smiling, faltering. 'Lilith got in too. She'd be better than me in interview,' she mumbled.

'Probably,' he said matter of factly. 'But your written work is generally stronger. The others didn't receive offers. It's an achievement to celebrate.'

'Thank you,' she said, unable to look at him, 'for the classes. Thank you. Thank you so much.'

'Oh –' he said, dipping his head at a beam. Mistletoe brushed his ear and he moved away with awkward rapidity. 'You'd have achieved it anyway –'

'No! I'd have had to have been taught by *Wiggy*. It'd have been experimental monologues inspired by Kerouac's travels,' she said, too fluently, reciting examples pre-prepared in fantasy conversations in the bath. She hesitated intentionally. 'Milton as viewed by Lawrence Ferlinghetti. I'd have ended up at Torquay Tech.'

He smiled.

'Mr Wigram, I'm sure, inspires certain students . . .' he said.

'Oh come on,' said Cecilia, helping herself to wine and filling his glass with a proprietary air. 'Students who want to create "narratives" to perform in the "drama space". He,' she said, feeling the renewed heat of alcohol pluming through her, 'he's the type to encourage the writing of horrible haikus when – when people should be studying their Shakespeare set texts.'

James Dahl laughed.

'Ridiculous place,' he murmured, sinking his words into his glass. His fringe fell on to his forehead. Laughter rose from the end of the room.

'*What?*' said Cecilia delightedly.

'Oh, I –'

'Come on, tell me,' she said rapidly with a new carefree happiness so that she touched his arm as she said it. 'Do you think so too? Oh God. I – I think it's maddening. Farcical. I'd love it to burn down. An enormous spontaneous conflagration.'

'Of course,' he said, looking at his feet, 'this is – a purely subjective view. But – I do think it's an absurd institution.'

Cecilia let out an abrupt gleeful laugh. 'Sit down,' she said.

She hesitated, then sat next to him on a chair near a bookcase. The babble of the party rose.

Patrick could be heard telling a nostalgic anecdote to a small audience by the woodburning stove at the eastern end of the room. Guests clustered on the rug around the flames of the fire on the other side: various artists whose wooden carvings and monochrome prints had been bought, ill-afforded, by Dora, were nodding, expounding with expansive gestures. Benedict and his friends were stationed by Patrick's old gramophone, a sheet of Indian printed cotton draped over the back of a young farrier met travelling and semi-encasing two others like a yurt in the corner of the room.

'I loathe it,' said Cecilia, her voice deeper as she drank wine.

'There is a bewildering culture of underachievement,' said James, pausing. 'I think it discriminates against those – the pitifully few – who want to learn.' He bent his head, seemingly addressing his polished brown shoes. 'I do find it self-indulgent and ultimately nihilistic. I'm sure many feel excluded. Far more than you may imagine.'

'But they all seem so . . . to fit in.'

'Of course. But an exclusion complex can be almost universal.'

'Oh . . .' said Cecilia. 'God. Yes. God.'

He looked at the ground, frowning. He hesitated. 'I feel as though I've been wasting time,' he said, a characteristic quarter-rotation of his head making his hair glow dully in the firelight. 'With – with exceptions, of course,' he said, lifting his eyes, nodding gravely at Cecilia, then turning to the floor once more. 'At least where I was – a, well, boys' public school – those boys were expected to learn, and so they did.'

'Why did you move to Haye House?'

'Oh, my wife, my wife wanted a change. To work. She had largely been a full-time mother until that point, and here was both job and studio. It was a promotion for me. A challenge.' He smiled wryly, faintly grimaced.

'Where is Mrs Dahl?' said Cecilia, looking around.

'I don't know,' he said, following her gaze.

'It's meant to be this idyll. It's not. One day someone should write about it.'

'You will,' he said.

'No no. So – do *you* write?' said Cecilia, blushing. She was aware of Diana on the outer edge of her vision, silently willing her to look up. Elisabeth Dahl was out of sight, the party extending to the kitchen and the other sitting room, shouts emerging from the garden, a cacophony of laughter by the fire. Most teachers were now behaving more wildly than they did at school.

Cecilia glanced down. James Dahl's long corduroyed leg was inches away from her on a chair; his shoulder was freakishly close to her nose and mouth. The experience seemed too intense and improbable. He shifted in his seat, apparently considering her question.

'Oh,' he said, shaking his head. 'No. No. I tried and tried. I think I had little to say. Or I had a *perfect* vision in my head and nothing could equal that. I was always surrounded by better works.'

'But you know that aiming for perfection can be an excuse for inactivity.'

'Can it?' he said, briefly turning to her.

'Of course! What a great excuse: Shakespeare did it better. You have to abandon that idea of perfection or you do nothing. Even in an essay. You must know that. It can never possibly fulfil that glorious complete vision lodged in your mind.'

'You're right,' he said, looking at her, pausing and catching her eye, then lowering his gaze again. 'You've worked that out before I fully did.'

Drumbeats vibrated through the floor. Lodgers were rolling spliffs in a huddled production line. A gardener, his Adam's apple echoing the movement of his knuckles, was tapping a group of slender drums pressed between his thighs like a clump of toadstools, his eyes closed as he nodded to the rhythm. A friend of Benedict's joined in with what was clearly intended to be an African-inspired cry, and Jocasta from Haye House began to sway, her hands closed in a praying position above her head as she undulated, laughingly glancing round for an audience.

'Lord,' muttered Cecilia. 'Take me to civilisation.'

He laughed, a laugh distinctively his that only occurred outside class: an almost silent shaking of amusement, his lashes lowered.

'You know ... one can never get it right,' he said. 'I fear we brought our boys up too conventionally. With my – my wife there was an artistic input at least, but what did I have to offer? Trying to teach them poetry. Latin and tennis. Then there are these more, well, bohemian upbringings, and so often they seem to instil a desire for convention.'

'At least yours had a *solid* upbringing. No phoney Communists in your barns. No wankers imagining they're African in your sitting room.' A smile crossed her lips. She drank more wine. 'God!' she said as the swirling jacket hem of a woman who had joined Jocasta flapped across her cheek. 'I'm going for a walk.'

She rose and the room swelled, woodsmoke meeting cigarette, skirts ballooning in front of her. A game involving monologues and clapping was interspersed with laughter. He was below her, a corner of his jaw visible at the outer edge of her eye; his wedding ring was smooth when she glanced at it on his thigh. Someone banged into her.

She looked at the window, colour rising in her cheeks. Branches were stacked in old silver vases from the Dublin Bannans, winter berries gathering on sills. He hesitated, then stood.

'I'll show you the grounds,' she said.

A warm cloud of dope smoke wafted from a little group gathered beneath them on the floor.

He half-nodded.

Dora registered Cecilia walking through the room with an averted gaze, and she began to call her for help, but the sound of a glass breaking set her searching for a brush as she smiled reassurances at the glass dropper, and it was too late.

In the kitchen, bodies hovered in clusters around food, and Dora pushed her way towards the smaller pantry where the brushes were kept. Her smile tightened. Elisabeth Dahl stood in the corner shadows talking to Cally, the science teacher, who had openly hinted for an invitation. *Why am I so passive? Why am I so stupid?* Dora muttered to herself. She entered the pantry, poked around for a dustpan, her spine contracting, her heart racing, and rested against the wall where she could listen.

'What?' Elisabeth was saying. Her voice, so defined, was quite audible to Dora. She remembered certain things she had said to her: kind words, loving statements, sudden sexual assertions.

'Come on now,' said Cally, and added something else in a murmur.

'No,' said Elisabeth. 'What do you mean?'

'I mean,' said the science teacher, 'I mean – you're not really talking to me.' She laughed slightly.

'What am I doing now?' said Elisabeth, barely patient.

'Talk to me *properly*,' she hissed.

'Cally,' said Elisabeth. Her voice dropped. 'I do not think it's – appropriate – to spend an evening *à deux* in the corner of someone else's kitchen.'

'Oh,' said the science teacher, her words lost among other conversations, and Dora waited, alert in the semi-darkness, until she heard Elisabeth being greeted by another teacher. She left the pantry and moved through the crowds, and glass was already ground into sisal, a grape crushed on a shard, and Patrick was veering into a chorus of a Van Morrison song to cheers and whistles. *Come back*, she thought tearfully as she glimpsed Elisabeth's shoulder.

Cecilia found her coat and took down James Dahl's without feigning uncertainty, the corner of it vividly recognisable among a pile of others. She handed it to him, walking with the ease of ownership out of the front door. The wine swayed in her head.

He stood on the path with his hands in his pockets, his fringe slanting over his forehead, his body tall against the long low house, looking as displaced as a soldier freshly billeted to an estate. The coldness, mild as it was for December, constrained their speech as the party boomed through the windows at one remove, the garden echoing with space to be filled. Guests stood shivering in groups on the front lawn, their cackles pricking the tension of the cold in a self-conscious attempt to transport the mood of the party into the garden.

Cecilia walked with James Dahl down the path to the gate. She heard her own chat as a chirruping in the silence.

He said nothing.

She talked on. Her voice echoed and trailed into the airy distance. She pressed her teeth into her lip and attempted to terminate her babbling.

He was silent still, walking tall beside her across the lane to the fence of the river field.

'Look,' he said finally, lifting his head, 'at the stars. Extraordinary. More than you ever see on the edge of the moor where I am. They light the sky, *the wings of night*.'

'*Take him and cut him out in little stars, / And he will make the face of heaven so fine / That all the world will be in love with night*,' said Cecilia in a rapid monotone.

'I look at the stars and think of that,' he said. 'And wonder who's up there. Who did someone – love – who's not here?'

'Wait,' she said suddenly. 'Promise you'll wait? Look – look at the river there. I'll be one minute.'

She ran back into the house. Ducking and burrowing through bodies, she pushed past guests, heads turning as she passed, and she grasped the handle of the door to the staircase, muttering apologies to force it open. She ran up two steps at a time, tripping, and sped into her room where she grabbed a book from under a pile of papers inside her desk. She kicked off her high heels, found other shoes and checked her appearance in the mirror: almost maddened with nervous anticipation, she made faces in the glass, widening her mouth and eyes as though expressing frantic, cartoonish incredulity to herself, her only audience.

'Celie!' called Dora, but Cecilia hurried to the hall.

James was still standing there, leaning against the fence and facing the river. The blot of a cow patterned the fields beyond. Night furred the thatches of the hamlet.

'This,' she said breathlessly, 'I got this for you.' Her feet scraped gravel in a small skid as she stopped beside him. She handed him the book. 'It's – I saw it. I thought you'd like it. Thank you. It's to say thank you for all that – all our teaching, those extra classes. Well ... Thank you.'

Her breath flared, wine-tinged beneath her nostrils. She shivered. *Calm down*, she told herself. She cursed him for making her shy. *Charm him*, she told herself. She made a promise. She dug her nails into her palm.

'*Lyrists of the Restoration*,' he read. 'Collected by Masefield ... 1905. This is a first edition. Are you sure it's for me?'

'Yes,' said Cecilia.

'What a fine and lovely book,' he said, shaking his head. 'I'm – I'm very touched.'

'I thought you might like – the Rochester, and the Abraham Cowley – and the Marvell.'

'I've never been given a present like this,' he said, turning the book over and smiling.

'Oh,' said Cecilia. She returned his smile; she shrugged. She felt the velvet of her sleeves rubbing against her coat lining. She drew in her breath and pulled her shoulders back.

'Thank you,' he said solemnly, his head slightly bowing.

She laughed. 'Come on!' she said. 'I have to show you.' She walked ahead. She turned to him. 'Here's where the stream goes under the lane to meet the river. Over here – look, over there – are the stables. I used to think I would keep Dalmatians in them.' She pulled her coat to her.

'Which Dalmatians?'

'Oh, stray Dalmatians kicked from Dartmoor farms – found in winter snows and rescued and groomed by me. They'd emerge all plumply silken from the mud of neglect, of course. Cadpigs would be kept inside.'

'A children's novel?' he said, and he smiled.

'Dodie Smith. This is the dove barn,' she said. 'I used to think I'd ...'

But she couldn't say it. She was unable, with anxious superstition, to say that here she had planned to house orphans. Orphans scuttling round in faded floral prints, rescued, reading her books, eating the flapjack she would deny herself and hide in there with stolen milk. The proposed orphans had once almost merged with animals in her mind: large-eyed infants covered with grime or fur, in heartbreaking need of petting and shelter.

'This is my father's pottery barn,' she said. 'A passage runs behind it. I used to think I'd find ingots down there, and that from the roof you could glimpse a secret garden. Full of Edwardian children.' She suddenly heard her own voice emerging, warm and animated into the night.

A laugh murmured in his throat. She walked close to him. She didn't pull away.

She opened the gate that led to the pond field. They began to talk as they had at Elliott Hall, the flow and intensity that had begun to develop there now deeper, flooding into the spaces and easing the sense of propriety. The night was still. She showed him places; she told him anecdotes; he laughed at what she said.

'How very wild it is here, Cecilia,' he said. 'You could almost be living at Haworth for all the human company there must be.'

'Just a few hippies in barns,' she said airily. 'I'd rather sheep. I'd rather parsons and women in attics and the odd ghost than those phoney beardies.'

'I can see they may be preferable,' he said.

'Tell me about *your* childhood.'

'Oh,' he said. 'Very, very conventional. Nothing like this.'

'No childhood is conventional,' she said. 'Tell me.'

'*It is the bliss of childhood that we are being warped most when we know it the least.* William Gaddis.'

'Yes. But what was it like, really? Yours.'

'I grew up – in a big brick house in Suffolk –'

'A *vicarage*?'

'It was once.'

'How I longed for a vicarage. A vicarage boyhood!' She dared herself. 'You'd have to be a poet or a relic if you were born in a vicarage. And?'

He paused. 'I grew up there,' he said, amusement tangling with possible discomfort. 'Prep school. I boarded at seven –'

'*Malory Towers* or *Tom Brown's Schooldays*?'

'There were no midnight feasts. Tom Brown.'

'Poor you,' said Cecilia emphatically. 'Poor little Mr Dahl –'

'James.'

'I can't call you James!' She shivered and pulled her coat tighter.

'You can here at a party, I think. I know your mother.'

'Poor little James. Oh, I can't! You are Mr Dahl.'

'And I will die Mr Dahl. For eight years I was "Sir". At Haye House, God only knows what else I am.' He cleared his throat. His breath was visible in the air. 'It was a mistake, essentially, Cecilia, coming here.'

'Don't you like Devon?'

'Oh yes. Of course. The wildness, the moors. But my heart and home lie in Dorset. We still have our house there. We often go there to spend weekends with our boys.'

'Do you?' said Cecilia with disappointment, her memory spooling back to Zeno's reports of the Dahls' weekend absences.

The fields were scored with sounds and airborne shadows. A fox ran past and disappeared near the hump where badgers lived. The sky was liquid in its darkness, sections of hedge rustling.

'You don't like it then,' she said dully. She saw his ring again. Her intermittent surges of hope, so heady and assured, descended with equal rapidity into humiliation.

'It was a brand of teaching – in Dorset – I understood. My wife – Elisabeth – enjoys the artistic element of her job, but I . . . I fear death of the soul here, frankly.'

'Oh but I'm so glad you came!' said Cecilia with spirit. 'Truly I am. You *saved* us. What would Nicola and I have done? We couldn't . . . you know, we couldn't really *learn* before. I was so miserable. You saved our souls!' She coloured, obscured by the dark.

He paused. 'If I feel I can have been of any help at all, then I'm gratified,' he said, his voice audibly moved. She could see planes and shadows of him, tiny details of him palpable in sounds and scents beside her.

He smiled, and threw his shoulders back and gazed up at the sky. 'How vast it is,' he said. He strode over the stream that ran in front of them with a slight jumping movement. Cecilia hesitated. He held out his hand and helped her as she landed, then let it go. She felt the brief passing of warmth of his hand on hers. They walked up the hill towards the sallow on the other side of the stream. Stray party noises drifted up there, smoke twining from the house.

'From here,' she said, catching her breath, 'you can see the tors. Corndon Tor. Wind Tor. Ravens and kestrels nest there.'

'Look at their immensity against the sky,' he said. 'I remember reading *The Hound of the Baskervilles* under my blankets and longing, longing to get out of that dormitory to see this strange wild place.'

'Strange and wild,' murmured Cecilia. 'Do you remember the *atmospheric tumult* of *Wuthering Heights*? The *pure, bracing ventilation*? I love that.'

A horse appeared almost silently beside her as a breathing shadow spilling on the night, then edged away. An owl flew over the pond. There was a silence. Her heart sped with urgency into the pause. She had a new sense, rising sharply through her body into a pitch of certainty that seemed almost to hurt her, that she could move him, attract him, possess him. The stars rolled in a dome over the valley. *Carpe diem*, she thought. *Carpe noctem*. Do what others would do. Which others? What?

She felt sick. Nerves beat through her body. It hurt when she breathed in.

'Come to the river,' she said quickly. 'The last part – of your tour.' She blushed. She blessed darkness. *To hazard all, dare all, achieve all*, she quoted to herself, but she could not hold on to the words.

He hesitated.

'It's down here,' she said smoothly, almost laughing at her own boldness, and she descended the stone steps cut into the side of the wall that led from the field into the lane. They rounded a corner. His feet were noisy on the gravel. She heard the rhythm of his breath.

Speedy was huddling before a fire beside one of the river field's roofless stables with the teenage sons of a neighbour. They were stirring something in a pot on the flames, crouching in a clump of ferns, now dried, that reared and choked the entrance to the stable in summer.

'Hey! Mr Dahl. Celie,' said Speedy. 'Try some of this.'

He added liquid from a bottle that Cecilia recognised as her parents' Stone's Ginger Wine, and scooped some of the drink from the pan into one of her mother's earthenware mugs. Cecilia took a sip, then another. It was thickly alcoholic.

'Go on,' said Speedy, dipping another mug into the liquid and handing it to James Dahl.

'I'm just showing him round the grounds,' said Cecilia unnecessarily.

'We must be getting back,' said James, tentatively consuming Speedy's beverage. 'This is rather good, Gabriel,' he said.

'It's fucking great stuff,' said Speedy. 'More.'

He took the mug, dipped it into the pan and brought out steaming liquid, spilling some on the grass and throwing his head back with uninhibited laughter as he handed it to James.

'The river,' said Cecilia.

'Where is it?' said James. He stumbled slightly; there was amusement in his voice.

'Just down here,' said Cecilia, leading him round a corner past the stable and climbing a gate. The voices of Speedy and his friends merged behind them, thinning into the silence of the field and the approaching fall of the river.

'Where? I can barely see a thing.'

'Down there,' said Cecilia, lurching as she jumped off the gate. 'In a cavern measureless to man.'

'I see,' he said slowly. 'Is it, then, a savage place? Holy and enchanted?'

'It has a mazy motion,' said Cecilia.

'I can't beat you or even, possibly, match you,' he said, listing as he climbed over the gate. 'And you are,' he said, his voice hesitant, 'a fraction of my age.'

'It's only famous stuff,' she said.

'And Enid Blyton.'

'Oh, I could quote to you very easily from *The River of Adventure*.'

He stumbled. The earth was soft, matted with growth, netted with the streams that traversed the field.

She slid on a slope of mud and let out a small scream. He caught her arm. She laughed as her feet sank into chilled liquid.

He slipped again. Mud slapped against his trousers as he walked. Water pooled into her shoes. The river glittered, ribboning at the end of the field. Cecilia looked up and saw it, like a live entity waiting for them beneath the density of the trees. The shifting weight of him was beside her as he slithered and helped her stay upright. He skidded; he mildly cursed and laughed. Her pulse seemed to burn just below her ribcage. *Carpe noctem,* she reminded herself, gathering her resolve.

The tumble of the river rose like mist. The orange-lit house crouched across the field. She wondered whether she could hear it boom, then realised that it was silent beyond the river's rush. Diana was in there waiting for her, she thought. Her mother. Elisabeth. All sealed from them.

She turned to him. The dampness of rock and chilled water lined the membranes of her throat.

'There's a little island,' she said. 'In spring it's full of bluebells and wild garlic.'

'It's beautiful; so beautiful. Listen to the sounds. We could be by the sea.'

'I think that at night sometimes.'

'You come down here at night?'

'Yes.'

'On your own?'

'Well yes. To think – I think about – people.'

The water threw a glow of foam where it fell over rock into rapid curves. It streamed past the island that was almost tethered to the bank, caught in a pausing spiral where its path was narrowest.

'You can jump on to it from here,' she said. She raised her voice above the flow. 'I always land on that rock first, and then sit against the tree.'

He stood, a leaning angle bent towards the river, the stars and moon rocking on its surface.

He jumped. He leapt in two movements, on to the stone, on to the island.

She swallowed as he went: a streak shifting through the night away from her into the river, his shoe squeaking on the grass by the bank. She leaned as she stood, the wine rolling darkly in her head. She jumped.

'Oh God,' she said. She caught her shin on the stone, felt it clatter and tug; she tilted, then twisted herself upright and launched herself from the stone on to the island, tugging at grass as she landed.

'Shit,' she muttered.

'Here,' he said, standing and helping her. Water stormed around them, its surface close to their feet, its noise amplified.

'God,' said Cecilia.

He didn't hear her. She feared she would vomit.

'Sit,' he said, clearly unaware that she had hurt herself, and she lowered herself beside him against the birch that grew there.

She swallowed. Her calf bone was ringing with soreness, layer washing over layer. Tears of simple pain had sprung to her eyes. Now they fell, invisible to him.

'It's a very mild, clear night,' he said, his head tipped back against the tree as he looked at the sky.

She nodded. She said nothing. She could feel blood running through her tights.

'We should go back, perhaps,' he said.

'No,' she said. Her voice wobbled.

He glanced at her. 'Are you all right?' he said.

She paused. 'My leg,' she said.

'Your leg?'

'I – hurt it.' Her breath was uneven. 'On the rock.'

'Cecilia,' he said. 'Where?'

'Here.'

He lowered his face nearer her leg, widening his eyes in the darkness. He pulled out his handkerchief and laid it over her. He began to knot it. He stopped. 'Tie it,' he said. 'Tie it tightly at the back.'

'Oh God,' she muttered.

'Can you do it?'

'Yes.'

'We should go back,' he said.

'No,' she said as the wound pulsed beneath his handkerchief.

'Are you all right?' he said in a concerned voice.

She nodded.

She couldn't speak. The pain in her leg was so strong, her emotions towards him so overburdening, that she couldn't regain her breath.

'How is it now?' he said, the water's movement loud beneath them. There was cool river mist in her mouth, flecks of leaf or insect in the darkness, the sharpness of winter against her lungs. The grass was cold. Her leg was swelling. She shivered with an uncontrollable tremor.

'It hurts,' she said, and she was relieved when she said it, and tears flowed hotly over her skin. She averted her face from him, her hair obscuring her. She cried in silence with pain and the misery of longing.

'Does it hurt still?' he said. He was holding her arm.

'No,' she said. Her voice was a shameful squeak.

'Cecilia?'

She was silent. Involuntary shivering still gripped her body. She was aware of it in the space of air between them.

'I'm all right,' she said. A sob rose through her, humiliating her.

He put his arm round her. 'Cecilia,' he said, 'you're hurt.'

'No,' she said.

'We really ought to get back.'

She shivered more violently. His arm was curved over her shoulder. She was pressed against his ribcage.

'No,' she said, tears flattening over her cheeks. She lay her face against him.

'You're crying,' he said, looking at her.

'Sorry,' she murmured. 'Sorry.'

'Does it still hurt?'

'Yes. No.'

Her tears heated her face, scoring her skin with irritation.

'Why are you crying?' he said in a gentler voice.

'Because –' she said. 'Because –'

She shook her head. Her hair was pushed upwards, rumpled against his arm as she moved. 'I can't say. I can't say it to you.'

'Can't you?'

She shook her head.

'Why?'

She was silent.

He said nothing.

She waited. She rested against him, breathing him in. She trembled still, unable to stop.

'I think I understand,' he said.

'Do you?' she said after a while.

'I think so,' he said with no detectable emotion.

She looked up at him. He gazed straight ahead. She looked again. He didn't glance down at her. Her mouth was open; her face was prickling with the after-effects of tears, small starbursts of soreness tightening her skin. She could feel his pulse through her hair. She was aware of the smell of his neck, traces of others' tobacco smoke, clean skin, mature male scents. He looked down at her for a fraction of time and pulled back from her slightly, jerking his body away from her. She shifted. She turned to him. He looked away. He turned back to glance at her and she murmured as their faces moved closer, and there was a noise from him, a vibration in his throat, the half-heard sound of relinquishment, and she pressed her mouth to his. For a moment, he was still. She drew in her breath.

His harder lips moved against hers. His stubble burned her. His cool mouth was on hers; she felt the edge of his tongue; she moved her mouth and she lay down, lay on the grass beneath him. She opened her mouth further, the inner surface of her lip catching his teeth, his tongue, his taste, and she felt the hardness of his body, the pain of his coat and weight against her, the animate scents of him.

'No!' he said, pulling his head away from her. He jolted upwards with a clumsy rearrangement of his body, hurting her hip. 'Absolutely not.'

River air spiralled over her neck.

She rose from where she lay, her vision seeming to follow her with a delayed movement. She murmured in confusion, her hair falling over her cheek. Fragments of dead leaf stuck to her coat.

'I'm so sorry,' he said rapidly. He caught his breath. 'Good God.'

'No!' said Cecilia.

'I'm so sorry,' he said, his voice higher, strained. 'I – it's unforgivable.'

'It's not!' she said, propping herself awkwardly, holding his arms.

'Absolutely – *unacceptable*,' he said with an abrupt shaking of his head.

'No. Please.'

He stood, his height an immense shadow above her. He bent over and reached firmly and almost roughly under her arms, making her stand. 'I must take you back home,' he said.

Thirteen
The Window Seat

WHEN DORA opened the staircase door, she heard her baby's cry as a keening blanketed by floorboards. The sound entered her brain with a hiss of panic. She ran up the stairs. He might have been crying since she had last looked in on him, she thought, but no one else would dream of extricating themselves from the warmth and music to negotiate their way through the corridors and check on him.

'Dora . . .' called someone as she tried to find a light above the staircase. She heard the crash of glass breaking.

'Barnaby,' she called, guided to his cot by his bee-shaped nightlight.

He was wet and hiccuping. She lifted him and pressed her cheek to the heat of his face.

'Sweetheart,' she murmured, stroking him.

He gasped against her neck. She kissed the mucus on his face, tasting the salt of his tears, murmuring apologies and comfort to him. He had wet through his nappy.

'Dora!' called Patrick up the stairs, his roar a distant vibration. 'More glasses?'

'Go away,' she muttered, her mind automatically roaming the pantry in search of spare glasses and landing on enamel mugs whose spider remains she wiped as she peeled the sleepsuit from Barnaby. Cannabis smoke edged along the corridor into the room and she questioned its effect on babies. Perhaps it would make him drowsy, she hoped guiltily.

He held out his arms to her when she settled him back into his cot, initiating a chug of protest while the party thumped through the floor, and she moaned through clenched teeth, producing a sound of frustration that was, to her ears, satisfyingly demented. She repeated it in a less pleasing echo. She went back and stroked his head. He sat up. She considered taking him downstairs: an infant plump in a sleepsuit to hand around. She hesitated. She knew it would cause chaos.

Benedict was calling up the stairs now, hunting her down and demanding her. She pulled Barnaby to her chest and sat there rocking. All she wanted to do was to lie in the bath and hide from them all, breathing slowly.

Someone walked along the passage outside Barnaby's room. Dora kept her head bowed, anticipating a lodger or Benedict, impatient for whatever it was he wished her to provide. There was a pause as the person negotiated the semi-darkness between the corridor and the bedroom, footfall muffled by the shufflings of the water tank.

'Dora,' came Elisabeth's voice softly.

Dora heard it with a delay. It was so unexpected, so outside her sealed cavity of misery that it was momentarily unwanted. She emitted a murmur.

Elisabeth was blurred in the shadows. Barnaby stiffened, straightened his legs hard against Dora's torso, and grinned.

'He's really rather sweet,' said Elisabeth absently.

Barnaby began jiggling on Dora's thighs, shifting his weight painfully from one side to another. He gurgled and laughed. He began to bounce.

'Oh God. Not now,' muttered Dora.

'Poor darling,' said Elisabeth in the rich old voice that recalled so many complexities.

Dora breathed slowly. Elisabeth's presence was now filtering through to her, stinging her with an erotic charge and its accompanying pain.

'Did you have to do this to yourself?' said Elisabeth lightly.

'It was – a mistake,' said Dora, biting her lip at the word. 'You know that. But I love him. So he wasn't. Just wait a minute.'

She lifted Barnaby, hesitated, the instinct to put him in someone else's arms forestalled in the presence of Elisabeth, and she went off to the bathroom where she dropped a Junior Disprin in a glass of water. Trembling, she fed Barnaby a full dose and then a dribble more. He licked his mouth, and let her stroke his forehead and lower him back into the cot. With uncharacteristic swiftness, he fell asleep.

Elisabeth looked at him and breathed through her nose with a cynical exhalation as if to say, *Really, what have you done?*

'Don't,' said Dora, kissing Barnaby's cheek.

'Don't what?'

'I know he put you off me.'

She heard her own statement, baldly expressed. The darkness covered her face.

'And what of your own endless shilly-shallying, my darling? Your ladylike horror? Your fits of duty?'

'It was my pregnancy that really put you off me,' said Dora steadily.

'Nonsense.'

'Nonsense back – really,' said Dora. 'What did you say when you heard? When you *guessed* in fact? You said – Our coffin nail. Our exit strategy. This is a message to us.'

'Well a torrid Sapphic liaison is barely compatible with domestic life as a mother of four. Of a newborn,' said Elisabeth, spelling their situation out so that Dora cringed.

'Much as I loved you. He's a little older now,' said Elisabeth, glancing at Barnaby. 'One tends to forget and forgive when they're sleeping sweetly.'

She took Dora's arm and guided her to the wide window seat with its brown cushions home-sewn in early days, its curtains forming a hiding place to the children who had played houses when younger; and she laughed and kissed her.

'Patrick – could come up,' hissed Dora. She wriggled away and pushed the bedroom door as far as it could go, but it was warped like most doors in the house, and she could not even kick it into place.

'He won't come up,' said Elisabeth, her lips closing decisively over her teeth. 'He's far too busy plucking that guitar.' She closed the curtains, enclosing them. 'Why am I thinking of Boccaccio?'

Dora shook her congested head.

'And of you,' said Elisabeth, and bit Dora's neck.

Dora sat very still, her skin flooding. She slowly breathed out to stop herself panicking, to prevent herself from protesting again. Her heart leapt. 'Cally . . .' she murmured.

'*Her*,' said Elisabeth impatiently, and kissed Dora hard on the mouth again. 'A temporary diversion. Barely even that –'

'Oh,' said Dora, unable to say anything else. 'Patrick,' she added once more, trying to stop herself, her inability not to fill a silence an affliction to her. The name hung between them, the child-snatching Bannans crowding into her mind until she was unable to gauge the ratio of terror to overwhelming excitement in the speed of her heartbeat.

Elisabeth looked at Dora through the moonlight that phosphoresced their created room and raised one eyebrow. Dora paused, then leaned forward and kissed her in return. It was the first time she had moved towards Elisabeth. Kissing her felt extraordinary. Was she actually going to have sex with a woman now, she wondered, so light-headed she worried that she might faint.

Elisabeth was hard and definite with her; swift, skilled; she made no allowances for her inexperience; she shocked and stupefied her. Barnaby slept. There on the window seat, Dora sank into Elisabeth's perfume smell, so intimately known to her, and felt the hardness and the skimming and was brought to a height at which all else subsided to irrelevance. A strand of panic sounded even while she relinquished, knowing the wrongness of such savage temptation. It felt almost too strange after so much longing, inevitably different from the softness she had conjured in her mind: spiky and veering towards awkwardness yet entirely necessary. Her pleasure rose in sliding steps. She dreaded the following days, the time in her life apart from her.

'Oh Dora, I don't know what to do with you,' said Elisabeth lightly.
'You do,' mouthed Dora into her hair, wanting not to be heard.

James Dahl had insisted on accompanying Cecilia home across
the field, barely speaking as she struggled along beside him. They
had entered the house in tense silence, Cecilia instinctively lagging
behind in the hall, and when she emerged from hiding in the downstairs lavatory, she saw the back of him as he addressed his wife. The
music and shouted speech was more ragged now, fracturing into
hysteria. She knew that the Dahls would soon leave and she needed
to escape him before he went.

She limped her way back down to the river in her soaked tights,
the pools of water that fountained into her shoes pleasing through
her electrified daze. She stood on the riverbank, looking across to
the island in moonlight for evidence she knew she wouldn't see: for
bent grass or blood from her leg.

She lay on her stomach close to the surface of the water with
its hissing ogees of foam and tried to breathe slowly. Invisible from
where she lay, she watched the shapes of people going home, saw
rectangles of hall light widen and narrow, heard distant car engines.
She stared and stared at the low swell and heave of the house and
wondered whether she saw him. She played the scene back, watched
herself with him from above. She was a girl in a dress with hair falling night-dark over white skin: a girl embraced and kissed for long
seconds by an adult man, older and tall and heavy in a coat. She saw
herself pressed beneath her teacher, her mouth being kissed, and
elation soared through her, followed by disbelief.

Her heart beat powerfully against her chest. She was trembling.
The need to vomit took hold of her more forcefully. She put her
fingers into her mouth, the back of her hand skimming the river, and
heaved. She tried again, and made herself sick, spewing alcohol and
turmoil into the Dart's waters.

Fourteen
March

S HE WAS hungry, Mara was hungry, Cecilia was sure. The baby Mara who lived in her head and haunted her. She saw her as a muddy baby. Her belly was swollen. Dark whorls of silt patterned her back and her focus was dark. She turned her head unevenly towards the woman who had been her mother, catching her hem as she passed.

Stop, stop, Cecilia told herself, pressing her hands into her scalp, but Mara was here haunting her. Mara was here, as she had never been in London: more raw and vicious and starving.

Cecilia glimpsed Dora setting off towards the bracken-clumped riverbank the other side of Wind Tor land, and wondered whether she might catch her on her way back. For the first time since she had returned to live in Wind Tor House, she made her way to the river island. She walked through the mud-sprung grass with less sureness of footing than she had possessed in that girlhood spent tramping about the moors, her body only marginally fuller than in those days, though pregnancies had taken their toll.

The field's foaming of new foliage was black-green beside the hazel and alder that lined the riverbanks, and she decided that perhaps the protagonists in the book she was writing could camp there on their way up the tributary. She entered the moss-brown shade so often suspended with gnats and saw that a baby tree now grew beside the original birch, arching away at an angle from its trunk and crowding the tiny island. She pulled up the leg of her jeans to look at her scar, examining it as she hadn't done since her teens, and saw the thin curve of paleness cut by the rock on to which James Dahl had jumped ahead of her over twenty years before. She pressed her nail into it and could feel nothing. She noticed how her leg looked older. She leapt on to the rock and then on to the island, the movements automatically known, and sat there while the water ran past her.

She leaned back against the tree and thought about James Dahl.

She remembered stumbling back to the island after kissing him and seeing herself as if from above, and replayed it now, but the picture was quite different. She saw how youthful she had been and had not known it. Photos of her from that time resembled a quaintly dated archive: a blur of freckles and health and unformed features, simple youth like a drug flushing the surface of her skin. That girl, that child in love, had lowered herself to the ground beneath her teacher. Antipathy rose inside her. Underlying it – always – twisted an old, primitive flare of excitement. She strongly and strenuously disapproved. Her feelings towards that long-estranged figure had periodically moved her to pure fury, the faintest notion of her daughters with a man so much older or more powerful inspiring rage. Yet she had never really got over it. It had been, at some intrinsic level, the most exciting time in her life.

She thrust the vision quite violently from her. She leant against the trunk, felt the remains of dew soaking through to her thigh, saw a tickling of water by the bank and an early vole. She fell half-asleep briefly, the sun touching her as catkins rippled above her, and wondered where he was now.

The house appeared sunken in its valley: a crusted hump of landscape cradled by new leaves. She wondered – when would the intruder come back? She shivered slightly. Her ghosts tangled, as they always had, warmth now rising with the riverbank.

When you were a baby a few hours old, you left here – left by the front door or the kitchen door? I don't know; I have no way of knowing. I was still lying on Dora's bed. You left with strangers whose smell was different and whose voices were not those you had heard in the womb. They fed you formula milk and you started your new life away from your parents. Where was it? Where are you? My little girl, you are somewhere in this world.

Dora was walking along beside the river field, a tall figure now bent and reduced, as though the sky itself might blast her. She wore red denim beneath a coat that was decades old. Her pea coat, thought Cecilia, and complacency somehow nestled in Dora's continued use of the term, in her general refusal to move with times, and made Cecilia twitch with automatic annoyance. She wished her brothers would visit their mother more.

Mara was still there, a layer of presence among the trees.

A goose called. The sound was as harsh as a newborn's cry.

Cecilia sat up quickly and ran across the field, its clumps and water-filled hoof pits making her stumble as she had beside James Dahl.

'Where did they take her from?' she said barely audibly, coming up behind her mother.

'Sorry?' said Dora.

Cecilia could smell Dora's breath.

'Did they take her out of the front door or the kitchen door? Or the door near the boiler room?'

'Celie, what is all this about?'

'Where?'

'I don't know.'

Cecilia paused. 'You do,' she said.

Dora closed her lips tightly, and Cecilia refused to fill in the silence.

There was continued silence.

Cecilia's heartbeat was painful.

'Please,' she said eventually.

Dora gazed at her with her look of mild bewilderment.

'Look Dora,' said Cecilia. 'I can't do this. Don't you see what it's doing to me?'

Dora hesitated. 'Yes, darling,' she said.

Fifteen
The Drama Hall

ISERY VEINED with hope seemed to soak into Dora's body, making her exhausted. She walked about school in a frenzy of anticipation: she had given in to her state, because she could do nothing else.

Patrick was evasive, spending evenings pottering around the house fixing the surface manifestations of far greater structural problems or driving to the pub in Leusdon where he sat barely drinking alongside farming men. She was aware that he was avoiding her in silent protest. She didn't know him any more; she knew him too well. Her guilt reared and receded in regular cycles, repressed during flares of excitement. Out of habit she viewed the decline of their marriage as a temporary phase: as something that could be mended, at least to a functional level, one day when she was no longer in love with Elisabeth Dahl. With a woman. An astonishing fact that she could still barely absorb, let alone understand.

Patrick avoided Elisabeth's name with what Dora sensed was a barely conscious disgust rooted in religious morals or simple disbelief. A rigidity came to both his and Cecilia's faces on the rare occasions that the Dahls were mentioned. He was more perceptive than she thought, Dora reminded herself, and anger sharpened his intelligence. Dora wished he would go away. During the times when Elisabeth was busy or caught by duty or simply fickle, Dora mourned until the absence tired her to sleep. The inconsistent intoxication of her relationship was like a glittering blackness in black January when the skies froze at four and Barnaby wet through his clothing to his frayed miniature duffel.

She felt she wanted to live now elsewhere: near lights and concerts, beside notices about book sales and lost cats, among echoes of exquisite-smelling skin. She pictured herself living in Wedstone with its shimmer of civilisation; in Elliott Hall even, tucked away with her love in a forgotten cell up in the hammer-beam roof where they would do nothing but absorb each other's limbs and urgently converse: two minds and bodies attuned in a haven of centuries-old wood. She thought of tangling with Elisabeth's small body with such urgent need that it conquered confusion and guilt: the almost ruthless sex in snatched hours at Neill House or in an office behind the sculpture studio. She knew already that she was the one who loved more, and that that would prove to be her curse.

Much as she loved Barnaby, she wanted him grown up, as the first three now were. She was waiting, and dreaming of a more manageable age. When Barnaby was four, even three, perhaps she and Elisabeth would consolidate what it was they had.

A fortnight after the spring term started, students performed a Lorca play they had been rehearsing since the previous autumn.

Speedy Sardo sat by his mother and waved in affectionate fashion at Dora across an audience that consisted of almost the entire school and parent body, adults crowding on the steps that served as seats, teenagers excitable on bleachers behind. Elisabeth entered. Her clothes, the rightness of them; her carriage, even when picking her way to a seat, made Dora's abdomen contract. Dora could barely contemplate the suspicions she surmised circulated through her colleagues' minds. What if the people surrounding them had seen what she did with Elisabeth? What would they think? The brushing of mouths, limbs, *genitals*? What would they all think? A hot fall of horror drenched her.

The fibreglass dome's rough inner surfaces were clung to by condensation that ran down the panels to pool on its metal ribs as the building boomed with such unstable echoes that it seemed as though it might explode like a toadstool. Its acoustics, the drama department unanimously agreed, were 'dodgy', and now the building screamed and reverberated as the band sporting crownless hats and pirate scarves tuned up. The keyboard player wore dungarees over a bare torso with one strap undone although it was early February. Dora watched them all: the band; Cally Cooper; Peter Doran, accompanied by a craggy, carmine-lipped girlfriend; the Dahls: James murmuring to Elisabeth, who sat very still in her coat. Flanked by colleagues and children, Dora felt lonely. Barnaby was with Patrick; she hoped he had put him to bed. The thought of her youngest child made her tighten with a guilt that she tried to soothe, but panic always cut into whatever comfort mechanism she summoned when she considered him: a difficult baby, the hardest of them all; her beloved accident. She was barely coping. At this moment, her shoulders bowed, she admitted it to herself. And her mind was flooded with distress.

Cecilia Bannan looked strained. Her eyelash vibrated with an underslept tic. She sat on the same side as Dora, pressed beside Nicola and another upper sixth-former at the bottom of the bleachers, taking vague comfort in the fact that her mother was there, reachable by crawling or shouting. She could be saved by her mother.

The band tuned up again, its discordance sawing at the air, and rows of hands covered ears.

'Shut the fuck up, man!' a boy called out to the trombonist, the silence in reaction followed by whistles. Stamping and catcalling delayed the opening scene, sound ricocheting off the ceiling and spreading into a muddy boom.

Cecilia closed her eyes. Diana's school was rehearsing *Iphigenia at Aulis* and had performed *Leben des Galilei* in German at the end of the previous term; Diana's school possessed cloisters, French clubs, debating societies, Latin classes; its Greek society organised orations. Haye House, which so often presented self-penned musicals and anarchic social commentaries, had now seen fit to mangle *The Billy-Club Puppets*.

She watched the collective breath sweat down the walls, wondering about the composition of DNA that swarmed in a sole drop. She skimmed the auditorium to establish where he was, relieved that she could look straight ahead at the stage without her gaze splashing against his. He was a blur pulsing on the other side of the room to the right of her eye line. He spoke to Elisabeth, both of them gazing abstractedly ahead, her nodding, listening and occasionally commenting.

He was wearing a chambray shirt without a tie beneath a jacket: his version of relaxed Friday night dressing. He looked tall, wide-shouldered, noticeably large sitting on the steps, his legs sharply bent. Elisabeth, so much smaller, sat beside him, her grey-black head indefinably challenging. Her gaze was occluded, as though she had no need to meet anyone's eye.

Two trumpets sounded and a boy entered the stage talking about 'the theatre of the bourgeoisie' in tones of privilege softened by the standard mock-London accent favoured by Haye House. Cecilia groaned internally. Her misery seemed composed of physical pain. She had spent the remainder of the Christmas holidays waiting for a call, a sign, a visit from the man who had kissed her. As time ground past unoiled by sleep, she had picked at sections of her body – scalp, heels, nails, cuticles – excavating and attacking. She wandered, sometimes, with Gabriel Sardo when he returned from his parents' house, telling him nothing yet soothed by his talk, up to the frozen moors where she thought James Dahl's old navy Saab might appear over the horizon.

A girl dressed as a puppet now sat embroidering on the stage. She sewed each stitch with loose jolting movements. The audience laughed. Cecilia remained silent. He had never driven on to the moor that Christmas. She had cut more holly in the woods, pricking her fingers, bringing branches home cradled in wool-gloved hands itchy with blood. Dora and some neighbours arranged a wassailing tour with lanterns for their children while she stayed at home listening for the phone. She had conversations with him in her mind with the frequency of a nervous tic: her thoughts tugged and flickered that way, so that she was forever talking to him, explaining herself, even as she railed against his silence.

The puppet-girl on the stage referred to her desire to be married, her head tick-tocking from side to side, and Cecilia froze, sliding her eyes further from where James Dahl sat.

Days had gone by. Dora had stuffed stockings with presents, welcomed her children's friends, cooked wholemeal mince pies, completed jigsaw puzzles with Tom while yanking Barnaby from the electric sockets. Gales poured along the valley. The phone cables were down for two days. 'What's the matter, darling?' Dora had asked as though incidentally, eclipsed by the demands of Barnaby.

The puppet was now singing, rolling her eyes, lifting her patched layers of skirt as she sang about breezes and sighs in a pure voice. Children in the front joined the chorus. On some days, Cecilia had woken in terrible excitement. The light was white on the curving plaster of her walls, the morning late and warm – they put the central heating on at Christmas, her parents; the only time because of the cost – and she was drugged with brief sleep after an interrupted night, and she woke and thought, *he kissed me.* She hugged it to herself in her bed.

Children from the younger classes now scattered glitter on to the audience's heads from a platform above, its drift scored with the heavier fall of cigarette ends and lollipop sticks and pellets of paper hankie.

He had written her a letter. The third of January, it arrived: a formal typed letter on Haye House paper that could have been written by a teacher regarding schoolwork, requesting that she phone him at three o'clock that Thursday.

She waited until three and a half minutes past three and rang from the phone in her parents' room. She trembled violently as she dialled.

'Cecilia,' he said. 'Thank you for telephoning me. I should –'

He was silent.

'Yes –' said Cecilia, interrupting him as he began to speak again.

'– felt I should call you to find out – establish how you are.'

As she absorbed the formality of his tone, she felt as though sand sank through her chest cavity, dark and sludgy, falling and falling and leaving an empty space.

'Oh!' she said breathily, audibly a teenager. 'I'm fine.'

'Good,' he said. 'I'm glad.'

He paused.

'So . . .' he said.

He stopped. He seemed to be about to terminate the call.

No, thought Cecilia, clinging on to the phone connection with knuckles and nails in her mind, knowing the self-lacerating regret that would ensue if she said nothing.

'How are you?' she asked simply.

The audience was clapping now as Time, represented by a boy dressed in a yellow bustled frock, skipped on stage and sounded the hour. Cecilia caught sight of a flash of blue shirt, an electric imprint of familiar features facing the stage from the other side of the room.

'How are you?' she had said on the phone, and he had hesitated, and she heard his breathing change.

'Cecilia,' he said, audibly coughing hesitation from his throat. 'I do regret – I wholeheartedly apologise to you for –'

'Don't,' she said, her voice dull.

'I do. I'm very concerned that –'

'Yes –'

'That you should be all right. In fact. Not upset. I mean –'

'Oh I – Can. When –' *When can we meet?* she wanted to say, but the sand was now at the pit of her body, almost weighting her to the ground and unbalancing her, and she could say nothing after a little further hesitant exchange but a polite goodbye. She cried against her parents' bedside table, knocking her head on its side several times intentionally.

Skeletons in luminous body suits darted on and off the stage as a boy stood playing cymbals attached to his knees, the performance veering further away from Lorca's text into the realms of the experimental.

He was never in Elliott Hall gardens any more: he kept away, just as she, to avoid him at school, a twist of hope still tormenting her, routinely went there.

The stage darkened as a group of smugglers carrying balsawood blunderbusses over-acted, inspiring faintly embarrassed merriment among the audience.

She could barely work; she could do nothing but work. Her essays were stiff, her handwriting altered; her reading was obsessive. She had lost weight. She sat in his classes, said nothing, and was not addressed. Rage rose inside her.

Children playing urchins now rushed from the stage on to the steps dabbing powder on to the audience's faces with brushes to screaming hilarity.

He had talked directly to her just once, on the stairs that led to the room where she studied French.

He had paused. He seemed to be about to say something. 'I —'

She smiled at him, fearing that she was baring her teeth into a grotesque grin. Her gaze alighted on the curves of a mouth that had touched hers, the jaw with its shaving shadow, and confusion coloured her face.

'I hope — you're well, Cecilia,' was all he managed to say. He looked tired. He looked more poignantly beautiful to her in his strained state. He smiled slightly and turned, hesitated, then went off to teach a class, his head lowered.

Speedy's laugh was now sounding through the auditorium among mounting hysteria as Furry the school dog tore round the stage with wings attached, representing a bird. Pupils screamed and called his name, whistling and competitively beckoning him. A parent from a formerly celebrated rock outfit sauntered on stage apparently unbidden and performed a drum solo to further appreciation.

How was she supposed to hand in essays referring to love in Shakespeare? He had smiled at her courteously as she passed him in the corridor. He smiled with similar restraint at Nicola and Nick.

A drama teacher wound the handle of a hurdy-gurdy as the skeletons launched into a dance of death on stilts, the audience whooping without reserve. Cecilia groaned, and at that moment her gaze met James Dahl's across the auditorium. They rolled their eyes to the ceiling in simultaneous derision. They smiled. Time halted. They looked at each other in a tunnel. It was a violet tunnel, filled with bright dusk. No one else was there. The raucous cheering was outside. She laughed. He broke into a bigger smile, looking directly at her. They glanced back at the stage again at the same time, Cecilia's mouth still twitching.

Nicola, sitting beside Cecilia, remained unaware.

The audience fell into a frenzy as the play ended and children cartwheeled across the stage with Furry storming among them.

'I'm going to stay with Zeno,' said Cecilia decisively, struggling down the steps, weaving through parents and touching her mother's arm.

'Oh!' said Dora. 'Are you sure?'

'Yes, yes. I'll call you tomorrow,' said Cecilia, and kissed Dora. She detected the exhaustion in the thinness of her face against her lips and felt a pang.

'Are you all right?' she asked softly.

'Oh yes,' said Dora, and smiled at her.

Cecilia walked from the damp heat into the contrast of night where students gathered in groups shivering and chattering loudly. Lights went on in boarders' rooms. Guitars could be heard. Solipsistic hysteria still reigned, thinning out in the cold.

Cecilia walked across the lawn, faces bobbing palely over the night grass, and there was camaraderie in the exchange of half-smiles with people who were still linked by the same recent experience. Voices sounded louder outside, clustered shadows walking, their delivery a controlled hush in the expanse of night. Laughter broke out across the lawns; two bicycles wobbled through the darkness. Cars were starting up on the drive in a clatter of exhaust.

She entered the main school building where corridors were lit and classrooms long-darkened, and pupils ran, skidding with their arms in surfing positions, around the hall. She walked unthinkingly from room to room, an unspecific sense of purpose driving her.

Teachers and parents chatted, their children lingering in groups and unwilling to leave. She walked along corridors, glimpsing the lights of the boarding houses and the spread of trees through windows; she passed Idris talking to Speedy, Annalisa's parents, and her French teacher Lavinie. Further lights snapped blinkingly off, making her jolt, and the school became quieter, its daytime atmosphere shifted.

She entered the corridor containing the cupboard in which she had so often sat in earlier days with Nicola and Zeno, and James Dahl appeared from the other direction. He almost passed her with the speed of his gait. He stopped, his footfall ringing on the linoleum as he paused mid-step. He turned, and his hand rested spontaneously, fleetingly, on her arm.

'Hello,' he said, surprise in his voice.

'Hello,' said Cecilia with a smile she couldn't repress.

'What are you doing here?' He smiled at her. Lines fanned pleasingly from the top of his nose, as they did when he smiled, his eyes catching hers.

'Just walking,' said Cecilia. 'Where are you –?'

'Walking. Thinking – I've been thinking about that performance.'

'What wankers.'

'What wankers.'

She snorted. He laughed quite openly. She laughed more, hysteria rising inside her. He looked at her, slightly wonderingly, hesitating.

The bell of the church outside Wedstone sounded from a long distance.

'It's beautiful, isn't it?' he said.

She could hear all the colours of his voice, the workings of air and tendons close up in the quietness of the building.

'I used to look at it sometimes during – Oxbridge. You could just see the tip of the spire from where I sat,' she said.

'Could you?'

'Yes. Just the highest point, right in the sky. I used to see clouds near it and think they were snagging.'

'That's lovely. I never noticed.'

'Your back was to it. I'll show you,' she said with a rush of boldness.

'Oh –' he said almost sharply, pausing. He stood still. The strangeness of being in the school building at night with its festive sense of abandoned routine dissolved the constraints of the day. Cecilia began to walk, and he walked beside her. He stopped; she walked on, then he walked again.

They went up the main staircase, darkness interspersed by the intermittent buzzing of lights. A door slammed below. A sole guitar sounded from somewhere across the grounds. It was an old route: left, right, a bank of lockers shimmering in the gloom, past the high window at the turn of the staircase on whose sill you could sit and be animated, profile arranged becomingly, in case of James Dahl passing; up further flights of stairs to the top of the building and right again, its details followed in her head so many times.

The room was dark. The tables in the centre, regrouped since the previous term, formed a grey bulk, the area by the door illuminated by the glass-shaded bulb on the landing. The plant curled down the wall from the sill.

'You see,' she said, pressing her face against the window, but nothing was clear in the blackness. He cast a shadow over her that spilled into the corner of her vision. The scent of him came to her in twists twined with radiator dust. They stood there.

He said nothing. She listened to him breathe.

'I love you,' she said.

He was silent. There was a click in his throat.

She heard herself with a delay, echo of sound lapping echo.

He drew in his breath.

'You don't,' he said.

'I do.'

'You can't,' he said in the same tone.

'I know,' said Cecilia blankly. She was cold.

She stood stiffly. She lowered her face. She was motionless, leached of thought or movement. Nothing more mattered: she could die, she could escape.

'Look at me,' he said eventually. He shook her shoulders lightly and placed his hands just below them on her back, reassuring her or comforting her.

'Silly girl,' he said. 'Lovely girl –'

'I –'

'– don't waste it on me.'

'It's not a waste,' she said in a thread of a voice. She looked at the floor. Her hair fell over her face.

'I have to go,' she said.

'Don't,' he said.

She stood still.

'I have to see that you're all right,' he said.

She looked up at him, his face lit by the hall and the spill of lights on the drive. She could feel the mobile warmth of his breath about her. The plant floated gently with radiator heat.

Her face tilted minutely, instinctively, towards his mouth. She stopped. She emitted a small sound; she stayed still, humiliated.

'You're very – fine,' he said. He frowned. 'That's not the right–'

He caught his breath with a snaggle of air.

'I think you have to keep away from me,' he said.

'No.' She shook her head.

'You – I think you should.'

She moved nearer him, or he pulled her further towards him, an adult comforting her, the side of her face pressed against his chest, his shoulder, and tentatively he stroked her hair. They stood still by the window. The Klimt was golden in the night. She rested there, his heart pulsing warmth into her ear from beneath his shirt, the size of his chest remarkable to her: he was the widest and tallest person she had ever felt. She tried to steady her breathing. The stroke of his hand on her hair was so rhythmic, so constant, she could barely absorb it; she was suspended by the movement into a state of milky tranquillity, past and future obliterated.

She felt the varying pace of his heart. She stared at the darkness that welled and retreated in the corner of the room when she focused on it.

'It makes me very miserable,' she said eventually.

'I know,' he said. 'I know what you feel.'

She paused. She detected the acceleration of his heartbeat again. She nearly spoke.

'Do you?' she said after too much silence.

He was silent.

'I think you – I think you should go down now,' he said.

She nodded.

His hand was still on her back. She turned her head and she pressed her mouth to his chest like a small creature seeking comfort with a gesture in which pride threaded supplication. He bent down and eased her away from him and as he did so she looked at him, and they kissed.

They paused. They pulled away, their mouths open; she glimpsed the reflection of light on his pupils as he looked at her, his eyes dark, almost unfocused; then they kissed again, the cool movement of his tongue against hers shocking, the realisation of what was happening surging to her head.

He was so much taller that in kissing her he half lifted her, his hand on the small of her back, her waist, his body bent to meet hers, and she pressed herself against him, kissing him fast, searching for breath, clutching at him for salvation after such grief: frantic, almost tearful in her need to eradicate that despair. Sharp spurts of anger at all that suffering rose, surfaced, made her faster. His hands moved down to her hips. She shivered. Her coat fell down one arm, his palm meeting her shoulder, her untouched skin flaring to sensation, and she pressed against his chest, finding his skin, his clavicle. They stumbled together round the desks: he backed, still kissing her, holding her as she moved with him, and they sank on to the small sofa on which he had once stacked books, moving in a slow awkward fall towards the arm. She kissed him faster, still startled by the rougher harder planes of a man, by the bristle and searching tongue.

'Slowly,' he said gently, his voice low.

'Yes,' she said, kissing him, playing with his ear, tracing the line of his jaw with her finger. Memories from films, from books, twitched through her mind informing her, making her momentarily conscious of cliché, of stock images that could either instruct her or humiliate her, but now he was kissing her, his mouth on her temple, cheekbone, lips, his body so hard and male-scented against her that extreme excitement edged with fear mounted inside her. He kissed her neck; he pulled her coat from her, her jumper, his own jacket, and she, her mind still flickering with cinematic sequences, unbuttoned his shirt and pressed her lips there.

'We – mustn't do this,' he said, opening his mouth against her hair.

'Yes,' she said, her face scraping against his stubble, distant panic rumbling beneath her elation. She wondered, unable to regulate her breathing, whether she might have to struggle away from under him after all, to run away and hide.

'I was looking for you – some part of me –'

'Me too,' she murmured, exaltation hitting her again.

'As I walked along the corridor. I knew I shouldn't –'

'Me too.'

'I – shouldn't,' he said, pulling his head back, gazing at her for one moment, his hair disordered, his mouth slack. 'Absolutely –'

'You should, you can,' she said, pressing her mouth to him, stopping his words. 'You've already kissed me,' she whispered. 'Already.' And he kissed her for a long time, long and focused, his hand moving over her body towards her hips, and her heart thudded; her body was liquid; she felt arousal move through her thighs in rising heat, spreading its tendrils upwards. Vague sounds from several floors below came to her through some outer skin: doors, passing footfall. A stereo thudded across the night from one of the boarding houses. She wondered vaguely where his wife was, but Elisabeth Dahl was a mere idea.

'You can,' she repeated almost coquettishly, laughing into his ear and feigning confidence so that she pressed her hand on his chest, lowering him further on to the small sofa, its fabric already blessed, and she lay across him, feeling the stretch of her body, knowing the power of the smoothness of the skin that was gradually exposed, and she kissed him from above, aware that what she felt was the hardness of his penis, and with the very idea – she removed herself mentally at that moment, saw him as her formal English teacher in his corduroys with his stack of Chaucer essays – a kind of delirium hit her. Her head raced. Triumph, rapture after the weeks of abandonment rose inside her, and she kissed him and murmured into his face again, telling him soundlessly that she loved him, she wanted him, she loved him.

His hand skimmed her breast.

'You're beautiful,' he said.

He was moving faster, his body wrapped with hers. Clothes were coiled or abandoned; the top she had worn under wool now snaked and caught above her bra. With one hand she started to undo his belt, the recalled images lending her certainty laced with self-consciousness, and she felt a flicker of hesitation in his response, but the pause was followed by a quickening of his breath. He said her name. The excitement of that fired her brain. She felt small, and carried by events, and riding over fear. He breathed. He burrowed into her neck. His hands were between her thighs.

She saw the concentration of urgency in his face: a play of expressions unknown to her. She wanted him inside her now with a fierce longing, and then a returning feeling that she might suddenly, after all, in such excitement, push him away in fear: she was being carried down an icy pitch and saw the ground sliding from her and knew that she would only go faster. It was inevitable. She felt him hard against her, felt him on her thigh, the hollow of her hip.

'Yes,' she kept saying in his ear, 'yes.' And when she said it, she felt an acceleration of his desire, a letting go of last restraints.

'Yes?' he murmured finally into her shoulder. 'Cecilia.'

She hesitated minutely. 'Yes,' she said, the sound vibrating against his neck where his skin was damp.

His hand was gliding over her pubic bone, making her gasp and move. She could feel her wetness, the new heat growing as he stroked her. She was profoundly shocked that he was touching her there. She pushed against his hand, rubbing against him harder. She felt as though her body was a separate entity, swollen and floating, her legs moving instinctively further apart.

'Yes,' she said again, encouraging him, and she felt the hardness nudging against her, utterly alien and surely large, larger than anything she had conceived of in her graphic yet hazy imaginings. His mouth was against her neck, skimming her skin, talking to her. She opened her legs further and she felt it, a block of flesh, a private thing, a part of him yet surely an entity with its own life. He looked serious, utterly absorbed, his jaw taut. The intensity of his expression in the shadows sent a fresh plume of fear through her.

I can kiss Mr Dahl, she thought, and, almost testing herself, summoning a picture of him in a lesson, she craned her neck and moved awkwardly towards his mouth, so that after a pause they were kissing. She was kissing James Dahl. His tongue was moving against hers. She pressed her hips more forcefully towards his, and now the hardness was against her, bearing down uncomfortably against her, pulling at her pubic hair, hurting her. She held it, her eyes widening in the dark almost to herself, this object in her hand, and she moved against him. He slipped away. He came back to her, his breath fast in her ear. She moaned. He pressed against her. She drew in her breath sharply. It was hurting, straining, an impossible obstacle.

'No!' she said.

'No?' he said, stopping, the sound broken into separate components. He paused.

'Yes,' she said. She swallowed. 'Now.'

He hesitated.

'Yes now.'

He kissed her breast. His hand was on her hip, lightly, his fingers on her buttock. She moaned, and he moved again, began to enter her, but it hurt; her scalp seemed to expand with the pain of it, the sharp stretched stab.

Panic hit her. She glimpsed shame. Her breath speeded; she shook her head. 'I don't know what's wrong – I –' she said in a high, rapid voice.

'Shhh,' he said, nuzzling into her neck, stroking her chest, his hand lingering lightly on her hip. 'Shhh, my darling.'

She drew in her breath. He kissed her, murmuring, holding off: she had a sensation of him swimming above her, touching her in a way he understood but that was unknown to her.

'I can't believe ...' she said, feeling the shape of his face.

'I wonder – about you all the time,' he said, arched above her, touching her, lowering himself to kiss her, his breath uneven. 'You're beautiful. Your hair.' He stroked her breasts, her hips. He moaned. 'If I don't see you I wonder ...' he drew in his breath '... where is she?'

The words filtered into her mind in little grains of amazed pleasure, like a drug settling into her bloodstream. Incredulity sped through her again. He stroked her, and she moved her hips, arched them towards him, encouraging him.

'Slowly, slowly,' he whispered, the tension subsided.

Her hips moved against him. 'Come – on. Now,' she said.

'Soon,' he said, his hand trailing joy, alarm hovering in one residual spray in its wake.

'Oh –'

'*Slowly*,' he murmured into her ear, and she could hear his voice breaking into fibres of sound.

She opened her legs, and he stroked her and then he paused, and she felt the straining stretching of her skin again as he partially entered her, and she called out, astounded, the pain of it, the largeness of it beyond all her anticipation or understanding. He stopped. He waited there, and she discerned the rate of his heart, felt his sweat, his desire, his maturity in close proximity. She was impatient for him inside her. She slowed her breathing with an effort of will, and he kissed her gently, their tongues mixing, the different currents of their saliva meeting.

'Very slowly,' he whispered and she murmured assent. She calmed her breathing. 'Yes,' she whispered. Slowly, with infinite patience, he entered her, and they lay there motionless for a short time while she breathed and he kissed her and his words emerged in fragments. That astonishing fullness, that stretched congestion she felt, filling her to her rectum, her abdomen, the base of her spine, nudging all her organs, her hips pinioned back, his weight hard against her, was a shocked revelation; and she thought, so *this* was what women did: Dora, Elisabeth, Zeno, all those mothers casually walking round school who knew the conspiracy of this, this extraordinary truth.

They began to move. She rose and drew in her breath and pressed herself against him. She was, she thought, connected to him for ever, in that merging of pleasure and pain.

Sixteen
March

I<small>T WAS</small> as if they were still camping. There were damp-aired cupboards and crannies, a jigsaw of small and larger rooms to decorate, their walls bulging and drifting; beams and alcoves half sunk in curving plaster, uneven doors on staggered levels. Cecilia could taste the dust of flaking paint as she folded piles of washing while attempting to plot her children's novel. The deadline was at the end of July, and it suffused her with low-level panic.

She could barely contain her daughters: they were city girls who, she feared, might become lost on the moor or frightened by the darkness where the trees and lichen knitted. She worried about them in unspecified ways, ways that nagged at her because she couldn't quite formulate them. Romy scorned anywhere outside London and took refuge in St Anne's; Izzie put announcements about cowpats and sheep shaggers on her Facebook page; and Ruth still followed her mother like a clinging dog.

Ruth had seen him again. He – she didn't know his name, or perhaps he had no name because he was a wild man – had seen her in the fields near school and talked to her. He spoke, just a little; he didn't expect answers; he asked no questions. Ruth couldn't talk when people asked her questions. She listened to him. He told her about the parts of the moor where the wind blew and the trees were goblins slipping down the gorse on their root feet to the streams to strangle sheep. He lived there, he said, among ravens and buzzards.

There were Hairy Hands on the Postbridge road that caused cars to crash. There was a wronged servant's grave whose flowers were always kept fresh. There was a prison. Had that been his house? she wondered. Was that meant to be his house? She pictured him coming down to Widecombe, crawling through Dockmell where the badgers ran and rats squirmed in stable drains. He said he would give her a wild baby rabbit to tame if she wanted one.

In the evening, Cecilia smiled at her eldest child, making herself traverse Romy's new aura of independence to hug her. Since the day Romy was born – since the day her first baby was born – her children had taken over her mind more forcefully than she could ever have imagined: preoccupying her, Ari informed her wryly, to the exclusion of himself or anyone else. She always laughingly denied this out of love for him, but she knew, as he knew she knew, that it was true.

'Was the scenery painting good?' said Cecilia, kissing Romy's cheek.

'Oh yes!' said Romy. Flames rose above logs behind her. With her bright red hair that fell just past her shoulders, her spray of freckles bridging a small straight nose set in an oval face, she looked, thought Cecilia, like a picture of a girl in a fisherman's jersey in a children's book bearing an ice cream and a novel, the sea breeze just lifting her hair, an art nouveau cloud scudding over the horizon. She was an old-fashioned kind of girl.

'And you think the art teacher's good?'

'Yes. Really. I – yes, very good.'

'I'm pleased, my darling,' said Cecilia. 'And your English teacher's just "old"?'

'Oh,' said Romy. 'Yes. An old weirdo.'

Cecilia laughed. 'Weird in what way?'

Romy laughed slightly in response.

'He – he. It's hard to say,' said Romy, and colour rose on her neck.

'Why?' said Cecilia suspiciously.

'He,' said Romy, glancing at the ground. 'Sometimes I see him kind of looking at me.'

'Does he?' said Cecilia. She paused. 'How?'

'Just – looking.'

'What's this man's name?'

'Mr Dahl.'

'What?'

Romy frowned.

'Mr Dahl.'

There was a silence.

'Mum,' said Romy.

Cecilia opened her mouth.

'Mum –'

'What's his first name?' Cecilia asked in a small flat voice, cutting across Romy.

'I don't know.'

'What kind of old?' Her skin was pale.

'Quite old. Fifties? I don't know. Prehistoric. Jurassic? Why?'

'I – I just wondered,' said Cecilia, her breathing unsteady. '*Jesus*,' she said, and it was almost a growl. 'Idiot. Me. I –'

'Mum! What's the – What do you mean?'

'*How* does he look at you?' said Cecilia, turning to Romy. She laid her hand on one of her shoulders, holding it hard. Romy twisted to look at the hand.

'Oh God, Mum, I don't know. It's – nothing. Like. I don't know. It's nothing. It's just the way he looks. Stop getting so fiery about things –'

'Well I'm going to the school,' said Cecilia rapidly. 'I'm complaining – immediately. He *cannot* –'

'*No!* Mum!' said Romy in a panic. 'No!'

'I certainly am. How does he look at you?' said Cecilia.

Romy jumped. 'Like – it's really all right. He just looks at me a bit. I notice because he's always looking down. He probably looks at *everyone* like that. You've gone mad!'

'I haven't –' said Cecilia. 'I – I – How long has he been teaching there?'

'*I* don't know.'

'Where's his wife?'

'There. *There.* She teaches me.'

'What?' said Cecilia weakly.

'Ms Dahl,' said Romy.

Cecilia hesitated. 'What's her first name?' she said.

'Elisabeth. She's the art teacher. The good one,' said Romy impatiently, rolling her eyes. 'Remember? There's a good one and a pathetic one. You've gone crazy!' she said, laughing.

Cecilia flushed angrily.

'No *teacher* can look at you – whatever way it is he looks at you,' she said, and she walked out of the room.

'James Dahl please,' said Cecilia, ignoring Romy's calls of protest from her bedroom door, the very enunciation of his name a disturbing plunge into the past; but some secretary – an officious trained impostor instead of the failed artists and part-time knitwear designers who had once worked in that office – informed her that staff were available to take calls between four and six in the afternoon. Cecilia argued impatiently while the voice repeated rules. Had she, she wondered, at some subconscious level known that he would be here? She doubted it. Then it seemed glaringly obvious. She dismissed it again. A memory of herself as a teenager came to her then: a girl the same age as her daughter Romy now: a man's mouth kissing her breast, a strong thigh against her smaller one.

The idea of Ari in close proximity to James Dahl worried her.

On Saturday morning, Dora heard the garden gate open. She glanced up, her body tuned to hope, but it was the helper Katya.

'I took a phone call for you yesterday,' said the taciturn Katya in a mumble, the local accent having survived university. 'Sorry. It was from your friend called Elisabeth.'

'What did she say? Did she say when she's coming?'

'No.'

'Nothing?'

'That she'd call again.'

Dora paused. The air felt cold on her hair. She knew that she would be waiting all day. *I haven't progressed*, she thought suddenly.

She felt frozen, her life an unmoving chunk of matter. She stood quite still as understanding splintered through her. Twenty-five years of intermittent pleasure and torment from Elisabeth Dahl. A quarter of a century. She reeled. Suffering and joy and sexual reunions weeks, months and even years apart. They were supposed to have a friendship – a friendship interspersed by heated moments at Elliott Hall, or by an annual night spent together in which Dora helplessly watched herself losing her year's worth of pride while her body and mind were relit – and yet, it seemed, they never could quite give each other up. Elisabeth's bouts of kindness, caring, unexpected vulnerability, always occurred just when Dora thought she had summoned the strength to push her away; because there were of course depths of humanity and even – most affectingly; most disastrously – sadness beneath Elisabeth's imperturbability. She was more fragile underneath it all than she could begin to know, and it had taken Dora years to understand this.

And now, since the diagnosis of breast cancer, Elisabeth was being more considerate. She would arrive, unannounced, with food or gardening and opera magazines. Dora felt a new softening. When Elisabeth visited her cottage, she made Dora laugh with her caustic asides and her boldness. She was generous: she brought flowers, always, and meals now that Dora was ill: surprising meals, hotpots and intense pasta sauces that she had, she said, left simmering for most of the day, transported and garnished extravagantly with herbs or edible flowers. The warmth, when it came, was touching. It was simple.

'I will look after you,' Elisabeth said to Dora, and she did – indeed she did. But intermittently.

There seemed to be no pattern but randomness.

'Come and drink the tea inside when you're ready,' Dora said to Katya, her voice croaking until she coughed. 'I made us some scones too. Do you mind brown flour in scones?'

★   ★   ★

That night, Ruth counted the gods and ghosts that peopled her room with a system to contain them, but shadows haunted the house and feet ran across the loft. When she looked at the river-gurgling blackness from her window, she saw the hulks of the old troughs and broken walls by the barn, like a crumbling city of stone and moss, and she thought about all the animals out there, the bogs and mists and bare-teethed horses creeping down towards her.

Cecilia slipped out of bed just after midnight.

'Hey gorgeous,' said Ari, grabbing her hand in his half-sleep.

Cecilia leant down and kissed him on the lips, then pulled her fingers away.

'Come here,' he said.

'I have to work.'

'Not now . . . Go and do it, then come back to me.'

'It's all very well for you to say *that*,' she said, then heard her own voice and softened and stroked his forehead. 'You have all hours all week to work.'

'Yes yes yes. I know. I'm sorry. Let's not have a fucking argument about it now.'

'I'll argue with you in the morning instead.'

'How I look forward to that,' said Ari, and groaned and pulled the duvet over his ears, and she walked away, ruffled. Words of self-justification ribboned through her mind.

She sat down in what was her old bedroom, now her study, and tried to clear her thoughts. Into the space flooded James Dahl the St Anne's teacher, followed by Romy, by Dora's radiotherapy, by the coal for the Aga, the draughts and leaks and scrabbling animals, and the needs of three uprooted girls. Had she, then – somehow, unwittingly, unknowingly – put herself back where she would be forced to encounter him again? She felt like a fool. Her face heated, she opened the file containing *The House on the Moor* and drove herself to plan her characters' journey up the Dart: three children with their pet wolves, their complex quest and their escape from a deranged butler. The door of her old bedroom bore Gallery Five stickers covered over in layers and layers of paint, their plump mouse and cat figures just detectable under cream gloss, and she thought how fitting but disconcerting it was that the writing of children's books had partially bought her back her own childhood home.

She forced herself to write, but she heard a noise as faint above the river rush as a scratching. The sound was not on the road this time: it was in the plants outside the window, nearer to the house.

Someone was outside again.

She didn't look. She made herself imagine a fox. She considered disturbing Ari and asking him to explore the foliage in his practical male way to tell her that the intruder was a product of her imagination, a chimera of weather and animal movement, but she couldn't, because she knew that someone was there.

'Darling,' she said, and she didn't know who she meant.

She tried to stop thinking. She attempted to write. Perhaps, she thought, she didn't want Ari to interfere because she was clinging to irrational hopes. People couldn't just disappear from this earth. The baby had gone somewhere.

Someone was out there. There was someone or something – a pony, perhaps? A hedgehog? – rustling in the tall grass that obscured part of the front wall and needed removing. She went to the window and made herself open it, the frame catching on the thatch, the stillness lining her lungs. She could see nothing. She turned off the light, knelt on the window seat and stretched out through the narrow opening into the night where she could taste the rinsed chill of the air. There was someone there. Mara, Mara. Was she coming across the river, reed-battered, hungry?

'Hello?' she called out urgently, but her voice broke into a croak.

She caught sight of a sleeve in the light angling from the landing window above the porch, saw a hand passing behind the bushes and grass near the house, a streak of paler substance as the figure moved swiftly away, crossing the garden and disappearing from sight on the lane.

'Oh God,' Cecilia said, holding the windowsill. 'Wait!' she called.

The person had gone.

She couldn't tolerate it. She rose clumsily and ran to the nearest upstairs landing window that faced the back garden, but all she could see was the ridge of Dora's thatch with no lights beneath it, the wind slicing through a loose pane onto her neck.

Seventeen

March

WHEN CECILIA woke, Ari had risen and it was almost ten o'clock. The sound of his voice fusing with Ruth's came to her, the rush of a game in the garden floating to the window.

A cluster of tortoiseshells moved sleepily, hibernating in a corner of the windowsill. Cecilia remembered then, those half-dead butterflies of childhood that had always slept in the house in winter, waiting in a drugged state for spring. However much you believed you remembered, there were always forgotten things; there were distortions.

She stretched, idling in the unaccustomed relaxation, and with the warmth of the sheets and the sudden unwanted intrusion of James Dahl into her life, she was reminded of the Saturday morning after the Lorca play all those years before when she had woken up in Zeno's room at school. She had stumbled in there in the night, Chase House, Zeno in a smoke haze asking little, and made a bed on the rug. As she turned on the floor on waking late in the morning, the over-extended pull of her inner thighs had filtered into her consciousness and informed her in her half-sleep of what had happened. A kind of bliss had filled her mind. She later thought that that moment, that drowsy waking passage of time on the sunlight of Zeno's floor when she remembered that she had had sex with Mr Dahl, had encapsulated the purest happiness she had ever experienced.

She had gone home that afternoon and walked over the moors for most of the day, all evidence there in the tugs and tendernesses of her body. She was loose-jawed, wide-eyed. She paced about in a disbelieving trance near Wind Tor, past Foxworthy and over the Ball, fast-breathed and careless, and she caught the scent of him on her arm, warm and private beneath the wind, her faint residual fear at the reality of sex overlaid by a progressively enhanced memory of arousal. He would be in Dorset from the morning, he had told her, solemnly and straightforwardly, and she had accepted that prearranged fact as she must, because she knew that he would contact her, though how she wasn't sure, and she felt wind-battered and alchemised as she ran, jumping over tussocks and marshy stretches, the tendons at the top of her thighs pulling as she leapt. She flew. She had never experienced such elation. She felt the soreness inside her every time she clenched her muscles – repeatedly, deliberately, nudging at the entrancing pain – a reminder that she had made love, that she had a lover.

The wind blew, and she carried on walking out there into the stirrings of evening, away from the phone, though he couldn't call. She played back moments in a disordered rush, certain she had remembered everything; and then images, as yet unexamined, would come to her with a vividness of recollection that made her emit small shouts as she ran that sounded mad even to her own ears: memories of his hand brushing her nipple; a word he had murmured to her; his finger lingering on the back of her neck. She was imprinted by him. An electric current seemed to shoot from the top of her thighs through her abdomen, and then again, and again, as she recalled scenes. She lowered herself on to a stone in a hollow with the wind tugging at her front to remember with enforced slowness, every prefatory detail arranged in sequence, the moment of penetration. She thought of their wedding, of how they'd plot it, and when they would run away. He would have to divorce Elisabeth first. Or could he become effectively engaged and then divorce afterwards? She was uncertain.

She pictured herself beside him in a carriage pulled by sturdy cobs making for Yorkshire or Scotland. They would stop at an inn on the way with her trunks compressing rustling layers, springing and starched and laced, and blood on her wedding night though she was no virgin now. Returning to school his wife. Would she do that? Facts seemed burdensome and muddling. Could she marry him without anyone knowing, and then on the day, the very day she'd finished her A levels, there would be an announcement and she would drive off, a bride in old ivory in a carriage being gazed at open-jawed by her schoolmates and wished well by the farming folk lining the lane. But then what of university? Would he accompany her? She saw herself taking notes in lectures wearing her wedding ring, the existence of her grown man of a husband known by contemporaries as she spurned drinks and student frivolity while he waited for her in their modest married quarters. Logistical vagueness set in. She looked at the bracken-choked Ball rearing above her and focused on the present. They would soon talk of the future, and then she'd know, again, that pleasure, that edge of pain.

And Dora had understood nothing when her daughter, deflowered by her teacher, had returned to Wind Tor House after pacing the moor all afternoon. She glanced at her, later hugged her in passing to acknowledge her return, and asked her above the sounds of Barnaby crying if she'd enjoyed the school play.

By early Monday morning, fear had begun to nibble at Cecilia's euphoria. She had found and reread suitably exalted passages of *Madame Bovary*, of *Anna Karenina*, of *Tess of the d'Urbervilles* and *Villette*; she had cried and felt her own skin where he had touched it and, afraid of being overheard at home, walked the mile and a half to the telephone box in Ponsworthy just to tell Diana, her only confidante, in a series of soaring, gabbled runs of speech. She felt as though she were drunk. She was agitated with ecstasy followed by waves of disbelief. She visualised the Mr Dahl of the classroom handing back essays; and then, in deliberate sudden contrast, summoned him entering her and whispering to her, the juxtaposition repeated and repeated with subtle variation.

Speedy had smiled slyly at her at supper as though he knew, yet actual knowledge was impossible. He grinned at her, raising his eyebrow in enquiry. She laughed, unable to stop herself, her over-excitement bubbling up like a dizzying series of steps rising higher and higher and emerging as a childish cough that ended in a snort of crumbs on to the surface of the table, causing him to wink at her when her parents weren't looking. But by Sunday evening, she had developed a stomach ache that wouldn't go away. She pulled her knees to her chest in bed and tried to squeeze the pain into submission. It was past two in the morning and she couldn't contemplate school. The suspicion that he wouldn't discuss marriage immediately after all, that he would be awkward and might even hide behind his teaching role, fanned coldly through her mind as a growing fear, and by four in the morning she wanted to lie barricaded in her bedroom and go back, back to her childhood, back to the time before this had occurred. She wished with panicking sincerity that it had never happened. She read some Enid Blyton to numb herself with descriptions of teas provided by cheerful cooks, with coastal paths and cornflowers and boys called Sooty Lenoir. Terror ticked through her. By the time Dora called outside her room, she had slept for just over two hours and had to be shaken awake.

And now Cecilia, lying in the same house over twenty years later, spring air tensing on plaster curves, daughters in varying states of frenzy or adolescent languor in the garden, looked back on that period with James Dahl more fully than she had ever wanted to – having been unable to contemplate it in its entirety; viewing it only in fragments of recalled joy or anger or regret – and wondered exactly how that relationship – if a relationship was what it had been, rather than a lopsided attachment or a series of colliding desires and misunderstandings – still informed her to this day. It was there as a flare that receded and returned at the periphery of her consciousness.

Poor girl, she thought now, feeling sorry for herself as she so rarely did. The poor buffeted eager creature that she had been. All the energy and obsession she had poured into literature, into studying, and into love for James Dahl, had, after that first night, been dedicated to him alone. She had seen her schoolwork through an obsessed daze. The affair with him had brought her very close to breakdown, she thought now.

Looking back, she realised that she had been, if anything, particularly inexperienced, raised on seclusion and bohemian ideals. She had never paid a bill or eaten a takeaway; she had barely been to London, hardly travelled; rarely even went, unlike so many of her school contemporaries, to a pub, while her sexual education was derived from *The Valley of the Dolls* and Dora's well-meant speeches about 'lovemaking'. Perhaps, after all, there was something dangerous, clotted, in that idyll that the Bannans and their contemporaries had attempted to create. And she, the seventeen year old with her denim skirts, her clogs and her hair clips, she the bluestocking virgin, had negotiated single-handedly the emotions of an affair with a married man.

'How are you? How are you?' he had asked rapidly when he found her alone by the lockers the Monday after the play. This moment, vividly prefigured as a series of arrangements for elopement, was now taut with anguish. She had avoided him, just as she had looked out in agony for him. The sleeves of his palely striped shirt were rolled up in distracted fashion although it was February. He breathed quickly through his nose.

'Fine,' she said, glancing at her feet, then meeting his eye with a smile crooked with irrepressible radiance. 'Oh – very well!' she said. She blushed.

'No.' He shook his head and exhaled loudly through his mouth, tension darkening his face. His sand-coloured stubble glinted in the landing-window light. 'That – that – should *never* have happened. Christ,' he said, sweeping his hand over his forehead. His breath was faintly sour. 'I'm appalled. I'm so deeply sorry –'

'No,' she said steadily. 'No. Please don't say that.'

And the next time he had seen her – and she had been repeatedly sleepless, had picked at her skin until she bled – he had apologised again in a strained and self-blaming speech, but he had asked more kindly after her, with audible concern. He had resumed walking to Elliott Hall gardens at lunchtimes, and she saw him there among the mulch and darkness and snowdrops, the occasional gardener marking horizons, and they began to find each other again. She knew, could see him trying to resist her, knew beneath all her despair that there was a compulsion that bound them; that she held some strong attraction for him; that he battled with himself over that. And so the affair had carried on even through the weeks of apparent indifference or propriety: the snatched talks and pretexts and assignations, the skimming of skin and flaring nerves with nowhere safe to go, and the rare, rare sex, snatched from normal rhythms of time and place.

On weekends, she had walked up high on blustery days, the wind and gorse scratches more alive than the slow dripping hours at home. *Yonder a maid and her wight/Come whispering by;/War's annals will fade into night/Ere their story die*, she had thought, her mouth moving rapidly with imagined dialogue. She would be glimpsed by him, she was certain, as he sped along that moorland road, and they'd walk together, a tall figure with a younger woman in an air-blue gown blown against him like a tethered spinnaker, his hand caught round her waist. '*Hail! Bright Cecilia*,' he would greet her, as he sometimes did.

Only twice in reality – once in March, once in May – she still remembered the months, even in adulthood – had he walked with her on the moors, hinting that he would pass the back route to Widecombe on a Sunday, and they had walked, talking in the sweet-smelling wind among the tormentil, skylarks calling, bracken rankly unfurling, ponies tugging grass.

Those walks were the exception: he seemed unwilling to extend the affair beyond the boundaries of Elliott Hall, since he would rarely do anything intentionally: it had to happen by chance, a collision of time and place in which events were driven by temptation rather than forethought. It had taken her months to understand this. So strong was his resistance to his own actions, his acceptance of any relationship at all only functioned if events occurred spontaneously.

It was illicit, apparently suspected by no one. Sometimes in her nervous exhaustion Cecilia even wanted her mother to know. 'Can't you see? Can't you *see*?' she wanted to shout at her, throwing herself at her feet so that Dora could put a stop to it, force an end to it entirely, immure her safely in a nunnery to sleep and recover and dedicate herself to her books – the books now neglected, the history and French sliding from her grasp, the English so unevenly studied – but she was simply too addicted. She was in a state of love.

'Mum!' Ruth called now. The light slid over the plaster, quickening on the silver of the mirror. Cecilia wanted to lie there unfound.

'Mama!' Izzie followed, some injustice demanding attention, the floorboards jittering the length of rooms. 'Ma!'

She would behave so differently now, Cecilia thought, and felt very old and knowledgeable with that realisation.

She remembered somehow, in some hidden sensory chamber, the smell of the school: the old-fashioned standards – wax, chalk, cleaning fluids – beneath the patchouli and damp Afghan coats, and James Dahl in those parqueted classrooms, teaching her – still her A level teacher with his formal patterns of speech, his exacting ways, his rows of pens, teaching her for two double periods a week – and the surreal awareness burning inside her that she knew what that wide-shouldered figure in a jacket was like uncontrolled, his breath in hot spurts on her shoulder. What if they saw it, the kohl-eyed cynics splayed over their desks? She was engorged with this secret. It swarmed through her. She felt chosen and illuminated.

'Cecilia, can you see me after the class?' he had said on one of three occasions, as he did to other students, fulfilling one of her most repetitive fantasies, and even then, as she waited for a relief teacher dashing in with an enquiry and stood behind a classmate whose essay was being returned, she had known that she was storing details for a scene that would be replayed during the droughts that would follow.

'I have a free period on Friday after lunch,' he said, tapping his pen, appearing to be studying his register before he closed it. 'I can spend it in the gardens.'

And in the pearlised light of winter at Elliott Hall, she understood at some level that youth carried her, that something in her flexible spine, her legs, her skin, her enthusiasm, was a primitive calling card, and that despite all the periods of self-hatred, the stuttering and blushing, she could at least intermittently radiate charm.

Then after those almost maddeningly rich interludes of dialogue and brushed skin, he would become merely her teacher for stretches – ten days, two and a half weeks even – passing her in the corridor in conversation with a colleague and ignoring her; glimpsed consulting Elisabeth, or stacking essays on his desk without glancing at her. She always felt that she had failed to control the situation effectively: that if she had taken a certain action, or said something, or not said something else, or been an entirely different person altogether, that he would come to her; that her own failure to act was allowing him to slip from her grasp. And so he went about his daily business. Just give me a *sign*, she begged him silently. She hurt her own flesh, punishing herself, and failed to work and sleep. She talked to him, without ever stopping, in her mind. She accepted crumbs.

Cecilia now shuddered. Yet it turned her on, still, that image of a girl and an older man: some remnant of it buried in her brain, hardwired beneath the resistance. Ari was her age; she had had brief relationships before him with men who were both older and her contemporaries; but it was that notion, that dangerous power differential that somehow remained her template for excitement, and combined with the clandestine nature of her affair, it possessed an intensity that had never been repeated. She was the one selected. However terrible its ramifications, there was some aspect she returned to, a time of extraordinary exhilaration that had formed her. It was, she thought, to do with more than age and power. It was to do with being picked out. Yet the truth was that she had been chosen and not chosen.

Eighteen
March

CECILIA DECIDED to drive to St Anne's early that Monday afternoon while Romy was attending a rehearsal. Feeling some doubts, she left Ruth in Izzie's care. Izzie's storm cloud of blackish hair was perfectly framed by the dark-red and green clothes she was wearing, and she seemed restless, and glanced out of the window. Ruth, wearing a dress that clung to her compact pot of a tummy, a row of badges attached just below its neckline, sat and knitted a scarf.

'That's beautiful,' said Cecilia, and went and kissed Ruth again.

'It's got holes,' muttered Ruth.

'It's lovely,' said Cecilia. 'I'll be back before supper. Don't stuff yourselves. Or only on *healthy stuff*,' she added, parodying herself.

'Yes, Ma,' said Izzie, who was hazily friendly and smelled of cigarette smoke. She had settled immediately into her comprehensive in Ashburton, swiftly finding friends and smoking companions, while Romy embraced the culture of diligence at St Anne's. Ruth, Cecilia worried, spent much time at the primary school in Widecombe sitting on a step where a beetle lived.

'Phwoargh, you look sexy, Ma,' Izzie called out.

Ruth blushed.

A dead badger lay rotting on the verge. Cecilia had, changing several times, dressed in the clothes she would have worn in London for a work meeting, out of self-protection and a need to prove herself, and she had not made an appointment so that he would have no warning. Already the idea of Ari meeting him at a future parents' evening filled her with an uncharacteristic instinct for subterfuge.

The bleached flickering of the hedges above her gave way to glimpses of river beneath oak woods, and an image came to her. She couldn't help it. It was a photograph in her mind. She had so few. What I remember, she thought, is a hand. It was as small and peaked as a button mushroom.

She walked nervously around St Anne's, still perceiving the grounds, with the standard adult shift of perception, as notably smaller than she had done in childhood. She saw that Neill House or its present incarnation was no longer his home, the blinds in the flat on the top floor clearly the choice of someone other than Elisabeth Dahl. The formality of the school – the borders and immature pergolas, the signposts in copperplate pointing to the Refectory, to the Beech Walk and other faintly bogus locations – amused her even as purpose increased her pace. The new theatre, in which Romy was supervising scenery, rose richly near the head's house; a science and technology block stood where boys had once stubbed out their cigarettes; a new clock in an old tower struck the half hour.

After almost fifty minutes, she caught sight of him. She began to shake with a steady tremor. As he walked across the lawn that adjoined the boarding houses, her image of him was realigned with a lurch of recognition. Some remnant of emotion merged with her anger, reminding her of the lost feeling of adoring him, though he was in truth diminished from the figure she had remembered: not so monumentally tall as she had thought, and simply human, and the shine of what she now realised had been comparative youth had gone. She felt relief, even perverse amusement, but she continued to tremble.

He was broader and visibly older, his hair a paleness between white and faded dark blond, his posture straighter, while his eyes, their lashes still contrastingly dark, seemed more blue than grey against the increased colourlessness of his hair. He possessed the suggestion of muscle of an older man who still exercised. At seventeen, she had considered him age itself, yet he had been thirty-six. She now had to adjust her notion of his age. She watched him before he saw her and she remembered how one leg of her tights, her schoolgirl's black woolly tights, had remained caught with her knickers, still attached to her ankle while they were performing that act that changed things.

He stopped. His mouth opened. He glanced down and looked up at her again.

'Cecilia,' he said. Colour washed his skin.

'Hello,' she said. He was just a normal man, she thought, almost in confusion.

He stretched out his hands, those square-tipped clean hands, and she lifted hers instinctively to meet his, then pulled them back.

He was wearing a dark-grey jacket with a shirt in a muted cherry colour – the work of Elisabeth Dahl, Cecilia could see with pitying exasperation – and pens lined his pocket, and his briefcase was fuller than it had been in Haye House days, its bulk straightening his arm, and in that moment she felt herself to be immensely tall and composed, her every movement adult and assured as she faced him here.

'How are you?' he said, looking her in the eyes as he so rarely had.

'I'm fine,' she said steadily.

'Good –' He gave her a strained smile.

'But angry.' Her voice was rich-toned.

'Oh –' he faltered. Blood drained from his skin.

'Romy,' she said.

'. . . Romy,' he said. 'Romy Hersch. I wondered –'

'I can request that you don't even teach her,' she said, yet even as she spoke, she knew that he would have no sexual interest in a girl so very much younger. She was, in effect, punishing him for the past.

The sight of girls passing, bearing the blurred lustre and unformed features that she must once have possessed, made her think of herself again then.

'You have been looking at my daughter,' she said.

'Yes,' he said, catching her eye and then glancing away. 'She struck me very quickly as familiar. I wondered – seeing her reminded me of . . . you.'

'Oh –' said Cecilia.

'I couldn't tell from her surname, but I wondered. Aspects of you came back to me –' He coughed.

They were silent.

'I thought I saw you in her,' he said. 'It was – strange.'

Cecilia paused. 'But you've made her feel very uncomfortable,' she said, still maintaining the same cold intonation though she knew that he told the truth.

'I'm sorry,' he said.

'I thought, surely you can't be looking at another girl like – And, you know, if you, anyone, laid a *finger* on her, I'd report them without hesitation.' She blushed.

He flinched. 'Of course I would never –' he said abruptly.

'Well how should I know?'

'Cecilia. Cecilia. What do you take me for? Some lecherous old . . . Good God. The girl – your daughter – Romy –' he paused, lifted his hands '– must be forty years younger than I am. I –' he said, shaking his head. His voice was more raised than she had heard it before.

'You're capable of it,' she said, then paused.

'Cecilia,' he said, his colour rising. 'That is entirely untrue. And you know that.'

He was silent.

'This is the thing that has haunted me the most,' he said, his voice faltering.

He raised his head and met her eye. She nodded. The mothers probably fancied him now, she mused; the grandmothers even. She pitied him: the small-town teacher who had never moved on.

'I sometimes see myself in photos from that time. And I was a child,' she said. She steadied her breathing. She blinked impatiently. 'Yes, yes, I was technically of age, but I was in your care: you had power over me.' She swallowed. 'I could never perceive you normally. Equally.' She suddenly wanted to cry. To weep for the first time for years over what she had been through. In her battle against her earlier shyness and vulnerability, she had become determined: demonstrative, expressive, as though any form of reticence or passivity were a sign of weakness to her.

He flinched. 'I –' he said, opening his mouth and then closing it again, as though physically unable to speak of the subject.

'It's a crime under the Sexual Offences Act.'

'I'm aware of that,' he said. 'I – have had to resolve this with myself. It has been . . . the greatest failure of my professional career.'

' "Failure"? Career? Good God, you pompous fool,' she said. 'It was a *failure* in so many more ways than that to me.' She was trembling.

'I'm sure, I'm sure. I'm sure. It was unforgivable. I've tried to apologise to you or explain, but I feel I never have entirely. You –'

'You were married. You were twenty years older. You had power over me,' she said.

He looked at the ground, then back up at her, his mouth a set line. He breathed slowly.

'Did I – did you –' he said, colouring. 'Did you feel I *forced* you?'

'No,' she said. She shook her head. 'Definitely not. I wanted to sleep with you. I wanted to be with you.'

His shoulders sagged with palpable relief. His breathing was faintly more audible, his fringe now a sparser fall. He whose every impulse, desire and mistake had once determined her own happiness was an ageing country teacher, and she felt precise, almost fiery, an outsider blown into his little world. It made her want to laugh, suddenly, with newly taken power.

'Oh God, you never could talk about things, could you?' she said. 'Sex, love: *emotion*. Too much the uptight English gentleman. But not too uptight to have an affair with a schoolgirl.'

He moved with his old characteristic quarter-rotation of the head, his features still immobile.

'You are very angry about this,' he said in a low voice.

'Because teachers should not sleep with their pupils, and then expect –'

'I have never again – never again.'

'You've never seduced a pupil again? I doubt that very much.'

'Never,' he said.

'You've been faithful ever since?'

He hesitated.

She nearly spoke. She stopped herself.

'Once – twice.' He looked up.

'It's all right,' she said impatiently. 'No one can hear you. Your *wife* won't overhear you.'

'I understand – believe me, I understand this anger. There have been years ... when I've wondered, regretted. Sincerely regretted. But you were the only one.'

'Really? I really do find that hard –'

'Truly,' he said emphatically. 'There have been a couple – two – other brief, brief ... but never with a pupil. You have my word.'

'I –'

She said nothing.

He coughed.

'Why is your daughter here?' he said.

'Because she wanted to come here. Because I had to move back. Because my mother is ill. I need to be here near her. My – my partner, boyfriend: there's no good word for that; he has a job here from October.' She heard the uncharacteristic coldness of her voice as she spoke.

'Your mother –'

'Yes, my mother.'

'How is –'

'She has had cancer.'

'Oh, Dora. What bad news. Dora. I'm really very sorry. How is she?'

'She's having radiotherapy. As you'd expect.'

'Please do – please send my very best to Dora. What a very good person.'

'Yes.'

'I was always full of admiration for her. I know Elisabeth still sees her sometimes but it's been some time since I have – She didn't tell me –'

He was silent.

'Are your brothers there to help?' he then said awkwardly.

'No,' she said. 'The youngest sometimes.'

'You're living back – back there.'

'Wind Tor, yes. I bought out one brother's share, pay rent to the other two. Dora's next door.'

He breathed heavily. 'Congratulations,' he said then, but without warmth, 'on your novel.'

'Thank you,' said Cecilia.

'I read about it.'

She paused. 'It's . . . absurd you're here,' she said.

He inclined his head. 'I thought you might have heard.'

'How could I know?' she said.

'Well,' he said, and he smiled. 'There's a grapevine. Now that you live in a *little one-eyed, blinking sort o' place.*'

'Don't do that,' she said quickly. 'Don't quote at me. It reminds me of – Haye House.'

'Yes I know,' he said. He looked at the ground. 'You know that I'm – truly sorry, don't you?'

She drew in her breath. She turned to him. 'I don't know,' she said finally. She looked at her watch. 'I have to go.'

He was momentarily silent. 'I have a meeting of the English department.'

Cecilia nodded. She left him standing with his briefcase beneath the oak at St Anne's and with her heart racing she collected her daughter and drove back to her work and her family and a house that contained a past that was unknown to her children.

Nineteen
March

S HAKING AS she chatted to Romy on the way home, Cecilia returned in her mind with a still-queasy lurch to the moment she had suspected she was pregnant.

She had been out food shopping with her mother and Barnaby one Friday night, noting in the metal strips below the supermarket shelves how blotched she was beneath rain-frizzed hair. Her very posture seemed bowed by alternating despair and euphoria. Her period was late.

They walked up the small high street towards the car carrying their bags, heads lowered in drizzle, and the headmaster's latest girlfriend, a Belgian dancer, rapped on the window of the wine bar favoured by Haye House staff. She beckoned, projecting her beam through the glass, and as they were ushered with little choice into the bar, Cecilia saw that he was there. The Dahls were sitting beside Peter Doran with Mike, an art teacher who had studied with Elisabeth Dahl, and Serena, the mother of three of Mike's children.

'Dora, my dear,' said Elisabeth, turning. She created a space on the settle.

'We must be quick,' said Dora, resisting and then sitting back in that place of dripping red candles and Liberty prints.

'How enormous that child has become,' said Elisabeth, gesturing at Barnaby, who snored, his curling 'M' of a baby's mouth glimmering rhythmically.

'More wine,' called a drunk Peter Doran with parodic lordliness. 'What kind of hostelry is this? A grotty dive. I require two more flagons now our music mistress has appeared.'

Cecilia shuddered. Mike tipped back beer from a pewter mug; James Dahl's sleeves were rolled up, his hair less orderly than it was at school, his jacket hanging from a settle arm.

'The bloody taxes are prohibitive,' he was saying as Cecilia sat down, and he raised his eyes and nodded at her, his fringe falling over his forehead. He drank. 'And basic socialist principles are there to claw you back if the Treasury doesn't . . . How are you, Dora? And – Cecilia.'

'Happy to be here,' said Dora.

'I –' said Cecilia. She scraped her chair as she pulled it in.

'You're a dinosaur, Dahl,' called out Peter Doran. 'Fuck the taxman – sorry, Cecilia, and –' he said, gesturing at Barnaby, '– baby – and polish up your avoidance strategies. Exile? Offshore assets? Short trips to Switzerland? I can see you striding around the Matterhorn, James.'

'You're shameless, Doran. Try paying normal taxes once you've accounted for the nice little spread of properties this charitable foundation owns in Knightsbridge.'

'I was there the other day,' said Elisabeth crisply.

'Why?' said Dora.

'I felt a Harvey Nichols recce was required.'

Cecilia's skin burned. She attempted to react, looked up, formed expressions that implied understanding, emitted a breathy laugh that elicited no response, interjected the occasional 'Yes!' and 'No!' that were ignored beyond a slight turn of a head in her direction, and then pretended to be too busy studying the feather motif on the table's oilcloth to listen. James Dahl took no notice of her. Subtly, she tilted a knife towards herself to check the inflamed patch of skin above her mouth while the adults discussed mortgage relief and educational policy and art world friends of Elisabeth's with drunken flippancy, interspersing their theories with semi-obscured sexual innuendo. Even her own mother entered this adult world, its codes unknown to Cecilia, who floundered like a retarded infant in her itchy skirt, her knicker gusset pressing against her, every minute creeping round on the forged-iron clock wittily constructed of bicycle parts. She waited for the tug of her period, her nipples sore. She was a child in a woman's body, her breasts curving grotesquely to mimic adulthood while her mind was unable to produce a single word of interest. A fear leapt at her and subsided.

'Thank the Lord it's Friday,' said James. He drank more wine and played a card game as he talked.

Elisabeth leant against him, nodding at one of his cards, and he smiled in appreciation as he played it while running his hand down her back.

'I'll meet you later by the car,' Cecilia nearly said to Dora, but even that one sentence was impossible to say in this company, catching and halting in her throat. She was only capable of whispering it into her mother's ear. She rehearsed the words time and time again as she stared at a candle; she arranged her bag on her seat in infinitesimal movements so that she could pick it up when she left without swinging it into a flame. She waited, but it was too noisy or too briefly silent to speak. She could say nothing.

And then later, in Elliott Hall gardens in late spring, when she had avoided thinking about the absence of her period through panicking denial, she had met him and walked along with him.

He smiled at her on the path. He put his hand on her waist – but too high, above its real curve – when they turned the corner where the Madame Isaac Pereire roses grew, and she quivered in response with a small delay in her reaction.

She looked up at this man with his faintly distracted air, his bristling of adult preoccupations, and a realisation came to her as though from nowhere.

'You're not ever going to leave her, are you?' she said.

His hand stiffened. He walked forward slowly.

She pulled away from him.

'Are you?' she said. She was suddenly light-headed.

He looked at the ground. She took it all in: his polished brogue, a piece of grass attached with dampness to one side; a frown which aged him; the blossom on the soil between the roses like sodden confetti. She noticed his faint gold stubble, the strong straight bone of his nose. Pain passed over his face.

'I can't do that,' he said.

She heard his words. She refused to hear them. A blanket, almost a smile, came down over her mind.

She made a little noise.

'How could I?' he said. His mouth was set in a straight line.

She felt herself tumbling inside. Nausea rolled up her throat and she swallowed it again, breathing its afterburn.

'You –' said Cecilia. 'Please –' she said, but she could say nothing more.

'I can't lose my ... marriage,' he said, his voice lowered at the word.

She said nothing.

'This is my life, my job,' he said without inflection. 'My – sons are still at school. You understand that, don't you? There is no other means of income. Cecilia,' he said, his breathing uneven.

'Yes,' she said. Her mouth was open in a small round hole. 'No.'

'I have to apologise. Profoundly,' he said, pale faced. His eyelashes were soot-coloured in comparison with the pallor. His voice cracked a little. He looked thin, intense, the bones in his face larger. 'We should – *I* should – never have even considered – never have considered this.'

'Please –' she said.

'You deserve much, much better.'

He looked up at the beech walk. He looked down at her.

'Do you want me to resign?' he said. He touched her sleeve very briefly.

'No,' she said. She shook her head.

'There –' he said, looking up at the trees, taller still in his greater height as he tilted his head, 'there is no justification ... I'm – grievously – to blame. I'm deeply sorry.'

She stared at him, her mouth distorting, and then walked away before he witnessed her tears. She knew then, just before she reached the arch that led to the courtyard: she knew as though she knew that she was dying: she was pregnant.

Dora had noticed Cecilia's changing shape in her last term of school, even marvelled at the fullness of breast, at odds with her increasing slightness. She noticed at the most subconscious level that Cecilia's curves resembled those of pregnancy, and her mind had scrawled into possibilities; she wondered about Gabriel Sardo – they laughed, those two; they colluded and chattered at night quite audibly – but she dismissed the notion, her naïve daughter with her crush on a teacher and her hours dedicated to books the last imaginable candidate for teenage pregnancy. It had been several more weeks until Cecilia had finally come to her and allowed her to know.

And all these years later, Dora chose not to remember that time if she could avoid it. It helped no one to dwell on it, she thought, yet she lived with sadness.

'What's done is done,' she had said to Cecilia so many times, hearing her own inflexibility. It was as though she couldn't stop herself saying it, though she hated herself for it every time the words rose like scum to her mouth. 'What's done is done.' She wished she had never done what she had done.

Dora had feared cancer all her life, assuming with a weary acceptance that she, like so many others, would one day find a lump. The only way in which it seemed destined to surprise her was in its timing, and she had been sixty-six, her fear beginning to drift into a blurry unease about strokes and osteoporosis, when cancer's fibrous grip on her left breast was detected by mammogram. Even then, after a lifetime of low-pitched dread, it managed to shock her. Surgeons in Exeter removed the lump and lymph nodes from her armpit, despite Cecilia's protests that she should be operated on in London and stay, for the first time, with the family. But it was too soon. Dora had preferred to live where she was, with what she knew.

She was now seeing an oncologist and counsellor and beginning her radiotherapy, but there was still an uncertainty over one of her lymph nodes and still she would have to wait. She knew that Cecilia would not be here if it were not for the cancer: Cecilia who had largely avoided the area since she had left home. Their reconciliation had been taking place in increments over the years, but it was still partial, so liable to incendiary episodes and periods of guilty recompense. She hardly knew her own grandchildren.

Dora lived a quiet life. She entertained occasional friends there in the little cottage, and she helped with a local children's string quartet. Sloe gin brewed; chick peas soaked; seedlings grew; the radio played. Her cottage was her refuge, the still point in her life. It was like a miniature version of the house, its ceilings yet lower and its staircase a coiling cranny built for stunted people, labourers centuries dead, its hobbled end wall engorged with weed and foxglove. It could have been as dark as some of the local farms with their tiny parlours and tack rooms but she had endowed it with light and old bleached wood, the children's paintings framed, the dresser in the downstairs room holding her old paraffin lamp, the cello standing polished in a corner of the bedroom.

Here the lodgers Moll and Flite had once lived, their washing dripping on to flagstones from self-plumbed pipes, their aduki bean trays misted with mould. She remembered the smell of must and Indian bazaars, the offerings of hibiscus tea, and the sarongs hung from lintels above listing doors. She had made it her own with her milk jugs and remnants of antique pine from the Wind Tor House days, her oak chests, baskets and Bannan rugs, and her flowers: vases and jam jars full of flowers in every room. Yet compared with the busy wild years of Wind Tor House, there was a silent passing of days. Only Elisabeth threaded time with brightness.

Now Romy and Izzie and Ruth came in to visit, letting themselves through the gate that led from their own back garden. Dora couldn't even touch upon the loss of years gone by without their company. They came in with youth's absolute assumption of welcome, and welcome they were: the red, the dark, the dully fair. They draped themselves, put feet on furniture, scoured the cupboard for biscuits – deliberately casual, knowing their informality to be a benison to an old grandmother – and thus they all happily played their appointed roles with this woman they barely knew but accepted as a family member.

'Hello!' called Romy, who was so like the adolescent Cecilia, Dora thought, but a brighter-coloured, elongated version, her body tall and uncoordinated. Dora recalled Cecilia, already largely estranged from her, stiffly informing her of the existence of Ari Hersch, with whom she had – stunning Dora with its unexpectedness, its inappropriateness – seemingly deliberately become pregnant before she had graduated.

'Greetings, Doreen,' said Izzie. She raised her hand. Dora, who had been taught to respond, lifted her palm, and Izzie slapped it, then pretended to tickle her grandmother with her other hand. She took out her lighter as she folded herself on to the sofa and called to Ruth to fetch her an ashtray.

'Your asthma,' said Dora mildly.

Ruth, the youngest, her squat figure contrasting with Romy's effortless height, sidled into the room unable even now to catch Dora's eye. Dora touched her shoulder in passing and knew that she might, or she might not, unfurl over sweet biscuits with bright monologues that contained no questions.

They chatted. Izzie fiddled with her iPod and rolled a row of cigarettes but planted smoky kisses on Dora as she passed her and urinated loudly with the bathroom door open, still talking at elevated volume into the sitting room with her earphones attached. Ruth gazed through biscuit crumbs as Romy talked earnestly about the history of art, asking her grandmother about the composers contemporaneous with the artists she was studying, her small nose and her many freckles neatly and touchingly arrayed on her face. It was clear to Dora that Romy was making an effort, that she was likely to be bound in a web of altruism and superstition about her illness, just as Cecilia's impulses of kindness and duty were similarly apparent to her. Such concern embarrassed her, but it was preferable to her sons' varying degrees of neglect. Benedict was now in Turkmenistan, Tom gardening for a monastery in Scotland, and Barnaby, the most frequent visitor of the three boys, taking a belated diploma in childcare studies at a college in Bath and turning up whenever he could hitch a lift. Tom wrote regularly, his large writing filling up postcards with spiritual content and news of apple crops, while Benedict's occasional emails from internet cafés would be followed by months of casual silence in which Dora fretted about him and studied the political situation in whichever country she believed him to be visiting. His hints for money sometimes changed to open requests, and she helped with the little she could.

She glanced at the sink. Katya had washed up and was now driving Dora's old car to Newton Abbot for its MOT. A movement caught her eye. She saw Elisabeth Dahl open the gate on the lane side of the cottage and enter the garden. She rose unsteadily and reached the door as Elisabeth was knocking.

'How nice of you to come,' said Dora. She smiled. 'That pasta you brought me was delicious.'

'Good. I rather hoped so. I have apples. You need more fruit.'

'My granddaughters are here.'

Elisabeth nodded. Romy stiffened at the sight of a teacher in her grandmother's house.

'Romy – of course ...' said Dora, gesturing at her. 'These are her sisters Izabel and Ruth.'

'Cool coat,' said Izzie. 'Where from?'

'Extremely ancient Jaeger,' said Elisabeth, turning her gaze on Izzie, pausing very slightly, and letting it swivel away with the same momentum.

'Nice.'

'I've brought you these,' said Elisabeth to Dora. 'I thought you might appreciate them. I don't think I've ever seen lilies of such a vibrant red. They brought to mind Emil Nolde.'

'Thank you,' said Dora, colouring in the presence of her grandchildren. 'How lovely. How lovely.'

'There are flowers everywhere ...' said Elisabeth. 'Perhaps even more than usual.'

'Just cottage garden stuff. Just the flowers of spring.'

'I'm going to start bringing you shopping, music. Books,' said Elisabeth. 'You need distraction. You need looking after.' She began to stack together some of Dora's Royal Horticultural Society publications with brisk movements.

'I have the nurses, and a part-time helper. And Celie now. Thank you.'

'I was very surprised,' said Elisabeth with a delicate pause, 'that she has come back.'

Dora held out her hands in a small shrug. 'This was the catalyst,' she said, glancing down at her chest. 'Her partner will follow later to take up a new post. He has a professorship in Bronze Age archaeology at Exeter.'

'Of course.' Elisabeth paused again. She walked into the kitchen and Dora followed her.

'I –' said Dora.

Elisabeth was silent. Was she going to touch her? Dora wondered. She never knew. Sometimes she did, embracing her or on rare, rare occasions kissing her deeply against a wall or holding out her hand and guiding her up to bed. Then for several visits in a row, she would not, avoiding even social kissing. Dora cursed her own acceptance.

Elisabeth Dahl was impenetrable, yet predictably that obdurate self-possession veiled, as Dora knew, defensiveness. Its origins possibly lay in the fact, inferred by Dora over time, that she was not from the background she would have chosen; her upbringing in the southeast suburbs of London was not exactly what the modulations of her faintly aristocratic inflections seemed to suggest, though some sense of entitlement was naturally hers. Yet in a fashion, thought Dora, they'd all reinvented themselves, those women who had flourished in the South West in the Seventies. With their crumbling houses, their alternative educational establishments, they had cleaved to a doctrine that involved a certain *laissez-faire*, a cultured class ease that she herself had never quite fully inhabited either.

Sunlight fell in smeared segments through the window with its deep-set old glass. Crocuses crowded and browned beside a pot with a Russian doll's face that Cecilia had made for her as a child.

'You deserve the best care,' said Elisabeth. 'The very best care in the world. You know that, don't you?' She looked directly at Dora until Dora flushed a humiliating dark red. She grabbed a bottle of wine by the neck though it was only mid-afternoon and, flustered, began to look in a mustard pot of pewter teaspoons and pens for a corkscrew.

'I'm just tired,' said Dora. 'How's – St Anne's?'

'Adequate. Stuffy,' said Elisabeth, frowning at the wine, on whose surface floated a speck of cork.

Dora smiled. 'I miss Haye House.'

'You,' said Elisabeth, smiling back and catching Dora round the waist so that Dora jerked her head in the direction of the girls lying around in the sitting room, 'you were born to play a lute in a pine studio with fine acoustics and children running round naked outside. You Arts and Crafts beauty.'

Dora laughed abruptly. She reached out and scooped some hand cream from its pot near the sink. She smeared a little on her lips when she had rubbed it in. Her hair was shorter now, her eternally dry skin sapped of life, it seemed to her. Her eyes, surrounded by wrinkles, were still fine and sea-coloured. Was there anything left? She saw cheekbones. Little else.

She avoided Elisabeth's gaze, but Elisabeth was looking straight ahead, only her profile visible, suggesting that she was now caught in some other line of thought. She was always darker than Dora remembered, shades of Italy or Portugal passing over the English and Scottish. She had dark eyes, a beak of a nose, the air of a small eagle. Aquila, thought Dora. Aquila Dahl. Mountain air. She was so familiar, and all the pain and glory that that implied stung Dora with a feeling almost of repulsion. Her stringy legs. Her sharp fierce ego.

'You were very lovely, I've always thought,' said Elisabeth as though delivering a factual statement, returning her direct eye contact. 'That long plait ... Your cello case ... I always imagined that you could hide anything you wanted to in there.'

Dora smiled crookedly. Is this what her other lovers feel? she wondered. Do they treasure these compliments of hers? Jewels glimpsed unexpectedly, then whisked away again.

Dora looked back at the young Elisabeth – surely different from today; hair a darker charcoal; fewer lines; but barely, it seemed, distinguishable from now – and saw her own younger self with something approaching anger: eager to please and impressionable, eternally trapped by the smell, voice, edge of the woman in whose presence she seemed to breathe oxygen, and who rendered others lifeless. Dull, dead, dull.

After the Christmas party when they had begun, so unevenly, that alarming fully sexual relationship, she had fallen into emotional servitude, and her life and her marriage to Patrick had never regained its equilibrium. Elisabeth was uncharmed by Barnaby with his tantrum-splattered toddlerhood, openly sighing at the interruptions he caused. He was so frequently ill with tonsillitis, summer colds, stomach upsets, it seemed at that time as though he were rarely entirely well, Dora wrestling with the contents of his nose, his discontented wrigglings, his snuffles and protests. Elisabeth had, it seemed, forgotten the most basic needs of young children and viewed babies as either dolls or monstrous obstacles to enjoyment. Dora – again, she cursed herself for this now – became pragmatic, compromising, occasionally neglectful of Barnaby in her efforts to secure time and location and harmonious mood.

Overlooking the chilled silences inspired by her little son, she had devised a future with Elisabeth. It held an element of fantasy, she knew – running away to create some kind of demi-relationship that embraced all aspects of her life – but it was driven by something more substantial, by a link that had kept them returning to one another over all those years.

'You are my calm maternal inspiration,' Elisabeth would say. 'My tranquillity. My sexy tranquillity. I need you.'

'I need you too,' said Dora. She looked away. 'It's exciting being with you.'

'Is it?' said Elisabeth and smiled, and sent a trail of quivers up Dora's arm simply by touching her.

They would build a female fastness. It would be like a Rossetti painting, Dora thought: all straw and gold and tapestry. So they plotted in ellipses their bright life together.

When Cecilia had wordlessly let her know about her pregnancy, her listlessness and bowed body compelling Dora to edge towards the subject, her reaction was not what she would have expected of herself. The Kentish Anglican village upbringing returned to her: the lives lived behind tended hedges, the fear of neighbours' talk. Pulling Cecilia to her in sorrowful sympathy even as a part of her wanted to slap her across the face as her own mother might have done, Dora ran out to the pottery barn and told Patrick. That was her immediate instinct. To share this family disaster with her husband. And Patrick's own Catholic past came rearing up in condemnation and humiliation, the two liberals bound by shock. He and Dora shouted at each other for a while in the barn. Who was the father? he always wanted to know, infuriated by Cecilia's stubbornness, but Cecilia persistently refused to talk about it, so eventually he pretended to ignore the subject instead, disturbed and unable to catch her eye through the entire pregnancy.

'Never mind who the father is,' Dora shouted at Patrick. 'What are we going to *do*?'

'This is preposterous!' Dora snapped at Cecilia. 'That – that baby will be barely younger than its – *uncle*. Who is the father? It's Gabriel. Isn't it. Is it?'

But Cecilia dropped her head in what could have been construed as a nod, and breathed rapidly to ward away tears.

'Is it?' said Dora several more times, and Cecilia kept her head hanging.

Dora considered and dismissed James Dahl as a ridiculous idea, though she did spend a painful morning wondering; various boys' names were raised, certain lodgers invoked, and always her suspicions returned to the obvious answer, to the boy she had once spotted kissing Cecilia playfully: Gabriel Sardo, whose behaviour remained unchanged. Dora only later acknowledged that the failure to establish the baby's paternity was somewhat convenient. The father or his parents may have had a view, and to Dora, other solutions were not an option.

She pulled Cecilia to her and they cried together. She took her to a private doctor in Exeter who wouldn't talk to neighbours, but it was, as she strongly suspected, too late: otherwise, she knew with a sense of steel entering her blood that she would have marched her off for an abortion and paid for it without telling Patrick, who would have strenuously objected on lapsed religious grounds.

Gabriel Sardo left after taking two A levels, puzzled by Dora's muffled hostility, Cecilia's pregnancy still invisible to his boy's vision, and the hot summer took grip. Even the grass in the river field yellowed, the flowers clustering round the septic tank drying. Benedict was travelling; Tom ranged, swimming in the river and making dams: the most rural child among them, with his intermittent West Country accent; Barnaby demanded; Cecilia stayed in her bedroom. She hid and slept and roamed at night.

Elisabeth was based in Dorset for some weeks with her sons, then back in Devon when they attended an Outward Bound course on the Dart. But wherever she was, she drove frequently to Wind Tor that summer – with more regularity than she ever would again, reflected Dora later – meeting downriver or in Widecombe or even in the long grass of the meadows to feed Dora's addiction to a pitch of euphoria. Dora saw all activity in her own house – the parched weather; the pregnant girl in the bedroom; the silences left by her absent children; Patrick ministering to the artists who crawled around the place, barns packed to their limits – with a filmy detachment, almost as an amusement. She set out baked potatoes beside lumps of Cheddar and coleslaw for the artists on the barn tables while girls from Leusdon and Poundsgate cleaned the bedrooms, but every activity was performed with Dora's mind quite elsewhere. She was bored unless she could see Elisabeth, talk to her; or, failing that, hear her referred to. All endeavour pointed towards her. One cancelled plan to meet threw her day entirely awry.

She took terrible risks with Patrick, she realised later. Even her guilt was blanketed that summer. In the insanity of her fixation, she told lies as a matter of course, and the more she succeeded, the more fluently she misled. She buried her head, as though the fact of Elisabeth's gender threw a cloak of invisibility over their activities. It did not.

'You have your own life,' Patrick said to her, with ominous variations, and Dora had learnt how to answer. As the principal wage-earner, she possessed some power, she realised over time. She was the provider. The exhausted cash cow. But the Bannans continued to terrify her.

Of Elisabeth's own marriage, she was not permitted to enquire.

'Your husband –' she had ventured with absolute lack of response. 'James – does he – ?'

Elisabeth had barely ever spoken of him. She referred to him with moderate regularity; she explained nothing; she offered no details. As a man he was not real to Dora: he was like a portrait: unbending, formal, unchanging.

Cecilia was in hiding, a madwoman in the attic, reading the same novels over and over with a new lassitude. She slept in the mornings and ate sugary food and became fatter and moved through that twilight place between girlhood and womanhood in near-silence. And although Dora discussed Cecilia and the pregnancy with her one confidante Beatrice and agonised for her daughter, her mind was not fully engaged by it. Years later, she was forced to admit that to herself. Whatever happened, her thoughts returned to one beacon. Had her house been on fire, she would have wondered about the conflagration's effect on the chance of contact that week.

When the pregnancy could no longer be concealed from Elisabeth and Dora had stumblingly revealed the secret, Elisabeth had said, '*More* babies?' with a raised eyebrow. 'Will this household ever stop reproducing? What do you expect if you keep a reasonably good-looking member of the male sex in the house?'

'*You* asked me to take him in,' said Dora.

It was not her conventional Kentish background that had made her do what she did in arranging for the baby's adoption. A roar of anger against Elisabeth, and against herself, now grew inside her.

'You're not well,' said Elisabeth, turning to Dora.

'I am not well,' said Dora, stating a fact, and her throat hardened with vulnerability. She, who always blessed her good fortune, felt sorry for herself. No wonder the cancer had found her, she thought.

It had never really changed. She had tried to look elsewhere, but no woman had ever hauled her in like this: they were too wholesome or homely or politically motivated, causing just a twitch of interest or a manufactured attraction, never acted upon. She had dated a few men after Patrick's death, without success.

Looking at Elisabeth now, Dora wondered who she was seeing, since Elisabeth never referred to her other relationships, or more accurately her discreet liaisons: brief and vivid, and quite extraordinary to Dora. They were so hurtful to her, she couldn't dwell upon them. Dora was aware that Elisabeth, progressively immersed in the Catholicism to which she had converted at some point in her forties, attended retreats in the school holidays; and there, Dora suspected, in those centres of self-denial, she indulged in intrigues of the mind and even of the flesh: contained liaisons that were disposable.

Elisabeth would never leave her husband. The workings of that relationship were an absolute mystery that Dora had long puzzled over, but the marriage was clearly more necessary to Elisabeth than anything else in her life. Dora had no doubt that Elisabeth's love for James was, despite routine infidelity and an assumption of independence, unquestioning. As her anchor and refuge, he had done what no one else had achieved: won the commitment of a woman who seemed to spend her time both inspiring and avoiding intimacy. Dora knew it couldn't be easy. She knew that James must, at some level, have detached himself from her in order to avoid the torment she would otherwise impose. In letting her fly, he secured her, but what of his own happiness in the marriage? Dora couldn't begin to know. Perhaps, she thought, he expected and required little.

'You're really not looking well,' said Elisabeth now, with almost clinical detachment. And Dora knew that she was not, her English-coloured hair thinned by age and hormone levels, her skin so dry after the bullying of cancer, her breast and armpit burnt.

'Yes. It's – I'm – not right,' said Dora, who so very rarely complained, catching her breath awkwardly. 'They're not quite sure about one of my lymph nodes. I'm tired. I'm meant to be feeling better by now, and I don't.'

Elisabeth nodded.

'It's just a matter of time, I suppose,' said Dora, minutely brighter.

'And at least your daughter's here,' said Elisabeth carefully. She rarely referred to Cecilia by name, Dora noticed.

'Yes, yes, I'm so *glad*,' said Dora, and smiled. 'And these –' She nodded at the next room. 'I used to see them perhaps twice a year, in recent years, in London. Now look. What a treasure. It's a gift.'

'Three girls. I can't imagine,' said Elisabeth. 'They're striking. Does she – their mother – look after you well?'

'Oh yes, yes, absolutely. But she's under such pressure ... she's often writing after they're in bed.'

'She was always committed. I hope she provides you with some company.'

'My relationship –' started Dora. She felt her mouth stiffen, almost physically sensed the lines around it deepen in an unpleasant mani-festation of age and grief '– will never be the same with her. Really, our falling out amounted – it amounted to an estrangement. You know that. I can't rely on her totally. I don't want to.'

'I do know,' said Elisabeth. The sounds of girls squabbling mildly, debating the identity of some animal seen through the window, grew louder next door. She glanced in that direction. 'What's this?' she said, delicately inserting her nail beneath a small section of peel-ing white paint beside the light switch. 'There seems to be some aubergine glaring beneath.'

Dora laughed, gulping a little, still constrained by unwanted emotion.

'I'd forgotten. The kitchen used to be dark. Dark and gleaming with condensation.'

'Gruesome.'

Dora gazed at the paint. She peeled a further flake away. 'I'll get Izzie to Tipp-Ex it,' she said. She paused. 'Does Tipp-Ex still exist?'

'Who did that?'

'Remember those lodgers?' said Dora. She glanced at the ceiling. 'Much as you tried to avoid them all. Hippies. True hippies who lived in this cottage when the children were growing up. On barely any rent. They were meant to fix the tumbledown parts instead. Moll and Flite. You remember them. They used to wander around naked on the lawn. But they were kindly souls.'

'They somewhat blur into one. I certainly remember that frightful fire thrower.'

'Oh, Stefania. I know who you mean.'

'What happened to them all?'

'They all left. They were all rootless, all those people who lived in the outbuildings here. I never stop thinking about them. About the past, really.' She pressed her fingernails into the wax wrapper of a Baby Bel discarded by Ruth, her nail tips meeting and bending.

'Oh Dora darling, you're so emotional. You think about everything too much.'

Dora paused. She felt flat, picturing a subsiding balloon, a drying mushroom. Her chest was like that: the lumpectomy had left a partially empty breast. I am dying, she thought. Am I?

'Do I?' she said with a catch in her voice.

'I think so.'

'Perhaps you think – not enough?'

Elisabeth coloured, unusually, the pink quickly contracting to two points on her cheeks that seemed to indicate displeasure.

'Perhaps,' she said. 'But you should be kinder to yourself, Dora. And I have to go.'

The aubergine paint now scabbed the wall, and again Dora thought of mildew, of a past that revealed itself even now, painted over but pushing through like malignant cells.

Twenty

March

CECILIA SAT in her room writing for a snatched half hour in the evening, but she put her work down. *It took me a long time, but I came back,* she wrote in Mara's book. *I look for you everywhere.*

In that book was the history of it all: letters from the private detective she had used, a copy of her enquiries to the social services, to the Salvation Army, charities, intermediary services; entries scrawled after fights with Dora: all evidence of her long search. There was the letter she had written to Mara on her eighteenth birthday but had been unable to send. There were newspaper cuttings on the overhaul of the adoption laws in 2005. There were postcards and objects and tokens instead of the photographs the others had had taken on their birthdays and glued into their books. For the adopted Izzie, Cecilia had included early photos given to her by her birth mother's father, who had died when Izzie was five. Mara's imagined existence was charted in sketches like a smaller echo of her other daughters' known lives.

She dreamed and pictured her first daughter's body quite beaten by battling through the uplands of the moor, where there was barely air: just liquid and cloud and ponies' breath, branches and birds flying through cataracts of rain. She held her soaking figure in her arms.

'Oh God,' she said, stopping herself. She turned instead back to Mara's book.

When you were born, she wrote, *facts could be obscured. A lot could be hidden in those days. Histories, records, people, could disappear, just as footways could vanish beneath the bracken; just as sheep were rustled, ponies stolen, farmers' children missed for days and barely questioned. The country had its own laws. There were no CCTV cameras, little centralised information, rudimentary computer systems, no internet. It was not so long ago, yet it was different.*

'You've been much more moony lately. Melancholy,' said Ari with the abruptness of a practised statement when Cecilia returned to the kitchen. He had arrived home from a meeting at Exeter University to spend the night before returning to London.

'You took up with a raving neurot,' said Cecilia matter of factly.

The son of an Israeli father and an English-Spanish mother, Ari was thin; narrowly, almost wirily built, and dark: there was an element of Gabriel Sardo to his appearance, Cecilia had thought when she met him, though his face was bonier. He wore glasses with dark rectangular frames that echoed his dark hair. With such closely cut hair hugging an elegantly shaped skull, grey-olive shades of skin, and emphatically brown irises, he could never appear English, a fact that appealed to Cecilia in a land of watery hues. She wondered whether she had first been attracted to him by his very contrast with James Dahl. He was more intense, more bristlingly energetic. Despite his wit and his sporadic grumpiness, his moods were consistent compared with hers, his level-headedness steadying her. The traces of pensiveness that she detected in him tended to be channelled into capability.

'You knew what you were getting,' said Cecilia. 'I was a basket case when you found me. The woman who thinks too much.'

'Yes I know,' said Ari. 'But still. What's going on? You've been in a strop. More moody.'

She hesitated. 'Have I?' she said.

'Much. You're distracted. Preoccupied.'

'You sound accusatory, you horrible man,' she said, her mouth moving into a smile.

He was silent. His jaw tightened in the manner that always made her body stiffen.

'Well,' she said then, heatedly. 'I can hardly be the life and soul of the party, can I? With three children to look after on my own and an ill mother to worry about? I –'

'Understood, understood,' said Ari.

'Don't do that thing of holding your palms up.'

'It's peacekeeping.'

'It's passive-aggressive. As though I'm going to hit you.'

'Well you look like you might. Cecilia.'

'I am not a husband batterer!'

'And I'm not your husband.'

'Woah!' said Cecilia. She took a deep breath. 'I can't believe you say it like that.'

'Well I'm not.'

'Is it so important?'

'To me. Yes.'

'To Mummy, you mean.' She winced at herself.

'That's not fair.'

'What are we arguing about? Are we arguing about something else?' said Cecilia, her voice rising, but, catching his repressed agitation, she stopped herself. After so many years she could read emotions that he seemed barely aware of himself.

'It's amazing, isn't it?' she said more gently. 'How we go straight back into exactly the same patterns. The same old arguments. They're often about *nothing*, essentially. Tone of voice. Or some – some imagined injustice.'

'I think you're disturbed by being here,' he said. His mouth was a line shadowed by stubble.

'Your voice is cold,' she said.

'Not cold. Concerned.'

'Well don't sound so stern then. You sound – heartless.'

'For God's sake, Cecilia! I did warn you. I warned you very strongly about coming here.'

'Well what was I supposed to do? Dora's ill. This might kill her, Ari.' She began to tremble. 'We don't know for sure yet if it's spread. Do you know how much this hangs over me? How much it must haunt her all the time?' Her shoulders dropped. He reached out and held her arms, and she shook him off.

'If it has . . . it spreads more slowly at her age.'

'I know. My darly. I know that. But it's a cloud over the house. Who can relax with this?'

'OK,' said Ari gently.

'I worry about the girls, then – genetically.'

'So do I. And you.'

'I know. I know.'

'You –'

'And you got the job you'd always wanted to go for. You got it! Relatively easily. It would have been mad to stay in London. What? You think that would have been a logical, sensible move –?'

'We could have. I begin to wonder about why –'

'And what is my poor mother to do?' Cecilia swallowed, determined not to betray panic about Dora. 'She needs someone, and none of my fuckwit brothers is going to do that.'

'You can barely bear to speak to her some of the time. Then you're rushing round for her.'

'Well I try. At least. I *try*. What can I do? I loved her so much, Ari. I really adored her. She was good to me when I was younger – I don't want to live with regret –'

'I know.'

'And part of me – it sounds silly – part of me wants to look after her for my father, because he loved her. Even though they had a distant, almost sad kind of marriage by the end, he loved her, and I think he'd want me to look after her, and I miss him, and – and – she needs someone to look after her.'

'I think you wanted to come down here.'

'I seem to remember that *you* did,' said Cecilia, warding away the truth that she could not quite repress: that she had come back to take from Dora what she knew, to immerse herself in where it had all happened, because she couldn't keep away any longer. She needed to pick at it, she thought. It was like stabbing herself to feel alive. She sensed, again, time running out.

'Of course I wanted to,' he said. 'But I warned you not to – become fixated by being here.'

'I'm not fixated. I'm – Why can't we even mention her name?'

'You don't know her name, Cecilia.'

'Leave me alone,' she said.

He stood and he gazed at her impassively. She stared back.

They had talked about the facts of her pregnancy and the adoption almost a year after meeting, when she had begun to realise that she would stay with him. He had accepted her reticence about the most sacred of subjects, but he had been less forgiving of her reluctance to talk about the father: an old boyfriend who had left her, she said, short-lived. He had mentioned this man – 'the *boy*' as he referred to him dismissively, in vicious prods intermittently, mid-row, over the years, trying to rile her, at times trying to trick her – but he was not given to extensive probing. It was one of the codes of their relationship, that combustible near-silence and their collusion in protecting their daughters from unnecessary grief. But, she had realised over time, he agreed to it, not even primarily out of consideration for her, but because this baby – or more accurately her continued disguised mourning for it – was a subject that never failed to inspire his discomposure.

She stared at him.

'Just because,' she said, breathing carefully, 'just because your mother was critical of you – and you know I'm sorry about that; you're the last person who deserves it – doesn't mean you have to fly off the handle every time Mar – she's – she's mentioned. It hits a nerve in you.'

'Well perhaps it does,' said Ari, running his hand over his scalp with an impatient gesture. He shrugged dramatically. 'Let's not have a therapy session now.'

'You've never really understood this.'

'Probably not,' said Ari steadily. 'It's likely to be impossible to understand it. It's a long time ago. I'm now just asking you to be sensible.'

'For God's sake, you're speaking to me as though you're my *father*.'

'You have anger-management issues.' His gaze softened. 'You need a firm hand.'

'On what blundering team-building course did you learn that?'

His mouth twitched. 'You need a firm hand,' he repeated, showing her his palm.

'Oh, you're such a pervert!' she said, and began to laugh, her shoulders bowing weakly. He moved towards her.

'It's like dealing with Medusa,' he said, putting his arms around her.

By eleven o'clock, Izzie's music still vibrated from her room, hanging on the breath of the river, and it brought back a memory to Cecilia of the old Wind Tor, with lodgers' shadows edging through the garden at night, and bass thudding into the small hours, and with it came the unwanted presence of James Dahl. Ruth and Romy were asleep; Ari packed up his papers, frowning. Cecilia could see small, appealing signs of ageing in him.

'You look . . . distinguished,' she said lightly.

He glanced up, blinking away tiredness. 'You mean I look extremely old,' he said, rubbing his forehead with his arm. His hair, beginning to recede, was a blackish stubble grazed with grey; his eyes were almost blank with darkness.

'I like you like this. Are you going to bed?'

'Yes. The alarm's got to be set for five.'

'God almighty. Go to bed. I'll follow.'

She went to check the house. She felt for the hall light switch and couldn't find it and moved slowly through darkness. The hall chattered and settled, its concentration of woodsmoke and beeswax streaked with night air. On the windowsill she could see pellets of dead wasp granular in moonlight among the drift of plaster crumb. It was the hall that most bothered her and had clawed at her memory. It was where she had laid her head against the wall to think about the fact that she was pregnant. There it was: a stone wall, and here was her own flesh, too solid or too sullied as it was, and once in this very spot there had been human cells multiplying to form a body inside her. Over twenty years before, she had had the choice. Her own body had enclosed the tiny beginning of that human; no one could have taken it away. She lingered for a moment, slipping back to that time, revelling in that moment of free will before her life had darkened.

But she had made the wrong choice, and she had given her baby away.

It was too late. As simple as that: too late. However much her mind might spin into the past and effect muddy rearrangements, the fact of it being *much much much too late* was what hit her like a crack of wood across the cheekbones.

It was too late, yet the baby was still here. That was what she hadn't accounted for. Her memory was here. A vestige or echo of her physical presence was here: a urine stain, a rush of heartbeats, a snuffled search for milk.

She walked back upstairs. The sound of a window swinging slowly in a movement of air made her stop. It was almost perfectly dark. She crept towards her bedroom. She saw the pool of Ari's imminent sleep, his easing breaths and clutched duvet, and she couldn't enter it, couldn't let herself be immersed in the intimacy of that shared life.

She sat apart, gazing out into the darkness, and remembered the summer of being pregnant with Mara and walking at night, emerging only as the light fell to wander up beyond Dockden and Dockmell to where a horse path led to a stone-strewn stretch of bog with no tors to break the horizons. She had never walked alone at night before, but she was not afraid, not afraid of the smudge of sheep bulk and breath, their lanolin dampness on the stillness; not afraid of the owls and foxes who seemed alone like she was. The summer nights were often high with stars. She needed the water in her shoes and the hours eaten into the dawn to prevent sleeplessness from getting her first.

The labour had begun before sunrise, when the light would have been a dull transparency on the Wind Tor fields and the sky full of tugging movement. After so much suffering and secrecy, the baby emerged sprawling in a bloody rush, Cecilia's body not split after all but beaten after five hours of labour, and she stared at her once; she saw her, her child, a lock of eyes, the haunting later composed of that one memory. She remembered the eyes, or just the dark sockets of her eyes. They had looked at each other.

Cecilia always claimed there had been no last moment when she was told to say goodbye to the baby. Of course there was, stated Dora. There was not. Others bathed and calmed her child and placed her briefly on Cecilia's bed for cradling, but Cecilia had no memory of knowing it to be the last time, though she had already signed the papers that haunted her from that moment. The girl was ripped away from her: she wasn't informed that it would happen so quickly. It was better that she didn't bond, she was told. She was a cat spayed. She was an injured elephant immobile and lowing, its grief – and soon its love; within days *love* – spilling out through its wound. The adopters were waiting, and very happy with her baby.

Twenty-one

March

RUTH COULD make herself disappear with silence and will-power, and her teacher never appeared to know her name. She left school at lunchtimes to sit where she was hidden by towering dock leaves as birds like eagles flew above, and no one noticed her absence. She saw the moor man wandering the lanes; he nodded at her, and sometimes he had the baby rabbit in his pocket, and he kept it in straw for her and told her how to feed it. Now she had shown him to Izzie, and Izzie knew where to find him in a caravan.

A note arrived from James Dahl addressed to Cecilia, asking to talk to her. It was on thick white headed card, the writing on the envelope so instantly familiar, it sent her tumbling back with a shock. He had email, jcdahl@btinternet.com, she noted, the idea of him embracing the century somehow faintly embarrassing. She put it aside, not wishing to see him until she was required to at a school event. She glimpsed it on her desk later and hid it, knowing that she would be unable to explain it to Ari.

She heard a knock on the back door, and went down to open it, but Izzie burst into the kitchen before her, muttering excuses, and snatched at the handle. Romy followed her.

A man stood in the doorway and leaned over Izzie. He was sinewy and unkempt, the brownness of his multi-angled hair and stubble rendering his eyes lighter in contrast. He wore a stained fleece and emanated a dull tang of unwashed body. Cecilia felt a moment of uneasiness as he held her gaze with pale appraising eyes. His smell alone ignited memories from the old days when there was always a travelling stranger in the kitchen, someone who had slept on a lodger's floor, or one of her brother's friends. She recognised him from the Friday market, she realised.

Izzie looked like a child drained of colour, but she glowed through the pallor.

Cecilia and the man said nothing. She tilted her head slightly. He was manifestly older than her fifteen-year-old daughter. Dear God, she thought. Protect her.

She turned unsmilingly to the man, ignored all Izzie's hints about inviting him in, said goodbye to him, and shut the door.

'You can't keep having him here. She'll find out,' said Romy, sitting in her bedroom in the evening, her chin resting on her knees. A candle burned, curving into the alcoves and drop-angled beams of the room.

'I don't keep having him. He doesn't come that much. He wants to be outside. Like basically live outside.'

'I just don't understand how Ruth met him,' said Romy.

Izzie shrugged. 'She said she sees him, you know, wandering around. She's been missing school. At lunchtimes and stuff? You'd have thought she'd be too scared. Anyway, I think she thinks Dan's a bit creepy, so she took me to meet him when he brought this lush little rabbit to the field.'

'Which field?'

'One near her school. He's really fit, but Ruth just thinks she's found Stig of the Dump kind of thing. He does live in a dump.'

Going by his descriptions, Izzie had stumbled over muddy tracts to where the moor seemed remote and cold-aired and animal-filled beyond anything she'd ever seen or understood existed, and a streak of uncustomary fear had threaded her breathing. Sudden mulchy gulfs of bog lay among the bracken, and the wind had chilled her ears, coming at her unexpectedly in what seemed like mobile cubes of air, as though boxes of pressure buffeted her from behind hills. She was about to abandon her search when she saw smoke on the air. It flattened and then disappeared. She walked faster towards it and saw a small copse, its alley of stunted trees bent behind a neglected dry-stone wall. A stream seemed to bubble in glassy bulges nearby, then snake among the gorse again, ravens picking around it. Beyond the copse and stream were miles of open moorland.

She had watched him. He kicked the fire on which he was cook-ing. He settled himself. He scratched his head. Eventually, he stood up and she watched as he pissed in a large windstrewn arc. She puffed on her inhaler, then left it on a rock.

'I saw him pissing in the wind up there when I skived off school?' she said, so that Romy had to nod as she was always compelled to do through Izzie's upwardly inflected speech. 'Like, I kept thinking of his dick! He had all this hair there. Hardcore.'

Romy laughed, and looked disconcerted. She pulled her duvet further up her chest and shuffled in it. An owl hooted.

'Shhh, sis!' Izzie hissed, her eyes widened in amused drama as the sound of their mother's footsteps made the floorboards whine, a creaking always travelling the length of the house through varying levels. 'She'll hear us.'

Romy nodded.

'Where is he now?'

'I don't know, sis. Sometimes I see him at the market. I looked all last week. He lives in this caravan in a garden centre near Widecombe where he works a bit! His caravan's called Turd Towers. I miss him a load. He just comes here when he wants. When I don't expect it.' She giggled. 'I want to . . . him,' she said calmly. She lay back.

'You can't,' said Romy stiffly.

'Ha! Virgin. Virginia, I'm going to call you. In front of Mum.'

'Oh God,' said Romy.

'Virginia. Virgin Virginia Vagina of St Anne's Convent with all the other scabby nuns and lesbians. Do you think Ruth's going to turn out to be a bit of a lezzer?'

'Leave Ruth alone.'

'She's getting weirder than ever, poor lame kid,' said Izzie, rolling up a new cigarette. 'She's gone really like deranged here. Emo. I think she's getting knockers. Hurry up or she'll out-virgin you. Out-un-virgin you. She'll get there before you and smother some farm boy on the bus while you dry up.'

'Shut up. Poor Ruth. Why is she so, such –'

'Such a weirdo? She's just shy. She always has been, hasn't she? She can't open her mouth.'

'And she wants to be with Mum all the time. But she's eight.'

'She loves Ma sooooo much. But old Ma can't be with her like *all* the time, stroking her head and reading all their sappy treehouse skating books together. Have you seen how much Ruth batters at Ma if she's in one of her moony dopey moods, all blank and not listening?'

'She needs some friends.'

'But she only loves Ma.'

'And you.'

'Yeah, and me. Ruth's a mute.'

'Oh Izzie . . .' said Romy. 'Shut up now. And if Mummy sees your Facebook photos she'll ban them.'

'Mummy? You've gone well posh. Anyway. She can't be bothered to go spying on me when she's clattering on her laptop. It's usually *Dad* who's the strict bastard? She was always the gimpy one. But I can't say a thing without her being really harsh at the moment.'

'She's got too much work to do,' said Romy. 'She's got to do this book.'

'Cocking book,' said Izzie, dragging on her cigarette. 'She needs to give me a break.'

'She always gives *you* slack,' said Romy, a tightness entering her voice.

'Yeah yeah, I'm the favourite,' said Izzie airily, dragging on her cigarette and hiding her expression beneath a cloud of smoke. 'It's just like because I'm a bastard. Bit of a darkie. She's a soft touch.'

Romy giggled. She heard another owl and shuddered.

'You really hate it here, don't you, sis?' said Izzie as though the idea had only just occurred to her.

'I hate it,' said Romy. 'I – I *despise* it.'

'I think it's wicked,' said Izzie. She got up and looked out of the window. 'Did you hear a noise?'

'No,' said Romy.

'I'm just wondering if he's going to come and see me.'

'Why would he? You're fifteen.'

'Exactly,' said Izzie. She twisted her hip in a provocative pose as she stood. 'I'm going to go and find him on Thursday. Double maths? Make him shag me. Think I might want a kid soon too.'

'I have to do some prep,' said Romy, ignoring her.

'You're a sap, sis,' said Izzie, gathering up her tobacco and Rizlas.

Cecilia worked on her book while Ruth read, then she went down to help her find her daisy-patterned pyjamas, which were hanging in the darkness of the boiler room. Once a dairy with its stone sinks, it was too swollen with shadow for children to want to visit alone. Cecilia held Ruth's hot clutching hand to lead her through the house, past piles of unsorted washed clothes on the stairs, a mess ever growing as she worked more urgently on her book, then she stroked Ruth's arm in bed, tickling and scratching it as she liked, and telling her of the pleasant aspects of the moor, the curlews, whortleberries and wild strawberries in the lanes, the cushions of emerald-coloured moss that she would find, to counteract Ruth's darker fears of bats and gales and malign spirits. She pulled her to her, feeling her flopping zigzags of mouse-coloured hair and stroking her forehead. She kissed her goodnight then went to Romy's room.

'I have to go to see Dora,' she murmured.

'Why?' said Romy distantly.

'She's received a letter from the hospital. I'd better be with her. Will you listen out for Ruth for me?'

Romy nodded, averting her face, and Cecilia held her shoulder, her head bowed. She caught sight of herself in Romy's mirror as she left. She saw, even in the evening light, that the shadows under her eyes had deepened into a kind of sooty spilling of tiredness on the fairness of her skin.

She made her way with a torch up through the back vegetable garden whose long grass was still damp at its roots, and remembered walking in that air-bent garden as a child, holding her father's hand as she stumbled uphill. She sent a little message to him. She let herself through the gate that led to Wind Tor Cottage, where Dora's head bobbed past the window at the sound of the latch.

'Darling!' she said at the door.

Cecilia smiled.

'Hello,' she said. 'Shall we open the letter?' She held Dora's arm.

'No!' said Dora with a lift in her voice. 'I just did it. Before – before you came. The fact that you might come made me dare to do it. That lymph node is clear, darling! They think I'm clear for the moment as long as I have the radiotherapy. No chemotherapy.'

'Oh! Fantastic!' said Cecilia, and hugged Dora and hugged her again. 'That is brilliant – wonderful news. Really wonderful. Oh thank goodness.'

'Isn't it?' said Dora. She lifted down a bottle of wine.

'I shouldn't –' began Cecilia.

'I've been saving it.'

'You have some.'

'Join me,' said Dora.

'OK,' said Cecilia. 'Thank you,' she added flatly, perceiving again the quiet power Dora exerted, a force that she had barely understood in youth.

'Oh good!' said Dora.

'Are you getting enough help?' said Cecilia. 'You know I could do more.'

'Darling, you couldn't. You couldn't possibly with three girls and a book to write. And that house . . . I remember – I remember how much work it took.'

'Until my deadline's over, I'm letting it do its own thing: drift, crumble. Collapse,' said Cecilia. She shrugged and smiled. 'I can't begin ... I don't think I could ever be like you were. You kept it so warm and lovely.'

'*Thank you*,' said Dora.

'You did. Does that girl help you enough?'

'Oh yes. She's really very good. Strong. How are the girls? Are they all in bed now? Are they tired?'

'They,' said Cecilia, 'they're fine.'

'I'm so glad,' said Dora. 'I think about them all at their schools and I wonder how they're doing, who their friends are, what they're up to in the day. They're all so different. I don't think I ever stop thinking about them!'

'Nor do I,' said Cecilia. 'All of them,' she said. She couldn't look at Dora.

'They're really wonderful!' continued Dora, her eyes shining, pausing as if to enumerate each girl's particular qualities in her head. She topped up Cecilia's nearly full glass, filling silence with activity.

'Thank you,' said Cecilia flatly again.

She took a gulp of wine. She half caught Dora's eye. Repressed emotion glinted from her. Something had set it off. Yet Dora skated over the danger patches, blithely ignoring them, debatably oblivious.

'All of them,' said Cecilia again, unsteadily. She waited. The words sat in the silence. The fire spat. She instinctively wanted to smooth it over, but she forced herself not to. It was all too easy to regress, to become irritated and sulky yet self-sacrificing in Dora's presence, using abnegation as a passive weapon in the face of Dora's intractability.

Dora pressed her lips together. She breathed out slowly. A possible glitter of moisture appeared and passed in her eyes. The muscles supporting her frequent smiles sagged and aged her instantly.

Grief passed over Cecilia's face.

'After – after, Celie – after fifteen or so years of such intermittent contact, I can't talk about it,' said Dora. 'I simply can't,' she said in more emphatic tones. She smiled. The very structure of her face was lifted again. She held her wine to the light, and she maintained the smile with determined focus. The glaze of denial in her eyes made her look almost mad, Cecilia thought.

'I never stop thinking about her, you know,' she said steadily. 'I am going to keep on asking you about her.'

'Who?'

'Who? *Her,*' said Cecilia, then softened her voice.

'Oh for goodness' sake, Cecilia.'

'I loved her.'

'You didn't know her. You really did not know that baby. It was just a few minutes.'

'A few minutes,' said Cecilia, her voice strained. 'Not even that. Seconds, perhaps. Even *cats* keep their litters for longer than that.'

'You agreed,' said Dora, as she had never said before in such direct terms, her lips tightly pressed together.

Cecilia shuddered. She fought against her own fear of her mother.

'Did I have much choice? Did I have the choice? I was seventeen. Eighteen.' Her voice weakened. 'I'd just given birth. I wasn't even booked at the hospital! No healthcare team – just a so-called "independent" midwife. I – I never even thought about all that until afterwards. *You* wanted me to give her up. You – you organised that, right – right from the beginning.'

'And you agreed,' said Dora, sitting down. Her chest rose and fell beneath her corduroy.

'I agreed. I agreed. And I will never forgive myself,' said Cecilia, as though talking to herself. She ran her fingers across her forehead, up through her scalp. Her skin was flushed. 'It was all arranged for me. I did agree. I agreed. I hate myself to this day that I did. But – You never gave me time to change my mind.'

'Well –'

'None of you, none of you did. You – you,' said Cecilia, catching her breath raggedly. 'You didn't give me any choice. I want to know why. Why, why? You were such a *mother*. Why didn't you want to keep her? Want me to keep her?'

'There is no why. It's so long ago, Celie,' said Dora more gently.

'I know, I know, that's what I can't bear!' said Cecilia, the clock, a hook, a pewter container appearing to enlarge to fill her vision. 'It's too late! It's over! She's twenty-three now – her childhood's over. And who knows what it was like? That's what I can't *bear*. I just cannot bear.' She drew in her breath. 'What was that like? I'll never know, I'll never know if her childhood was all right. I just want to find out.'

'It would have been –' Dora twisted her fingers. 'You know, you did agree at that time.'

'Would have been what?'

'Nothing,' said Dora, shaking her head, closing her lips.

'*What?*' said Cecilia urgently, taking Dora's arm, spilling wine as she moved. She stared at the drops on the waxed surface of the table. 'It would have been what? Why won't you tell me?' She said more calmly.

'Celie,' said Dora.

'Tell me who took her,' said Cecilia. 'Who adopted her?' Her mouth was an oblong of pain.

'How can I tell you that? How can I?'

'You can. You've got to. I know you know! I know. It's too late now. I'm not going to do anything.'

'Then why do you want to know?'

'I want to know if her childhood was – passable. Jesus.' She put her head in her hands. 'At least all right.'

'I'm sure it was.'

'How do you *know*?'

'They wanted a baby very much.'

Cecilia flinched. 'Oh God,' she said. 'Oh God.'

'They couldn't get pregnant. It wasn't happening. The – contact I used told me. And there were you pregnant. Not wanting to be –'

'I know. I know. I was –'

'What's done is done,' said Dora, as she had said so infuriatingly frequently before.

'That's right. Sweep it under the fucking carpet. Pretend it doesn't exist. Pretend everything's nicey-nice, oh lovely, lovely, candles and wine. Schubert on the radio. Three lovely girls. *Pretend*,' shouted Cecilia, shocked by the sound of her own voice, by how she was challenging Dora, the only person who could silence her.

'Cecilia,' said Dora.

'Well tell me *who*,' said Cecilia.

'Adoption is anonymous.'

'It fucking well wasn't, though, was it?'

'It was as good as,' said Dora.

Cecilia clamped her hands on Dora's shoulders. They were startlingly thin. She let them go, shocked.

'I lose my temper,' she said, ashamed. 'I can never be as calm as you were. I'm sorry.'

Dora nodded.

'I tried *every* channel,' said Cecilia. 'All the agencies, social services departments, records, everything I could find, and my name never came up. No child. No indexing number. I wasn't even a registered pregnancy. You know that.'

Dora gazed ahead.

'This was an "unofficial adoption",' said Cecilia slowly as though spelling it out. 'It was by no means an adoption in the legal sense. You can't even really call it that. Even though we refer to it as an adoption, there was no *legal* change of family. "Illegal fostering" at best. For God's sake –'

Dora looked at her. Her lips parted.

'I don't know why you're so interested in that,' she said eventually, swallowing and emitting a strangled little compression of air for which she covered her mouth with her hand in apology.

'I'm "interested",' said Cecilia, 'because that means you arranged that so-called adoption without proper paperwork, let alone authority – without an interim period for me to change my mind; without, without all the counselling, fostering, the access, all the normal – the normal procedures. Dora. Dorothy. Social workers. You know, all that other birth mothers are granted because they *might see sense and change their minds*.'

Dora shuddered. She opened her mouth. She closed it again.

'It wasn't so odd in those days,' she said in a voice weak with defensiveness. 'Things were different. Less formal. It wasn't all signed and sealed; there wasn't all the bureaucracy of nowadays, you know.'

'You talk as though it was after the war, with babies being given to barren sisters, to neighbours,' said Cecilia, her voice rising.' "Eee, we've got too many mouths to feed. Here. Have one, why don't you?" '

Dora shook her head. Her eyes seemed glazed.

'When I was young, even in Kent, it happened a lot more, you know. A friend's sister – younger sister – the mother had to go and work and she was left behind with relatives and just never taken home. It was about who could and who couldn't.'

'I don't care –'

'Many babies fell outside the system, you know.'

'It was the Eighties by the time you –'

'It was not so very odd. It seemed a suitable alternative to an agency.'

'I couldn't even put my details on a register to show I wanted to contact her! What do you think I felt when that became legal? No indexing number system attached to the adoption. And all those years, no official way of her finding me – either.'

'You wouldn't have been able to adopt Izzie if it had been official,' said Dora, and again the steel entered her voice.

'I –' said Cecilia.

'Do you think they'd have let you adopt if you were already on record as having given up a child?' said Dora. 'Not a chance in hell,' she added.

Cecilia flinched.

'You know. You know very well. That's *why* I couldn't pursue it,' she said desperately. 'You know that –'

Cecilia recalled a sliver of the past with clarity. Oxford would not defer her place. Her A level grades having fallen well below her teachers' predictions, she had no wish to take the entrance exam again, and had applied to Edinburgh University for the following October, simultaneously ashamed and indifferent, wishing only to live as far from home as possible. In her last year there, she had stood in a phone box, the whirr, clunk, swallow of the coins, the plastic against her cheekbone as she phoned the local authorities in Devon and asked for her baby, after having written a letter to social services with her enquiry. She was three months pregnant with Romy.

'We have no record of a baby of that name,' came the voice. 'Can you repeat the mother's – your own name?'

Questions and delays followed, the ten pences, fifty pences hesitating with that rollercoaster pause before they lurched into darkness and silences were filled with the beating of her own pulse. She blew breath on the glass; hills stretched above her; students meandered past. She had known bleakness, dullness, what she had later realised was depression, in those first years after the affair and pregnancy. Her haunting by Mara began there. She saw her baby in Edinburgh, in little limbs suddenly visible in the clatter of New Town tea shops, or clinging to her as she walked the Pentland Hills, trying, trying so hard to forget the recent past. Her missing baby was in the university corridors as a piercing of guilt behind swing doors, blooming with no warning in a room and making her head grainy with panic. She was a face projected on a cloud of almost-happiness in a pub with students. She was there in other people's buggies. She sat, fleetingly, lightly, on Cecilia's lap in seminars.

'Are you sure of the birth date?' came the official voice.

'Yes.'

'You couldn't have got it a day or so out? That sometimes happens.'

'No.'

'Then we appear to have no birth certificate.'

Cecilia was silent.

'Nothing?' she said.

'No record of adoption or registration of a baby to that mother on that day,' came the voice, and Cecilia could by then hear suspicion begin to stir. She could imagine slammed filing cabinets, alarm bells, letters winging their way to her and various authorities, and yet all the while the conversation was not entirely surprising to her: something had nagged at her, some knowledge that it was not quite right, that there had been no midwives from the hospital, just the apparent 'community midwife' who was one of the lodgers and who only appeared for the birth; no efficient women from the local services, just Dora wielding a piece of paper while she lay in physical pain and confusion. She had barely noticed at the time. She hadn't wanted to notice. She had only one thought as she lay there: she was abandoned by the one she loved, and so her life was useless.

'You got Izzie,' said Dora now, steadily.

'I "got" Izzie? As compensation? My replacement for my child?'

Dora shrugged. 'If you want to see it that way.'

'I needed to have Izzie *because* of – of the other. I'm so glad, so very very glad about Izzie,' said Cecilia, her voice faltering. 'But surely you can see I had to make up – some pathetic attempt to make up for the dreadful thing I'd done.'

'I know.'

'And there was this little girl – there, in the council's care, as soon as we registered,' said Cecilia, smiling despite her pain through her blurred vision. 'I heard about her. That scrawny crying baby. How can you even –'

'I know.'

'It was Izzie! Imagine life without her! I always thought – if I can care for her, perhaps I can make up. Perhaps, then, M – the baby – was being cared for in the same way as I cared for Izzie. It would all work out, mothers sharing the care, spread across the world, linked but unknown. It sounds mad, but I thought it.'

Dora nodded.

'Do you see?' she said, hearing again that she sounded almost unbalanced. 'And the more interviews with the social services we had, the more I wanted *her*, this Izabel, and it seemed so miraculous when there was no enquiry, no discovery of the other one. But we know why, don't we?'

Dora exhaled loudly.

'Your eyes are glinting,' said Cecilia slowly.

'Well really,' said Dora. 'I feel quite beaten, Celie.'

'Well you –' said Cecilia. Her hair had become tangled with her nervous tugging. 'If it were known that you – you of all people –' she laughed incredulously '– organised an "informal" adoption, there'd have been a police inquiry, and you'd have been arrested, wouldn't you? To spell it all out.'

'I –'

'Without a doubt. And, you – It's the fact you got me to *sign* a piece of paper you had dreamed up that always kills me. I think it was just a typed piece of A4, not a printed form, wasn't it? I've tried to remember it so often. Fool that I was.' She took a deep breath. 'You know, it was only when I started the process of adopting Izzie – all those interviews and assessments, hundreds of forms and statements and so on – that I realised that mine had been nothing like a *normal* adoption. It took years for Izzie to be legally ours.'

'If it had been formal, you wouldn't have been allowed to adopt Izzie,' repeated Dora.

Cecilia paused. 'It's interesting how you never mention this "contact" you always claimed you used,' she said. 'This contact you used to give my baby away. It's strange there's no trace of her, isn't it?'

'She died.'

'But no one seems to have known anything about her. How long do you think I spent trawling through Ashburton for someone whose name you couldn't quite remember, just to find that there had been a children's home there years ago, all closed down, that woman seemingly non-existent, rumour after rumour, leads confirmed and contradicted with equal certainty? And yet nothing. After all that, always, nothing.'

'I know, I know,' said Dora. She breathed heavily. She shook her head.

'I wonder if she existed.'

Dora was silent. 'I –' she said, and then clamped her mouth closed and said nothing more.

'How –' said Cecilia, steadying her breathing, her voice emerging weakly, 'how am I supposed to relate to you? To *love* you? I want to look after you. I do want to – ease all this. Despite everything, I do.'

Dora's shoulders sank. She shook her head again. Her throat tightened with a spray of wrinkles as she swallowed. 'I know,' she said eventually.

'Tell me,' said Cecilia, again shocked at her own outburst towards Dora.

'Gabriel,' said Dora, clumsily trying a new track. 'Gabriel never stood by you, looked –'

'Gabriel? Oh. God, you can leave him out of this.'

'Well –'

'Just tell me,' said Cecilia. 'Just tell me. Do you think she had a nice childhood? A reasonable one?' She glanced away. She pressed her nails into her palm.

'I don't know,' said Dora, swallowing again, her eyes shining with moisture. 'I think so. Every chance was there.'

'And you're not going to tell me any more than that?'

'I don't know any more than that,' said Dora. She looked up at Cecilia, and her chin moved forward, the jutting chin of determination that made Cecilia queasy, and her eyes took on a skin of confusion until she appeared, thought Cecilia, quite stupid.

Cecilia slammed her glass down on the table. She stood up.

Dora looked at the table. She raised her chin again as Cecilia reached the door.

'I don't believe you,' said Cecilia.

Twenty-two
March

THE STARS, more stars than Cecilia had seen for so many years, were soaking, spraying the thatches of the hamlet as she ran back from Dora's cottage. The raw air caught her breath. She is somewhere in this world, she thought into the darkness stretching over the tors and the spaces beyond.

A guitar was being played with expertise on the other side of the house, bringing back her father. A light dimmed.

'Hi Ma,' called Izzie, opening a bathroom window that scraped against the thatch and looking down, grinning.

'That man's there, isn't he?' said Cecilia, and hurried towards the back door. 'He has to go.'

'What? Who?' said Izzie, hastily closing the window.

Izzie ran back to her bedroom, quickly locked the door, and scuttled back to Dan. He sat crouched cross-legged on her window seat where the snow-soft plaster threw his body's angles into relief, and he brought in an air of dirty clothes and new mud. He plucked at a guitar, threw her smiles, and lay his head back listening to the rhythm as it slid through the air.

'I can picture a bab on your lap as you play the guitar,' she said.

He nodded, and didn't reply, but he smiled at her again, and her lamp shone in his pupils. She gazed at his cattish pale eyes and graceful body in black clothes faded to patches of brown and silver-green.

On his rare visits to the house, he landed upon her, alerting her from outside her window or scaling a wall and throwing earth at her pane, or he let himself in through the back door and crept socked inch by inch through this house of lengthy creaks. He possessed a tense-shouldered vitality that made him restless.

He eyed her lazily.

She sidled up towards him, glancing almost shyly at his feet. He had brought skunk. He ruffled her hair, and drew her to him, resting his head against her, then he reached out and circled her wrist.

'Let's hide you,' she said in a low voice as she heard her mother on the stairs.

Dora sobbed for two minutes in her cottage. She rubbed an old Bannan tea towel against her eyes, then pressed it harder into the lids until her eyeballs ached.

There was a knock on the door. She had heard no one on the path and she jumped.

'Elisabeth,' she murmured as an automatic whisper in her own head, but wearily, the hope weighted with anticipated disappointment. It was Katya. Dora patted her arm and guided her in.

I am lovesick, she thought. I am radiation sick.

'I've got oranges,' said Katya. 'Potatoes. And peat.'

'It's late,' said Dora, and put her to bed in the little iron bed made up in the slip of a spare room beyond the bathroom. I wish my boys were here, she thought, a flicker of resentment repressed. I wish she was Elisabeth.

Ruth, with her yellow-dun curls and dark-brown eyes, had woken in the moonlight to lie on her back in obeisance to the week's spirits and rituals, counting bumps on the tentish plaster of the ceiling as an act of homage to the swarms. She switched on a torch. She worried at night that her mother might be sad. Her father wasn't sad. He was impatient and fun and he got cross, but he wasn't sad. She stroked her collection of bogies on page thirty-one of her mother's old copy of *The Borrowers*, where they now formed a range of sharp fierce little mountains. Outside on the moor with its battered sheep and ponies, badgers waddled, bracken rearing, trees arching, eyes in hedges, poachers coursing the trout streams, mink hidden in barns. Mist twined over the moor and dripped in the lanes. The mountains slid, like the trees slid towards the Railway Children. If Ruth could faint like Bobbie did, then her mother would never die.

Cecilia knocked on Izzie's door and pushed impatiently against the lock when she didn't answer it.

'Open it,' she said with an authority that even Izzie found hard to defy.

Izzie had bundled Dan into the back of her wardrobe, snorting with laughter as she piled nightclothes and underwear on top of his head.

'Where is he?' said Cecilia, looking at the wardrobe.

'Uh?' said Izzie with an exaggerated frown. 'Who?'

'Your unwashed friend. Where is he?'

'You're hardcore curious.'

'Tell me.'

'On the moor?' said Izzie.

'I heard him.'

'I didn't. Where?'

'Playing his guitar.'

'Hey Ma, you look rumply. Flushed and stuff. What's the matter?'

'Nothing,' said Cecilia. 'Where is he?'

'*I* was playing the geetar,' said Izzie.

'You?'

'Yes.'

Cecilia was silent. 'Well, you've become very accomplished. He's a lot older than you,' she said, automatically picking up one of Izzie's tops, shaking it out and folding it. 'You're underage,' she said, and her voice was unsteady. 'To – to have sex with him.'

'I didn't.'

'I could report him,' said Cecilia, straightening a school skirt.

'Do,' said Izzie lazily.

'I —' said Cecilia. 'Why?'

'He wouldn't do it with me.'

'Should I believe this?'

'He said I'm too young.'

'How do I know that's true?'

'Do I lie to you?'

'All the time,' said Cecilia. She frowned. 'No you don't. But you omit. Your omissions . . . amount to lies. But . . . But I'd rather you told me about him than sneaked out to see him.'

'Where?'

'Out on the moor. Look at the state of him. He must spend a lot of time outside. How can you, you idiotic girl?' she said, but gently. 'If you are seeing him I'm going to start issuing punishments. Groundings.'

'I don't even like him that much,' said Izzie scornfully.

Cecilia looked at Izzie. She said nothing. 'I'll think about this,' she said finally.

She went to her bedroom. She splashed icy water on her face. She dialled Ari's mobile number, but the phone rang until his voicemail came on. She rang again, but there was no answer.

The following week, Cecilia wrote at home and Ari worked in London. Dora read a biography of Eric Gill, a passion of Elisabeth's, in some discomfort from radiation. Ruth wrote a story about an ant colony at the village school and felt the thickness of her thighs in the girls' toilets, while Romy practised fonts and Izzie sat through classes desultorily, reassuring herself that she could feign sickness in the afternoon. Cecilia wrote in a fast nervous swoop with the time pressure of the Monday St Anne's run, but when she arrived at the school, Romy was full of enthusiasm for a new sculpture society that Elisabeth Dahl was organising. She begged to be able to attend the first meeting, until Cecilia agreed to turn back to school after dropping off the other St Anne's girls on her shared-lift rota. She rang Izzie, who growled, 'You owe me, Ma.'

She would go to Elliott Hall gardens for that spare hour, she thought. Spring in the gardens, where her characters would lie in a hollow imagining they could live on out-of-season nuts and petal juices when they shook off their pursuer. She drove quickly to Wedstone and parked and hurried, her heels scraping on gravel, so that she could span the entire garden and make notes, ingrained though its landscape was in her memory. She instinctively put on lipstick in the car mirror in case she bumped into anyone she had known at Haye House or in Wedstone, the urge for self-protection still strong. She was not ready to look up people she had known, and at times she doubted whether she ever would be.

As in Wedstone with its mini-roundabout and flashing Go Slow reminder, all had changed at Elliott Hall: there were signposts to a restaurant and sympathetically designed additional buildings outside; an air of busyness, of restoration and richness, of larger festivals and summer schools. She had to override her faint annoyance: a possessiveness about the place's shabbier past. Spring covered the gardens with petal light.

She took a shortcut through the café and glimpsed the other side from the window: new roses, perhaps too many roses, falling over the old masonry; yews tamed, and a marquee, testament to a corporate present, rising in one corner. Sections of passed time were clear entities to her, almost visible now in front of her, sealed with nostalgia and a rare sense of her own progress. She stepped into the sunshine with its density of warming stone.

'Cecilia,' came his voice behind her and she jumped.

He was standing on the other side of the café, the door closing behind him. She had to narrow her eyes through the light dance to see him. He held a pile of papers and a laptop; his jacket lay over his arm, his car key in his hand. Briefly, caught in a timewarp, she saw him as a teacher, perceived his papers as essays.

He smiled at her. New lines fanned around his eyes.

'I was going to work here,' he said, walking towards her.

'So am I,' she said.

'Join me for a coffee.'

He stood in front of her. There was a small hesitation, as though he had considered touching her arm or kissing her in greeting, and then withdrew the impulse.

'Do you work all the time?' he said.

She remembered his voice with its natural depth and resonance, the appealing intimacy of his tone. Girls had commented on his voice, all those years ago.

'I don't *get* all the time,' she said, and her brows drew into a sharper line. 'I have children.'

'Of course.'

'I work during the school day. Like you. Then – I start working again, often into the night.' She lifted her hand, defensively.

'How very fine it is that you make a living out of writing. You actually did that, Cecilia.'

'Very belatedly,' said Cecilia. ' "Fine"?' She smiled, despite herself. 'You sound like Julian of the Famous Five.'

He paused. 'Ah. Well. I think I am such a character after all. You make me nervous. You were not as belated as ...' he said, glancing down at his computer.

'You're actually writing?' she said.

'I don't know,' he said, averting his gaze from her. 'Who knows? Critical theory.'

'Oh good! Something changes,' said Cecilia.

'You are hard on me,' he said.

She was silent. She made herself maintain the silence. She would not fill it.

He floundered, and still she would not fill it, though it was difficult.

'I haven't seen you for over twenty years,' he said. 'You know, Cecilia ... It's very strange for me to see you here.' He hesitated. 'Like a time lapse. I've thought about you often.'

'I was just a shag.'

He winced. He closed his eyes momentarily.

'You were not that,' he said, uncharacteristic anger colouring his speech. He turned. 'I'm getting us coffee,' he said.

'I don't like coffee. Do you remember that?'

The sun caught his hair, his cheekbone, bleaching him as it had once done in the Oxbridge room when she had sat studying with him, floating on the progression of his words.

'I do,' he said, frowning. 'But perhaps I thought that that was because ...'

'Because I was virtually a child? Children's tastes change as they get older,' said Cecilia. 'But I prefer tea.'

'Do you really see me as some monster?' he said, lifting his gaze slowly to look straight at her. 'As some – Humbert Humbert who plundered your youth?'

'Not really,' said Cecilia, with a semblance of composure. 'But there are touches of the dirty old man to this story, aren't there?'

'Good God,' he said. Colour rose to his cheeks. 'There is that view. I suppose. I find it –' His lips parted. 'Extremely hard to think of it in this way.'

She pulled a strand of hair away from her forehead. He glanced at her hand as it moved across her face.

'Don't worry,' she said. 'I was seventeen. I've told you already I don't think of you as some child abuser. A "kiddie fiddler" as my middle daughter would say.'

'Good lord, Cecilia,' he said.

As he fetched drinks, she sat on her own where once there had been a room full of gardening implements instead of a café, on an estate where workmen had burnt leaves in gardens so little populated that walks and hollows had made places for touching, and she watched people coming in: the middle-aged subscribers to the festivals which now seemed to have made a cultural epicentre of this former backwater. They formed a highly strung, self-satisfied rabble at the bar, hailing each other loudly, feigning demotic largesse as they bought four o'clock beer or brown bread sandwiches and chatted about certain conductors with an implied familiarity. They think they have discovered this place, thought Cecilia. She wanted to tell them, those strangers. She wanted to tell them that she owned these gardens in her heart: that in the earth's history was the wooing and rejecting of a girl by her lover.

He came back.

'I got you tea and this,' he said, handing her a cheese scone.

'Thank you,' she said.

'What are you doing working here – attempting to work – at this time?'

'My daugh – Romy – is attending a sculpture club. With your wife.'

'Ah,' he said. He looked uncomfortable. His face, which had tended towards narrowness, had resolved itself into later, older proportions so that his features were somehow more settled. He breathed slowly, perceptibly composing himself.

'So you're married still,' said Cecilia, toying with the scone on its plate. 'It lasted.'

'Yes,' he said.

'But you've been unfaithful,' she said.

Her bald statement sat in the silence. His expression stiffened.

'She must know,' she said.

'I suspect that she does know; but not with whom,' he said eventually.

'So what do you two do?' She heard the richness of her own voice, the adult timbre, noticing it again as she hadn't for years because she had once attempted to charm and keep this man when she spoke in breathier, darting tones. She paused. She tried to shake off the undertow of remembered despair.

'Oh,' he said, with the partial rotation of his head she knew so well, its exact choreography returning to her. 'Much the same.' His expression was closed. She glanced at him. It seemed impossible to her that she could have loved him: she felt neither revulsion nor residual attraction, only absolute indifference. Perhaps, she thought, his appeal had been only the product of hormones, of collective hothouse hysteria.

'Go to Dorset.'

'Yes.'

'Read Shelley. Tennyson. Joyce. Gaddis . . . Whitman. Trollope.'

'Well yes. But –'

'You don't still live at Neill House?'

'Thankfully no. We moved to one of the staff houses shortly after – after you left. Over by Meadowbank Lane, behind the Copse. I'm sure you remember.'

'I do.'

'And then we moved to a small house we bought – right near here. By Elliott Hall, towards the moor. We do still go to Dorset.'

She nodded.

'I thought you would move back there. I was sure you would have done so by now.'

'Oh yes. Yes. But when the offer of teaching posts at St Anne's came up . . . And we already had the Devon house, and really, such a school was everything I'd wished – naïvely – that Haye House could be. Well, I was keen to stay.'

'I see. What else do you do?'

'Oh, I . . .' He tapped his fingers on his paper, his wedding ring glinting. It filled her with a tense feeling of recognition.

'You fish. You play tennis with your boys. Your grandchildren now. Are you a grandfather, James?' she said, unable to enunciate his name naturally after all these years.

'I – yes. I am about to be again.'

'Congratulations,' said Cecilia.

'Yes I – We are pleased.'

She prodded him further with questions designed at some subconscious level to reveal the limited nature of his existence, or to prove to herself how well she had once known this man, as though possessing him finally after the event, and then discarding him. Is there always this with old lovers? she wondered. This accounting and mental placing of each other, this pleasure and partisan adherence to the present, to one's current love?

'I see I'm unimpressive to you,' he said eventually, his mouth set in a faintly ironic line.

She lifted her face, hesitating. 'Do you want to be impressive?' she said.

'I'd like that very much,' he said. 'But primarily I just want . . . peace.' He breathed slowly. 'Resolution if you like.' He looked strained.

She exhaled through her mouth.

'Peace?' she said, her lips barely moving. 'Resolution? How – how is that possible?'

'It is possible,' he said. 'The nature of my friendship with you –'

' "Friendship"! For God's – It was never that.'

'I was about to correct that,' he said, lowering his voice. 'My relationship – my ill-advised – with you. It was not something I'm proud of. I mean, I'm proud of you, Cecilia. Of your work, of what you've – become. Look at you . . . But we have progressed. We have different lives.'

'Our affair affected lives.'

'It was folly on both our parts, almost exclusively mine. But life continues. I'm pleased to see that you have had children.'

'It affected –'

'We have survived. Flourished even,' he said, nodding somewhat awkwardly at her.

She struggled for composure. 'So it's all good, dried and dusted, then?'

He hesitated. He made a movement with his mouth as if about to speak. 'There doesn't seem much more to add,' he said eventually.

'You're like my mother,' she said.

He paused. 'I regret the past. I wish it could be forgotten now.' He glanced at her. He caught her eye, seemingly appealing to her. He looked weary. 'It was regrettable, but there were no – major ramifications,' he said. He shifted in his seat. 'Well there were of course. Emotionally. I do see that. I'm very sorry that I hurt you. But –'

'You kept your job, your wife, your nice little existence, you mean? You have no idea, do you?' she said, anger straining her voice. She began to feel the unsteadiness of her heartbeat.

'What –'

'What it did to me. It – it did my head in. I couldn't cope with it at all. You left me. You simply abandoned me. In these gardens. You let me be dropped . . . you barely spoke to me again. After – after our last conversation.'

'I understood it was a mutual decision,' he said carefully.

'I had no choice! Absolutely no choice. You never dealt with it. You just let me go.'

'I –' he said, slight alarm crossing his eyes. He bowed his head.

'Believe me, it fucked up my life in many ways,' she said. 'What do you think – ? I was seventeen and eighteen, my mind profoundly disturbed by – by you, you and me. I threw away the chance of Oxford –'

'I know,' he said. He bowed his head again. 'That was regrettable.'

'It was,' she said, trying to speak evenly. 'It was. The least of my problems. A knock to my pride. That was all. What do you think you were doing?'

'I ask myself that. I often have. I think the answer is – I – I was attached to you.'

'I was *obsessed* with you,' she said, shaking her head.

'I didn't know –'

'You have to be so careful with teenage – young – minds. It's a monstrous time of turmoil anyway ...'

'I see that. I do see that.'

'That dangerous vulnerability.'

'You're right. You're right. I was blind to some of that. Of course. I had thought I was doing my best in unwise circumstances.'

'I think you were. I think you were in a way,' she said, pausing. 'But what madness –'

'We are here. We have decent lives,' he said.

'*We* have "decent" lives but –' Colour flooded her face. She began to breathe rapidly. 'You, you let me leave like that – here, *here*, in the gardens! I was lost. What do you think I was going to do with that? You never said anything – not one valedictory thing, any word of regret. Explanation. You said you couldn't leave your wife – *of course* you couldn't, wouldn't; I could see that later – but then that was it. You never sought me again. You let me leave school saying nothing further about it. For God's sake, we didn't even use contraception! What *were* we – you – thinking of? I knew nothing, nothing! I was the most naïve silly old-fashioned teenager you could imagine.' She glanced at the table.

'I should have tied it up,' he said, his mouth set. He met her eye. 'I didn't know what to say. What to do. I'm so sorry. I missed you more than I'd ever imagined – after, after you'd left school and we were out of contact.' A flicker of awareness crossed his face. He looked briefly to one side. '... Contraception?' he said.

'I'm going,' said Cecilia. She pushed her plate away and stood up. She was forced to shuffle sideways along a bench to reach the end of the table. The wood banged into her hips. She almost tripped.

'No. Stop,' he said.

She grabbed her bag, shook her head, her throat tight with a lump that stopped her speaking.

'Contra – Are you saying? Surely nothing – ?'

'I'm going now,' said Cecilia, and she walked quickly out of the French doors into the garden. It came to her with a dazzle of greenery and light. The new grass was bright. Birds seemed to line the branches. They thickened the sky.

'Stop!' he said, coming after her. 'You must stop, Cecilia.'

'Leave me now,' she said, walking on, talking without turning round to him. Warmth hit her cheeks.

'Is there something – I should know?' he said, catching up with her. His breath was cool and fast on her shoulder. His voice, the movement of his hair, seemed to boom, amplified, right beside her. She jerked away from him.

She said nothing, her heart racing. A larch soared above her. Rooks were deafening in her ears.

'Cecilia. You have made me worried now. Was there some – unfortunate result?'

'Result?' she cried. He was beside her, touching her shoulder. She shook him off roughly. His hand returned to her shoulder. She turned round abruptly and hit his upper arm. 'Result?' she said and she laughed. 'A human, a human, a daughter. She was not *an unfortunate result.*'

He opened his mouth. He held his upper arm.

'A –' he said, his mouth still open. He paused. 'A baby?'

'Yes. A baby. That's it, isn't it? A baby.'

Birds soared above her. They seemed to climb, evaporate beyond sight.

He was silent. He gaped. His mouth closed. It opened again.

'A baby,' she said. Her voice rose. It was laughably simple to say it. 'A baby. *My* baby.'

'Oh God. No. No.'

'You selfish cunt.'

'I – you – have a child? A girl?' He took her arm. 'Are you saying I've got a *daughter*? Are you sure? Where?' he said roughly.

She gazed at him with hostility. An expression of denial, of panic, seemed to pass over his face.

'Who is she? When? Where? Cecilia. Good God.' He was white. His voice was congested. He cleared his throat with a form of growl. 'Why on earth haven't you told me this?'

He stood there. He looked at her. He was a silent statue in his unchanged place in the sun.

He rotated his head. He said nothing. He looked at the ground.

He's going to leave, thought Cecilia in disbelief. This is what he wants. His undisturbed life. He is going to leave.

'Go on then. Go home. Go home. Go home to your marking and Elisabeth.'

'I can't believe it.' His expression was entirely impenetrable. He was silent.

'Goodbye,' she said. She began to walk.

He grabbed her upper arm. She pulled away. 'My God, Cecilia.'

'Yes. I'm going now.'

'No! No you're not. This is awful, terrible. A *daughter*, you said? A girl.'

She nodded, her mouth slack. There was a shout from across the garden. Crows cried. There was silence.

'Good God, a girl,' he said. He ran his hands down his cheeks. He looked gaunt. He buried his face in his palms. 'We had a daughter?'

Cecilia nodded again, her face crumpling at the sight of him.

'Where is she?'

'I don't know,' said Cecilia.

'You don't – how?'

She shook her head. She was crying.

'She – she –'

'She's alive?'

She gazed at a peacock without seeing it. She turned to him through her tears. 'I think so. I –'

'Was she adopted?'

He was crying.

She nodded. She turned from him and covered her face with her hands.

'No. Come here,' he said, and he held her and she heard him cry as he stroked her shoulder with rhythmic movements so firm they almost hurt.

'Why didn't you tell me?' he said at last, gently. She heard the effort of his breathing.

She shook her head.

'I just can't understand why you didn't tell me. Good God. You needed to *tell* me this,' he said in a groan. 'How many years ago? So many years ago.'

'I couldn't –'

'You couldn't, could you?' he said into her ear at the same time, holding her head and then pressing it to his mouth, the wetness of his face on her scalp.

She shook her head.

'I thought you wouldn't care,' she said.

He gazed at her.

'. . . You wouldn't want to know,' she said.

'I think,' he said slowly, 'I'd have loved a daughter more than anything else in this world.'

She nodded.

'You should have told me,' he said more forcefully.

She nodded, silently.

'Has she gone? When – ? Oh, it's – she's grown up. It's almost twenty-five years. Oh my God, Cecilia. What you . . . Cecilia. You should have told me. What an uptight fucking fool. Me – I mean me. I let you go.'

'I had no choice,' said Cecilia. She could barely open her mouth.

'Perhaps you didn't.'

She cried into his neck.

'And you were pregnant. Good God. What did I expect? Oh, Cecilia.'

He kissed the top of her head. 'Poor sweet – Poor Cecilia. Do you know – where? Where she went?'

Cecilia shook her head. She looked up at him, straight into his eyes, as though she could find sanity there.

'What's – her name?'

She shook her head again, still looking into his eyes.

'It's not your fault,' he said.

Her shoulders sagged. Sobs shook her body.

'Isn't it?' she said. 'It is.'

'No no no,' he said, stroking her. 'It's my fault. It's – youth's. You are so obstinate, courageous – But you should have told me. You should have. Oh my God. What a waste, a tragedy.'

'I thought you wouldn't care,' she said again. Her body felt drained and supple, as though it were not her own.

'I do care,' he said.

'I know,' she said in a small voice.

'What – whatever I can do to help. It's too late, isn't it? What can I do?'

Cecilia paused. 'Understand,' she said.

He nodded.

'You can understand my – sorrow. Regret.' She shrugged, exhaling with a small hopeless laugh. 'It's – you know, it's too late to find her. You can help me just –' She raised her hands in the air. 'Celebrate her. Mourn her.' She rested her head against a tree and saliva rose to her mouth.

'I will,' he said.

Twenty-three

March

'**Y**OU'RE PALE,' said Romy when Cecilia collected her from her sculpture society.

Bracken-scented air flew in from outside. Cecilia glanced at Romy, taking in the long and still ungainly limbs. She was destined to be taller than she was, she saw. She looked like a camping kind of girl: a far more wholesome and restrained teenager than Izzie.

'You're really pale,' said Romy.

'Oh,' said Cecilia abstractedly. 'Yes.'

'Are you OK?'

'Yes, darling. Thanks.'

'Have you been crying?'

'No,' said Cecilia.

Romy turned and Cecilia saw the smile on her lips reflected in the passenger window.

'What did you do? Did you actually do some sculpture?' she asked.

'Oh,' said Romy. 'I – we. Not yet. She – Ms Dahl – showed us different materials and we just began to work, to choose I mean, one of them.'

'What's she like?' said Cecilia after a pause.

'Who? What?' said Romy.

'Mrs – *Ms* – Dahl. Is she good? Do people like her?'

'Oh. Yes,' said Romy, and turned back to the window. A section of her hair was twisted into a clip that raised it into a discreet beehive which lent her a haughty appearance.

What is it about that bloody woman? Cecilia wanted to ask. What *exactly* is it about her? What quality? What power? How does she influence people?

She stopped herself. She felt irritated and uneasy. Or perhaps, she thought, what she was experiencing was simply age-old jealousy of a rival. She and Elisabeth Dahl had given birth to half-siblings. They were linked in antipathy by that hidden fact. What, she mused, would that frosty and determined woman think if she knew that she was teaching the half-sister of the half-sister of her own sons? Hugh and Robin, she mused, Robin and Hugh, and the flavour of those names recalled a different time. Everything, she thought: everything led her to her lost baby.

That baby, her lips a suckling bow, lived in her mind as a snapshot now turned black and white and crocheted as though it came from a different era. She remembered a little alien, head unbalanced, gazing up at her; she remembered her beauty too, the lock of blue eyes on to hers for seconds before the baby was taken away. Yet she could not grasp the features of her face; all she retained was the knowledge of a gaze.

I say sorry to you, thought Cecilia, staring out of the window. So very sorry. I would do anything in this life to change that.

A buzzard stood on a telegraph pole and flapped away in a soar across the windscreen as she drove past, throwing a shadow. The helper Katya was there on the lane as Cecilia and Romy arrived home. She retreated swiftly at the sound of the car, walking the back way that led to Dora's cottage, her hair with its green tinge from the water's copper drifting about her small solid body. New leaf thickened the air. The liquid bubbling of skylarks was high above the thatch.

Cecilia stood in the kitchen with Romy, picked up a cup and put it on the rack by rote.

He would have wanted our child, she thought, her conversation at Elliott Hall playing past her like a film that hadn't stopped, and she held on to a section of tongue-and-groove that had always been there at the end of the work surface, Dora's PVC bags once hanging from its hooks, its varnish layers now toffee dark. The very idea made her stomach plunge. She scrabbled for justification.

A daughter. I'd have loved a daughter more than anything else in this world, he had said. He had wanted a daughter. The baby she gave to other people.

She should have told him. They could have brought her up together.

But it was not true, she thought; whatever he said now, it was not true. Was it? Was it?

She had been living in her parents' house, not an unmarried mothers'-and-babies' home of an earlier era. She should have acted. She could have turned up at Haye House overtly pregnant and made him do something; she could have begged; she could have demanded, got him sacked, told Peter Doran, kept her baby. She felt she might retch.

She breathed with more effort, warding away nausea. She turned to Ruth. 'I'm glad Izzie has cooked for you both,' she said, and she smiled absently at the astonishing mess, the ragged pile of pancakes in maple syrup.

Ari came back from Exeter at half past eight after another meeting with his future department, walking into the sitting room as he would every evening from October. Cecilia jumped as he arrived through the door, as though her thoughts could be read or the effects of her earlier tears seen, and she moved rapidly towards him and kissed him on the mouth, then awkwardly on the temple.

Izzie perched near the fire and Romy sat beside her making notes in pencil on a book, the fireplace so large it had always been perceived as a separate room by children. They were regathered, thought Cecilia, trying to calm herself by focusing on the scene: there was no running out with an Oyster card for a night in Camden or a sleepover in Finchley. The intense family dynamic had not yet reshaped itself, with its shifts and hidden meanings, its annoyances and attachments and rituals. How long would it last? She did not know how to begin to explain the existence of James Dahl to Ari.

She glanced at Ruth who was sitting stiffly and breathing shallowly in the belief that she must remain motionless as Izzie divided her hair to make plaits. Ari fingered Izzie's scalp while looking over Romy's shoulder at what she had written. The girls perched around him. Woodsmoke and Izzie's cheap perfume drifted through the room. Cecilia watched Izzie – her good deed, her salvation, the one who filled her with ferocious protective love – and remembered how her desire to hurt herself, to donate parts of herself, had subsided to more bearable levels when she and Ari had rescued that cross and laughing baby. She had wished with a missionary zeal to save Izzie from a life of foster care.

Ruth sidled up to Cecilia wearing one of her hand-knitted scarves, its swaying edges and clumped purl heartbreaking. 'Can you read to me about treehouses?' she muttered, her hair a fountaining explosion of plaits that emphasised her flat dark eyes.

Cecilia put her arm round her, pulling her closer and inhaling her childish smell. 'We could read *The Swiss Family Robinson*,' she said, and Ruth nodded.

'I want you to put a treehouse in your book,' she said, and Cecilia smiled at her.

'What did you do today?' said Ari, looking up at Cecilia.

Cecilia glanced instinctively down at her lap. 'I wrote and – I collected Romy from her school sculpture club. I –' she said, opening Ruth's book, and said nothing more.

Ari seemed to be waiting.

She looked up at him and smiled briefly and glanced away.

I'd have loved a daughter.

Ari ate in front of the fire and talked to Romy about the finding of Mesolithic flint tools on the moor. The fire emphasised the shadows under his cheeks and below his stubbled chin, his narrowness defined by the blackness of his eyebrows. It pleased Cecilia that the man she had met at a party in Edinburgh who had first caught her attention with the word 'Dartmoor' – he had just been there, he said; he loved that wilderness, its barrows and reaves and pounds – was now in the place itself.

'Dartmoor . . .' she had echoed spontaneously in that Georgian basement so long ago, tailing off, because it had been buried for her after her escape. She thought that she hated it.

'A lot of my digs are there,' said this stranger who was, appealingly, not connected with the university, but the recent boyfriend of a history student.

'Have you ever seen it in deep winter?' said Cecilia, tilting her face towards him. She was surrounded by people, in the middle of a group of students, but she spoke to him alone. 'Not in the snow, but in the wettest most lifeless January when the riverbanks burst and the rain falls horizontally?' She said it challengingly, sifting the tourists from those who knew that its essence lay in its very bleakness, turbulent and gritted, cloud shadow streaming across bog.

'I love it maybe the most then,' he said. 'I've taken digs out in January and no one wants to come with me, but on those days I return more alive than on any other.'

'Well –' said Cecilia, pausing.

'You think I'm some day-tripper bussing in for cream teas in Widecombe?'

'Widecombe ... I went to Widecombe Primary,' said Cecilia absently, even the name lost to her, unspoken during the last years.

'A Dartmoor girl,' he said. 'I've never met a real one.'

The fire shifted now in their house on the moor, lighting Ari's face.

'I thought I heard something,' said Cecilia, and she walked towards the hall.

'You're jumpy,' said Ari. 'There was nothing.'

She's there, thought Cecilia. She's in the hall, crawling under furniture, butting her head at corners, waiting and catching the hem of my skirt.

'Ari,' Cecilia said, coming quickly back into the sitting room. 'I –' But she didn't know what to say.

James Dahl rang in the morning.

'How do you know my number?' said Cecilia. A whinchat flew and brushed a branch against the window.

'I looked it up in the school records.'

She was silent.

'I'm glad you called, though –' she said.

'I'd like to see you again,' he said, uncharacteristically interrupting. 'To continue talking.'

She paused. 'OK,' she said.

'When?' he said.

'I could do Monday again.'

'I'd like it to be sooner.'

'No,' said Cecilia with certainty. 'Monday.'

Dora knew that more would be said. Every day she sensed her increasingly fragile grasp on the concealments and evasions that had shored up her life. For the first time, she had taken to locking her door when she needed privacy.

She heard the movements of Cecilia's family: the car starting up as Ari drove to London on Sunday evening or Monday dawn; the exhortations to hurry in a morning chaos of sports kits and instruments and packed lunches. She heard her granddaughters' clear voices rising in protest and mockery through the valley, their scents – their urgent teenage hormones, their deodorants and foundations and canned drinks – clashing with the rinsed air of the moor. She wondered whether they were running wild, these city girls let loose. She had spotted Izzie, sometimes, on the lanes in school hours, Izzie's answers to her questions disarmingly persuasive. Once she had seen Ruth alone in Widecombe. Ruth sat in a field with her legs drawn up in her anoraked coldness like a fat little tepee, so Dora had gone to the National Trust shop and bought her an expensive rug of the Bannan factory variety that cost half a week's pension, and lowered it over the wall with some biscuits, an apple and a bottle of water. She never saw the rug again.

She was lonely.

How it all changed, she thought. People had left her: Patrick had died so prematurely of emphysema followed by pneumonia, their marriage having never recovered but settled instead into increasingly fond compromise once they accepted each other's limitations, so that over the years she loved him again, quite calmly, almost cynically, through the guilt – he was destined to be her life companion, she realised – and his death had unexpectedly devastated her. Gabriel Sardo, to whom she had rarely spoken after the birth of Cecilia's baby, was now living with a long-term girlfriend and employed as a camera operator in London. Her great friend Beatrice had died at fifty-nine, cancer claiming her before it migrated to Dora. Beatrice's daughter Diana was still in almost daily contact with Cecilia in a friendship that had remained intense, living in London, unable to conceive and enduring her fourth bout of IVF. How Beatrice would have loved the almost preposterously delightful reward for living that was grandchildren, Dora thought, and she felt such pity for her friend: love beyond death, an awareness of the wrongness of the world.

Katya, at least, came in to help, her hours erratic in a way that suited them both because uncertainty afforded Dora stimulation. Dora was caring towards her, would take her in for tea and speak to her in the cheerful compassionate manner under which her Haye House tutees had flourished: even Annalisa the lachrymose Swede had sent her chocolates from Stockholm for almost a decade after leaving the school. Dora saw many things: she saw the movement of the sky and birds, watched for hours; she saw Dan on the lane one dawn; she glimpsed Cecilia working into the night, the light of her study smudging the back garden.

'We have fifty minutes almost,' said Cecilia on Monday afternoon, looking at her watch. She glanced around. She still felt a nervous alertness in the school grounds, her need for self-protection strong in the face of James Dahl. She had changed her clothes several times before meeting him, frustrated by her sudden inability to put an outfit together.

'So tell me –' he said.

'Not here,' she said. Even the sight of what had once been Neill House, and Chase House where Zeno had lived, made her skin tighten. Could you ever be natural with ex-lovers? she wondered. Was it possible to behave without an awareness that before this time of polite greetings, the two of you had been pinioned together, mouths, hands, genitals linked?

'Let's go along the water meadows and follow the river down,' he said, guiding her, the familiar muscle beneath his shoulder visible as he moved, and he began to walk ahead, noticeably more assertive than he had been.

'I have thought about little – almost nothing – else,' he said as they reached the boundary of the St Anne's grounds and climbed over a fence into fern and long grass leading to the Dart's more tranquil reaches.

She was silent.

'Oh Cecilia,' he said suddenly, turning to her, putting his arm briefly around her. Colour appeared on his cheekbones. 'I can't bear it that you went through that.'

He reached out to her and then seemed to change his mind and dropped his hand.

'I think of this girl,' he said, and his chin tilted downwards. 'I do keep wondering how she is.'

'I'm surprised by your reaction,' she said eventually.

He shook his head. 'I'm intensely shocked.'

'No,' she said, looking to where the river curved and a jay drank from its shallows. 'I thought you'd be – awful. To be honest. Terrible. Uptight. I thought you might even say nothing about it again.'

'On the contrary –'

'I find I do want to punish you all the time.'

'I know,' he said, then shrugged slightly defensively. 'But you deserve – relief. Some kind of abatement. No one, *no one*, could blame you for this. For what happened later,' he said gently, taking her arm and holding it. 'You know that, don't you?'

She said nothing. The grass beneath her shone with bright green clarity, daisy sewn.

'I gave her away,' she said.

'I'm sure you had no choice. You were extremely young. Eighteen?'

'I did the wrong thing. Exactly the wrong thing.'

'You couldn't help it.'

She hung her head. Tears sprang to her eyes. She concentrated on minute fissures and bobbles of earth. She stumbled slightly as she walked.

'Did you –' he said, a rush of waterfowl curving from the river, 'did you think of telling me?'

'No,' said Cecilia.

She steadied her breathing. He put his arm out, laid it on her back, then dropped it.

'You were entirely happy for me to remove myself,' she said.

He paused. He looked down. 'I was – relieved – guiltily relieved you made no fuss,' he said slowly. 'I admit it. I was . . .' he frowned '. . . grateful. But I always felt guilt and I always missed you.'

She was silent.

'But of course I'd have wanted to know. I wish I'd known. I really do strongly wish that you'd told me,' he said, in a less conciliatory manner.

'You'd have wanted me to later, perhaps. I don't think, I really don't think you would have liked it at that time.'

'I think you should have given me the choice.'

'I think now that I should have. But at the time – well,' she said, and her voice faltered, 'I was in denial anyway until – until it was too late. Too late for an early abortion,' she said. 'I just felt dropped by you. I didn't really care what happened to my life. I wanted to die, a lot of the time. I just wanted to disappear. In a way, you were the *last* person I'd have told,' she said more combatively.

He was silent. 'Yet I wish you had.'

'What exactly would you have done? Installed your schoolgirl mistress with illegitimate offspring in a cottage in the grounds? Don't lie to yourself,' she said. 'You would – I suspect – have agreed with Dora. There is no way you'd have wanted me to *keep* my child. You'd have lost everything! Don't lie to yourself. It makes me angry.'

'I wish you'd told me,' he said, shaking his head. 'But I suspect – fear – you're probably right.'

'I couldn't tell you,' said Cecilia. 'I kept my head down; I hid. I barely saw you in those last weeks,' she said tonelessly. 'I can't really tell you what that was like. I left after the last exam.' She paused. 'I didn't even collect my things from my locker. Then I stayed at home for the summer and autumn.'

She breathed slowly, warding off that remembered abandonment, that hot panicking knowledge of a pregnancy that wasn't yet showing. In the weeks after their last meeting in Elliott Hall gardens she had studied and taken her exams in a daze, and only forming letters on a page, the bleeding of ink on paper fibre, the rumblings of her own intestines through the perpetual grief, had possessed any sort of physical reality.

'How did you do it? How did you manage?' he said, and a pained expression passed over his face.

'I don't know. There was a kind of scary passivity. I was pregnant, but I couldn't believe I was pregnant. I was relieved – pathetic, malleable – when Dora took the situation out of my hands. There was no question about the solution in her eyes. I thought, my mother will clear up the mess.'

'If only it were not so –'

'What I've never understood is how I, as the baby's *mother* – her own birth mother – could have –'

'Cecilia, is it so terrible to allow a child to be adopted? In certain circumstances, I mean? Many – many women did it in the Fifties and Sixties. The men gone. The world doesn't view it as you do.'

'I think of that. I know. I tell myself that. I did the wrong thing.'

'Families have always done this,' he said gently. 'Standard practice even. Think of Jane Austen's brother, given away –'

'Don't talk to me now about Jane *Austen*,' she begged.

He paused. 'What was she like?' he said. He stopped by a fallen tree, and his face was grey shadowed.

'I hardly even saw her,' she said guardedly, because she was not going to share her one vision: that dissolving gaze. 'Less than minutes.'

She stopped. She stood back.

He nodded slowly, his mouth stiff. He gazed back at her, standing still by the river in his pale trousers, his faded blue jacket, his eternal tie. The movement of air above the water lifted his hair. She still loved him, she thought, then the notion disappeared, replaced by blankness and that resistance to him that so swiftly flared into anger. She gazed at a fish basking by the brown-slimed stones underwater. 'I have to go back soon.'

He nodded.

'I read about you after your second novel was published,' he said. 'I read about your – new life. Your family. It was very strange. I felt a . . . surge of possessiveness, of jealousy. After all that had happened.'

'Did you?' said Cecilia, raising one eyebrow. She looked uneasy. 'You know, I fear, I fear that talking to you will somehow mess up my head,' she said in a rush. She played rapidly with her fingers. 'It took me so long to stop being devastated by you and angry with you. I think it's . . . dangerous for me to see you again. It stirs up the past. It took me so many years to get over that.'

'It won't be dangerous,' he said. 'We need to talk about these things.'

'I don't know what to tell Ari.'

'Ari is –'

'Yes. He doesn't even know . . . of your existence, really.' She smiled. She looked down. 'I don't want to be late for Romy. I need to go,' she said, and she turned abruptly and began to leave. She wanted to look back and wave, but she stopped herself, and left him walking along the riverbank, in her wake.

Twenty-four
April

YOU GREW to fear your children, Dora realised. You sensed what they must secretly feel about you. With their generation, you were aware that they could at any moment turn and accuse you of primal psychological damage, and you danced to their tune, both villain and encumbrance.

Since their argument, Dora had begun to acknowledge that she was, indeed, afraid of her own daughter. For all her knowledge that Cecilia's strength had been gained through grief and earlier powerlessness, she was still intimidated: by her apparent certainties, her urban style, her Londoner's over-fast way of speaking. She feared too that the delicate structure of her own life could be dismantled by her enquiries. Had she clung to consistency – to Wind Tor, to Elisabeth – to prevent that edifice from collapsing?

Because here she was, still waiting for Elisabeth. Today, this very morning, in early April, when the ash gleamed lime and she had gently probed her armpit until it hurt in her dawn bath; today when she would fetch a new supply of inhalers for Izzie from Newton Abbot and set aside baking recipes for Ruth; pay bills, tread down smaller weeds from the path, bank some outstanding lodgers' cheques from Wind Tor House, though many would never pay in her lifetime; take a phone call, perhaps, from the String Society: today her mind was still set in the direction of Elisabeth Marianne Dahl, née McGill.

'Come to me,' Dora sometimes murmured in the garden. 'Keep away from me. Come to me,' she had muttered in a hospital bed, tender-skinned with radiation. 'Come *on*,' she murmured today, a recent phone call from Elisabeth indicating a proposal to meet.

The phone rang. It was not her.

'One of us needs to move away,' Dora had once said to her, wearily.

'One of us needs to move away,' Elisabeth had echoed, turning to Dora chilly with implication.

She will come tonight, she thought. Would she?

'I'm *sick* of this,' she said out loud to the mirror in a growl full of coughs, so unused to speech was she in her cottage. Next time, she thought, sitting down and weeping very suddenly, she would tell her to go away. *Go away, go away, go away*, she thought, muttering it to herself. Somehow, that day, she had had enough. The very idea of Elisabeth faintly nauseated her. Nothing had happened to cause it. No event. No epiphany even. Just an end of her tolerance. From past flurries of effort followed by capitulation, she knew that it would be grindingly hard, but, almost superstitiously in illness, she promised herself that she would try. She would try to end it.

There was silence behind loud birdsong.

The phone rang.

'It's me,' said Elisabeth.

Dora paused.

Elisabeth paused.

'My love,' Elisabeth added lightly in her opulently layered voice. 'How are you?'

'Hello,' said Dora.

'I can't come over till later. I'm sorry, my darling. It'll be late. It will be after supper now. Nine thirty?'

'Don't,' said Dora, faltering, softening, driving herself. 'I mean, don't come over.'

Izzie pulled on her inhaler, wheezed a little, saw that her hair was roping rather than curling and doused it with products, then dressed up. Having not seen Dan for some days, she walked north of Wind Tor and stormed across a section of the moor where military planes shot overhead and tors were merely falls of broken rock. This time, he flicked his eyes up to her, pointed to an adder in the gorse, chewed on a burnt sausage, and told her he might feel her up to her shoulder if she was lucky.

Ari was back in London after spending some of the Easter holiday at home. Cecilia walked with James Dahl to the spread of willows beside the river, the weather unseasonably warm, but she projected a small figure in the space between them, the river casting swelling discs of light.

This is the secret of my baby, she thought. I gave her away. I gave her to strangers. She lives with me, strapped to me as she would have been.

'Come and see where the badgers walk in summer before dusk,' he said.

She hesitated, and he walked ahead, his gait more relaxed than it had been in his thirties, his body more upright, as though he accepted the advantage of his height and no longer apologised for it. He still emanated a faint sadness, a suggestion of vulnerability at odds with his size that had once pulled her to him.

'I did some research,' he said. His shirt was open, with no tie. 'I found out about the local adoption agencies, the council's policy, various facts about that time.'

She gazed at the ground.

'I did all that too,' she said with a smile, but she avoided his eyes. 'I looked into it early on. I know all Norcap can ever tell you.'

He was different again from the man she remembered, or remembered in her imagination: more three-dimensional, betraying edges of a febrile nervousness beneath his apparent calm, but she was projecting her earlier vision, she realised. There was a defensiveness to his reserve; something less assured than she had imagined in all those times when he had appeared to her at Haye House as a professional talking to colleagues or as a teacher who taught her in a classroom with no flicker of communication.

'I don't know you, do I?' she said. 'It's just occurred to me. I *think* I know you.'

'Perhaps you shouldn't investigate too far.'

'You look discomfited! I'll find out about you … I have *no* idea how your marriage works, for example.'

'I'm not sure I do either.'

'I always wondered. I always wondered. Now you can tell me.'

He stood in the sun among blossom and plant filaments, watching the water, the light from the spaces between the trees landing like flames on his skin.

She smiled to herself. 'Let's walk along the other side,' she said.

'It's not school property,' he said.

'Why does that matter? You think we'll get prosecuted? Shot by the military? Have you never swum here?'

'At night … Perhaps I've done more than you imagine since you consider my life tremendously limited,' he said. He looked up at the trees, then turned to her again.

'Well, if you would tell me about it —' she said, heatedly. 'Tell me where you've been in all these years.'

'Here of course and Dorset, and visits to London and France —'

'Where else?' she said.

'After Haye House ended, we had a year or so of pay, and we stretched it to two. So Elisabeth and I travelled —'

'Did you?'

'Yes. Sometimes together, sometimes separately. When we were offered jobs here, I wanted to stay – more than she did.'

'Why? More your type of school?'

'Yes,' he said, catching her eye with a glance that reminded her of their time of shared mockery. 'St Anne's – the ease, the relief of it! Working here was almost a holiday after Haye House. I'd taught at boys' schools before, never girls', and that was different. And after two years away, I was ready to come back to Devon. I think it's my home now. Finally.'

'Where did you go?'

'We went to Europe for a while. Into North Africa, but then back to Spain and Italy. Elisabeth's – her faith – she wanted to spend time in Italy, immersed … We spent a lot of time in religious accommodation, in hostels. We walked to Santiago de Compostela. We crossed borders so many times.'

'Did you?' she said, her surprise audible.

'Yes,' he said steadily. 'Italy was the loveliest. Near Ravenna. I can see,' he said, 'that I appear to you like a cautious, reserved pedagogue – a crashing bore, even. You had your life in London and elsewhere, your writing, your family. But I hoped for some little remnant of your – esteem.'

'Oh – no. No.' She smiled. 'Tell me more about what happened.'

'I think I was a chillier soul when you knew me,' he said.

'Oh,' she said, hesitating. 'Why?'

'I didn't know – didn't know what to do,' he said, twisting his head self-consciously.

'Tell me. More.'

'Privacy was all I understood. By the time I realised I was in a ridiculous institution, it was too late, and I experienced a kind of giving up –' He paused, his mouth twitching with apparent pain.

'How?'

'There were tensions between Elisabeth and I about staying, rather than returning to Dorset, but in the end we remained there. And then you came in. You – for all the events that followed, for all the damage . . . you, young though you were, you gave me some sense that I could be a living person rather than a shell.'

'Did I?' said Cecilia with a tone of disbelief.

He turned away. He looked at the ground to speak. 'I don't think anyone had ever asked me so many questions –'

'The tip of the iceberg!'

'Well. I responded to all that. And you were kind to me, you know, in a funny way,' he said, speaking rapidly as though he wished to explain himself. 'You brought me things, looked after my somewhat damaged soul, though I'm sure you didn't know it. I've wanted to say all this to you for a long time. And then I missed you terribly.'

Did you? Did you? . . . Thank you, she wanted to say. 'I was young flesh. No challenge,' she said instead. She winced at her own words.

He stared at her, then turned and walked on.

She caught up with him.

'I regret it. It was deeply wrong. In a way, I was taking advantage of an opportunity. Of – timing. Of you. But I also had feelings for you,' he said stiffly.

'OK,' said Cecilia, her mouth opening.

'I could be accused of being some thoughtless cad, but it was never without care or distress – or regret.'

Her mobile rang in her bag, vibrating with Ari's ringtone.

Dora waited still. She had told Elisabeth not to visit, and Elisabeth, her surprise readable only in her pause, had agreed with a gelid detachment. She did not ring, and she would not ring, Dora knew. After perhaps two weeks, three weeks, she may, piqued and almost impatiently roused, appear in Dora's garden; but too much suffering would have occurred in the interim, and Dora knew through years of experience that it was not worth keeping her distance merely for the sake of pride. Pride was a subject she thought about frequently.

Instead, Katya came, with her usual self-possession, and at her own instigation found all Dora's shoes to polish and banged and brushed away old mud, her hair wobbling with her movements in the air. Dora watched her. Her freckles gave colour to her narrow face, the effect like cinnamon and milk, a pale gold that matched her eyes.

'I'm feeling a little better today,' said Dora, smiling, standing in her cottage door with her old striped apron.

She looked at the hill beyond the thatch of Wind Tor House and a vivid image of two decades before came to her.

The phone rang. It was not Elisabeth.

'I need to take this call,' said Cecilia to James, and she walked away from the river towards a hazel copse where the whispering of leaves enclosed her in what seemed to be silence, her heart racing with guilt as she heard Ari's voice. Her own voice was light and over-enthusiastic as they discussed practical matters, daughters and work. She could hear traffic, all the tangles of his breath and the amplifications of his mouth close to the phone.

'Where are you?' he asked.

'Where am I?' she said, and she looked up at the river foliage arch-ing, the plates of cow parsley, cattle moving in slow motion on the field beyond and James Dahl disappearing into shade as though he had never existed other than in her memory.

'Where are you?'

'I'm here near the school, by the river. I'm waiting for Romy; she's sculpting,' she said.

James had walked ahead. He was pacing a little further downstream.

'How did you meet your wife?' said Cecilia, without preface. 'There are things I've always wanted to know.'

'Oh,' he said.

'I must go soon,' she said. She recognised his watch, his father's watch.

'It's many years since this ... since I talked of this.' The canopy of trees swallowed him temporarily in shadow. 'She was – she had thought of being a nun.'

'Oh my God!' said Cecilia, laughing for some time. 'Elisabeth Dahl as nun!'

'She had been brought up very strictly in the Anglican Church. It was only later that she turned towards the Catholic faith.'

'I see,' said Cecilia warily.

'She was at a last dance, so she thought. A quaint, supervised dance for girls living in this kind of boarding house in Kensington. *The Girls of Slender Means* – very much like that. And I was there, training as a teacher nearby. I had been invited with a group of friends, and Elisabeth was standing alone in a corner. And I started to talk to her.'

'And?'

'And I danced with her.'

'How –' said Cecilia.

'How what?' he said gently.

'How romantic.'

'Yes.'

Cecilia paused. She found, to her consternation, that she was blushing.

'And now. Does she look after you? Interest you?'

'She is – good to me. We are very happy.'

Cecilia began to laugh again, unable to stop herself, becoming embarrassed. Her eyes moistened. 'Are you?' she said.

'Well . . .' he said. He coughed.

'Are you happy?'

'We are . . . contented.'

'Doesn't she have her – dalliances?'

'Cecilia,' he said.

'Well?' Her mouth straightened. 'Well I'm very happy you're so domestically fulfilled.'

'Oh Cecilia,' he said. He sighed. 'We make our choices.'

'I know,' she said, and, no longer laughing, she looked up at him and nodded. 'I know.'

'Tell me about your relationship with –'

'Oh no,' interrupted Cecilia defensively.

'– with Dora.'

'Oh,' said Cecilia. She paused. 'Elis –'

'No. Dora.'

'Dora,' she said impatiently. 'Oh. I – I wish to have a relationship with her, as you know. But to this day we can't really talk without it being there, because she knows – I'm a woman without my child. I'm like all those women in documentaries who gave up their babies in the Sixties: haunted. It never goes.'

'I know,' he said. 'I know.'

'I think – I think you do. I –' She swallowed. 'I hadn't realised for some time that Dora had organised this entirely outside the system. In the early days, I used to walk away from any discussion of adoption because I'd instantly panic, start breaking down, so I simply didn't know –'

'That could easily happen. I'd have no real idea what the – the procedures would be.'

'Nor did I. I thought you gave up your baby, and that was it. Then you went mad.'

He took her arm for a moment and guided her through a clump of old bramble on the path, though she stiffened. She looked at the river driving its glittering angles as she talked to him, and felt the strange release of it, of words she had said to no one but Diana in fragments over the years. It soothed her to explain to someone, even to him.

'Why didn't you contact me?'

'I thought it wasn't my place,' he said. He looked at her directly in the eyes; she felt a glitter of old awareness, embarrassment, in looking straight at him. 'I'd already caused you enough disruption,' he said eventually. 'Though of course I had no idea how much.'

She was silent. Perplexity crossed her face.

'You don't understand,' he said. 'It was simply not allowable, not done – not wise. Even there. It seemed anything went – but not that. Of course an establishment can't employ teachers who … Though in fact there were, had been instances over the years, I came to know, the longer I taught there –'

'Who?' said Cecilia instantly.

'Oh, I'll recall and report. Some time. But it … was, is, never advisable. Of course.' He coughed.

The water snaked as they passed with the speckled shiftings of stones beneath a slow yellow. Cecilia soundlessly turned and began to walk back. 'Will you meet me another time?' he said.

'Yes,' she said. 'Next Monday.'

Romy was not at the school. A note was tacked to the studio door, stating that the sculpture society had taken a short trip to Danver Sands to observe wave formations and may be a little late returning, the paper signed in a large, careless fashion by Elisabeth Dahl. 'Fuck Elisabeth Dahl,' Cecilia murmured, and glanced at her watch. She walked fast towards the car, hoping that if she drove to Danver Sands now she might meet the minibus on its return to the school.

She parked, turned a corner beyond the fence lining the fields that led to the beach, walked down a slope beneath a windless sky, and came upon them: girls in the waves.

Girls in dark-blue uniforms ran and rushed with the movement of the sea. They bobbed and gathered, surged with the waves until they came in as one, water stained black, their hair dragging behind them as they were carried in and thrown on to the sand. They were part of the sea, galloping together, climbing back in, screaming soundlessly.

'Romy!' Cecilia cried. But no one heard. There on the beach stood Elisabeth.

The girls in their uniforms looked like figureheads, crests becoming horses, sodden and breathless, hair streaking mouths, faces wet with foam as they reared and plunged. Cecilia stood and watched with her lips parted. The self-contained Romy stormed through the swell, wild-eyed. Girls clumped and gripped and pulled one another under, emerging choking, laughing, battered by the movement. Elisabeth, tiny and still, stood in front of them and watched.

These girls love her, thought Cecilia. My lover was in love with her. In a corner of her mind, something formed. *My mother was in love with her.* The idea seemed to bloom at her as a vivid certainty, then disappear.

On the return journey, the car reeked of seaweed and sand, and Romy's mobile kept beeping with texts. 'How –? How did that happen?' Cecilia asked eventually, and Romy told her between gulping breaths and collapses into laughter that they had talked about the shape of the waves in detail until Elisabeth had said, 'Go in then. Go in and feel them.' One girl could hardly swim but she followed the others. Her mother would complain to the school if she knew, she said, so she wouldn't tell her.

Katya was in the field in front of the house. Cecilia parked the car and hurried a shivering Romy to the garden path, but Katya had already slipped down to the river and only a section of her back was visible, her hair waving. She turned and paused momentarily, and Cecilia, catching a glimpse of her face, thought with a sudden acceleration to her heartbeat, *Is this my daughter?* Was it she who hid at night? The thought melted.

Twenty-five
April

'WHERE'S IZZIE?' said Cecilia.

Ruth shook her head. She tapped seven times under the kitchen table. She saw the colours in the air. A solitary apple that she had been noticing in the fruit bowl was losing its freshness as it contracted unevenly with age, and she worried about who, if any, its fruit friends were. Is it autochthonous? she wondered. That was her safety word. If something was autochthonous, it was protected.

She gouged her nails into the surface of the table. Cecilia noticed her and was reminded of herself, the old soft pine sedimented with children's pasts. She saw again that Ruth was suffering and pity clutched at her and sent a trail of uneasiness through her that she couldn't shake off as she wondered, as she so often wondered, how to help. She was problematically shy. An educational psychologist in London had made little progress; neither had her teachers, Ari or she herself, despite her hope that country life would be beneficial. Nightly, she slipped into Ruth's room and talked to her quietly, stroking her forehead, willing her words to be heard in the passage between consciousness and sleep.

Did I get this sweet child as my punishment? she wondered. Is she disturbed because she knows, somewhere, about the missing one I mourn? Does Mara take up the space in my mind?

And she resolved, as she had resolved before, to love only Ruth and Izzie and Romy. She banished the ghost.

Izzie then burst into the kitchen, reeking of a confusion of elements and substances: wind, woodsmoke and alcohol.

'You're here,' said Cecilia. She breathed slowly. 'You've been on the moor.'

'Mm hmmm,' said Izzie. Her nails were covered in chipped silver varnish. She gaped at Romy. 'Why're you in your dressing gown? Why's your hair wet? You look like a housewife about to shag the milkman.'

'Why?' said Cecilia. 'You said you would look after Ruth.'

'She's cool. Dors is up the garden. So's her weirdo servant.'

'You said you were cooking beans for supper. Where is he?'

'He –' said Izzie. 'I don't know, Ma.'

'You are *fifteen*,' Cecilia said, old alarm gripping her as she looked at Izzie in all her youth.

Izzie reached out, squinting, and grabbed an apple.

Ruth watched her teeth: they had become horse teeth chomping and sinking into skin.

'Eurgh,' said Izzie.

The abandoned ageing apple rocked on the table displaying its flesh wound. Ruth sent it blessings and medicine in vibrations through the air. Everything is lost, she thought.

In the morning, Dora woke early after a night of deep sleep, satisfied at her continued silence towards Elisabeth, but so very solitary in the light that bounded against her walls.

This longing for Elisabeth would hurry her death, she thought suddenly, tears springing to her eyes and humiliating her. She blinked. The pain of wanting Elisabeth – banished through will-power; returning with vicious teeth – was brutal. She would, would, would, continue the journey away. She promised it to herself as a brand of insurance against death. If she kept herself from this person, the cells would not metastasise.

She looked out of the slip of a window facing Corndon Tor and saw the boy arrive outside. It was the first time Izzie had brought him so close to the house in daylight, though she had been aware of his van sometimes, a vehicle belonging to a Widecombe garden centre, parking in the first light of the morning: early, early, when the cows were tossing heads and shouting at Dockden Farm and the nettles were astringent with dew.

He walked along scuffing stones. In the chill tinged with gold, the flecks of dirt were just visible or imaginable in the peaks of his hair as she watched him. She caught one glimpse of his face and she softened because he looked disquietingly thin and paler than she had remembered. Izzie walked silently beside him, eyeliner smeared, her arm around his waist.

Later in the morning, Izzie took the bus to school, attended registration and first lessons, then wandered the back route over a nettle-choked railway bridge to the market square in town. She thumped Dan's shoulder in greeting as he stood at his stall subtly mimicking his customers' nodding speech and weighing up the carrots he had bought in bulk from the large Asda outside Plymouth before spending happy minutes with Izzie immersing them in mud. They added snails to the boxes alongside a display of leafy carrot tops from the garden centre, a rabbit imported on one occasion in a supplementary show of authenticity. He had produced a printout explaining how the carrots were organically produced on his smallholding in accordance with the moon's phases. Izzie doodled badly drawn crescents and stars on the margins.

In his guise as artisan gardener, Dan nodded earnestly with his captive clientele while Izzie fought back burps of laughter and silently admired. She loved his shoulders. She reeled at his mockery. Mid-conversation, he turned with a conspiratorial smile for her. He had fashioned bowls from straw and horse dung which Izzie baked in the slow oven of the Aga. 'They look like shit; they are shit; but we'll call them Aboriginal,' said Dan, whose stock of carrots, potatoes and cheap cheese disguised with walnuts or wrapped in leaves was bringing in a healthy profit. He sold random pieces of rock as healing crystals, employing a series of delicately parodic gestures as he discussed their 'properties'.

One week he invented a moorland enclosed community which produced objects of wood and clay, eliciting questions and cynical comments, yet still a handful of these knobs and lumps and non-functioning instruments were purchased. On occasion, he wore a sack as an apron or a borrowed medieval outfit with no sign of embarrassment, while Izzie snorted behind him. A regular buyer lost faith, held a carrot up to the sun to examine it, and threatened Dan with a fight.

After visits to a pub off a sharp slant of track behind Widecombe, where a vicious local beer was served beyond closing time to old men who sat silently with their sheepdogs but greeted Dan with handclasps, he was more leisurely and affectionate with her. He curled up against her in her bedroom and they kissed and chatted, and he told her solemnly that she must do her schoolwork.

'Or you'll end up like me,' he said.

'How?'

'A wazzock.'

She giggled. 'Didn't you go to university?' she said.

'Two terms, then couldn't afford any more,' he said matter of factly.

'No way am I going.'

'Well you should,' he said, looking her straight in the eye. His mouth had a vulnerable cast to it. 'You're clever.'

He stroked her softly, reaching just above the knee, and refused to go further despite her urging. 'You're not old enough, missis,' he always said.

She had found her husband too young, she considered reasonably; but that could be overcome, and they were likely to have a baby soon. On some nights now he was inching up her forearms to her elbow; on other nights, he merely curled up against her and they held each other, murmuring and lazily laughing into the night, and kissed necks and chins as they fell asleep.

Dora's cottage was cold even after the warmth of the day. The slight dip in which it was built – a workers' afterthought to service the main house – was, when the light went, a chilled pool, lightly rank, its mosses and rich-earthed succulents overgrown and clinging to the walls.

That evening, Dora sat at her table and watched her daughter, and perceived how over-stressed or burdened she was. She saw the Irish Bannans in her, in the brown eyes, the country colouring beneath the later sophistication. She was reactive and alert, emotion transparent on her face and a barely perceptible trace of freckles across her nose, so strongly reminiscent of girlhood, suddenly visible in the light of a candle that burnt near her. Dora had noticed that she had been wearing make-up more often in the day. Her eyebrows were darker, more emphatic lines, contrasting in repose with the faint look of sadness to her eyes.

'You need some sleep,' said Dora.

Cecilia smiled, and shook her head.

She built up the fire. 'Izzie can bring you logs,' she murmured. 'This horrible radiotherapy. It's hard.'

Dora hesitated. 'It's just tiring,' she said.

'Poor you, that you had to go through this,' said Cecilia, her voice unsteady, and hugged her.

She sat down and filled Dora's glass.

'Ooh! Enough!' said Dora, causing Cecilia, despite all her pity, to cringe internally with the primal irritation that could be precipitated by every intake of breath, every tonal variation, every moment of generational behaviour betrayed. She stopped herself. She took a gulp of wine, and took another, only alcohol enabling her to dare to confront her mother this evening.

'You know I've protected you,' she said then. 'For a long time.'

'Cecilia.'

'You know I absolutely blame myself as much as you. More so, much more.' Her voice was unsteady again. 'But you ... I ... I think you need to search your memory now and tell me something. Please.'

Dora paused. She tipped back her wine. Her lower lip trembled. 'Is that a threat?' she said eventually.

'No. No. Please. Dora. I need to know.'

'You do, don't you?' said Dora. She fiddled with an old enamel ladybird in a bowl.

'Yes,' said Cecilia, her heart speeding at the subtle change of gear she detected. She would not pull back, she pledged. However much Dora filled her with guilt, with duty, with fear even, she would push ahead.

Dora poured more wine into her glass, spilling a sizeable portion on to the table. 'It has to do with that time,' she said uncertainly. 'Nothing,' her lip trembled, 'nothing was very formal. Do you remember what it was really like?'

'Hippies lining the loft, signing on under three identities, growing ten acres of dope, then getting grants for tinpot courses at Torquay Tech they never attended, you mean?' said Cecilia, still becoming heated even after all these years.

Dora's mouth twitched. 'Yes. But seriously. Do you remember? Farmer Hillier's child wasn't his, for instance. That boy Timothy was his nephew.'

'Really?' said Cecilia.

'Brought up as his son. Inherited the farm. Everyone knew; no one really commented after a while. It was moorland law. Our own laws, wild, cut off down lanes.'

'Oh —' said Cecilia.

'Yes. You know. People living outside the state in converted cowsheds; wood dwellers, putting up log buildings illegally. And many people around Wedstone had that system of bartering with their own currency instead of tax —'

'Five acorns equals a back rub,' said Cecilia impatiently.

'I know you've always scorned these country ways. Well. Anyway. Now there's a sense of this area being discovered, and known to Londoners — known about, more expensive, desirable. Second homes. Restaurants in Ashburton. It wasn't like that then, Celie darling. You know that. You could have these big crumbling manors with not so much money, and live off your . . . your ideals, making do. There wasn't a sense of the state being after you, if you like, then. So — so —' said Dora, her voice faltering, 'when — when your baby went to another home, it wasn't such a strange thing.'

' "Strange thing" . . . ?'

'Oh Celie, you do intimidate me.'

'I realise,' said Cecilia sombrely. She shook her head.

Dora paused. Her chest rose.

'So it was all rather informal.'

Cecilia swallowed. There was silence.

'But what about the birth certificate?' said Cecilia. 'That's what the adoption support agent I spoke to asked immediately. Where was the baby registered?'

'They must have – arranged that.'

'Faked it, you mean. Took my baby, said they gave birth at home, and got her registered as theirs. Or that fucking hippie midwife who kept running in and out signed the documents for the birth certificate under their name. Did she?'

Dora shook her head, her mouth thinning, the old glitter of tears that had silenced Cecilia for so many years coating her eyes.

Cecilia stiffened. She breathed deeply. She gazed at the ceiling. 'And you know what's odd,' she said slowly. 'This "friend of Patrick's" you said you arranged it through – after you said the baby went to a "contact", that is – though odd how I could never find any trace in Ashburton. Well, I don't recall many friends of Dad's at all. My Irish uncles couldn't remember this person either. Where did this "friend" live?'

'Nearby,' said Dora stiffly. 'And – Ireland.'

'What was his name?'

'– Aiden.'

There was a brief silence.

'You said Padraig before,' said Cecilia.

She hesitated. 'How could I?'

'You did. I remembered, very clearly. I wouldn't forget that anyway. But I particularly noticed because he had the same name as Patrick,' said Cecilia rapidly.

'I – I –' said Dora, her mouth goldfishing in repeated circles. 'I don't know,' she said. 'I . . . I . . . I'm sorry. I just don't know, I don't know.'

Cecilia was silent. She breathed slowly.

'You don't know?' she said eventually to Dora, who had her face in her hands.

'I don't know,' said Dora.

'So you lied to me.'

'I didn't.'

Dora sank on to the sofa and then lay against the cushions and pressed her face into them. Cecilia felt her heart plunge with pity. She began to rise, to throw her arms round Dora, to appease her, to withdraw. Forcibly, she stopped herself.

'Celie, I can't cope.'

'You never could, Mummy. That's what kept me away, kept me from asking. I called you Mummy. Why did I do that? You can never cope. That's what you always say. That's what silences me.'

'I'm sorry.' Dora's face was pressed into the sofa, her voice staggered snuffles.

'Who took the baby?'

'I think I gave you the wrong impression.'

'Who?'

'I – I – I don't know.'

'Then I'll initiate a missing person inquiry.'

'Oh Celie, you wouldn't do that,' said Dora, exhaling with a whistling sound.

'I wouldn't have before, but you've left me – you've left me nothing else I can do. And really.' She looked around wildly. 'Why shouldn't I do that? Izzie's almost sixteen. After that she can choose, and – and she'll live with me. There's not that particular threat over me any more. Even if you're in the middle of radiotherapy, you can tell me . . .'

'I'm ill. I can't –'

'Then tell me.'

'I –'

'You can.'

'Well there was –'

'Yes?'

'I don't know how to – Celie,' said Dora, swallowing clumsily.

'Tell me,' said Cecilia, looking straight at Dora. 'Tell me, please.'

'There was – were, was; which do you say? – a couple.'

'Where?'

'Here.' Dora sat up. She sounded mildly drunk. Her hair was pushed into a new position from lying down. Deliberately, Cecilia filled her glass.

Dora was silent. 'It was urgent.' She spoke in a croak.

'Why?'

'Because we – I – didn't want you to bond with the baby. If you had decided to give it up, I thought it was better for you that it was immediate, or it would break your heart.'

'It did break my heart.'

'I know.'

'Do you have to stick your chin out? You look so obstinate. So hard –'

'Oh Celie. I'm not; I'm not . . . Perhaps I am. Perhaps I am. Why did this happen?' said Dora, mildly slurring.

'So you took her immediately. But instead of an approved adoption . . .'

'I just didn't want to go through the formal channels and find some unknown couple,' said Dora, breathing in broken gusts. 'Random, unknown. And these two. They were there all along.'

'There all along? Waiting for my baby?' said Cecilia loudly.

'Well they – they were involved with it. The woman was a midwife, you see, darling. A – a community midwife. She couldn't – couldn't conceive,' she said, swallowing. Her hair was wilder. 'I just couldn't stand the idea of you having to go to hospital, and then some official coming along. I don't think you could have stood it –'

'It would have given me a chance to realise my mistake,' said Cecilia. She felt the blood drain from her face.

'But the parents could have been anyone. Vetted, but a risk. Anyone. Whereas I knew – them. It all seemed more – homely.'

'*Who?* Who were they?' said Cecilia rapidly.

'I told you. They lived here.'

'Here. Here in this house?' She pulled a cup towards her suddenly, pushed it back.

'Yes.'

'What?' Cecilia groaned. 'What were their names?'

Dora hesitated. She took more wine. A large amount spilled on the table and spread. 'Moll and Flite.'

'Moll and Flite? What?'

'Don't you remember them?'

Cecilia paused. Her eyes searched the ceiling, as though scanning the past.

'No,' she said in a small voice.

'He had a black beard. No – with no moustache. She . . . Well, she was brown-skinned, from the weather. Always outside. She was – big. Wore long skirts, layers of them. Do you remember?'

'You gave my child to –'

Dora bowed her head. 'Do you remember them?'

'There were so *many*.'

'And always passing through,' said Dora, nodding.

'I don't remember,' said Cecilia, breathing slowly to quell the nausea. 'Moll and Flite?' she said in a monotone.

'Yes.'

'What were their real names?'

'I don't know.'

'Don't know?'

'I never thought about it. Well,' she said, swallowing, 'I've never known.'

'What was their surname?'

'Jones,' said Dora quietly.

'Oh God. Didn't she have a different name?'

'They both went by Jones as far as I know. Women did in those days,' said Dora faintly defensively. 'Even . . . alternative ones; alternative livers. Oh you know what I mean.'

'Moll and Flite?' she said again in disbelief.

'Yes. Flite was a gentle soul.'

'They all were. *Gentle*. Filthy useless workshy morons. You gave my baby to one of those?' Cecilia's voice began to rise. She caught her breath unevenly.

'They were a nice couple. They wanted a child very badly, and there you were – You, you, my poor love. You were so *young*. You shouldn't have been pregnant at that age. You forget that.'

'But why didn't you tell me?'

'How? You wouldn't speak to me for years.'

'You didn't exactly try.'

'We're not the same as you. Your generation. I find it – hard to speak about things, Cecilia. Ask Diana. Beatrice was the same.'

'*Why* didn't you tell me before? You knew how desperate I was.'

'Oh Celie.' Dora paused, sighed.

Cecilia sent the bowl in front of her spinning across the table. It fell on to the floor, and failed to break.

'You're very difficult when you're like this,' said Dora.

'What did this "Flite" do for a living?' she said, turning back to her, a look of disgust stiffening her face.

'He gardened. Gardener, really. She was a midwife –'

'Was she *that* midwife?'

'That midwife?'

'Oh *you know who I mean*.'

'Cecilia –'

'That dirty-haired bitch who was around when I was having my baby. Christ, I think I remember her. Remember her smell or something. I don't remember her face. Christ, Christ. You must have been out of your mind. So you let that woman *pull my baby out of me and take her?*'

Dora shook her head, nodded, her eyes glazed.

'You are insane. Off your head!'

'Celie . . .'

Cecilia looked at her. She laughed with a small hiss of air. 'There's little I can believe any more.' She slapped her hand down. 'Where are they now?' she said abruptly.

'I really honestly have no idea, darling,' said Dora, sounding drunk. 'No idea. No idea. I'm sorry. I looked for them over the years. I still ask the odd – person who comes by, who might have known them. A few people saw them occasionally –'

'Where?'

'At – fairs. Or just around. It seems they went to Wales and then abroad. I looked.'

'You *gave* my baby to a couple of infertile old drifters renting this cottage and then let them –'

'They were very, very gentle, loving. I had no doubts they would nurture a baby well, darling.'

'And you didn't keep in touch, didn't have any address? Where did they go?'

'They gave me an address, darling. But – but – I thought it was best. A clean break. I wrote to them there – Wales, Pembrokeshire – and they'd long gone. I knew you'd be angry,' said Dora weakly.

'Angry?' said Cecilia, her mouth open. 'I can –' She shook her head. 'I can barely – I can barely articulate – This is monstrous.'

Dora recoiled.

'My child. Your granddaughter. You – I cannot believe this. Dora. What did you do to me – to her? Did you *hate* me? Was the child not good enough? Not good enough for you? She was, she was perfect. I remember. I remember that lovely face. Little cheeks, face. I saw her. Why did I agree to anything? *Why* did I agree?'

'I knew I shouldn't tell you. I *knew* I shouldn't,' said Dora, biting her lips and shaking her head hard. 'I always knew – I can't – can't lose the girls.'

'Good God. You expect – what now? How could you have done that in front of me, under my nose? Cooked it all up with them?'

'I thought it was best for you.'

'For you.'

'For you.'

'Well, you're always going to deny everything,' said Cecilia. She hit the top of the table. 'I'm going to look for them. Give me everything you've got. Now. Now.'

'I have *nothing*, Celie,' said Dora weakly. 'Really, darling. I – I looked.'

'Well I will look. "Moll and Flite". How fucking ridiculous. What were the names on their cheques?'

'Oh darling, they always paid cash –'

'– Cash,' said Cecilia at the same time. 'Of course they did. If you were lucky. Or they paid in quiche and childminding. *My* child. *My child.*'

Dora clamped her mouth shut. 'I can't tell you any more,' she said. 'I looked for them. For – you. I didn't think it was the best thing for you, but – But I looked for them.'

'Why?'

'Because how could I not? Given your reaction.'

Cecilia said nothing.

'Oh this is a terrible mess really,' said Dora. She sounded slurred. 'I knew – always. I knew I should keep it as it was.'

'Where is she?'

'There's nothing more to say,' said Dora, her hand wiping her eyes, her mouth.

'I'm asking you once more,' said Cecilia.

Dora was silent. Her chest rose and fell.

'That's it,' said Cecilia, reaching for the door.

She went to the house and threw herself on the bed. The pillow smelled of Ari. 'Why aren't you *here*?' she said, thumping it, and she picked up the phone. 'Ari,' she said, sobbing into Ari's voicemail. 'Oh why aren't you *there*? I need you – Need to talk – Oh God. Call me.'

She put the phone down, glanced at her alarm clock, pressed her eyes to her pillow until she saw slow starbursts, owlish irises staring back at her in the darkness, and rang James Dahl's mobile. After several rings, he answered.

'Sorry, sorry,' said Cecilia in muted tones, fighting tears. 'It's too late?'

'No.'

'I – I – I need you. I want to talk to you –'

'Of course –'

'Dora told me things about the baby. I need you.'

'I'll drive out.'

'Oh no – Can you?'

'I can't really talk now,' he said steadily. 'I'll see you in about – forty minutes.'

Cecilia paused, her chin dropping to her chest as she stood there. 'Yes. Can you? Yes.'

'Of course,' he said.

'Don't knock, don't knock, the kids are in bed,' she said rapidly. 'I'll look out for you and come down.'

She paced the bedroom, tensing her fingers as she heard herself speaking clusters of words out loud, the floorboards straining with every movement until she feared her daughters might wake, and she attempted to quell her panic as anger bolted through her agitation, leaving her nauseated. With a jolt, she recalled her impulsive voice-mail message to Ari. She couldn't talk about it to him, she realised with fresh clarity. It had only ever been productive to mention the baby in the early years; his gruff sympathy turning into resistance over time. She scrabbled for another reason for her call, conscious of how her lies proliferated.

Moll. Flite. Wales. Midwife. Adoption, she Googled frantically, making no progress. She searched blogs, tumbling into a barely literate netherworld featuring the ramblings of self-justifying dropouts, elaborate conspiracies, theories on festivals, raves, drugs, without success, and listened for James Dahl's car as she tapped in further futile entries. She would walk in the river field with him, she decided, hidden from the girls' bedrooms by a barn, but sufficiently close to check the house. She waited, emailing all her brothers to ask them if they remembered who had lived in Wind Tor Cottage, barely able to write the lodgers' names and enclosing them in inverted commas.

She heard a car engine and ran to the window. The phone rang behind her.

She stopped. She hesitated, waiting for several more rings. She snatched it up to answer it, aware that Ari would continue to call and become concerned if he couldn't reach her.

'Hi,' she said, her own sudden huskiness taking her aback.

'What's happened?'

'Oh darling, sorry, I – I overreacted. I had a horrible row with Dora. I –'

The sound of the car was audible, the engine cutting, the door closing. Cecilia stiffened. She covered the phone with her hand and pressed it to her ear.

'What was it about? Was that a car?'

'Oh – usual stuff. Sorry. I was upset,' said Cecilia, walking back to the window. She opened it. 'Very upset. I – I got all flustered.'

'What are you doing?'

'I –' she said. James stood outside the gate, a pale-tinted shadow. She tried to gesture to him through the darkness of the lane but he was looking in the direction of the front door. 'Oh I – someone's out there,' said Cecilia, trailing off. She put her hand over the mouthpiece. 'Just a moment!' she called softly out of the window.

'Who is out there at this time of night?' said Ari, amusement lifting his voice.

'Oh God,' said Cecilia, unable to think. 'It's – oh, it's the neighbour.' She cringed.

'What's he-she want?'

'I don't know.'

'Which neighbour?'

'He's . . . I think he's the one with the lost dog.' Her voice weakened. She blushed, alone.

'*What?*' said Ari.

'– Oh golly, I think he's that weird one – farmer. There's an advert about his dog.'

' "Golly". Since when have you said "golly"?'

One minute, she mouthed at James, holding her finger up.

'Why's he – now?' said Cecilia.

'Don't be ridiculous,' said Ari, amusement now tangling with hostility.

'He is,' said Cecilia weakly, unable to stop. She widened her eyes.

'In the middle of the night?'

'I think he wants to ask me about his missing dog. It might be in the barns? I've got to go. *Coming*,' she called.

'This is ridiculous. Why are you saying this? Phone me back,' said Ari brusquely.

'Yes yes, I will. Thank you for calling. In a – minute.'

Ari said nothing.

'OK – OK, darling?' gabbled Cecilia. 'In a minute. Oh *please*, Ari. Please don't go all silent on me. Thank you. A few minutes.'

'This is just stupid. You don't need to talk to him now, whoever he is.'

'I'll – darling. In a few minutes.'

She ran downstairs in bare feet, wincing at the creaks that pursued her, and she and James instinctively moved forward to embrace. He held her; she rested her head on his shoulder and talked in fragments of speech, and they walked through the field, Cecilia glancing with almost metronomic movements at the house and making no attempt to hide her tears.

'I think this will only torment you,' he said eventually.

'Help me,' she said, closing her eyes quickly, looking abruptly to one side.

'I will find this daughter for you if that's what you want,' he said, and he placed his hand on her back and held it there steadily. 'I'll spend the rest of my life doing that if that's what you want, and I'll find her. But I –' He shook his head. He raised his arms.

'. . . it's too late?' said Cecilia.

'That's what I think.'

They were silent, the tumble of river at the end of the field increasingly loud.

'There it is,' he said, turning to the island.

'I know,' said Cecilia, but she moved away from it. They circled the field, picking through tiny streams interspersed by spongy sections of grass.

She caught her breath. 'James, somewhere a girl bears my – our – genes. And the loss that I caused in her. The rejection lying some-where in her.'

He stopped.

'It's likely she was loved and looked after,' he said. 'However you perceived the parents. Or their type.'

'Is it? *Is* it?'

'If people want a child so much . . . They usually – not always – do their best by the child, don't they? She's twenty-three.'

'Well into adulthood. You think it's too late. I keep saying that.' She glanced at the house. She remembered, with vague concern, that she hadn't phoned Ari. 'The investigator I found. And the adoption support agent,' she said dully. 'They both said that without a legitimate birth certificate or known adoptive parents' names, there is no search worth doing. Do you think she wouldn't want to be disturbed now?'

He paused. 'What do you think?'

'She never contacted me.' She felt unobtrusively in her pocket for a tissue. 'She might be too hurt or wounded or angry, and if I found her now I would disturb her life. She could find me, I think, if she wanted to.'

'I have to say that that has occurred to me.'

'Do you think she could?' she said, her delivery more rapid.

'More easily than you could find her. Her – par – adoptive parents would have friends she could ask, I assume, given – who they were. They themselves would possibly be willing to tell her at this age.'

'I think she's chosen not to,' said Cecilia in a monotone.

'It is, well – my conclusion too,' he said, and he drew her towards him. 'But she doesn't know you. It's not you. Don't ever take it personally. Absolutely not.'

'You're kind to me.'

'I think it would be cruel, perhaps – to pursue her.'

Cecilia nodded. 'I just need to know,' she said. She bit her lower lip, hurting herself until the pain brought relief. 'I just need to *know*. I have to know, that's all. Have to know if she was all right. That's all I'm desperate to know. I don't think I'll ever be calm until I know.'

'You must protect yourself. Not hurt yourself so – so brutally. Remember . . . *which cost Ceres all that pain / To seek her through the world.*'

'I told you not to quote at me.'

He paused. 'What happens when your husband's home?' he said lightly.

'He's not my husband. Then I can't reflect, I can't search, I can't pursue Dora like this.'

'You need to stop now,' he said.

Twenty-six

April

T HE FOLLOWING night, Dan threw leaves from the bay tree
outside the house at Izzie's window. Izzie smiled, ran down
along the low-ceilinged passages with steps that still made
her stumble, and let him in through the kitchen door, which Cecilia
now kept locked.

In her bedroom, Dan made a brew of magic mushrooms on his
small stove. He coughed and shook.

'You've got flu,' said Izzie.

'Man flu,' he said dismissively, but he put his arms around her and
rested his head against her shoulder, and she stroked him as though
he were a large animal who softened under her hands.

'You're really huddled over that lame little stove,' she said.

'Well we don't all have an *Aga*,' he drawled.

He wore Izzie's towelling dressing gown unselfconsciously, his legs
knobbly and defenceless beneath it, his body long and shivering.
Izzie glanced at the bottom of the dressing gown from time to time.

'Come to the radiator,' she said. 'I've put it full on even if they're
stingy with heat.'

'It costs a *fortune*,' said Dan in an aristocratic falsetto.

'Shhhh ...' said Izzie, Cecilia audibly walking to the bathroom,
pausing outside her room. 'I think she's in debt or something because
of this house?'

'Your mum is well hot,' he murmured in a growl, raising one
eyebrow.

'Oh gross. You total perv. She really really is not.'

'She is. I'd give her one.'

'Dan!' said Izzie. 'Are you serious?'

He shook with laughter, arching over his stove, then began to cough, his back trembling.

'There's a fit nanny goat on that there hilltop too,' he said. 'Don't worry.' He softened, and kissed her for a long time. 'You're my girl.'

'Why won't you – do it?' said Izzie in a small strained voice. She blushed a fiery red.

He stroked her hair. 'You know I'm not going to run around with a schoolkid. You need protecting from yourself, my girl . . .' He said it solemnly, twisting her hair round his finger.

'I'm sixteen in June.'

'We'll move up your body inch by illegal inch till then.'

'And then?' said Izzie, turning away from him.

'We'll do it as the clock strikes. I'll have your mum first, though. See how you lot go. It must be in the blood.'

She hesitated. 'It isn't though.'

'What?'

'In the blood. I'm adopted,' she said in a quieter voice.

'I forgot that bit. Poor little orphan. Not. Southern softie. You're a milk-fed *princess*!'

'Fuck you –' began Izzie automatically, but she stopped. His eyes had their faint threatening cast to them.

She swallowed. He held her to him, and stroked her.

Cecilia and Ari spent the day engaged in snatched conversations between voicemail messages, their arguments curtailed by Ari's time-table. 'What kind of buffoon is going to believe there was a man outside after midnight looking for his dog when he's already advertised its loss?' he said in incredulous tones in his lunch hour. 'Do you think I'm a total idiot?'

'He was,' persisted Cecilia, now unable to invent an alternative scenario, shame battling with indignation as she temporarily persuaded herself of her story for a show of veracity. She promised

herself, ritualistically and guiltily, not to lie to him again. 'I – I think
he was drunk.'

'Dogs to rescue,' boomed Ari later down the phone.

She laughed, then disarmed him by inventing ever more improbable situations that inspired further merriment, but still he returned
to the subject, and returned again. She shuddered. She bit her lip
between her words.

How are you? James emailed as she talked.

Later, after work and the school run were completed and supper
cleared, she sat by the fire and heard the wind tugging its blackness against the panes, stirring the air into a storm, and she remembered a time she had never fully allowed herself to return to. A time
when she had walked across many miles of countryside at the age of
seventeen.

I drove past the Clapper Inn, he had emailed. *Do you remember it?*

She recalled it very clearly, the logs now radiating idly in the fireplace as they had once in an inn that spring night on the other side
of the moor. She had plotted the visit to the inn, the only time she
had ever known in advance where Mr Dahl would be outside the
school. Even later, in those years when the grief had abated and she
thought about him quite infrequently, the night in the Clapper Inn
on one of the bleakest stretches of the moor towards Princetown,
where the prison was situated, remained unrevised in her mind as a
bright stretch of exaltation.

'The Clapper Inn ... Do you know it?' he had said to her in
Elliott Hall gardens. She had concocted an elaborate tale about staying with Diana at a friend of Diana's, and once there, she had set off
alone with a map. On her own, on foot, the moor seemed a place
of impossible dimensions: tropical, rank, yet desolate enough on its
higher stretches to batter any human who approached it in fog or
storm. Terrible doubt assailed her as she traversed it. Had he been
telling her intentionally? Had he been hinting? Knowing him as
she did, she was certain that he had been. Confusion then hit her
again. She thought of nothing else as she walked those miles, a kind
of madness fuelling her. She wondered and analysed, and finally she

was sure that she could not tolerate it if he had been hinting to her and she had thrown away her opportunity. She would risk all. *No coward soul is mine.*

She could barely find the way when she came to smaller cross-roads, unmarked and leading to farm tracks. Damp air rose as the light fell, and she walked and walked, travelling with a torch through a land of fog and silent sheep, tors jagged on the horizon, her footfall muted and wet, only her own breath thunderous in her ears. She changed torch batteries; she applied deodorant from her bag inter-mittently; she was fluent and sinewed with purpose. It was an eleven-mile journey, she worked out later by obsessive map gazing, though she had walked considerably further by losing her way. He may not be there, she warned herself repeatedly, preparation for disenchant-ment by now automatic. He may be horrified by her arrival. The entire event seemed impossible to believe: one of her more garish fantasies. If he wasn't there, how would she return? She imagined walking back all night in the dark alone. She pictured herself with a broken heart, curling up on the roadside.

I remember it, she emailed him. *Of course.*

He had been there. A storm was beginning, the wind stirring, as she arrived. She had entered the tunnelling porch and emerged into a warren of lintels and panelled half-rooms silhouetted by three fires, her tights mud-splattered, hair scrawled with mist.

He was sitting by the fire in his country clothes: his sepia-coloured trousers, his dark-blue jumper, his face somehow ageless in the fire-light. He was writing. He frowned a little and looked down, paused and wrote. He was to rise at dawn to find the source of the Dart at Cranmere Pool, he had told her. She wanted to run out of the inn, exhaustion coming to her as a blanket. She stood a few feet from him and still he didn't see her. *James*, she could not say. *Mr Dahl*, she could not say.

His bedroom, when they finally went to it, was up a tiny stair-case sealed behind a door. There was a high bed with a wool cover, a Victorian etching of Exeter Cathedral framed on one side, a stained watercolour of bluebells on the other, a window set in a three-foot-thick wall, and an old fire that dreamed in the grate. They stood looking out at the storm over that bleak expanse, at how it tore at the windows, slammed doors below, shrieked and vibrated through a building that stood solidly still.

'I could have been out in that,' she said airily to him. He shuddered quite openly.

She was awkward with him. She didn't know how to touch him, or whether she should. They fitted themselves into the window-sill and watched the storm throw branches, twigs, leaves, as though gazing at a screen, pressed against each other.

Twenty-seven
April

'CECILIA!' CALLED Ari up the stairs. 'Darly!'
'Yes, darly?' she said, and she heard herself and noticed how absurd their old habits seemed.
'Can you come here?'
'Why?'
He paused. 'Because I need to ask you – how this boiler works.'
'It's complicated,' she called down.
'I'm going to put it on the automatic setting.'
'No!' she said. 'It takes for ever to put that back if you get it wrong. Please, Ari,' she called in a sharp tone.
'You have your routines,' he said stiffly.
'What choice have I had?' she sang down the stairs.
She landed in his arms at the bottom with a bump and he hugged her. She pulled away and went to set the boiler.
'Just wait till I come back and I'll sort you all out,' he called in a parody of manliness designed to provoke. She paused, then laughed appropriately, but as she looked around that little series of linked utility rooms, washing still toppling, walls damp with sections crumbling, doors shut against leaks and old lawnmowers, she knew that she liked this independence. It was living and rawness and a fight with elements, and it brought it all back in a rush: the intensity of young life.
'You're . . . a bit wired,' he said.
'I'm not. Please can we not talk about this now?' said Cecilia in an intentionally weary voice.

'You're becoming more remote from me,' he said, appearing outside the door and speaking flatly.

'I'm not,' she said. She paused. 'Well, we don't share a life,' she said. She softened her tone. 'It's that – it's the daily story that bonds people.'

'Does everything have to be a story with you?'

'No,' she said. 'No.' She shook her head. 'I'm sorry.'

'I want us to be us again when I get back,' he said, and she nodded.

'People,' said Ruth to Izzie in the river field by the alders. 'They live in wigwams and tepees. Charles and Carey and Paul, they went to the South Sea Islands, all on their flying bed.'

'Nerdy people in books,' said Izzie.

'But it must be – it must be because you can do those things.'

'What, sis, like finding moving statues and going all gay about bedknobs? I don't *think* so.'

'Oh,' said Ruth quietly. 'Can you help me with my island wigwam?'

'Not now,' groaned Izzie.

'Please. It would be a brilly place to smoke,' said Ruth.

'I suppose,' said Izzie, and she bent down, a cigarette in one hand, and gathered long sticks for building the conical shelter that Ruth had begun on a large flat stone a little further downriver where a section of water ran fast and smooth through the ivy-draped ashes, the surface now bright, now black.

Izzie hopped across from the bank still holding her cigarette, upsetting Ruth's jumping order that prevented the Dart from becoming the Stygian depths. 'Libation,' Ruth mouthed.

'That's lush,' said Izzie, nodding at the wigwam.

Ruth beamed, seeing herself as Bonnie Willoughby skating the river in flying tippets, but she couldn't say it. Instead, she imagined herself floating with her hair fanned like Ophelia, that dark-light painting with river-soaked flowers, because then she could be beautiful.

You count the hours and then the days, Dora advised herself. You tick them off, like a substance abuser, and eventually abstinence becomes a habit.

Would everyone leave her? she wondered. She glanced in the direction of the house. *My daughter will leave me again*, she thought. She summoned the faces of her sons, none of whom had had children. Benedict was largely silent. Barnaby did visit, irregularly, and Tom's cards came roughly fortnightly from his monastery; but she sensed duty behind their actions. No one. That chilled realisation. No one. She wondered whether her punishment was to be stuck in time: to be kept forever frozen at the point at which she had made her greatest mistake.

Her own shortcomings crowded around her now, with their choking wings and stings. She had, she realised, never quite managed to get over both the horror and the perverse excitement of the fact that Elisabeth was a woman. Whereas Elisabeth, it seemed, was blisteringly casual about her own sexuality, uninterested in discussing what she perceived as a perhaps mildly racy yet unsurprising aspect of life: merely nature's pleasing diversity.

'It's dull. Get over it,' Elisabeth had said dismissively. 'Or back to your husband.'

'Do you have no guilt?' Dora had said, trying another tack, shuddering at her own terror of Patrick's discovery. 'Do you ever think you should tell – James?'

'Goodness me, why would I rock the boat?'

Dora now walked stiffly up the stairs, her breast sore as she knocked into the newel post, and she summoned the memory of Moll and Flite: the multi-panelled skirts, mud-choked boots, dog, chickens, but no child. Dora had indulged Moll, talking for hour drifting into hour, because Moll was a woman who, even wet-faced and almost ululating about her childlessness, was prepared to hold the squirming Barnaby. Dora would, at that time, do anything to have Barnaby held. To save her back. To free her arms. To be able to drink a cup of tea without him grabbing and spilling.

'Just give me a sign,' Dora had said to Elisabeth on one of those hot dry summer afternoons.

She had smiled.

'I love you so much.'

'You don't,' said Elisabeth. 'You love this –' She gestured. 'Your house, your family. You are of the moors. I've told you. You are the family woman.'

'I'm not,' Dora said, and even then, before the giving-away, she experienced a twinge, knowing that something in her had been altered. 'Give me – something,' she said, quite choked.

'I'm giving you myself.' Elisabeth smiled again, planted a kiss on her lips, then she began quite easily to talk of something else.

And all the while, the pregnant Cecilia stayed in her bedroom. 'The ghost in the attic,' was how Elisabeth referred to her with casual humour, and Dora defended her, but there was relief in the irreverence. When Cecilia went for walks at night, appearing only as the light fell and the owls emerged, Dora observed that Cecilia seemed to have no fear and it occurred to her that she wished the baby or herself dead. Her days were unchanging. She functioned. She seemed heavy-footed and without expectation.

Ruth made her way through the kitchen door to the river, clinging to the shadow of the hedge. She dared herself. If she were to float, one day, like Ophelia in the ink-dark flower glow, she had to summon all courage. The place was, Cecilia had told Ruth, like *a cavern measureless to man*. Ruth had peeped at her novel, and seen that the river had become a tossing torrent spewing rapids. Horses bared teeth; snakes riddled the water; foam threw mergirl shapes.

Ari returned on Friday. He and Cecilia both frequently said that they missed each other. They emailed several times daily, sent romantic and provocative texts among the practical instructions and day-to-day news bulletins, repeating the message that they wanted each other back and that this period of partial separation was trying and unpleasant. Yet within half an hour of his return that Friday night, they began to argue. Small, unresolved sources of irritation were unleashed by proximity, the romantic haze cast by distance almost instantly dispersed.

'Amazing, isn't it,' said Cecilia, her mouth twitching, 'that within moments of you arriving back, we're bickering. It's all your fault, you old bastard,' she said, thumping him lightly.

He held her wrists in the air and laughed at her, but she could see that tension tightened the tendons of his neck.

'God, you need handling,' he said. 'You've gone more untamed in the sticks.'

'I can handle myself,' she said. She arched her eyebrows at him.

He looked tired. Shadows formed under his eyes, enhancing their extreme darkness; grey was sprinkled through his almost-black hair. For the first time, she noticed a slackening of his neck as he turned. He was still lean, as he had been in his early twenties in Edinburgh, but faintly filled out, a small stomach forming over his belt.

'Your hair's like Action Man's,' she said.

'The barber went a bit overboard last week,' he said, running his palm over one side of his chin, a nervous habit of his.

'I like it. You look sexy,' said Cecilia.

On Monday morning, the verge choked with hawthorn and stitchwort, speedwell shading the trees on the far end of the field, Ari stood in the porch and swept with exaggerated movements. 'This will be my last night here for near on four weeks,' he said in a generic West Country accent. 'So tell me what you want doing, Mrs Bannan.'

'Nothing, nothing,' she said, laughing at him. She kissed him thoroughly; she was connected with him again. He banished the stain that was Mara coming to get her.

They walked along the garden path.

'In four weeks, I'll live with you,' he said.

'Under,' she said.

'Twenty-six days,' he said, frowning. 'How can I leave you for twenty-six days?'

'They'll be the busiest twenty-six days of your life. Packing, marking, sorting your whole department. But I'll miss you.'

'Be good,' he said.

'I am,' she said, and she turned away from him. Swallows soared about them.

'Why,' said Ari after a pause, 'are you working in this archive now?'

'I so much prefer it.'

She had begun to write on her laptop in the small music library built under a slope of roof in Elliott Hall after her morning St Anne's drop-offs. It soothed her to leave home and work in a carrel among industrious music students and occasional visitors who spoke in muted voices to the librarian or searched the music archives.

'Are you escaping your mother?' said Ari with a faintly knowing expression.

'Perhaps,' said Cecilia.

'Are you being kind to her?'

'I'm doing what I can for her. I'm here. She's not the saint you think she is. Not always, anyway.'

'I'm aware of that.' Ari turned. 'And why are you wearing those clothes, darly?'

'Because – because I like to dress up somehow here. I don't know, it's just an instinct. In case by osmosis I start wearing fleeces and wellingtons like a country person.'

'To show all your old friends and enemies how sophisticated you are, you mean?' he said.

She paused. She smiled and took his arm. 'Something like that,' she said. 'A frantic, desperate attempt to show I once left. I wasn't always a country bumpkin.'

'God forbid – a farmer or a hippie, eh?'

'I have to go. I'm late. Romy!' she called.

'Well don't do your mad driving. I wouldn't want you stuck behind me, revving and then storming past, killing sheep.'

'Well I wouldn't want to be stuck behind you, my love,' she said. 'Crawling along as if you're in a cul-de-sac with speed cameras.'

'I suddenly realised,' he said. 'No wonder your London parking ... leaves something to be desired. You've never had to park. Just grind to a halt in a pile of mud or wait till you run out of pink diesel.'

She laughed. 'Your Country Ways talks are very amusing, but I've got to go,' she said.

He caught her round the waist as Romy appeared at the door. 'I've been missing you.'

'Goodbye,' she said, suddenly serious. She kissed his mouth. 'I'll miss you. Three and a bit weeks.'

'Then I'm back for ever!'

'For ever!' she said, and kissed him again, self-consciously.

'What?' he said.

'Nothing,' she said.

' "Nothing",' he said at the same time in imitation, pre-empting her.

She pretended to push him away, smiled at him, hugged him again, and Romy threw herself into his arms to say goodbye.

James Dahl drove along the upper moorland route that he had taken on those rare occasions when he had walked with Cecilia in the past, and now she looked out of his car window: the air-blue gown she had imagined still there somewhere, moving by itself, time-tarnished like silver; and words, words, words, a young mouth, unformed voice, lips kissed, evaporated in the moorland air.

'Did Elisabeth know? Does she know you've been meeting me?' she said now, pushing him. She had written fast in the music library that morning, her deadline so imminent that it caused intermittent insomnia, yet she had slowed her work by frequently glancing out of the window with a loose expectation of seeing James Dahl in the gardens, illogically surprised that he wasn't there. Her mobile had vibrated on silent mode. *I want to take you out to lunch*, he texted.

'Does she know?'

She turned to him and her hair flew into her mouth.

'No,' he said flatly, changing gear and driving fast through the sunken shadowed lanes beyond Holne. Spring charged up, toppled over hedges into choking banks, deranged with growth.

'I still don't understand how this marriage works,' she said. She glanced at him. 'Does she dominate you? Make you behave with coldness and – caprice? Or do you control her with stiffness? With reserve and expectation?'

'Do you really expect me to be able to answer that?'

'I have no idea. I just want to know.' She leaned her head against the side of the car. Ferns rattled against the doors.

'To a certain extent, I suppose we lead parallel lives.' He frowned as he changed gear. He drove, climbing above the steep-sided valley, old ivy clutching at the trees and making a rush of darkness, of bright air.

He stared ahead.

'Is it a matter of opposites?'

'Perhaps.' He paused. 'But perhaps more a matter of expectations. I expected to be married for life, and it would be dishonourable, wrong I suppose, to do otherwise.'

'Yes.'

'I think it's about – determination. Doggedness maybe. Do you think I sound appallingly old-fashioned?' He had to shout above the car's engine.

'No. Did you fall in love with her?'

'Yes. Oh yes.'

There was silence. She bit the inside of her lip. A feeling of the past came back to her, of insecurity and rejection.

'I feel I should explain myself to you more,' he said into the silence. He coughed. 'I've wanted to explain for a while. Since you quite openly believe that I was a heartless old lecher.'

She gave a murmur of a laugh.

'The point is . . . Never in my life did I think such a thing would happen.'

'I can imagine.'

'Really. I knew it was *madness*. You see. Every minute of it. The feeling of insanity surrounding it was overwhelming. It preoccupied me all the time.'

'Did it?' she said, recalling the air denting his shirt as he, this adult man, walked calmly past her without a glance.

'It haunted me daily. I would wake up with nightmares, sweating, heart racing, and think, it can't be true; and I'd go over every room, obsessively, every room I'd – been with you in. There was this empty, all-embracing fear that I'd thrown my life away, for a teenager.'

She nodded.

'And –' he said, frowning as he drove, not catching her eye, 'and yet, despite all that – in its midst – a strand of it seemed like the most exhilarating, extraordinary thing in the world.' He slowed the car to be heard above the engine. 'It seemed like living. And ... fantastically, unwisely, it was as though this had endowed one – me – with a different character. A rash character that I perversely liked. It made me feel young. I know that's not how you saw me,' he said, smiling.

'This isn't how I saw it all.'

She glanced at him, but he wasn't looking at her. All she could see was the shadow of his eyelashes, his strong statue's nose. The light shone through his ear, showing a network of red capillaries. She heard the melody of his voice, its rich pauses and falls.

'Look, James Dahl. I know where we're going now. The Clapper Inn.'

'You can't call me James, can you?'

'No. I must have been pregnant by that time.'

His mouth tensed.

'It was the only time you used a condom.'

She heard a text arriving and checked it.

Hello darl, how everyone, what you doing? wrote Ari.

All fine, not sure re R tho, just having lunch after Rom drop-off, she texted back quickly, and her omission disturbed her. *How work?*

Love xxxx she wrote on a new text as an afterthought.

The road disappeared in front of the car, over fast bowls of land, tors rising in the distances. He parked on a verge. There was the Clapper Inn, huddled on the escarpment and scoured to softness. She stared until she found the window of the bedroom.

'Let's eat there,' he said. He was looking straight up at the inn, his profile older in the afternoon light. A military plane stormed overhead, buzzards circling. He dropped his gaze, then looked at her again and smiled. The lines that had radiated even in his thirties from the bridge of his nose when he smiled appeared now, emitting a flicker of what it was that had once bound her.

'I don't want to,' she said, '– yet.'

'I understand.'

'Yes.'

The window of the bedroom in which they had merged their bodies gleamed blank with afternoon sun, but all those years before, a storm had gathered and thrown itself at the same glass.

They were concealed together in a bedroom in storm gloom with a fire that turned while thunder shook rain horizontally at the window and tiles shattered outside. A tree was flattened, cloud falling through the sky. The bed loomed, a source of awkwardness.

He sat down on the bed, and she sat beside him, and they kissed, and they lay down in one movement and kissed more deeply, moving against each other, their hands gliding beneath clothes, his evening stubble hurting her cheek and his bulk unbalancing the mattress with its soft bulges, causing the bed frame to creak. His palm sent a trail of tight trembles over her torso. They pulled clothes off piece-meal, obstructed by the mattress's squashy dells, until she was entirely unclothed beside him for the first time, and quivering and cold and pressed against him, instinctively hiding her face in his chest. He was quite naked, the hair and weight of him, the density of his thigh against hers, so that she drew in her breath at the shock of skin against skin.

In the chilling air of the room, smoke-streaked by a fire that provided their only light, she could hear the rapid vibration of glass in old wood and she thought, as they moved together, the battering of the wind disguising the creaks and protests of the bed, the fast eddies of air through the window cold against the heat of his breath; she thought that they were out on the moors, fucking in bracken, gorse, lichen as they sailed on their bed of wind.

She imagined kissing him now. He looked up at the inn and she glanced at him on the seat beside her and examined him as though strongly magnified, followed the exact shape of the bone of his nose, his irises' confusion of pigmentation, rendered lighter in sunlight; wayward eyebrow hairs, a faint sheen of moisture on his forehead; the outer line of paleness that traced his lips, the strong cleft above the mouth, the sun-shot curve of his ear and a tiny scar on its outer edge. She could see the twitch of his pulse in his neck. He turned and she blushed, and the notion disappeared.

'I found a poem for you,' he said. 'Emily Dickinson. You'll know it – don't you? *You left me, sweet, two legacies –*'

'Oh yes. And I have one for you too,' she said. '. . . "The Summer Day" by Mary Oliver. It's the ending that moves me. *Tell me, what is it you plan to do / With your one wild and precious life?* Do you know it?'

'No.' He shook his head. 'I like it very much. Can you give me a copy?'

She nodded. They were silent, and the breeze played and ponies toothed at the grass. He turned the ignition.

'I'm glad. I'm so very glad to have found you, met you again.' He paused. 'I miss you,' he said in a straightforward manner.

'When?' she said, out of slight awkwardness.

'When I don't see you,' he said.

'You see me now more than you ever did.'

He began to reverse the car. High clouds ran reflected in the bedroom window of the Clapper Inn.

The girls from the school run were loitering at St Anne's, waiting for their lift. Cecilia walked swiftly towards the sculpture studio, apologising for her delay, but Romy remained inside. Cecilia saw her through one of the tall windows, her ponytail soaked in light, Elisabeth Dahl holding a sculpting tool in her left hand and showing her and another girl a photograph in a book while reading out loud to them. Cecilia absorbed the navy artist's smock smeared in paint, a faintly absurd quasi-turban on her head, the flesh on her face still clinging tightly to the bones, and realised that she looked like a mannequin from a different era, her frame as slight as a child's, though that small body had produced sons who rose in manly height above her. She should somehow, thought Cecilia, have had daughters.

When she emerged, Elisabeth merely nodded at Cecilia; Romy smiled while still talking, and Cecilia found herself awkwardly following, as she once might have done, right there near the drive. She would not have it.

'We have to go now,' she said in a clear voice, and Elisabeth paused for a fraction of a beat, then inclined her head.

'Why are you late?' said Romy with a frown in the car.

'I had to drive somewhere. The garage,' said Cecilia, colouring, and when she spoke to Ari later, she assented to his assumption that she had worked as she waited.

She snapped at him, in guilt.

Ari snorted. 'Don't do that to me,' he said. 'This isn't good, all this separation.'

'I know, I know. Sorry,' said Cecilia, and her lip wobbled. 'I know.' She caught her breath. 'I think you need to come back to me,' she said. Her voice sounded vulnerable.

'It's only weeks now.'

Twenty-eight
May

THAT NIGHT, the first of Ari's longer absence, Cecilia heard the voice of Dan along the passage. She tugged open her bedroom door with a violent movement, then stopped, turned, and ran back to ring Ari.

His voicemail came on.

'Oh!' she said in distress. 'Where are you? Fuck shit you're not there. There's that man in the house again – Izzie's man. He's – he's much older. Look, look – this is the one thing I *can't* deal with without you. Ring me as soon as you get this. Love.'

She heard Dan's voice at full volume again, walked rapidly from her bedroom with bare feet and caught sight of his back disappearing towards the stairs.

'You!' she shouted. She tripped on the landing step in her haste. Izzie stood slack-mouthed in a long T-shirt just outside her bedroom. Cecilia ran towards Dan, catching his shoulder with her hand at the top of the stairs and absorbing his sweet-musty odour in proximity. Beneath the light, she saw details of tendon and hair on the back of his neck, skin that was palpably rougher and dirtier than her daughter's. She thumped him, awkwardly glancing the side of his shoulder blade and hurting her own knuckles without hitting him as hard as she had initially intended, detecting in that tiny interim some vulnerability or human appeal that curbed her. 'Get out,' she hissed.

'Bitch,' he said with force as he turned and looked directly at her.

There was a sideways sliding of faint implication in his holding of her gaze, the corner of his mouth tilted.

She paused for a fraction of a second.

'Get out!' She pushed him, shocked yet invigorated; he stumbled at the top of the stairs mid-escape and ran, light-footed, down the steps two at a time.

'What were you doing outside, scaring us?' she called after him, her voice breaking up, but he had left.

Dora couldn't sleep. She didn't sleep.

The dawn seeped scented with dog roses and damp grass and she yawned through the film of nausea of an unslept night, thought of Elisabeth, and put her away. The emptiness was almost unbearable.

She lay in bed and dozed, thick dribble on her pillow.

'I don't think I can do this,' she murmured through the window to an unhearing Katya, who had arrived early and was gardening, and she dressed and gathered a shawl around her, drove slowly to Widecombe and waited for a café to open and sat with her chin in her hand and a newspaper unread, observing the first tourists, watching the jumping children who were like lambs to her and remembering. When she returned to the cottage through her tangled arch of honeysuckle whose beauty only saddened her, there was a risotto sitting on the doorstep. There was no note, though she searched, but she instantly recognised the pan as one of Elisabeth's from Cadiz.

'Elisabeth,' Dora murmured.

Should she throw it away or use it? What, she wondered, were the rules of her attempted exile from her half-life with Elisabeth? She barely knew the answers. She microwaved a portion and ate it. She put Bach's *Magnificat* on the record player, an anachronism that caused amusement in Romy and Ruth and professed admiration from Izzie. She had managed weeks away from Elisabeth, a cruel and grinding apprenticeship; an experiment in a different form of pain. The jasmine that grew in a too-small pot outside the front door was turning rank and spreading a strange scent, of urine or of old Chinese takeaway, through the house. She counted off each day in her head with a sickened sense of accomplishment and went to bed early to foil the temptation of the evening.

The voices in the *Magnificat* merged and rose; Thérèse Ráquin experienced passion in an attic with her lover; an O'Keeffe reproduction that Elisabeth had given her glowed, picked out by a shaft of sunlight in the shadows beside the fireplace, and she could have her, Dora realised. Her hand trembled. She could have her. *I can have Elisabeth*, Dora thought, tears pricking her eyes. *I can be with my lover.* She is a joy, an extraordinary thing, a one-off in this world, she thought in a rush. Why should I deprive myself of that? Why am I doing this? Relief tumbled into excitement. She put her hand on the phone receiver, violently trembling. It was a revelation. She put down the phone. She picked it up again, her mind ricocheting. She started to press the buttons. Her heart hammered. She slammed it down. The devil was talking to her. She saw him glowing close to her ear with his scarlet-forked temptations. She swayed. It was addiction speaking. She lowered her head into her hands and gripped her scalp, pressing it harder and harder with her fingertips.

Ruth watched Izzie slipping through the garden and on to the field above the pond at dusk where the hawthorn clouded. Izzie loved him now, that man, more than she loved her, just as their mother loved Izzie the fairy child she had found the most: most most most because she hadn't grown in her tummy and that had to be made better for ever. After Izzie, she was a runt, a mute, a wriggly cadpig like in the novels her mother read to her. Her mother told her in half-sleep that she loved her when she wasn't supposed to be listening, but she knew that a different daughter would have been a better daughter. Someone like Sara Crewe or Laura Ingalls. She prayed to the ceiling that her parents would never die.

Izzie met Dan in the grass where wild poppies grew, and he murmured into her ear. He had brought a tape measure and, laughing so much that he and Izzie rolled around on the field together joined in mirth, he measured her body, and swiftly drew an outline of it with calculations on paper, working out how many days were left until her birthday and sketching plans with arrows of intent on his diagram.

'Are you having an affair?' said Ari with husky, freshly woken abruptness the next morning as Cecilia picked up the phone.

'God, Ari! Of course not!'

'Really?'

'*Yes!*'

'Well I . . . detect . . . there's some kind of unhealthy obsession.'

'Do you?' said Cecilia. 'Don't be silly, my darly.'

She lay back in bed for the few warm minutes available before Ruth ran in carrying her clothes, thrushes and blackbirds sang through the open window, and she was back at the Clapper Inn, where the weather had been quite different, and her body much younger, and her mind barely her own. He had kissed her deeply there, as rain heaved by wind was pitched against panes, and murmured words of love that she had never heard before, and in their unprecedented leisure, he lingered.

In his half-sleep afterwards, he was seemingly bothered by guilt, moaning little questions to her in mutters and sudden twitchings. He woke with a jolt and gazed at her. 'Shh shh,' she said and they kissed, their lips sticking together, and he moved his hand over her and caressed her until she juddered in sharp pain and sharp pleasure, and only then did she sleep, in that last partial hour before dawn, and he had to wake her through her thick drowsiness, through the dawning consciousness of his lips on hers, into a cold room.

She rose now as Ruth came scuttling in, and nervously changed her clothes several times the moment Ruth had left for the kitchen. Once Romy was dropped off, she wrote in the music archive with clouds clinging to the cedars across the lawns below, and then read what she had written with a fuzzy dissociation, the memory or anticipation of him swimming over her words so that she drifted and wasted time. When she heard his footsteps, slotting them into a sense of recognition in her desire that they should be his, she continued writing as she once would have done as a teenager, then resisted her own behaviour and stood and raised one eyebrow.

He put his hand on her shoulder. 'Let's go out somewhere different,' he said in a low voice as they walked outside the room. 'I've got my deputy to cover my next class.'

'I need to work,' she said automatically.

'Have life outside this too,' he said calmly. 'Writing's not living. I can meet you some lunchtimes. Or other free periods.'

'Aren't you catching up with – preparation – then?'

He shrugged. 'I talk to you in my head every day.'

'I do –' she said, but she stopped.

'You're not angry with me any more?' he said as they walked downstairs, his feet drumming loudly on the wooden steps.

She shook her head. 'No. Or yes, yes, always. A bit of me. But I forgive you now.'

'Then we can be friends.'

They stood in the entrance of Elliott Hall in grey brightness. She laughed. Blossom shivered against the sky's glare. She was glad she had worn the skirt she had chosen. She could only deal with him in certain clothes.

'We are friends,' she said.

'I'm always prepared – steeled – for you to turn round and suddenly –'

'Look, the sky is full of rain about to fall.'

'– feel a vigorous need to defend yourself. A desire to punish me for the past.'

'I have. I've done that. A line has been drawn under it,' said Cecilia. 'You want more?' She smiled at him.

They huddled together in the porch where the air was close and smelled of grass clippings and the walls had taken on a slatey darkness. Petals trembled. Large raindrops began to fall and flatten in explosions on the steps in front of them.

'Let's sprint to the tree there, then we're halfway to the car,' he said, shouting above the rain and grabbing her hand and running so that she stumbled a little on the step. They stood below a cherry tree breathing fast and the rain slid over the blossom in a perfumed fall about them and dripped in fatter strands on their heads.

'My hair is soaking,' she said.

He looked. 'It reminds me of when you were younger and it was curlier,' he said.

'Would you like that?'

'No. Of course not,' he said. 'I find you more beautiful now.'

'Oh –'

The rain churned earth into puddles and splashed up against their ankles, blossom weighting branches like snow clumps in the green shadows. The world beyond the tree seemed to have disappeared behind a curtain of falling water, but a young woman of about Mara's age passed them in a dark blur through the rain and smiled directly at Cecilia, and Cecilia turned her head in a billow of irrational hope as the girl passed and went on walking towards the hall.

She watched her back. She was silent.

'Oh Cecilia,' he said. 'You're crying.'

'I'm not.'

He cradled her in his arms. Their breath rose as steam. He kissed the top of her head.

'Sorry,' she said. 'Something – set it off.' He stroked her. 'She was warm,' she said into his shoulder. 'After they bathed her. I just lay there.'

'You'd just given birth.' His shirt clung darkly to his shoulder blade.

'And now . . . Do I keep on battering my mother, even though her cancer may return? . . .'

'Leave it, Cecilia. Or keep her with me. We will always – *always* – talk about her.'

'Yes,' said Cecilia and tears spread into cool rain on her cheeks. People ran from cars emitting muffled laughter, cries barely audible behind the downpour.

He put his arm on her back. 'I'll talk to Dora,' he said. 'I'll see how much she will tell me.'

'What!' said Cecilia, jolting her head up. 'She – you can't do that. She doesn't know. Elisabeth – Good God. You could lose your job even now?'

'I don't care,' he said, shrugging. 'I'm happy to talk to her. I can drive there right now. The sixth form can wait!'

'Oh no no. Thank you. No, I don't want – I want you to be safe. I want to protect you.'

'It doesn't matter.'

'It does to me. You won't get more out of her. I begin to think she really doesn't *know* where those fuckwits are. There's not much she's hiding.'

Petals tumbled and stuck to her skin. She lifted her hand and smelled them, wanted to eat them. The cleanness of him rose to her nose, the subtle laundered-shirt scent of him, his freshly bathed old-fashionedness. His eyelashes were wet.

More cars arrived in the car park, their wipers frenetic. Blossom fell in sopping clumps on to the gravel.

'Let's make a run for it,' he said.

'No.' She shook her head. Rain trickled over her eyebrows and into her eyes. She licked it. She could hear only his breath and the sheets of rain.

'I have to kiss you,' he said suddenly, and he leaned over and kissed her, his mouth warm against the chill of the wet air.

'My little chickadee,' said Dan, lazily stroking Izzie. 'No – not yet.' He scrabbled in his pocket, tipped back his head and swallowed a beta-blocker, and kissed her lingeringly. He smiled down at her, then he scrambled up, and went to the window, watching the arrival of Cecilia and Romy below through the rain.

'Is it my sister you fancy?' said Izzie suspiciously. The downpour was noisy on the thatch.

'No,' he said, laughing and giving her a wide kiss on the mouth, his nose knocking into her cheek. 'Wait your time.'

'You're cold,' said Izzie, touching his hand.

'I'm always an ice block,' said Dan, and he curled up against her, embracing her, holding her so that her back was pressed hard against his torso, and she felt his shakes and tremors against her skin.

★　　★　　★

I return a kissed woman, Cecilia thought in bemusement. She drove back through hedgerows and hawthorn that toppled and tangled with rank growth, arrived light-headed at the house and regathered her expression. Her lips had been kissed, illicitly. She felt disbelief. Did it show, unfaithful kissing? How did it change one? She glanced at Romy and Izzie, but all seemed ominously normal. She went to the bathroom to look at herself in the mirror in silence without Ruth's presence. She gazed at her own face. In almost twenty years, she had never kissed anyone but Ari. She contemplated her kissed mouth and she seemed to sleepwalk into the kitchen to arrange supper for her daughters.

The phone rang. A plunge of dismay hit her at the thought of Ari calling, of the simple fact of speaking to him with a mouth that had kissed someone else's, and she banged her hand on the sideboard in her agitation, but the call was for Izzie, and she floated, both dazed and hyper-alert, through the evening, the flavour of being seventeen, and kissed and incredulous, returning to her.

It came true, she thought now of her longing followed by her affair with him, the concept like a slide of mercury inside her all those years later.

Dora pondered over the tension that hung like a forcefield between the cottage and the house. She stood for a few minutes, her mouth pursed, then she began to write Cecilia a note. She wrote three lines and surveyed the stilted sentences that Cecilia might despise for their lack of grace, then she read some more of *Thérèse Raquin* in front of the fire, finding, these days, that she craved the cloying torture of romantic entanglements, wallowing in the mistakes and disastrous exultations of someone else's love life to take her away from her own.

But there were limits to how far she could be distracted. She put her head in her hands. She could only remember, and justify.

'Where's my baby?' Cecilia had said at the age of nineteen, the voice of the gentle daughter vicious.

It had taken Cecilia nine months to turn into a hellcat, a spitting creature denuded of her child. Only then did Dora, in trepidation, contact the adopting parents; but they had gone, they had already taken off, living outside the system with no National Insurance numbers, no property owned and no benefits claimed. Various travellers had assured her they would track them down at the fairs and in the lanes and on the fringes of a loosely formed society on which they collided – she had something belonging to them that she must urgently give them, she said – but they were elusive. They had gone to Wales, then Ireland; they had returned to Wales; they had disappeared.

The lies had started at the beginning. Oh, what a tangled web we weave ... Dora had let the words snake through her mind again and again down the years, cringing at her own use of cliché. The lies escalated, in desperation, out of necessity. A month after Cecilia's fury had emerged, Dora had found a private investigator through contacts of friends of Beatrice's in London. She had blundered into the process barely considering the legal ramifications, assuming that names would provide sufficient information; but once the questions started – her own rapid fudging in response, her ability to lie increasingly easily first shocking her, then shaking her and eventually hardening her – she scarcely knew any more which was the truth and which was her invented version of events. The detective had quite palpably been aware of omissions and distortions, but he could extract nothing more from her, and in panic, Dora had paid the bill for the entire, truncated search out of a cobbled-together loan from her in-laws, and hastily withdrawn before the travesty could progress. It was only over the years, with her slowly growing awareness of what she had done, that she realised that a missing person inquiry could have been instigated at that point.

Dora groaned now, into her hands. 'Celie,' she murmured. 'I'm sorry.'

Twenty-nine

May

THE NEXT afternoon, Dora saw Dan appear in the kitchen yard of Wind Tor House. She had glimpsed him more frequently in the last few days as he slipped in among the shadows by the back gate at night with a strained vigour that tensed his shoulders while his movements had the grace in nervousness of an overgrown adolescent. Now he was clearly waiting for Izzie to arrive home from school on the bus ahead of Cecilia and Romy in the car, bending over and coughing.

Dora almost ran out of the front door. Wild garlic pulsed through the air, making her breathe through her mouth. She longed for company, she always realised when someone appeared: Katya, a neighbour, above all a granddaughter. She couldn't think what to say to a young man who seemed so guarded and self-contained. 'Are you unwell?' she called through the gate to the yard, where he was cutting logs.

'A few sniffles,' he said in a strange high voice, and she wondered whether he was mocking her. He chopped wood with flimsy movements.

'Are you making a fire in this weather?' said Dora.

'I'm freezing my —' He stopped himself with theatrical exaggeration. ''Scusin' me, ma'am,' he said in his parodic Devon accent.

Dora's mouth twitched. 'You can sit by my Rayburn,' she said. 'And I'm cooking soup.'

He unbent to his full height. He hesitated.

'It's quite *warm* today. You must have a terrible temperature. Your name's Dan, isn't it?'

He nodded, his shivering subsiding a little. Dora nudged the kitchen door back in place.

'Let me get you a lemon and honey.'

'This needs bay leaves,' Dan said, leaning heavily against the Rayburn and stirring Dora's soup. 'Pinch of thyme. There's plenty of other things growing out there you could add to this.'

'What?'

'Oh. Nettles. Wood sorrel. Germander. Garlic leaves.'

'Well how fascinating,' said Dora approvingly. 'We used to eat these things, or think we did – at least we bought books about it!'

He said nothing. She detected the edge of sarcasm in his expression.

'So,' she said, caught awkwardly and floundering for something to say. 'You're Izzie's boyfriend?'

'I'm her friend,' he said shortly. 'She should be doing her schoolwork.'

'Oh,' said Dora. 'Yes, I agree. She's a wild spirit, our Izzie.'

'Not as wild as she thinks.'

'Oh,' said Dora again. 'You are an outspoken young man,' she said somewhat testily. She paused. 'Where do you come from?'

'Last place was Doncaster.'

'I can hear some northern.'

'Ay,' he said. 'Coal pits. Whippets. Incest.'

Dora smiled uncertainly. 'So what finds you – here?'

'I only ever wanted to be here,' he said, still in a convincing northern accent. 'I heard about it, always wanted to come 'ere,' he said, now switching back to broad West Country. 'My dad took me here once when I was thirteen, like, and proper job I thought it was. Dark day I rememory, 'em bleak great moors spreading out, ooh argh.'

He dropped his gaze. He looked cold and unwell. There was something endearing about his narrow back, Dora thought.

'Would you like a jersey or a blanket?'

'No ta, ma'am.'

'And what have you been doing recently? I see your garden centre van.'

'Making shoes,' he said.

'Really? How fascinating.'

'Any pillock can do it,' he said, banging the spoon on the edge of the pan. 'Easy. Shoot a cow, skin it, tan its hide, sew it together with brightly coloured thread.'

'I am not sure when you're mocking me,' said Dora carefully.

'I don't know myself,' said Dan cheerfully in his Devon accent.

'Don't you – didn't you – want to go to university?'

He raised his shoulders stiffly so that he looked long-armed and large-handed, stirring the soup again. 'I did a couple of terms. Couldn't afford it.'

'I suppose that is the case these days,' she said. 'When my children – they got student grants. Though only one of them went,' she said slightly ruefully. 'What date is it?' she said, looking at her calendar and changing the subject. 'I'm glad to say my son-in-law is about to come back.'

'Where's he been? Out shagging his students?' he said.

Dora said nothing.

He gazed straight at her. 'I wouldn't stray if I had that at home.'

Dora paused. 'I think I'm going to go and do some filing now,' she said. 'You can sit on this chair if you wish to. I think the others will be back soon.'

'I'll pep up this here soup, ma'am, and then I'll be off,' he said.

Dora opened the door, turned round and glanced at the back of his head with its random, flopping spikes of hair as she started to walk upstairs. She noticed the dull sheen of the telephone as she went, the fact that it hadn't rung.

'I'll have you as the clock strikes midnight,' said Dan to Izzie in her bedroom. He absent-mindedly moved his fingers in a soundless clicking movement and gazed around the room until he seemed to become aware of his own lack of focus and turned and smiled at her, his eyes crinkling.

'I was born in Israel,' said Izzie. She lay back. 'Is it, like, midday there or something?'

'It'll be a couple of hours ahead,' he said. 'Find out for me, and I'll do something to you every minute between midnight there and here,' he said, spreading rapid kisses with little suction movements over her body until she laughed, uncertainly.

'Nothing else happening here,' she said. 'I look forward to it.'

'Bored, are you, my brat?'

'Yes.'

'You don't know you're born. Just a pretty little spoilt sap who wants adventures. You've got a fucking girt great roof over your head,' he said, suddenly stroking her hair back from her brow. 'You've got a family that thinks that the world revolves around you.' He paced back to the window, and threw a beta-blocker at his mouth with a swiping movement.

Izzie winced. 'You look like you're hitting yourself.'

'I'm going.'

'Don't go now!'

'I'm off.'

'No don't,' implored Izzie.

'Why not?' he said, hesitating.

'Because Mum might see you.'

'*Mum might see me*,' he said in imitation. 'Mum might see me and kick me up the arse for laying a hand on Princess. I'm going.'

He left the room, walked through the house with his usual silent lope, and opened the door. 'Stop!' shouted Cecilia from her bedroom window. 'Not again, not again,' she groaned.

Dan slipped through the front gate, a tall streak darting past the garden wall. He turned slightly, ran, keeping close to the wall, and disappeared beneath the tumble of foxgloves at the end.

'Get out of here,' she called, hurting her throat. Rage seemed to grip her scalp. She felt as though she were shouting at a dog.

'I'm going,' he said contemptuously, re-emerging and staring up at her through the darkness near the gate.

'I think you *want* to be seen by me!' shouted Cecilia.

'Shhh!' said Romy, running into the bedroom.

'You've come out of the front gate when you could go through the *back*,' called Cecilia in a garbled shout, leaning out of the window. 'You're just rubbing my nose in it.'

'I could rub your snooty nose in worse,' he said.

'Get away and stay away,' said Cecilia. 'Or I'll call the police.'

He snorted with laughter. 'And they'll come down the lanes sirens a-blaring to handcuff your brat's man friend, will they?' He disappeared round the corner of the lane.

Cecilia cursed. She put her arm round Romy's shoulder and swiftly murmured reassurances to her as she ran along the passage to Izzie's room.

'Izzie!' she called. She rattled at her door until it was opened. 'This has got to stop! You are fifteen!' she said in a rush. 'You cannot have an affair. Must not. Can't. It will wreck your life.'

'Chill, Mum!' exclaimed Izzie.

'If you're going to do this, I'm going to have to give you contraception *now*,' said Cecilia rapidly. She shrugged with a defeated gesture. She was pale-faced. 'That is not permission to do it.'

'I told you,' said Izzie dully. 'He won't shag me.'

Cecilia paused. 'Good. But we don't know how long that will last. Is that true? I'm going to put some bloody condoms in your room. I'm not encouraging you. But don't get pregnant, don't – don't get diseases. Don't get pregnant. You know that you could, don't you?'

'Duh,' said Izzie.

Cecilia shut the door abruptly.

There was more time by the river now that the weather was warmer and bird-strewn. Cuckoo pints grew, herb robert, bacon-and-eggs; celandines marked the way in scattered ghee, thought Ruth. Ram Das had never transformed her bedroom, but the living world was outside, and she could eat wild strawberries now from the hedgerows. She went to a hidey-place of coppiced hazel and dawdled and she was happy; Ophelia was in the water, and the water was black. It gleamed black, green, white, black through the trees. Ruthelia, she thought. I am Ruthelia, Rothelia, Rophelia. It sat on her tongue and almost choked her, autochthonous Ruthelia, and the damselflies pressed bubbles into the surface.

Thirty
June

'Y OU DON'T answer my calls,' said Ari, a recent repeated
theme.

'I do,' said Cecilia, her pulse speeding. 'When do I not?
When don't I?' She caught sight of her reflection in the window
and saw that she had coloured, and tensed her fingers against the
phone.

'Not for hours. And I texted you today – at lunch. You didn't
answer for a couple of hours.'

'There's not always reception. I told you.'

'Well Romy texts me from school. You work right near.'

'I'm trying to work hard. To finish,' said Cecilia. Shame hit her,
followed by rapidly manufactured indignation. Thistledown drifted
past her. She grabbed at it. 'My deadline is just a few weeks.'

'You text less.'

'Don't be a moron,' said Cecilia in affectionate tones, although guilt
seemed to filter through her and crystallise in her head. 'Sweetheart,'
she said after too big a pause.

Later in bed when the darkness smelled for the first time of
summer nights, of cuckoo spit and grass dew, and her guilt was
stifled by surges of irrational excitement, she had a certainty, almost
a knowledge, that she would see James Dahl almost daily until Ari
came home. She knew that she needed to carry on with that cease-
less, time-travelling talk, that sharing of blame, the first halving or
unburdening in her adult life.

In the day, she wrote in a kind of semi-productive trance, only her deadline fuelling her, sensing, time and time again, the shoulder tapped before it was. She wanted him there. She refused to want him. She couldn't stop thinking about the astonishing fact that he had kissed her. It brought it back: the Clapper Inn, embraces in hidden corners, his mouth moving against hers, exhilaration overriding caution. In a daze, she wrote of brooks, haystacks, secret passages through the meadows. The children's hunting buzzard circled while they searched for their mother, and they encountered wolves, found-lings, slips in time. Always in Cecilia's mind, a baby hidden in a basket appeared in the depths of the story, bobbing, almost swept away in the dark-reeded waters like Tom the water baby. She inserted it; she excised it; she reinstated it; she deleted it again, wracked with superstition.

He would arrive at varying times, postponing all work that could possibly be completed in the evening, and in the short time carved out, with challenge and ingenuity in the devising, they found differ-ent places to go, sitting on banks and bridges and hollows as the late spring turned to summer.

In a boat, a sharp breeze scudding across the water, he said, 'I always wanted to do this with you.'

'We are doing it now. Now is now.'

They took a trip to Danver Sands, almost unfeasible in the lunch hour, merely to glimpse the sea.

'You are taking me away from my work,' she said.

'I'm sorry,' he said.

'I'll make it up in the evening,' she said, and she wrote at night, but through a filter of distraction, finding sand in her sleeves.

On Tuesdays and Fridays he had a free period after lunch, and they drove fast to the moor and lay on sprung prickling ground and followed the clouds racing, the meadow pipits and the skylarks ascending and he teased her and called her a blithe Spirit and she called him a star of Heaven, and she lay on his arm on purple moor grass, and sometimes they looked at each other straight in the eyes for seconds, heard the insects crackling by their ears, the rush of sap, the leaves, the mosses, and she knew that they would kiss if she leaned very slightly towards him. She almost moaned to herself, made herself look at the buzzards circling in the sky to resist kissing, and then let it happen in her fantasies later instead. The days soaked into one another in a green blur of time; she was very young again: she remembered it, he brought that back to her.

'How can you get away with this?' she said as they wandered through the moss of Becka Falls.

'I cut down my teaching hours – to live. What a non-life it would be confined to a classroom.'

Ari texted more frequently or rang unexpectedly, and despite her former resolve, she continued to answer him with semi-lies in the form of omissions and evasions; or to ignore his calls but to text him more vigilantly, implying that she was in the archive where she couldn't speak. She began to create fabrications more instantly and easily, the damage already done, while clinging to some superstitious understanding that this would be limited – a finite holiday, a self-indulgence – and she would pay penance, or absorb it, with time, seamlessly into their lives. Remorse flared up when she least expected it.

'Come out with me in the evening,' he said.

'What?' she said. She paused. 'How?'

'Why not?'

'I can't,' she said.

And she realised that with no Ari at home, she could meet him during an evening with Romy supervising. So she lied to her girls and to her mother. She was seeing Diana, she said: Diana was in Devon. She went to dinner with James Dahl, her one-time lover, for the first time in her life.

She was learning. Since her moment of clarity and the promise to herself that accompanied it, Dora was learning to live with gut-tightening emptiness, her resolve punctuated with seethes of outrage that Elisabeth did not defy her by contacting her, and at weaker moments she moaned audibly with an appalled sense of desertion. The loss of hope was what gradually came to her. A glimpse, a glimpse only, of comfort that she had chosen the better option. That she could, after all, manage this and survive. It had to become a habit. A lesser life, a better life.

A car stopped outside on the lane; the gate to Wind Tor Cottage opened, the honeysuckle shaking, and Elisabeth Dahl walked across the garden. She stopped, even today, to bend and examine some campions that had seeded themselves, and she appeared to be absorbed in the scents of flowers as she wandered up the path. She was like a mirage, but the apparition was sharply outlined and over-vivid.

Relief and excitement tumbled through Dora. She wanted to cry. She hardened herself.

'Hello,' she said uncertainly. She glanced at her watch. It was almost five o'clock.

'Hello, darling,' said Elisabeth, and kissed Dora on the cheek, then pulled her into a hug.

'Come in,' said Dora, without meaning to say it.

'How are you?' said Elisabeth, openly surveying the cottage.

Dora cursed the habitual mess, the jars of old flower water, the spots of shadiness and nests of unexamined clutter. Only now did her eye land on dead flies from the previous year on the window frame, on a mousetrap just visible beneath the crockery cupboard, on piles of seed catalogues, hoarded bags, newspaper cuttings, reading glasses and post-surgery exercise sheets. In truly not expecting Elisabeth, she was unprepared. She ran a hand through her hair. She searched ineffectually for wine that might suit Elisabeth's exacting tastes. Then she stood up abruptly. She took in a deep breath that seemed to hurt her chest with tiny barbs.

'I asked you not to come here,' she said.

'You didn't.'

'I did.'

'I don't recall this.'

'As good as. I asked you not to call.'

'And I believe I haven't. I'm here instead. I was on the moor. I thought I would see you.'

'Well —' Dora held her hands up. She walked to the door, opened it, went out into the garden with its settling light. Her shadow was alarmingly elongated on the grass; death's companion. She looked up at the tor and Elisabeth lifted her head in an echoing gesture. Romy was in a field below, a flare of hair against the green.

'She looks like her mother at that age,' said Elisabeth.

'Do you even remember her mother at that age?' said Dora sharply.

'Of course,' said Elisabeth after a slight hesitation.

'Because I am realising that what happened to her at that age has halfway wrecked her life.'

'What do you mean?' said Elisabeth, her features barely moving as she spoke, her eyes occluded, still trained on the tor.

'You know what I mean,' said Dora.

There was silence. Dora habitually broke such silences. The silence continued. Dora said nothing.

'What is the point of unearthing *this*?' said Elisabeth eventually. She was visibly ruffled.

'Because it has become clearer to me, the mistake.'

The air was restless, blowy in sudden gusts. They stood in silence.

'I don't need you here,' said Dora. 'I don't *want* you here. I need to do this now.'

'Oh Dora,' said Elisabeth, and pulled her to her and held her for a long time, running her hand from her brow and kissing her head. The breeze lifted their hair.

'You know it's — it's — let alone others' lives — it's — it's pretty much wrecked my life,' said Dora clearly into Elisabeth's chest, breathing in that remarkable individual scent. She felt paralysed by it. 'That's an exaggeration, but it's also not.'

'What has?'

'What what?'

'What has wrecked your life?'

'You really don't know?'

'Me? You mean me?' said Elisabeth, raising her eyebrows, her mouth twitching. She sounded humbled, or vulnerable.

'No. Well yes, that too. But I blame no one but myself for that. That has been my choice; my …' she trembled '… failing.'

Elisabeth was motionless.

'It's the other … this other …' Dora stumbled over her words. 'The fact of not keeping Celie's baby. It was a monumental mistake.'

'Don't be ridiculous!' said Elisabeth. 'Good God. Isn't that all buried and past? It must be what – I have no idea. A good twenty, twenty-five years. She has three others!'

'It was a catastrophic mistake. This is what has become clear to me.'

'Oh of course it was not a mistake to give a decent home to the child of a child! Good lord, the house was overrun with babies. What did you want to do? Set up a nursing home? Drown in nappies? *You* would have been left with that baby. Yet another baby. Don't indulge your delusions, Dora.'

'You really don't understand,' said Dora, hearing Cecilia's own phrases coming to the fore. 'You don't understand at all, do you?'

'I don't think I do.'

'Well you should,' said Dora in a strangled voice.

'And why is that?'

'I did it for you,' said Dora.

'Me –' said Elisabeth. 'You did it for me?' Her eyebrows shot into a disdainful arch. 'Don't be utterly ridiculous.'

'I did,' said Dora, beginning to cry.

'It was your decision, your –' Elisabeth said with icy distance '– family's. I made no demands. Nor could I have.'

' "I loathe babies, especially of the male variety" was how you greeted Barnaby's birth,' said Dora.

'And?'

'I've never told anyone,' said Dora steadily. 'I've never told anyone. I can barely tell myself … But I did this because of you.'

'Don't be ridiculous.'

'I did. It was my weakness. I take all responsibility of course. No one made me do anything, but I· did it for you, because I loved you so much. And yes, I was very worried that it would be too much for

Celie. But ... really, it was that I wanted you so much. I wanted to be with you. Nothing else.'

'Oh Dora, I cannot believe you would say –'

'Don't you remember all the things you said about babies? As though you'd never had one yourself. "*Boy babies are the worst.*" Mother of sons. There was poor snotty Barnaby. You were vile to him.'

'You didn't want that child either.'

'I know, I know,' said Dora in a half-wail. 'But I loved him. I suffered for him but I loved him. And ... I wanted him once he was there, of course. But I wanted you. You, *you*.'

'This is irrelevant now.'

'It's all I can think of.'

Elisabeth raised one eyebrow.

'That, and you. Which is an awful – sinful – waste of time.'

Elisabeth said nothing, a flicker of pain passing her eyes, but she drew Dora into her arms again. She was motherly and caring; she was wearing her perfume; her strokes, skimming and kneading over Dora's back and shoulders, were firm and comforting. She held her against skin warmth in a shelter of intimacy. Dora felt, at that moment, that she could die from having wanted this so much.

'I thought you would leave with me and we'd be together,' said Dora. 'It's shameful to admit. But – I don't care what I tell you now, really. Everything you said indicated that. Didn't it? All those plans we made.'

Elisabeth gazed at the horizon as though remembering, or denying.

This was my world, thought Dora. Into that, that child-friendly world, a baby came and went.

The baby had grown upstairs. Its mother stayed up there in hibernation. It was fed: a slow, sweet feeding like a spider dopey in its web. Speedy had gone by that time. Patrick was shocked into near-silence, yet love for his only daughter who adored him underlay his deep disapproval, and he and Cecilia would hug without speech for minutes on end while he continued to ignore the pregnancy and never once asked about the baby. He absorbed Dora's assurances that the matter was in hand with the passive acceptance that was increasingly his recourse. Dora watched the baby bump's progression through the late summer and autumn with exhausted dread while lodgers detained her, children required feeding, and Barnaby's demands began at dawn.

There was one incident that settled it, a routine accident that made the decision slot into place like a seal over a hatch. It had all been creeping towards a conclusion for some time, the tentative discussions becoming more frequent, their patina of pure fantasy now taking on a tangible reality. The childless couple, considerate and desperate, waited at the back of the garden. That morning, at breakfast, the tray of Aga ashes was over-filling. Benedict had occasionally emptied it; Patrick usually forgot; Cecilia could no longer be relied upon. An excess had built up at the back and Dora had to kick the Aga door hard to secure it over the container's front, attempting to crash it into place. Strong kicks no longer worked. Growling, Dora started to empty the tray, but hot ashes spewed out on to the floor, and Barnaby, grizzly with one of the bouts of tonsillitis that increasingly kept him awake at night, grabbed at them, pressed them to his mouth, and screamed.

'Barnaby!' Dora cried.

Barnaby shrieked, more ash captured in a fist and retained with a furious grip despite its heat. He wiped it over his mouth. It stuck to the snot running beneath his nose, fell over his hands, his face and the floor while he screamed. Dora grabbed him, doused him with the dirty washing-up water that remained in the sink, his screaming instantly amplified to a level of hysteria. His clothes were soaked with cereal-logged water that now dripped over the floor creating runnels through the ash, while the moment he was released he bolted towards the open Aga door. Dora caught his ankle, fought him physically to remove his clothes as he roared and kicked, fresh ash attaching itself to his wet body, and with a sudden movement that made his head fall back, she picked him up, swearing out loud, and ran with his struggling, wailing form up the garden path. As she stumbled, she saw Cecilia, hollow-eyed, behind a window. This was motherhood. Her daughter would not go through this at eighteen – as a *child* – she thought with a tearful determination.

Dora made for the cottage, panted a word, barely distinguishably, to Moll and Flite, and bent over by their kitchen door to catch her breath, Barnaby now flailing with fury. 'I've decided,' she shouted above the caterwauling.

Elisabeth was due at one.

The breeze now blew through the dying jasmine, dispersing its worrying scent. Dora returned with Elisabeth to the cottage. Elisabeth linked her arm with Dora's and, passively, Dora allowed her to.

'You're very thin,' said Elisabeth.

'The radiotherapy somehow makes me not want to eat.'

'Poor sweetheart. I will look after you.'

'No you won't.'

'You know I'm very good at that,' said Elisabeth.

'You are, you are. In the moment. But not in the long term.'

'Oh –' said Elisabeth, silenced.

There was a pause.

'I can't see you any more,' said Dora in a voice that seemed to sway and snag.

'Don't cry,' said Elisabeth rapidly.

'I think,' said Dora, carrying on, 'I think – I know – Cecilia thinks I'm hard. Callous. I can't express anything that I really feel about it at all. That's all I want now, really.'

'Well –'

'With her, it's dangerous to admit anything about it. It's too – too, much too dangerous. But she thinks I don't care. I do care. I do care. So much. I can never tell her that. Isn't that pathetic, really?'

'Oh Dora.'

'Why can I *not* explain my regret, my sorrow, offer my sincere and everlasting apologies to her? Why can't I just do that? It feels as if it would kill me to do that. I just – I just can't. And I'm – a coward. I'm too scared of losing her, of losing those lovely girls again.'

'Oh sweet Dora, how can I help you? Just tell me how I can help you.'

'You can't. You can help me by keeping away.'

'You don't want that,' said Elisabeth, smiling.

'I do. I do,' said Dora.

'Oh I —'

'Think of all the lies I had to tell Celie to protect her,' said Dora, swinging round wildly. 'I — I wrecked her life — unwittingly wrecked my life in the process — by doing the wrong things. By attaching myself to someone who cannot be pinned down. And you know,' she said, jabbing at a stained ball of Blu-Tack from the table, 'you know, my own weakness in this astounds me. I think I was half afraid of Moll and Flite. I was afraid that if I enabled Celie to start a real search, it would unleash the terrible anger of Moll and Flite. That they would be my nemesis.'

'Moll and Flite?' said Elisabeth mildly, as though it were obligatory for her to ask.

'Don't you dare say that,' said Dora, her voice thick with gathering rage. 'You know very well who they were.'

'I —' said Elisabeth, unusually silenced.

'I thought that *all* I wanted to do was save Celie's youth. I thought it was for the best.'

'It was,' said Elisabeth firmly.

'It wasn't,' said Dora, and she took Elisabeth's arm, half-grabbing it, half-punching it. 'It's my own fault, of course, my own fault that I took that decision. But *you* encouraged it, in your silent, proud — haughty — way. You can't deny that. You were a force too behind the — the giving away.'

'I had good enough reasons!' said Elisabeth.

'What reasons?'

'I —'

'What reason could be good enough?'

'Surely it's perfectly obvious to you whose that child was?' said Elisabeth, her mouth a tight line. She trembled almost imperceptibly.

Dora turned to Elisabeth. The world – the tors, the jostling tree-tops, the clouds – seemed to roll around her in a speeding globe, all understanding accelerated and crystallised.

The certainty went.

She shook her head dumbly.

'Surely –'

'Speedy,' said Dora. 'Gabriel Sardo. It wasn't?' Fire rose in her cheeks.

'Oh you poor sweet innocent. You sweet fool. I thought – truly thought we both knew. I assumed we *both knew*.'

'What?'

'That it was my husband's.'

'It was your husband?' echoed Dora.

'James.' Elisabeth smiled, wryly.

'Oh God,' said Dora.

'Yes. Inconvenient.'

'Do you – do you – know that?' said Dora, stumbling. She felt spots of colour coming to her cheeks, precise and burning as welts. 'How – how?'

'How do you think?'

'But she was – she was eighteen. Seventeen.'

'I know. It was regrettable. A period of madness, I always thought. But I suppose the poor chap had to misbehave at some point.'

'Misbehave,' said Dora. 'He told you?'

'No of course he didn't,' said Elisabeth sharply.

'Well how?'

'You only had to use your eyes.'

'How do you – know?' said Dora with a croak.

'Your naïvety is astonishing, Dora. It was not hard to guess.'

'Oh God,' said Dora, whiteness now drenching her face.

'What?' said Elisabeth. 'Dora.'

'And – that's why you wanted the child out of the way?' Dora swallowed. A thin surge of vomit burned in her throat.

'It was not an insignificant factor,' said Elisabeth in her ironic voice.

'So it was nothing – I mean ... It was not to do with – us?' said Dora with awful slowness. 'With us – us being together?' Even now she blushed as she said it at her own infatuated presumption. She gripped her own thigh. 'It was because it was – his?'

'Yes, yes, of course it would have been easier – more pleasant – if we could have been left in peace,' said Elisabeth.

'Oh God,' said Dora. She felt dizzy. 'I thought – I thought – We talked so many times of running away together. Being together. Almost endlessly.'

Elisabeth nodded, a slight smile on her lips that seemed to indicate that this was now a faintly onerous fact. 'A fantasy life can . . . help.'

'So,' said Dora, glancing out of the window, looking at the table, feeling around for something to press or bend. 'So you had even more reason to encourage me.'

'I never did encourage you.'

'You did. Oh you did. With silence.'

'I can hardly be accused of encouraging with silence.'

'You can. Poisonous silence. And with the odd well-placed word. Amounting to a demand. You'd say these damning things, then fantasise about our home together. Our home of sculptures and music and forbidden love, do you remember? Alternative. Golden.'

'I remember. But not like you do. This is quite skewed.'

'You wanted that child away and made it quite clear. You could only just tolerate Barnaby. But then you didn't leave with me after all. After – the baby. After all that, *you didn't leave with me.*'

'And how could we? Where would we live, exactly? Up in the roof in Elliott Hall in accordance with your endless fantasies? Playing the lute for a living?'

'We – we –'

'And what would you have done with Barnaby?'

'Taken him with me.'

'And with the older son?'

'Taken him . . .' said Dora dumbly. 'He was getting older.'

'I couldn't have stood it frankly,' said Elisabeth. 'I'd already done that. Two sons. Dear. But quite enough.'

Dora breathed in with a suddenness that left her coughing against the intake of her own saliva. '*Well why didn't you tell me at the time?*'

she said, and broke off in a volley of coughs, swallowed, and spoke through strained muscles. 'Why, why did you lead me to believe? Give me hope? Good God, I'd have changed my whole life for you. I did change my life. And ruined my daughter's –'

'How much clearer could I have been? You expected me to be encumbered with all those children? I was supposed to bring up my husband's child by his teenage mistress?'

'He was Cecilia's *teacher*,' Dora hissed suddenly.

'I know. It was hardly commendable –' Elisabeth lifted one eyebrow. 'It's easy to judge. I'm sure she was all over him like a rash.'

'Don't speak about my daughter like that.'

Elisabeth's mouth curved into a thin-lipped smile. 'Well – they all were. Are. They masturbate over the IT master now.'

'You should have disabused me. And not given me hope. So much hope.'

'Well I've always loved you, Dora. Been attracted by you. Cared for you.'

'That is not love.'

'You're in my life for ever, my Dora.'

Dora's mouth trembled. 'Do you remember?' she said abruptly. 'Barnaby wet himself, all through his clothes, just as the baby was born?' Her voice faltered. 'His trousers soaked. I remember the stain on the stripy cushion in there. I was helping Celie give birth while thinking, I must change him, must change him. As though further proof were needed that I couldn't cope.'

'I don't remember. No.'

'The baby went – that very afternoon.' Dora swallowed. 'And then you didn't stay with me – didn't commit to me. After all that. And I realise now that I have wasted my life. That I will never be rid of you, even if I never see you again. All I want now is peace.'

Thirty-one
June

THERE WAS Mara in the hall; the air, heat, breath of Mara. She was under the oak chest, Cecilia was certain. There was an uneasiness to the air, a stain there, spilling fingers and retreating. If she wasn't under the chest, she was in the bedroom with Cecilia as a pool of light, but the pool had claws. I am going mad, thought Cecilia, and when she saw James, he spilled into Mara and into sleeplessness and loss of appetite. She held James in her mind at night, just sometimes, when she let herself, as she once had so long ago, remembering him with her; but it was Mara who melted into him and clung to her and grew cold.

June heat burned her skin. Insects were a rabble of sawing and scratching. She and James sought the shade of the willows where the water meadows were bright and sodden, and he kissed her, and she hesitated, unnerved, his taste and scent shockingly familiar, and it came rushing back to her, the memory of desire and the old leaping response.

In the night, she moved about in bed. She couldn't sleep. She called Ari, and chatted and laughed with him in what she noticed was a slightly hysterical fashion. She pressed her eyes to the window and watched bats pour from the fern-choked trees in the river field to circle the barns. She felt tearful as she spoke to him, her fingers taut, guilt alternating with defensiveness, and she could speak normally only by hurting herself in the dark with her nails. Hearing his known voice, she could barely understand how she could have done what she was doing. *Thank God I haven't slept with him,* she thought, an icy fall of relief that she used as a warning to herself seeming to pin her to the bed, and she was loving with Ari, her awareness of hypocrisy intensified in all her affection.

But when she put down the phone, an old scene shot back into her mind. She remembered kissing James Dahl when she was seventeen in the dank chlorine-fugged section of garden near the Haye House swimming pool with its dripping evergreens and moss-silled glass. His hands were on her waist; the sexual power of two hands on the dip of a waist caught her now.

She made the picture blank, and Mara flew at her. Like a figure flying in wind and rain slapping against her. She was where their kissing had led.

There was a loud sound outside the bedroom on the ground below.

She ran downstairs, tripping a little. Mara was in the hall, turning to her, moving towards her, disappearing.

There were no wellingtons by the door so Cecilia ran out in bare feet, drawing in her breath on the garden path. She saw Dan's figure clearly in the moonlight. She hobbled rapidly, following him towards a feed barn sunken in a pit of nettles and old builders' sand behind the roofless stables in the river field. Stars stormed. The figure and the sketch of bracken behind him were silhouetted, the summer night like a version of daylight, the moon tipping brightness.

'Wait! Stop!' she shouted.

Dan crouched in the hollow of the broken-walled garden that fronted the stables where rat poison and grower bags gleamed. Cecilia glanced at the ground, almost expecting to find the ancient charred remains of Speedy's Christmas fire among the tangle of dock and grass, then watched him as he stood up, tall and purposeful.

He turned round; her breathing slowed.

She could see his face clearly in the spread of dull silver from the moon, and it seemed less threatening now; it was already so very familiar to her from glimpsing him that she felt an unexpected rush of intimacy upon meeting his gaze. She looked into his eyes and she was momentarily moved by his presence in the midst of her rage.

She paused.

She gestured at the lane. 'Leave her alone,' she said, the fury regathering.

He didn't move. He smiled very slightly. He raised an eyebrow and smiled again at her, almost affectionately.

'I'll get you taken away, I'll call the police. I mean it,' she said in a quieter voice.

A flash of pain passed across his eyes, as though he had been physically wounded. He recovered his equanimity. 'Would you do that?' he said.

She hesitated. 'Yes. I would.'

He nodded. He raised his head, and faint pain seemed to linger in his expression, but he looked straight at her. Bats wove and dipped behind him.

Her heart ticked, and an instinct to hold him came to her.

'You look beautiful when you're angry,' he said. 'That's what they say in *The Railway Children*.'

She stood still. 'Yes, I know,' she said. 'I know. Phyllis says it in the novel. How do you know that?' She was suddenly tearful.

'I read it.'

'Did you?' she said.

'I can read,' he said in his odd accent.

He looked into her eyes, then at her mouth. He kept his gaze trained on her, shifting smoothly between her eyes and her mouth, and a smile lifted his lips. He continued to focus on her mouth. She looked at his. James Dahl's lips came to her in her mind. The air was silent. She stared at that mouth; it filled her frame of vision, a Man Ray mouth in silver bromide, its curves sculpted but strongly male; she could see nothing else; she wanted to kiss it. She leaned very slightly towards him. He moved towards her. James Dahl's mouth was placed over his, merged, a memory of kissing it.

'You little cunt,' he said calmly, but still he kept his eyes trained on her, and their lips parted in an echo of each other's as they stared.

'You can't call me that,' she said.

Sweat broke out on her forehead. She wanted, now, to take it all out on him, all her hidden longing for James Dahl; to couple with him in this rearing garden, her thighs light from suppressed desire, her heartbeat rapid. Her chest rose and fell. She wanted him, in all his sinuous thinness, to take her now, and she would hold him and kiss him and bite his lips.

'Why did you call me that?' she said, barely hearing what she was saying.

'Because you are.'

There was silence.

'You stalk us.'

He said nothing.

'Why? To see Izzie?'

He nodded.

'Why couldn't you be more open?'

He shook his head. He seemed to smile with his eyes.

'The way you speak . . .'

'Yes,' he said.

'Where are you from?'

'Lots of places. Mishmash. Horrible stew of accents.'

'Army?'

He laughed. 'No.'

Dog daisies glowed. She glanced down and saw that he had been cultivating plants. A row of what she thought were potato leaves lined a dry-stone wall in that little garden so choking and enclosed, it seemed to her now like a Victorian horticultural case, species crammed against species, frothing but tamed. How could she not have noticed? she wondered.

'You've been planting,' she said, her tone still without variation. She felt a pang of tenderness that someone had bothered to cultivate living things in this forgotten knot of a garden where bats gathered.

'I try to pay my way,' he said.

'But you can't be here,' she said, and then she felt the cruelty in her words. 'Izzie is only fifteen,' she said, as if in explanation.

'So you're going to chuck me out? Just chuck me out again?'

She lowered her head. They caught each other's eye. The ripple of attraction returned.

He smiled.

He came closer and she caught a tinge of unwashed skin and slept-in clothes. Panic bubbled through her brain. The desire to touch him subsided, thinned, disappeared.

'Yes,' she said.

His eyes shone.

She waited.

He looked over the wall. He smiled at the horizon.

'I'll have your daughter first,' he said.

'Don't you *dare!*' she said, her voice rising, but he turned and began to walk with a fast loping gait across the garden, and she ran after him, her feet hooking woody stems, her toes stubbing on gravel which pressed wincing sharpness into her heels, his walk turning into a run that became faster as she chased him to the lane's corner and lost him.

She stood, bending over, trying to catch her breath, then she went inside and checked her girls and left a rapid message for Ari.

Mara was not there that night, and so she slept.

Thirty-two
June

D AN RETURNED to the house some time later as a rumpled shadow outside the kitchen door. He alerted Izzie, making no attempt to disguise his perturbed state, his eyes restless as they landed on her.

'What's the matter?' she whispered. He stood stiffly on the doorstep, not entering. She frowned. 'You stink. Sweat.'

'Nothing,' he said shortly, but his shoulders dropped.

'Oh babe,' she said. 'Something's wrong. Come to my room. Babe.' She ran her hand through his damp hair, travelling from his neck down his back and circling his vertebrae with her fingers. 'I love you.'

'Do you?' he said. He looked her in the eyes for a few moments, then cut his gaze and followed her silently up the stairs.

'You know I do.'

'I don't know,' he said. He lowered his head momentarily, as though pausing to contemplate his actions, then he turned to her. 'Get on the bed?' he said.

'Uh?' she said.

'It's only what – two weeks?' he said.

'What? My birthday? Yes. Less.'

'Let's do it,' he said. 'We're not going to wait any more.'

'What, like, do it?' said Izzie, sounding stupefied.

'Do it.'

'Oh God. Like, Dan. I'm – Yes.'

'Get your rump up there then. Where did we get to last time? Your left hip. None of this pissing around. You're gorgeous,' he said, reaching up under her night-time T-shirt and feeling her with a fidgety circling movement.

'There's this – I don't know? – though –'

'What?' His breath still emerged unevenly, though his eyes were bright and focused on her face. She felt his sweat cooling in the dew-scented air from the window as she stroked him, sensed the coiled tension of his wide-shouldered back.

'It's not really me – it's like it's not really me you like?' she said, stumbling over her words. 'Like you don't really know me?' said Izzie, colour travelling up her neck, and she turned away from him. An owl hooted outside, its call returned.

'No princess fits,' said Dan. His arm muscles were tensed. 'Do you know me?' he said.

'Yes,' said Izzie. Smoke twined in the air, the end of her cigarette drifting near Dan's head. 'Fuck. Sorry. Yes.'

'Really?' said Dan, his voice thickening, and he stretched himself out on the single bed beside her, his left leg on top of her, and sank his mouth on to her nipple.

'Yes I do,' she said, her words disjointed, and as she met his eye and saw anxiety blow across his face, she covered his lips with a series of kisses. 'I really love you,' she said.

He was trembling. He placed his mouth on her neck and his hand curved down her body; she took it, guided it, pressing it harder against her, and afterwards, his head was a dense weight on her shoulder.

'You've dribbled over me,' she said, murmuring little sounds of laughter as she kissed him, and then she saw that it was his eyes and not his mouth that had left her skin wet.

'Don't,' she whispered, and felt the spasms of his suppressed sobs, his legs heavy against hers.

Ruth lay by the river. It was the latest she had ever been out there: past midnight, *Tom's Midnight Garden*. Dog daisies glowed, stitch-wort, meadow grass, and all those petals could form a radiant nosegay garland when she floated like Ophelia-Ruthelia; but when she lowered herself into the river as she had promised, she could still only swim instead of float. The coldness made tears storm to her eyes. 'Mummy,' she muttered but water filled her mouth. She flapped, gasped, floundered and wriggled to the bank in breaststroke. She didn't float, and floating was what she needed to do to appease, silently and flower-logged.

He is coming, thought Cecilia, and a beam travelled down the lane. She could see lights arriving, widening and falling through knotted canopy, thinning on to the sky, just as months before they had left. The back of the car was visibly chaotic with books and boxes. Moths swooped towards the headlamps. The door slammed, Ari came into the house and Cecilia walked rapidly into his arms.

'My darly,' he said.

His short hair grazed her nose; she smelled the enclosed breath of the car on his comforting skin; she drew him closer to her and they embraced, her head pressed to him so that she couldn't see him but stared into the room, stiff with a horrified awareness now that he was here and solid and familiar beside her. He put his hands on her waist, and the action felt intrusive.

'It's my turn to take charge,' he said airily, though he suppressed a yawn of tiredness. 'I'll cook you some massive pastas. Tortillas, paellas. Enough of these country grubs and shrubs.'

'Oh my darling,' she said, and she buried her face in him. 'I love you,' she muttered.

'I love you, missis.'

An image of a kiss shot through her mind. Heat rose up her neck.

'You've been on your own too long. I'll take my turn now.'

She kissed him on the lips.

'I want you,' she said slightly awkwardly, looping her arms round his neck, a foggy pang of guilt rising through her. 'Come to me,' she said, trying to correct her breathing.

'I'll have you,' he murmured in a whisper into her ear so the girls couldn't overhear.

'OK,' she whispered. 'Then I'll have you.'

She froze again. It slammed into her only now, how far she had gone in the infidelity of her thoughts, kisses, the ripeness of her body. Ari hugged her and she looked into the long-known patterns of his eyes.

'It's different here,' he said suddenly, turning to survey the room, a trace of discomposure lifting his voice.

She dropped her gaze, then tried to meet his eye again, but he knew her too well and she saw him detect a stiffness in her expression.

'I think –' she began, to distract him.

'Perhaps you don't need anyone else –'

'I do – I –'

'It's strange. I think what it is, is ...' He furrowed his face in contemplation, looking momentarily almost ugly. 'Is that this is *your* house, life. Past. You don't need anyone else in it. Perhaps.'

'Oh I do, of course I do!'

'I sometimes feel here that I'm in someone else's life. This isn't my life.'

'Oh Ari, don't be so melodramatic. You've only just *got* here. Are we going to start debating, arguing immediately?'

'No,' he said in a low voice, and stroked the base of her back.

'Good God. This is a little heavy the moment you return. You sound like a lecturer with some new construct to propose. Couldn't you have told me that you're living "*in someone else's life*" when we first decided to come here? ... Is this some male pride issue?'

'Not everything is about gender politics.'

'Give me strength, you curmudgeon.'

Her mouth opened. She was heated. She could discern pain in his expression, and it made her swallow.

'Thank you for being so good,' she said, without knowing quite what she meant. 'Thank you for standing by me, for being a great father. I love you. I appreciate all of it.'

There are very few times I don't think about you, wrote James Dahl in a letter that arrived in the morning, because he had taken to writing to her, even while he saw her daily, and she wondered whether she would ever be able to look at those distinctive cramped loops without recalling how she once would have longed and longed for such words in this very handwriting.

June dusk was falling, and with a small escalation of energy, Dora wandered across the fields above Wind Tor House, taking a walk to regain her strength. Cancer, she thought, had hollowed out the remaining structure of her life. She stumbled a little over the uneven grass and clumps of hawkweed, but skylarks ran in pairs through the sky, their song bubbling high, meadow pipits dashing past her, and the trees were in full leaf, gathering the first shadows of falling light. Dora wiped her brow, felt the paperiness of her skin, tasted the hay baked by day twined with comfrey on the air, and hastened her pace. She planned a dinner to celebrate Ari's return; she had asked an old friend from her music group to meet her for lunch at Elliott Hall later in the week, and she was trying to read novels she had never managed before. Vigorously filling in time was a partial solution. Sadness sounded a high thin note at the back of her brain. She had not heard from Elisabeth; nor did she expect to.

Her mobile beeped in her pocket. She had reached the spot above the depths of the Dewdon valley at which reception was possible on a clear day, and now she glanced at her screen. *1 message Elis* it said. *I'm on the moor and looking for you. Not at home. Where?*

Dora hesitated, returned the mobile to her pocket, and continued to walk where the field wrinkled over the hill's brow and the earth radiated warmth. She breathed in still air. She would walk further, further away from home, where the houses in the valley were a crumble of thatch against a blur of green. She could hear the roar of oxygen in her ears.

'Dora!' came the voice of Elisabeth, strained but impatient, and Dora looked up, and there she was by the gate of the field wearing a fitted narrow dress of the kind that suited her small figure, Dora noted automatically, a cardigan slung over her shoulders. Dora waved and continued her walk round the edge of the field instead of diverting straight towards Elisabeth, and for a while, Elisabeth was a dot at the side of her vision, a figure that eventually climbed the gate and came towards her.

'Dora!' said Elisabeth, taking her shoulders and lightly shaking them. 'I have looked far and wide for you!'

'I was walking.'

'Good to see it,' said Elisabeth after a pause. 'Shall we go back to the cottage?'

'Not now,' said Dora. 'Look at the sun.'

'Why not?'

'I'd rather not. I'd rather be out here, really.'

'I had some supper for you in the car,' said Elisabeth, a light frown implying admonishment. 'It'll be cold now, or at best lukewarm.'

'Thank you,' said Dora. 'It's kind of you, but please don't. I'm feeling a bit better now. And – I have Katya and Cecilia, who look after me very well.'

Dora breathed deeply and watched the last sun light a stonechat on top of a gorse bush as she walked past. She looked up at the trees.

'Wait for me,' said Elisabeth eventually. She caught up. She ran her hand down Dora's arm. 'Will you really not go back to the cottage?'

'You sound a little bit Scottish sometimes. What a lovely evening. Who knows how many more of them I'll have,' she said matter of factly.

'Oh darling Dora, do you really think that?'

'I don't know. I have to be on Tamoxifen from now on. It's likely it will crop up elsewhere in the body.'

'The beautiful body.'

'You haven't found my body beautiful for months. Years by now – over a year,' said Dora levelly.

'Oh I do find it beautiful.'

'Because,' said Dora, smiling at Elisabeth, but barely looking at her, 'you know you're safe.'

'Let's go back,' said Elisabeth firmly. 'I want to take you to bed.'

'No!' said Dora. She glanced around. 'Look, the bracken's taken on a life of its own.'

'You won't come back with me?' said Elisabeth, a thinness appearing in her voice.

'It's so beautiful out here,' said Dora, not looking at Elisabeth.

They walked along a bracken-lined path trodden by cows that led to the trees beside the river, leaves reaching over their heads. The Wind Tor land could be seen from there across the water, the river field visible through the little island with its branching birches.

'Let's sit down,' said Elisabeth and she created a space in the bracken a few feet from the river, trampling down stems and tugging at fronds, but they were too young and strong and resisted her. 'I have green streaks on my hands,' she murmured. 'I was trying to make a nest for you.'

'I need to go home soon,' said Dora, sitting down. 'I have to wrap Izzie's present.'

'I'll take you back.'

'Thank you. No,' said Dora, and she managed to make her voice steady.

'You really don't want me to come there today, do you?' said Elisabeth, an element of soft teasing entering her voice. 'What are you hiding?'

'No. Thank you,' said Dora.

'Always so polite. Well brought up. My Kentish good girl.'

'I don't think my mother would think I had been good.'

'For consorting with me, you mean?' said Elisabeth, and ran her hand lightly up Dora's calf, skimming her thigh.

Dora knew in that moment what she was going to do.

As the dusk deepened, Ruth began to yawn.

'Are you tired?' said Cecilia, stroking her forehead.

'Yes,' said Ruth, avoiding her mother's eye, and she went to bed at eight o'clock in order to placate the ceiling gods before she floated to cleanse herself in a river where her skin would whiten and become flower-tangled.

Cecilia came up and hugged her in bed and kissed her cheek with small kisses in a row.

'I want Daddy too,' said Ruth.

'He'll come up in a minute and tuck you in,' said Cecilia. 'Goodnight,' she said, then sensed Ruth watching her and veered back to hug her again. 'Goodnight.'

Cecilia shut the door and glanced down the corridor. Hearing Ari energetically unpacking and stacking books in what would now be his study, she recalled a fire juggler with henna-purple hair who had once inhabited the room and alarmed Patrick with her practice. 'The thatch,' he always said to her. 'The thatch.' Cecilia thought with a small twinge about how straightforwardly she had always loved her father, and still did.

She checked her emails in her old bedroom. There was one from James Dahl.

Can you talk? it said. She glanced at her watch. He had emailed her seventeen minutes before.

Yes briefly, she wrote back. *Ring now?*

She shut the door and sorted through papers by the phone, waiting for ten minutes in a turmoil of anticipation and guilt, then picked up her laptop with an abrupt movement, still strongly averse to behaviour that recalled the past. *Too late*, she wrote. *Talk tomorrow?*

The phone rang as she sent the email.

She snatched up the receiver. 'Hello,' she said in a voice intended to be hushed but which merely sounded odd.

'Hello,' he said. 'Is that you? I'm glad you're still there.'

'Yes I – just briefly,' she said.

'How are you?'

'I'm fine.'

'I miss you,' he said.

She was momentarily silent. 'Me too,' she said, glancing in the direction of the room where Ari was unpacking.

'Your husband is back,' he said.

'Yes,' she said.

'I'm not sure I like it,' he said.

She hesitated.

'You'll have to get used to it.'

'I'm not sure I shall be able to,' he said.

'Well *you*,' she said, 'you live with your wife, as you have for decades. You *work* with your wife even.'

'I'm sad he's back,' he said levelly.

Cecilia hesitated. 'Well *you* –' she said, seemingly unable to vary her tone. 'In any case, it's irrelevant. You would never leave Elisabeth.'

He paused.

'*You're not ever going to leave her, are you?*' she had said, at seventeen, in Elliott Hall gardens. She remembered it with absolute clarity, that stupefied inability to process the death of hope in his answer, its intimation of later pain. She remembered blossom wet on the ground; his shoes; the Madame Isaac Pereire. '*I can't do that,*' he had replied.

'Yes I would,' he said now.

'Oh –' said Cecilia.

'Yes.'

'Well I – I should go now,' she said rapidly.

'Yes,' he said. 'I'll come and find you in the archive.'

'Sixteen tomorrow, sweet bint,' said Dan to Izzie, and smiled at her.

'Oh my God!' said Izzie. She grinned, radiantly. 'Like, adult. You look like a calf. Your eyelashes. Calves' eyelashes.'

'Still a pampered little dipstick,' he said, but he kissed her, and they laughed and rolled around in a heap. He placed a magic mushroom on her tongue.

'Because *you* are so hard, naturally.'

'Cosseted. Milk fed. Spoilt sick,' he said, tapping a different part of her body with every word. He hesitated over her pubic bone and then formed a small precise circle. He threw open the window, the bedroom an overheated fug of hash and tobacco smoke. 'You need to stuff that crack,' he said, nodding at the door. 'Look at that gaping girt great crack, my lover.'

Izzie bent over to press a T-shirt from her bed into the space between the door and the carpet, swaying as she did so, and Dan came up to her and put his hands against her hip bones. 'At least you're legal later.'

'Sixteen!' said Izzie. 'Sixteen whole years since I came shooting and shouting out of my old mother's fanny. Then she dumped me. Like, thanks, Mum!' She grinned.

'Not that story again,' he said.

Footsteps sounded along the passage, coming towards the bathroom.

'That kid,' he said. 'The little shorty strange one. What's her name again?'

'My sister's not strange,' said Izzie.

'She's not your sister.'

'What?' said Izzie.

Dan gazed at her.

'Oh!' said Izzie, screwing up her face. 'She *is*. Of course she is. God.'

She knelt and peered through her keyhole. She rolled away the T-shirt with her toes and opened her door very slightly. 'Ruth!' she hissed.

Ruth jumped and turned round, her eyes distracted in pinkened skin.

'Oh!' she said.

'It's all right, little smelly,' said Izzie. 'I'm not going to bite you. Quick! Come in.'

She grabbed Ruth's shoulder and hurried her roughly into the room.

'It smells weird here,' said Ruth, her eyes widening at the sight of Dan. She wore a white traditional nightdress that was now too tight so that it clung to her chest and stopped short of her knees. Her hair flopped over her shoulders, its waves even angular ridges as though she had slept in plaits.

'Don't stress about it. Here's Dan,' said Izzie. 'Don't worry. *Don't* tell Mum or I'll . . . I'd be gutted. And no way tell Dad. OK? Then you can play with us.'

Ruth nodded. She was silent.

'I have to go to bed,' she said. Her eyes were so dark, they looked magnified, her pupils seeming to merge with her irises in the shadows.

'What? Normally you want to stay up and play and stuff,' said Izzie. 'Sit down. Dan's made it so this is a super-nice place to chill.' She put up the volume of the music. 'We're thinking we might have a baby?' she said, glancing at Ruth. 'It would be really lovely for it up here.'

Ruth said nothing.

'Don't you think?' said Izzie.

Ruth nodded. Her hair wriggled in the dull light.

'Have some,' said Dan gently, and held out a tooth mug of magic mushroom tea.

Izzie put her hand out and took it from him instead. She hesitated, glancing at Dan. 'You can have a bit,' she said then, turning to Ruth.

'What is it?' said Ruth in a croaky voice.

'It's just this tea Dan makes. It's awesome.'

'What is it?' repeated Ruth.

'It's magic mushroom tea. Magic. You can only have a tiny bit? It makes things all glittery and floaty and sparkling. You'll love it. All that stuff you like. Kind of magic stuff like in those books?'

'Oh,' said Ruth.

'You're smiling!' said Izzie, suddenly hugging Ruth, and took a sip. 'I love you, sis,' she said.

'Float?' said Ruth.

'Makes you feel floaty. It makes your head all light.'

Dan took the cup from Izzie, filled it, handed it silently to Ruth and waited. She blushed and, tentatively, she sipped.

'Would the water glitter?' said Ruth.

'Yes,' said Dan.

'You weirdo. Have another,' said Izzie. 'Then that's enough.'

Ruth nodded. She took a mouthful, gazed around the room, then picked her way across piles of clothes towards the door. 'Look at those moths,' she said, inclining her head at a lamp and smiling. 'They love your lights, don't they?'

'You don't have to go yet,' said Izzie, glancing at her alarm clock. She started to roll a cigarette.

'I need to go to bed.'

'This is *soooo not like you!*' said Izzie, and laughed and blew Ruth kisses as she left the room. She stuffed the door with the T-shirt.

'She won't know what's hit her,' said Dan.

'It's not, like, dangerous, is it?' said Izzie.

'She'll just have a few pleasant hallucinations and giggle herself stupid.'

'Cool,' said Izzie. 'She needs to chill a bit. Poor kid.'

'None of you are poor kids. You're all brats. You the most. Queen brat of brats.'

'You never fucking stop,' said Izzie, dragging on a cigarette and passing it to him. 'Give me a break. You're probably some lord git yourself. Most likely a snooty. *Django.*'

'How do you know that?' said Dan sharply. Moths beat against the window with solid taps.

'Saw it on your driving licence. Django! Tragic!'

'I know. That's why I don't use it,' said Dan in a steady voice. 'A tosser's name.'

'Um. *Ye-es* ... What were your parents thinking?'

'I don't know,' said Dan.

'Why not?'

'I don't know what they were thinking about most things.'

'Don't you get on with them?'

He shrugged.

'You never, like, *talk* about them.'

He was silent. He gave two rapid blinks.

'Well?'

'They weren't up to much,' he said bluntly. 'They're OK.'

'How?'

He shrugged again.

'Go on,' said Izzie. 'Tell me about them.' She took him in her arms and stroked his shoulders. He softened, and stayed still until she stroked him more, then he kissed her suddenly on her arm.

'They're all right,' he said gruffly. 'I just didn't really see the point of them.'

'Not see the point of your parents?'

'We didn't really – suit each other.'

'What is there to suit?'

'Oh you haven't got the first idea,' he said dismissively.

'Dan! Don't be so harsh! You get all like really furious the least thing I say? At least you *had* your parents. No one dumped you.'

'How do you know?' said Dan, moving abruptly.

'That hurt!'

'What did?'

'When you stood up. Who dumped *you*? No one!'

He stood still and shook his head at her with the slightest movement, radiating hostility with the set of his lips and his stiff-spined stance. He wouldn't meet her eye.

'I'm getting out of here,' she said, and scrambled to her knees.

'Same as you.'

'What do you mean?'

'Who dumped me? My mother dumped me.'

'What?'

'You heard.'

'Who – how? Do you mean –'

He pulled a face. A moth collided with the window and they both looked up.

'You – you're adopted? Too?'

'Not *too*.'

'What do you mean?'

'Not like you.'

His breathing was rapid.

'Like how?'

'Not all cosy cosy, ooh Mummy.'

'Don't say that.'

He scratched his scalp hard.

'What, then?' she said.

'Taken in by some woo-woo arseholes.'

'Who? What?'

'My so-called parents.'

'God, Dan. Why didn't you tell me?'

'Why? What have I got in common with you? A princess case whose "mother" thinks the sun shines out of her arse?' He shifted his weight with a jerking movement on to one hip.

'Dan, don't.'

'Don't you want to find the real ones?' he said.

'These are the real –'

'How did I know you'd say that?' he said abruptly. 'Don't you just want to *see* who you grew inside? Who – gave you –? I always did.'

'Mine's dead,' said Izzie in the lowered voice that angered him.

He shook his head at her, his lip stiff with undisguised derision.

'I'm going to fuck off now,' he said, kicking a pile of clothes so that they flew through the air and landed slowly, a sock catching the door handle. 'Now the old man's back. He might shoot me.'

'He doesn't know you're here.'

'She'll tell him.'

His eyes shone. He bent over and began to cough, wheezing with a phlegmy clearing of his throat.

'Dan! Who?' said Izzie.

'That cow. Bitch. Cunt.'

'Who –' said Izzie breathlessly, still crouching near the door.

'Her.'

'You mean Mum?' said Izzie, her mouth open. Her eyes were wet.

'That whore.'

'God, Dan. Dan! Don't *speak* about her like that!' said Izzie, beginning to cry.

'I'm going.'

Izzie stared at him. She shook her head at him.

'I want you,' she said quietly.

He was silent. A streak of cooler air ran into the room.

'I really want you,' she said, crying again. 'I thought you might, like, stay here. You were going to – hold me. Stay with me.'

His face softened. His lower lip was unsteady. 'We were going to do it again,' he said, almost absently.

'At legal time.'

He peered at her clock in the gloom. He turned to her, blank-eyed, and picked up a lock of her hair.

'You're just about legal,' he said. 'I'll have you illegally again now. Then when the clock bangs ...'

'Then?'

'Then we'll fuck. Again.'

'And then?'

'And then I'll fuck off.'

'No *no*!' cried Izzie, throwing her arms round his chest, clinging to him.

Thirty-three
June

DORA AND Elisabeth had walked back towards the cottage in the half-darkness to the sound of late birdsong above the trickle of streams.

'Let me come with you,' said Elisabeth.

'I don't want you any more,' said Dora, the shadows cast by arching bracken lending her boldness.

'I don't see why not.'

'You don't?' Dora shook her head and smiled. 'No, darling.'

'Oh,' said Elisabeth, at a loss.

'We can talk in the garden,' said Dora as they approached Wind Tor Cottage and she pushed the gate against the topple of honeysuckle that slowed its path.

'Why?' said Elisabeth.

'It seems artificial but . . .'

The gate tore stems with a straining sound.

'But I'm too dangerous to be let into your house?' Elisabeth emitted her rich laugh.

Dora caught the edge of her breath. Elisabeth appeared human, vulnerable, as she had so rarely seemed, and even faintly ordinary in her mortal form.

'Yes,' said Dora.

'Breathe,' said Elisabeth, ignoring her. 'It smells of hay, but with the damper grass that's always in your garden.'

'This is a damp spot,' said Dora. 'I always wonder if I'm being punished! The past seeping in.'

Elisabeth pressed Dora's arm. 'You are more fanciful than your daughter, I sometimes think.'

'You don't know my daughter,' said Dora stiffly.

'My husband does,' said Elisabeth, and paused. She raised one sharp eyebrow. 'I suspect he meets her more than he lets on. I've seen them together.'

'Oh, she told me she'd met him,' said Dora.

'He goes off every lunchtime. He never did that before. Free periods –'

'She's working very hard to finish her book.'

'Is she? I wonder. What trouble . . . Of all teachers . . . Wouldn't one have imagined James would be the last?' said Elisabeth, stretching delicately as if to demonstrate her indifference. 'I almost admire him for it sometimes . . . And that she would have been the last pupil . . .'

'I cannot bear to think about this,' said Dora, holding her hands over her ears. 'There's no point now. It's appalling. I will be angry.'

Elisabeth laughed, but gently. 'There's a lot you can't bear to think about.'

'And yet,' said Dora. 'Now that I'm not sure how much longer . . . Things seem clearer. I do think.'

She walked around the garden with Elisabeth beside her, warm clusters of gnats shadowing the hedge and trees. Elisabeth took Dora's arm.

'Clearer. About what?'

'About the baby.'

'What baby –?'

Dora turned on her impatiently, extricating her arm. A blackbird sang loudly on the hedge above them.

'There is only one baby in my life. The others all grew up.'

'Certainly not a baby any more.'

'But he was,' said Dora, bowing her head. Her hair fell forward and she pulled a strand from her mouth, lifting it impatiently from her tongue. 'And I never ever forget. That face.'

'You know I've never particularly cared to talk about this. And I don't care now,' said Elisabeth. 'It was unpleasant. It was done. We have to move on.'

'You're hard,' said Dora slowly. 'But then I ... it's true that I couldn't talk about it either. Not to Celie, who was the only one who *did* want to talk about it. For years, she did, and – does. I used to think, I'd rather die than address the big things.'

'My Dora,' said Elisabeth, putting her arm round Dora's shoulder. 'You really do think too much sometimes.'

'Do you remember?' said Dora, turning round and shrugging off Elisabeth's arm with a small movement as she did so. 'Remember the day the baby was born? How I was just after? Wild. Mad. You arrived in the afternoon; I remember. How do you think Celie was? Do you think I ever stop thinking about that bundle disappearing through the back door?'

It was that, that bundle, held by the woman who had just assisted the birth and who was now suspended in some luminous daze of gratification, Cecilia alone in bed: it was that one image that came back to her, the blanket-wrapped baby a little breathing package, a fuzzy sad picture as though caught on CCTV. It was the last time Dora had seen her grandson. She watched them leave, Moll and Flite, their tears falling; watched their backs as they went out through the door, across the yard up to the cottage, and then left, as arranged, in their van that very afternoon: the new mother arriving in Wales having ostensibly just given birth. She looked the part, Dora always thought, the solid Moll in her layers of skirts – the baby in its sling, bottle feeding due to early mastitis, the ruffled glow and tentative movements of the new mother. Moll would say that she had given birth at home in England, register the baby as hers and Flite's, producing documentation from a midwife friend of hers, and start their new life as parents in Wales. And then – as Dora knew now – beyond Wales: beyond, and beyond.

'I was such a fool,' said Dora, her head in her hands.

'Let's go to bed,' said Elisabeth.

'No!' said Dora.

Elisabeth breathed sharply through her nose.

Dora smiled. She shook her head. She breathed deeply. 'I think it was only ever sex that could make me stop thinking about this,' she said. 'You and sex, I mean. Love, what I thought – sometimes – was love. They were the only time I could escape the truth.'

'I did love you. Do. You're my sexy maternal calmness. I tell you so often. The opposite of me in so many ways. And yet not.'

'Maternal,' said Dora bitterly.

'You were. You are. Too maternal for me – for my liking, I mean,' said Elisabeth and kissed Dora suddenly, briefly, on the lips. 'Can you please try to get over this? I had absolutely no idea you continued to feel like this. My darling one, it's *years* ago. You were a sweet fool to give it to those unpleasant hippies, of course. If you'd have discussed it with me . . .'

'You didn't want to know. You resisted, didn't want any of the details.'

'I just wanted it out of the way, frankly. Like you did. Let's not kid ourselves. But it was terribly home-knitted of you to arrange that adoption yourself!' She laughed with a nervous awkwardness. 'You'd be clapped in jail now . . .'

Dora flinched.

'You know, it was only over the years I realised that,' she said with something like a small gasp.

Elisabeth rubbed the back of Dora's head, alternating light fluttering movements with harder strokes, and Dora pressed her eyes into the ridges of the knitted cotton on her shoulder and in her mind she saw Cecilia's face – as it had been; as it was now – the two faces merging.

'*Where is she?*' Cecilia had said, waking and confused, when Dora and Moll had returned from bathing the new baby and dressing him in a nappy and sleepsuit.

Dora hesitated.

'She?' she said.

Cecilia held out her arms.

Dora glanced at the baby, wrapped up.

'Here,' she said.

Cecilia stared down at the baby's head, blinking. She kissed it, nuzzled it. The baby started to turn to a nipple, and Dora moved quickly towards the bed.

'Say goodbye,' she said quietly, not looking at Cecilia; or she thought she'd said it.

'*I never said goodbye*,' said Cecilia time and time again over the years. 'She just left.'

She, Cecilia called the baby from the beginning, having, Dora surmised, misheard, or simply assumed. Throughout the pregnancy, Dora noticed, she had instinctively and then increasingly unquestioningly believed that the baby would be a girl.

'You cuddled – cuddled . . . her,' said Dora, staggering over words the first time.

'I didn't!' said Cecilia. 'Only for seconds! I wanted to say goodbye to her.' She wailed square mouthed like a red-faced child, her breasts full and, to Dora, alarming, spilling out of her nightdress. 'I'd been asleep. I didn't know you were taking her *then*.'

'She . . . her,' Cecilia continued to say, within days expressing regret and asking barely rational questions, and Dora had allowed the mistake to prevail as a further disguise, another level removed from the truth, along with her hazy official adoption story. She would not, could not, engage with the facts.

'I honestly hadn't planned to lie,' said Dora now, tears running from the corners of her eyes and flattening sorely over her face.

'You did it in panic,' said Elisabeth soothingly.

'And then I couldn't get out of it. I told her wrong things about the parents. I thought she might be less attached if it wasn't a real person in our lives.'

Elisabeth patted her.

'I never corrected her on the girl thing . . .'

'Sweetie.'

'I *wanted* her not to be able to find him. Do you think I was a coward?'

'No,' said Elisabeth, shaking her head as she stroked Dora's shoulders. 'It's getting colder out here.'

'I was. I was a terrible coward.'

'No.'

'I was afraid of them – Moll and Flite,' said Dora. 'But I wanted to save Celie's youth, wanted to – protect us all. But oh God, Elisabeth, she has built this myth of this daughter. This mythical daughter. I would never know how to ... I didn't *expect* her to be so relentless about it. Ever.'

'Could you tell her now?'

'My God, she would never speak to me again,' said Dora, and cried loudly into Elisabeth's chest. Elisabeth palpably stiffened, and then softened, against her. 'And worse – I admit worse than that – I'd lose the three girls.' Her speech faltered between tears. 'After it took me so many years to begin to know them. I love them so much.'

Elisabeth shook her head.

'There is no need now.'

'I tried and tried to track Moll and Flite down,' said Dora weakly. 'Once I really understood the grief of Celie.' She swallowed. 'One of their friends threatened me once when he came past here and I asked after Moll and Flite and the baby. He kept talking very aggressively about "their kid". About, I don't know, "people leaving them and their kid alone". I used to be afraid of arson.' She shrugged hopelessly. 'Threats, exposure, of all sorts of revenge. They were quite scary, some of those people.'

'Yes,' said Elisabeth.

'And I was always terrified – for the future – of Celie being declared an unfit mother,' said Dora, her words now tumbling in a barely coherent stream. 'What if they put her on an At Risk register or something? I don't know how these things work,' said Dora, tailing off.

'You were protecting her,' said Elisabeth gently.

'The worst thing is, I failed them both so badly, but Celie has *no idea* I've spent a lifetime grieving and hoping,' said Dora. 'Once she said to me, very coldly, "All I need to know is that you cared about her." And I wanted to say to her, "I can't tell you how I cared, can't tell you." But I knew that I would break down. And all I said to her was, "It's over." My mouth was a small tight hardness. I know it. And the grief on her face. I just couldn't – *could not* – talk about things. Oh Elisabeth, why are we such fools?'

'Enough now, enough,' said Elisabeth, stroking Dora harder.

'I really –' Dora shook her head. 'I – Why could I never tell her I truly, truly did care? I was sorry? It was a mis –'

'Well tell her then.'

'What?'

'Tell her that,' said Elisabeth. 'Tell her just that. What you just said to me.'

'What?' Dora's mouth was open.

'*I truly did care. I'm sorry. It was a mistake.* Just say that.'

'I couldn't.'

'Yes you could.'

'I could – Could I?'

'Yes,' said Elisabeth, taking Dora's shoulders.

'I don't think I –'

'I challenge you.'

'Oh –'

'If you do anything, tell her that. Tell her it was a mistake, you regret it. I challenge you,' said Elisabeth briskly. 'If I can give you anything, I can give you that. The courage to do it if you want to – that's my challenge to you. I've had enough of this now.'

Dora was silent. 'Thank you,' she said. She lowered her head. Her shoulders sank. She exhaled with a loud rush of air.

'Hush hush hush now,' said Elisabeth firmly. She kneaded Dora's shoulders hard. 'It's a little cold.'

The day had fallen into a flimsy summer darkness, the thatches of the hamlet humped in uneven ridges in the tucks of the valley.

'Sit in here,' said Dora, indicating the summerhouse at the back of the garden.

Elisabeth hesitated and glanced at the cottage. Dora opened the summerhouse door. The breath of still-warm wood and tomato plants enveloped them comfortingly, remains of spider and leaf skeleton crumbled in corners. They sat on a bench.

'I can show you late love,' said Elisabeth.

'What does that mean? "Late love"?' said Dora.

'I think I can commit to you . . .'

Dora smiled. 'I can't even be bothered to laugh,' she said, without emotion. Elisabeth's arm was round her; she sat back against it. 'Just think of all that time.'

'I didn't want to rock the boat.'

'There has been no boat to rock for years.'

'I want you.'

'Yes,' said Dora. 'You only want someone who hasn't got long.'

Elisabeth glanced at her knees.

'I don't know why I always – push people away,' she said, her voice minutely uneven.

'Oh Elisabeth,' said Dora with affection. 'You will never be fathomed. Let's not try now.'

Elisabeth paused. She shook her head and looked at Dora with a small crooked smile. 'I won't,' she said. 'Come here.'

'Any time I've got left, I just want to dedicate it to my grandchildren,' said Dora in an unsteady voice. 'Helping them and loving them. I'll be on my own and look after my grandchildren. That's what I'll do.'

'Oh my Dora,' said Elisabeth, and was silent, then moved towards her lips, and Dora allowed her to. Elisabeth kissed her harder. Dora opened her mouth.

She knew, as she had known earlier that day by the river, that she would let Elisabeth make love to her once more. She was cynical; she was fully aware; she was safe. She would use her even, she thought, her mouth twisting with the notion. She knew that this would probably be the last time she had sex in her life; it would certainly be the final time with Elisabeth. She swallowed against a tightening of her throat.

Together they found her pile of camp bed mattresses beneath a bench, damp with the incense-tinged grime of the drifters who had slept there over the years. Dora felt a fierce desire returning for sex: pure sex, animal sex. Their bodies were light-sculpted under early-summer stars as she glanced in momentary wonder at their entangled limbs; the dent in her breast smoothed over, the skin seemingly ageless.

I've had this, I've known this, I've had this richness, thought Dora with exquisite pain as Elisabeth bit on her nipple and her thighs were stroked, and the old fire, the almost unbearably hot rising began to spread through her, her breathing shallowing and her nerves swarming to alertness. She took her pleasure. There was nothing to lose, all circumspection gone. Elisabeth stroked her hard, almost brutally, but she could touch her only with this heat, this buoyant burning. As she shuddered down those long hot steps, she turned her face into the mattresses to soak away the tears that came afterwards.

Thirty-four
June

THE NIGHT grew cooler, foxes crying out from near the river with their strange child-like call, and a bird singing that Cecilia recognised as a nightjar because in a different time, Patrick had taught her their song; she remembered hearing the nightjar in early summer as she prepared for exams in this very room, and it brought her father back to her again. It summoned a feeling of the house as it was, the retreating to her room after school, winding past the wax surface of old pine and oak furniture so cold to the touch, its fragrance twining after her, past fires, glimpses of bright sky or snow, along twists of passage and stair by low-lintelled doors towards her bedroom, Dora creating big meals downstairs and much shouting between rooms. She sank her head in her hands as she remembered it all, and Mara came to her. The created Mara, with her fair hair. In Cecilia's mind, she had hair that was not quite blonde, but of a light rained-on straw colour, falling over a thin face, a strongly sculpted arrangement of features. On haunted days, she saw her crouching on the moor trying to get back to her, the poor colourless hair a mass of knots and pony scurf. Instead of working, she wrote to Mara.

Tears pressed against her eyes; she made herself flick between documents and focus on her children's novel. She pressed her right fingernails under those of her left hand, then threw herself into her work.

The river rushed, loud in the hushed night. Her characters sailed. *The Water Babies*; *The Little Mermaid*; *The Selkie Girl*, she thought. She must check on Ruth. She worried about Ruth and was unable to subdue the anxiety, no matter how she tried, because there seemed reason for it. She walked along the passage and opened Ruth's door. Her bedroom was empty.

'If you were adopted,' said Izzie, stroking Dan's hair, 'where's, like, your real parents? The ones that brought you up, I mean.'

He lay against her chest, his lips parted against her breast after sex, his breathing snagging with early sleep. She prodded him and he grunted.

'Where?'

'On the other side of the world ...' he said in a sleepy voice, rolling his eyes.

'What do you mean?'

'They went to bum-fuck nowhere. New Zealand. Classic,' he said, lifting his head in stages, his hair flattened into sweat peaks where he had slept against her. 'They followed a couple of their moaning mates to live up some mountain.'

'And you didn't want to go with them?' Izzie tickled the back of his neck.

'Mmm,' he said. 'More. More. I like it.' He lifted his shoulders towards her. 'What?' he said through a new yawn. 'You think I'm likely to go and shear farting sheep and catch a flat-as-a-cowpat accent?'

Izzie laughed. 'Do they talk like that? Don't you like them?'

'Not *like*,' he said into her breast. He kissed her and blew a raspberry against her skin.

'Eurgh!' said Izzie. 'You soaked my tit. What then?'

'My old man's quite a nice geezer. She's a bit of a harridan underneath the earth-mother bit she does. She's OK, she fed me and everything, but well –' he said, turning stiffly beneath her and catching her eye, his pupils blankly reflecting the bedside lamp.

'You want to find your first mum,' said Izzie, drawing on a cigarette.

He stood up, shaking Izzie off him, and opened the window until it jammed against the eaves, scattering straw. 'Yes,' he said shortly.

The river's tumble poured into the room with a stream of cool air. 'Water's quite high,' he said. He pushed the frame harder, scraping away further clumps of straw.

'Hey!' objected Izzie, sounding puzzled.

He stared out into the night.

'I'll help you,' said Izzie.

Dan was silent.

'I knew where she was.'

'What?'

'I wanted to see her, always.'

'What do you mean? Like –'

'See her. Shake things up a bit for her, maybe. What –'

'Have you got other kids in your family? You've never told me all that stuff.'

He yawned. 'They sprogged years after they took me. Just me and my so-called brother. Zeb. He's cool.' He shook his head. 'He's gone to New Zealand.'

'Where's your mum? The old one, I mean?'

Dan was silent again.

'Babe,' said Izzie, getting up. She stroked his back. 'Come on, babe. Come away from the window.'

'I knew I'd see her. When they'd tell me where she was.' He was shaking minutely but perceptibly beneath her fingers. 'I thought she might want me. Miss me. I can't –'

'Babe,' said Izzie again, and strenuously, half toppling, she pulled him down until he sat against her on the bed. 'You're all shivery. It's cool, it's cool. When did they tell you?' she said, holding him. She kissed his eyelids. He kept them closed.

'Well, after Zeb was born. Made sense. But I knew anyway.'

'How, sweetie?' said Izzie, kissing him again. 'How?' He lay across her and she held him in her arms, almost cradling him. 'It's freezing in here now. How?'

'The oldsters said they were planning to tell me when I was eighteen. Eighteen? Why the fuck, man? But I heard one of their flyblown old relatives referring to it when I was about fourteen –'

'Like how?'

'Some unsubtle reference to "biological offspring", meaning Zeb, thinking I was as thick as they were.'

'You're not thick.'

'I know, my little princess.'

'You're one of the cleverest people I know.'

'Well let's not push it too far,' he said. 'But – yes, well, I knew I was a bit more switched on than those thick-as-pigshit dipsticks.' He started to laugh, coughing with exaggerated sounds. 'Brains fried.'

'Don't do that! You spook me sometimes. They'll hear. What else happened?'

'We moved everywhere, and I was always yanked from these smelly village schools, these pits, just as I'd started a halfway interesting project or something. Drove me mad. Then they tried to "*home school*" me,' he said in a stronger version of the accent he adopted for the clientele of his market stall. 'But they couldn't teach me the first basic thing. Oh well.'

'It must be really, really weird not to know always who your parents were,' she said, and she stroked his cheek, his unshaved skin rough against her fingers. 'My mum told me right away.'

'I always guessed,' said Dan, 'always kind of knew I was adopted, must have come from somewhere else, but turned out so did half the other people at school. We couldn't all be little unwanted bastards.'

'So where is she? Your mum?'

He shook his head and suddenly looked weary, his mouth a tight line that gave his face an unfamiliar expression.

'You don't want to tell me? OK, babe,' said Izzie, running her hand through his hair and watching its tufts spring back up in the wake of her strokes. 'Who was your dad?'

'No idea. I used to dream about her, never him. Some cock. Someone who fucked her when she was a kid.'

'My real dad was a randy waiter! Ha ha.'

'Who can just *give away* their baby?'

'Mine was a teenager,' said Izzie, fiddling with her tobacco pouch.

'Mine was a whore.'

'Dan,' said Izzie. 'Babe. Come on. You get all harsh. You've got me to look after you now. No one else matters.' She kissed him. 'You're a bit shaking still.' She stroked him. 'Babe?'

'Ruth!' shouted Cecilia. 'Ruth!'

She swerved out of Ruth's bedroom into the bathroom on the children's side of the house, but she could see in the moonlight that it was empty. She rapped on Izzie's door, and when there was no answer, she pushed her body against it and tripped into the room, wrenching away the lock that Izzie had carelessly attempted to hammer into place. She looked blankly at Izzie and Dan lying in a tangle on the bed, the tang of sex on the air.

'Mum,' said Izzie in panic, staring. Dan gazed at her, then turned away.

'Where's Ruth?' said Cecilia rapidly.

'I don't know,' said Izzie.

'*Where is she?*'

'She went to her room. Like, a couple of hours ago.'

'She's not there.'

'Fuck,' muttered Izzie.

'Oh God. Ari!' shouted Cecilia, racing along the passage. 'Romy!' she called as she ran past her room. 'Where's Ruth?'

'Ruth?' said Ari groggily, emerging from bed.

'She's not in her room.' Cecilia clutched at him. 'Where – Where is she?'

'Search the house,' said Ari, beginning to run down the stairs, two steps at a time. Romy followed.

Cecilia ran into every room on the upper floor, shouting Ruth's name, calling out endearments rising to commands, pleading, '*Come to me.*' Floorboards vibrated in a chaos of thumping and whining the length of the house; Izzie emerged crying; doors banged open.

'She's not here,' shouted Ari. 'Run to the cottage.' He whipped round. 'Look in the gardens,' he said to Romy.

'Oh God,' said Cecilia. She ran down the stairs, stumbling and nearly falling on the last two steps.

'Ruth! Ruth!' Ari called loudly.

'Darling, darling,' called Cecilia. 'Come back. You won't be in trouble. Come here. My darling. Ruth!' she shrieked, hurting her lungs.

'I'm calling the police,' said Ari, and picked up the phone.

'Quickly, quickly,' said Cecilia. 'Ruth!' she screamed.

Izzie stood in the garden in her night T-shirt, sobbing. 'Go to the pond,' snapped Ari, pushing her back quite roughly. 'No – I will. Look up the lane. And Dora's. Shoes on,' he snapped. He began to run.

'Oh God,' said Cecilia. She bent over and hot liquid trickled up her throat. She ran through the garden. *Please please*, she thought, memories of the last hour of melancholy and conjecture slapping at her in garish tatters, punishing her. *These are my children. Here. Now.* She tasted vomit in her mouth. She ran faster. *I chased shadows. Oh, God. Please.*

'Ruth!'

Dan sidled out from the porch as a tall slanting shadow, his footsteps barely audible, and Cecilia saw him from the corner of her eye and jumped. 'Help me,' she shouted at him.

'She wanted to float,' he said flatly.

'What?' said Cecilia.

'She was talking about floating,' he said in the same voice. 'Go to the river.'

'God,' said Cecilia, beginning to run down the path. 'Ruth!' she screamed again.

Dan overtook her. 'Get a torch,' he hissed. He ran ahead of her, dissolving into the shadows of the river field.

'Izzie! A torch!' Cecilia shouted, and dashed back into the house, where she snatched the torch from Izzie's hand, then ran, shoeless, slithering on the mud and waterlogged grass of the field. She fell, her toe catching a root, bit into her lower lip and tasted blood. 'Oh Ruth,' she said. She prayed. She begged. 'Ruth.'

Her feet plunged into a stream, a stone cutting her ankle; she slid on the mud bordering it, clambered out and ran towards the river whose rush threw up a mist of sound.

'I think she's there,' called Dan from further downstream, beginning to lower himself into the water. 'Can't see. Shine it.' He pointed towards the flat stone mid-river on which Ruth and Izzie had constructed a wigwam of sticks. Cecilia shone the torch across the black curves of the surface with its jostlings of foam, illuminating a tangle of hair and arm submerged in water by the rock. Ruth's hand clutched the stone, her head bowed, plants dragging over her neck, the purse she had knitted tangling with leaves. Cecilia scrambled into the river.

Dan plunged ahead of her.

'Ruth, Ruth!' Cecilia called.

The water had twinkled to Ruth when she had arrived there, shining at her, and it was so soft and warm and smooth-wrinkled like a bed. He had said it would glitter, the strange man. The water wanted her and she was ready and she glowed. She couldn't stop giggles rising like fizz bubbles in her brain. She remembered words of Izzie's and laughed aloud in little coughs.

She had hovered on her way there. However many times she had fallen in the river field and hurt her ankles, she floated above it and saw new things, and the water folded her in. Libation. Ophelia. She had read now of river gods.

The water froze her to icy heat. She was stiff, hot, splintered. Soon, she knew, she would float because she would be a board, a stiffness of ice like an iceberg, and she half-lay on a rock midstream like a polar bear and watched the water storm past. It rushed rushed rushed. How lovely, how beautiful, how funny. She was almost tired. The South Sea Islands. She folded herself in, bit by bit.

The river carried her.

She floated. She swirled. The flowers from the field wiped her face. Hot tears sprang from her as she reeled with the coldness, and the river carried her.

Then the water gulped into her lungs with a choking of weed stink, and she gasped and burped and struggled, and the petals were in her mouth, and Mummy was not there, and Izzie had left her, and she screamed a black mouthful of Stygian; the water's back reared like a whale, threw her and crashed her on to the wigwam stone. Autochthonous. Her leg was like metal, anvil on the horse's shoe, and the flowers had fallen and drowned.

'Hold her,' said Dan, and he steadied himself on the rock and then hooked his arms beneath Ruth's and dragged her with Cecilia supporting her legs as they pulled her to the bank.

Her face was puffed and white yet more pinched than it had ever been. Her lip ballooned. She looked like a dead girl, swollen and bloodless.

'Talk,' instructed Cecilia, putting her mouth to Ruth's.

Ruth moaned.

Oh God. Please please please. Thank you.

'Talk,' said Cecilia, kissing Ruth all over her face, licking water from her, bending over her to warm her.

'I can't,' murmured Ruth.

'Give me your clothes,' Ari shouted at Romy and Izzie as he arrived on the bank, and he stripped his top off, and the older girls stood there, hesitant as they undressed while Cecilia unpeeled what wet fabric she could from Ruth and covered her in their dry clothes.

'Don't move her,' said Ari. 'Her back could be broken.'

'Run. Phone for the ambulance,' said Cecilia, stuttering, and Romy ran.

'Darling,' said Cecilia, pulling Ruth's hair out of her eyes, kissing her frozen cheek, blowing, kissing again, attempting to warm the flesh with her own stiff lips. 'I love you.' She shivered violently. Ruth tasted of mucus and river weed, blood seeping from her mouth and catching the edge of Cecilia's tongue.

Thank you. Thank you, God.

'Jesus,' said Ari. 'Ruth.'

'I think she must have broken her leg,' said Cecilia. Ruth's blood met her tears, the river water dripping from her own hair. She wiped it with her fingers from Ruth's face.

'So do I.'

The other one doesn't exist.

'Ruth Ruth Ruth,' said Cecilia, covering her in kisses and breathing on her. 'Talk to me.'

'Thought I'd float,' said Ruth, her voice a small husky shivering. Mucus streaked with blood shone beneath her nose and on the bulbous swelling of her lip.

'Where's that boy?' said Cecilia suddenly. Bats flew in a staggered arc from trees lining the river.

There was silence. 'He was further up the field,' said Romy.

'He's gone,' said Izzie in a croak. Ari turned abruptly to her.

Ruth shivered more steadily.

'You'll be in bed soon,' said Cecilia, holding her in her arms on the grass, her tears sliding into her hair, her breath warming her face. 'Oh I love you.'

'We'll take you back,' said Ari gently to Ruth. 'Wait for the ambulance.'

'I'm cold,' Ruth whispered.

Cecilia arched herself over her. 'Get a blanket,' she said, not looking up.

I've abandoned two of my children, the first and the last. I've barely seen what I have.

She leant over and covered Ruth with kisses again. 'I'll do that till you're warm,' she said.

'We have to check if you've broken other bones first,' said Ari. 'Does your back hurt?'

Ruth shook her head.

I will do anything. I will do anything. Here they are. My children.

'Darling,' she said. She brushed her own tears impatiently so that they didn't fall, hot and alarming, on Ruth. She heard an owl; a second answered it from beyond the hill as the river tugged relentlessly behind. Shivering took over her body.

'I need a wee,' said Ruth.

'Do it,' murmured Cecilia into her cheek, the river water pooling from her hair into her ear as she lowered her head.

'I can't.'

'Just do it here. You mustn't move.'

Ruth smiled up at Cecilia through her big gappy teeth. 'It's warm.'

Cecilia whispered in her ear and kissed her. She looked at her family, gathered on the bank, bent over Ruth, stroking her and kissing her. She clung to Ruth. She smiled at them.

Thirty-five
July

'I MISSED YOU,' James Dahl said, placing his hand on the small of Cecilia's back and steering her towards the azalea path. The afternoon was mobile with rising warmth and insect crossing. Hay from the meadows banking Elliott Hall drifted on the heat into the gardens, moving over honeysuckle baking on walls, and in her tiredness, the scene looked like an illusion to her, rippled and unsteady.

'I missed you as I lay on my hospital camp bed,' she said. 'That creaking little cot.' A butterfly landed on the toe of his shoe. It seemed to bloom to magnified proportions. She remembered the grass on his shoes in a different century, petals wet on the ground. 'Ari is sleeping on it tonight.' She glanced at her watch. 'I have to go soon to pick up Romy.'

Tension passed rapidly over his face. 'Don't leave.'

'I won't yet.'

'How is she now?' he said.

'Romy?'

'Ruth.'

'Ruth,' said Cecilia, and she bent towards him and he held the back of her head, running his fingers against her scalp so that her hair clung hotly with electricity to his hand and her temple lay against his shoulder. 'Ruth. I –'

'It's all right,' he said, stroking her without stopping.

'It's all right. It's much *more* than all right. She's alive,' she said with elation into his shoulder. 'She's alive,' she repeated, superstitiously.

Hot tears streamed over her cheeks, unseen by him. She bit a ridge of his shirt, rumpled it and let her saliva soak it. 'She's safe. That's all that matters. Thank —'

He drew her further towards him. 'How is she now?'

'The worst are the breaks in her leg. They operated on the one on her wrist,' she said. 'Only one stitch on her lip, the rest inside her mouth. Why did she do this? It's so terrible that she could do this.'

He shook his head.

'I think I begin to understand,' she said in a flat voice. 'Partly.'

He pressed her head, and his shirt warmth mingled with the breath of hay, with the old roses that clambered over the arches by the azalea path.

'I need to be with her. Even more. Much, much more. Oh God. Ruth. She was always my troubled little girl,' she said, and he settled her head closer to him, on to his shoulder, against his neck. 'There'll be months of physiotherapy.' She breathed in a skin scent known for over twenty years.

'Poor you,' he said. He kissed her.

'No, no. Lucky me. We're so lucky,' she said.

'I hate to imagine.'

'She can have all the counselling in the world, but . . . I need to focus on her, to forget — forget — you know.' She couldn't look at him. 'I won't see her again. I know —'

'But we'll keep her alive by talking about her.'

'Even that, I'm not sure. I think I have to put her away. Oh, that sounds so cruel. Let her rest in my mind.' She spoke more rapidly. 'I loved her. I — Even the house,' she said, pulling her head away from him. 'You know, even that house, I think being at that house isn't good for me. It's past; it's in the past.'

'Perhaps you should go somewhere new,' he said.

'I think I should. I think I should. Not too far from Dora, though a little distance . . .' She brushed her eye. 'We don't get the life we thought we wanted, do we?'

'We should all change,' he said.

He gathered flowers as they walked – stolen roses in a rough silky bundle, lilies, anemones, ferns – and he continued to hand them to her one by one.

'The gardener's over there,' she said, tilting her head. She smiled.

'Do I care?'

'Last night, lying in bed,' she said, 'I realised how very short life really *is*. We all like to say it, but it is – it really is. Whole portions of it suddenly gone.'

The light that angled from the sundial passed over his face and he walked to its far side and stopped and looked down at her.

They both paused.

'Tell me,' she said playfully. '*Tell me, what is it you plan to do/With your one wild and precious life?*'

'Be with you,' he said.

The following afternoon, Elisabeth Dahl let herself in at the gate and walked through the garden of Wind Tor Cottage. Dora was bending over, ineffectually hauling up Japanese knotweed in one of her old denim skirts, while the squat figure of Katya mowed the further section of the garden, her hair floating.

'I've come for you,' said Elisabeth, her mouth curving into a smile of suppressed exhilaration or agitation. Her hair smelled damp with recent washing, and her movements were subtly jerky as she picked up a dropped key and walked towards Dora.

Dora stood up, easing the base of her back with her palm, and gazed at Elisabeth through the haze of sunlight while high in the sky a buzzard hovered and, momentarily, she perceived it as an eagle. On the lane behind the gate Elisabeth's car was parked, its back windows obscured with piled-up cases and boxes, sun swarming across its windscreen.

Elisabeth laughed.

Dora paused. She frowned.

'Take me,' said Elisabeth, her mouth twitching with a self-conscious irony that threaded the smile. 'I'm all yours!'

Dora remained motionless.

'I'm free! I'm truly free,' said Elisabeth, and caught Dora in her arms. Unusually, Dora could smell her perspiration.

'You're not,' said Dora.

'I am. He's gone. He's leaving me. All yours.'

'He's gone? You're not,' said Dora, her voice cracking, then trailing into uncertainty.

'Silly darling! You don't understand, do you? I really am free. *Yours*. He says he wants to leave. I can't say that this hasn't been brewing for some time . . .' She glanced at the ground and her features seemed to sag, or age, then harden; she smiled again, looking Dora directly in the eye.

'I can't believe it,' said Dora. Elisabeth's perfume seemed over-heavy in the warmth.

'We can be together. We can *live* together if you want.'

'No,' said Dora thinly. She eased herself into a straighter position.

'No?'

Dora shook her head, trying to smile, but she was veiled by the shadow of her gardening hat, which seemed to form a barrier between her and Elisabeth.

'Come on,' said Elisabeth, smiling with an almost disquieting radiance into Dora's eyes, and took her hand. 'Come with me. You're coming with me.'

'I'm not,' said Dora. The sound of the lawnmower rose behind her.

'You're not?' said Elisabeth, a first chill seeping into her voice.

'No.'

'You don't believe me,' she said. 'I can see why, my darling, after all these years . . . I can see why! *Mea culpa*.' She tilted her head in wry acknowledgement and smiled in a softer fashion. 'I think I've pushed you away. I never quite know my own mind. Forgive me. If you can. But truly. We've – separated.'

Dora opened her mouth. The lawnmower chattered loudly by the hedge.

'Come on, darling,' said Elisabeth. 'My love! Where shall we go? Shall we go out in the car? To lunch? To celebrate? Or a hotel? For a few days? Or here? I feel like getting drunk on something very good. You tell me.'

'Nowhere,' said Dora, taking Elisabeth's arm gently.

'Nowhere,' said Elisabeth.

'I want to stay here.'

'Do you?'

'Yes.'

'And me? – I?'

'You – You go back home. Elis – I don't know. I wish the best for you.'

'You're not coming with me?'

'No.'

'Oh Dora, you don't need to play games.'

'I know. I'm – I'm not. I'm sorry.'

'You really don't . . .'

'No.'

'Come with me now,' said Elisabeth more insistently. 'I'll make it lovely for you. I know I've . . . I've, I must have been difficult.' Shame seemed to pass over her face. 'But it will be different.'

'No,' said Dora, shaking her head, trying to smile at her.

'I can't stay here with you? Be with you? My love.'

'No.'

'Truly?' said Elisabeth, her face motionless.

'No,' said Dora. Her lip trembled. 'Really. No.'

All afternoon, she lay in bed. She lay in bed, dreaming, dozing, half-asleep, waking to moments of clarity and then tugging sleep to her again. The past came back to her. Cecilia, little red-headed girl in a mulberry-coloured smock dress, and her boys, her many boys, and Patrick, and the old Elisabeth, and Haye House, the sunbathing flagstones by the pool above Cantaur's Fields with children lying in a naked heap against Furry the dog. The wobbling depths of that pool seemed to play to her as she lay in bed, reflected in passing refractions on her ceiling, and finally she rose sticky-headed and walked downstairs and fetched lemons from her vegetable rack to make a jug of lemonade for her granddaughters. The afternoon was still hot.

She boiled lemons. She played an old and much-loved recording of Vivaldi's *Gloria* on her record player, and attempted her arm exercises as she stirred sugar into water, the heat of the Rayburn scorching the already hot day. 'Gloria, gloria,' she sang to herself, noting that her voice warbled unpleasantly like an old lady's.

She heard footsteps on the lane and automatically wandered to her front door to look through her gate, and glimpsed Dan passing. Tentatively, she called his name, having never used it to address him. He glanced up at her, his gaze expressionless.

Dora walked down the garden path. 'I – I understand you helped to save my granddaughter,' she said before she reached the gate. 'I'm more grateful to you than I can say.' Her voice quivered.

She opened the gate and pushed herself through the aura of faint hostility that surrounded him to give him a brief awkward hug, and to her embarrassment, tears instantly sprang to her eyes. 'Thank you,' she said, unable to look at him. His stiffness and his tang of unchanged bedclothes seemed designed to repel.

He shrugged.

'I can never thank you enough.'

He said nothing. A flicker of awkwardness crossed his face.

'Come in and have a drink,' said Dora, and he paused for several seconds and then followed.

He picked up a wooden spoon and began to stir the lemons simmering on the Rayburn. 'Do you have mint for this?' he said. 'Or a tiny bit of ginger will heat it.' He lowered his head, focusing on the pan, and Dora added a kettle to the hob. There was something defenceless about his back, she thought, as she had thought before, unhooking cups from the dresser and recalling the teenage Benedict's vulnerable torso as he stood poised to dive into the river at Spitchwick. Dan lowered the heat slightly on the ring, and then silently began to twist a bracket into place on a shelf beside the oven.

'Do you have a Rawlplug?' he said.

'Yes,' said Dora. 'I think that's been broken for about four years.' She smiled. 'I notice it every single day. As – as I cook. But I didn't know how to mend it.'

He nodded.

'Give me the tools you've got and I'll do it,' he said. 'Proper job,' he added in a Devon accent, as though obliged to inject mockery.

'Oh thank you,' said Dora. 'What a relief that would be.'

He coughed. There was something about the blinking of his eyes as he coughed that reminded Dora of a different time, of the era that had come to her so vividly in her bedroom and still seemed to rock and settle in her mind as a film of memory. Patrick, she thought.

'Where do you come from?' she said.

'All over,' he said. 'Told you, ma'am.'

'But all over where?'

'All over these miserable little islands,' he said.

'*All* over?'

'Where do you want me to start?' he asked, switching to what appeared to be a Welsh accent.

'From the beginning.'

'I – This'll need some Polyfilla.'

'Why did you come here?'

'Why not?' He shrugged, turning from her, and hammered into plaster that spurted crumbs while dust floated thickly on the air until he began to cough, his back arching thinly so that Dora could see the outline of his vertebrae through his T-shirt.

'I don't think you should be living in that caravan,' she said gently. 'If you're still coughing like this.'

He shook his head.

'Though I understand how expensive rents are.'

'I'm not paying off some tosser's mortgage for the pleasure of creeping round their worst bedroom while they resent me,' he said. 'I'd rather live in Turd Towers.'

Dora paused. 'Turd Towers?' she said. She gazed at the shape of his eyes. He coughed, and she watched again. She found heat, unaccountably, flooding to her face.

'My caravan. May as well live in a swamp,' he said cheerfully, reverting to his exaggerated Devon speech. 'Chuck us that chair. It's going to collapse if you don't realign the leg.'

He smiled at her for the first time. She gazed at his eyes when they creased, at the grooved channel above his mouth.

'Where were you born?' she said suddenly.

'In Devon,' he said boldly, then he shrugged and averted his eyes. She nodded. She sat down.

'Why are you here now?'

He shrugged once more. '– Had to see it again.'

She steadied her hands on her knees.

'Have you – have you been here before?' she said, frantically searching for questions in her desire to maintain the flow of conversation.

'I went to Exeter for a couple of terms. I couldn't finance it.' He shrugged again. 'It was full of braying idiots anyway. No loss.'

'Why – why there?'

'I wanted to be near the moors. It seemed the way then.'

'Oh –'

'Had enough of buggering about.'

She glanced surreptitiously at the way he moved his mouth while his face was in profile, his expression as he closed his eyes sounding a note in her brain, the ghosts of gestures shadowing the room.

'How long were you here for?'

'No time,' he said gruffly, staring straight at the screw he was turning.

'But you felt – you felt – you had to see? Where you were born,' she said, but her voice was beginning to weaken. She stayed sitting, although the kettle was whistling. He reached over and removed it from the ring with one hand while still working with the other.

She gazed at the table. She was trembling steadily. She looked up at him again.

'You can stay here while you get rid of your cough,' she said. Her voice was thin and seemed to come from a distance so that she heard it as though someone else was speaking. 'If you'd like to? I have a spare room.'

Dan said nothing. He began to dismantle the broken chair.

'It's empty this summer,' she said, but she didn't look at him. Her hands were shaking uncontrollably. 'Sorry. Could you – could you make the tea?' she said, but she kept her face turned from his.

'Coming,' he said.

'Did you always – always want to come back?' she said, and again her voice seemed barely her own.

'I've told you that,' he said abruptly. 'I wanted to look. I found out where.'

'You started out in Wales?' she said.

'Why yes, *bach*,' he said in a theatrical Welsh accent, as though to insert a distance, and she saw again the movement of his mouth. It stiffened as he stopped speaking. He kept his face averted.

Dora's tears fell through her fingers and she watched them fall, barely registering what she was seeing as they gathered in the grooves of the table and formed beads on the wax.

'Did they – tell you?' she said, her heart racing. 'I mean, where we – where she was?'

He tightened a mug hook on a shelf. He said nothing. The silence continued. Dora froze.

'I'm sorr –' she said eventually.

'They wouldn't tell me who,' he said at the same time in a monotone. 'I knew where. Where they'd lived. And then I found out who.'

'Please do stay here,' she said.

He was silent. 'Thank you, ma'am,' he said, and made tea. He placed a mug in front of her. She saw that his hand was shaking.

'Sit down,' she said.

'I can't,' he said.

'Sit down. Please.' She held out her arms to him.

He stood stiffly. He wandered to the window. 'I came up once to look at the house,' he said. 'I heard when she – they – were coming back.'

'Did you?' said Dora in a whisper.

'I used to dream about her.'

'She dreamed about you.'

He turned round angrily.

'She didn't,' he said. 'I thought –'

He stopped.

'You thought what?' said Dora softly.

His shoulders were shaking. 'I wanted to see her,' he said, still gazing out of the window.

The sight of his trembling shoulders in all their muscular width made a ball of grief rise in Dora's throat.

'I'm sorry,' she said.

'Don't worry,' he said, and he coughed.

They were silent. She peered through her fingers at him. He was motionless.

'Are you going to tell her?' she said.

'Oh –' said Dan abruptly. He swallowed tea and spilled some, then lowered the cup unsteadily. He coughed. His voice was strained. 'I haven't the balls.' He dropped his gaze. 'I thought I'd storm right up to her – I can't do it –' His hair stood in peaks.

'When shall we tell her?'

He shook his head. 'I thought I –'

'I'll help you.'

'I'm – I can't – Fucking her – I'm – I'm terrified.'

'There's nothing to be scared of,' said Dora, through her hands. 'Come on,' she said, and looked up, aware of her tear-blotched face, her thinning rumpled hair. 'We'll tell her tonight.'

Thirty-six
July

L ATE SUN slanted into the kitchen of Wind Tor House. As the meat hooks on the ceiling cast growing curves and girls spoke in a babble, Cecilia remembered her father at the same table, Dora stirring at the Aga with Barnaby in one arm, brothers plucking instruments, lodgers passing, while she herself remained mute, unstable with the glow of her secret as she was kissed on a loop that seemed to discharge a bolt of electricity inside her.

A recent memory of kissing James Dahl shot through her now. She lost her focus, misheard what Izzie was saying, got up quickly, and brought Ruth a glass of water with a straw. Ari brushed her shoulder as he passed with plates.

'*Euch*,' said Izzie, screwing up her nose in melodramatic horror and backing away from the meal Ari placed on the table.

'Thank you,' said Romy.

Ruth lay propped on the small sofa that had been dragged into the kitchen, her leg supported by cushions, and ate from a tray while Izzie knelt down and cut her food for her. 'Makes me feel pukey,' said Izzie indignantly.

Cecilia smiled in the direction of Ari, who caught her eye and grinned at her, raising one eyebrow. She made a face at him, and he returned it in exaggerated form. Unsteady tiles of sunlight patterned plates, and three girls squabbled lazily as they ate. Cecilia sat back, watching them through the light.

The phone rang from the sitting room.

'Oh, ignore it,' she said.

'No!' protested Izzie.

Ari pulled a pan from the ring, went out of the room and returned carrying the cordless phone.

This is all I want, thought Cecilia, and she pressed her fingernails into the edge of the table and sent a jumbled prayer of gratitude to the sky.

'James Dahl, for you,' said Ari in slight enquiry, raising his voice above the sound of talking and a knocking at the door.

All I want. She turned from the sunlight. *Isn't it?*

Acknowledgements

W ITH MANY thanks to: Louie Banks, Luigi Bonomi, Moray Bowater, Carol Briscoe, Holly Briscoe, Ariel Bruce, Marta Buszewicz, Liz Case, Eleanor Clarke, Mark Cocker, Tina Cotzias, Sarah-Jane Forder, Martha Lane Fox, Peter Grimsdale, Helen Healy, Simon Henson, Erica Jarnes, Clementine Mendelson, Rachel Mendelson, Theodore Mendelson, Victoria Millar, Mary Nightingale, Elaine O'Dwyer, Tinah O'Reilly, Melissa Pimintel, Kate Saunders, Louisa Saunders, Vincenzo Scocchia, Gillian Stern, Sarah Stogdon, Rick Stroud, Oliver Sweeney, Katie Troake, Alison Wilkinson, Ellie Wood; and with much love and gratitude to Charlotte Mendelson.

And most of all, thank you to Alexandra Pringle and Jonny Geller and everyone at Bloomsbury.

A NOTE ON THE TYPE

The text of this book is set in Bembo. This type was first used in 1495 by the Venetian printer Aldus Manutius for Cardinal Bembo's *De Aetna*, and was cut for Manutius by Francesco Griffo. It was one of the types used by Claude Garamond (1480–1561) as a model for his Romain de L'Université, and so it was the forerunner of what became standard European type for the following two centuries. Its modern form follows the original types and was designed for Monotype in 1929.